Praise for *The Mexican Flyboy*

"[Alfredo] Véa dives into magical realism headfirst in this hallucinatory fantasy
that reads like a blend of John Steinbeck and Robert A. Heinlein. . . . It's a
dizzying novel that combines Véa's solid prose style with a vivid
imagination and an authentic cultural brio. A lush fantasy in which
a man must unwind time itself to right the world's wrongs."
Kirkus Reviews

"Dreamlike and fantastical, yet strangely earnest, Alfredo Véa's *The Mexican
Flyboy* is a magical realist tour de force. . . . It is more an experience than a book,
a piece of literature that grabs and transports . . . [and] is not to be missed."
Foreword Reviews

"This impressive novel . . . gives a human-rights spin to the familiar science-
fiction theme of time travel. . . . The vividly fanciful and intensely passionate
story grapples memorably with the long history of human violence
and the need to escape or redeem it."
Publishers Weekly
starred review

"With heart, imagination, and wit, Alfredo Véa gives us a rollicking tale of
magical realism and science fiction, historical acuity and human truths.
If Gabriel García Márquez were to magically collaborate with E. L. Doctorow,
Luís Alberto Urrea, and Ray Bradbury, the result would be something
as delightfully moving as *The Mexican Flyboy*."
Rilla Askew
author of *Fire in Beulah* and *Kind of Kin*

"Alfredo Véa writes with the pen of a magician, the heart of a saint,
and a truth seeker's passion for justice. I'm in awe of this
brilliant and moving novel."
Elizabeth McKenzie
author of *MacGregor Tells the World*

THE MEXICAN FLYBOY

Chicana & Chicano Visions of the Américas

THE MEXICAN FLYBOY

ALFREDO VÉA

University of Oklahoma Press : Norman

Also by Alfredo Véa
La Maravilla (New York, 1993)
The Silver Cloud Café (New York, 1996)
Gods Go Begging (New York, 1999)

This book is a work of fiction. Names, characters, places, and incidents are either the product of the author's imagination or are used fictitiously, and any resemblance to actual events, locales, or persons, living or dead, is entirely coincidental.

Library of Congress Cataloging-in-Publication Data
Names: Véa, Alfredo, 1952– author.
Title: The Mexican flyboy / Alfredo Véa.
Description: First edition. | Norman : University of Oklahoma Press, 2016. |
   Series: Chicana and Chicano visions of the Americas series ; volume 16
Identifiers: LCCN 2015042861 | ISBN 978-0-8061-8703-7 (softcover : acid-free paper)
Subjects: | BISAC: FICTION / Literary. | GSAFD: Science fiction. | Fantasy fiction.
Classification: LCC PS3572.E2 M49 2016 | DDC 813/.54—dc23
LC record available at http://lccn.loc.gov/2015042861

The Mexican Flyboy is Volume 16
in the Chicana & Chicano Visions of the Américas series.

The paper in this book meets the guidelines for permanence and durability of the Committee on Production Guidelines for Book Longevity of the Council on Library Resources, Inc. ∞

1 2 3 4 5 6 7 8 9 10

For Stella Rose Véa

We can't repair our world, our present or future, until we fix our past—
pin it down in time and place; shine the brightest light on it,
measure it and study it with an unflinching eye—
then name it for what it was.

CONTENTS

THE MEXICAN FLYBOY

PROLOGUE

No wind is ever tamed. A few are cursed by being named: le Mistral, Sirocco, Blue Norther, and Neshama. The strongest, most ill-tempered gusts bristle with ire when they are called the winds of change—they wail in anger when they are charted, mapped, and treated as though their journeys were as predictable as the seasonal movements of geese. Their lifetimes have become windage; their droppings are called windfall; their resting places are dubbed the doldrums. But be warned: These are fighting words.

Most winds are blissfully ignored, so happy to be forgotten—free to fly unencumbered by strange appellations so fervently called out by small voices far, far below. It is the anonymous breeze, the sudden cross-current, the evanescent gust that is the most liberated of all—uncharted, unmeasured, unseen. It is unmentioned by any verse, any testament, psalm, or sermon.

It is the sudden appearance of one of these vagrant winds—blowing across a battlefield that is still heaving with horror, or ripping open the flap of a Bedouin's tent—that has, for ages untold, been so often mistaken for the presence of god. Slip a modest flurry into a swelling bodice of billowing curtains, and men will see angels. But these gusts are deaf to praise and oblivious to prayer. They never hear words of supplication. They linger in a sail merely as a whim; they turn a heavy millstone and lift an airplane only in passing. Then they twist away, laughing in dizzy whirls of delirium, gleefully unchained to any covenant—unwed to any tempo or measure, any chronometer, any latitude or locality. Freer even than the idea of freedom.

1

THE MEXICAN FLYBOY

1961, in a vineyard somewhere in California.

According to the local newspaper, the day the skydiver died had
been the windiest day in the history of the valley. Two residents
claimed to have seen a funnel cloud touching down near the winery.
The speculation was that the winds had caused the skydiver to fall
to her death. On that turbulent day, all of the Mexican farmworkers
had been rudely harried from their assigned rows—driven out like
trespassers and vagrants. With bandanas lashed across their faces
and hands clutching their hats, fifteen half-blinded men had tripped
and bumped their way back into the bunkhouse and slammed the
door behind them. Inside the building, two old men who were
standing in the kitchen watched as the workers stumbled toward
the door, peering at them through a window and through thick
clouds of dirt and debris.

"There goes six inches of topsoil. Too much dust on the leaves
means no sugar in the grapes," muttered one old man. "This wind is
going to last awhile. I can feel it. I smelled this kind of wind once on
a job in Argentina." He flared his nostrils and inhaled deeply. "Yeah,
it's going stay for five, maybe six days. Maybe more."

"No birds can fly in this," said the second man as he leaned even
closer to the window and squinted his eyes. "Shit! No birds can fly
in this! I've never seen this kind of storm. It's a good thing all of the
men are inside. I counted all fifteen of them, but look! I think I can
see someone else out there," he said, almost to himself. He raised a
gnarled hand, pointing vaguely, while his friend strained his eyes in
that general direction.

"I don't see a thing." Then they both saw it. They glimpsed something moving in the middle of the dust storm about a hundred yards from the bunkhouse. The small form seemed to be walking unerringly toward the entrance of the Quonset hut. "Is it a lost fawn? No, it's a man."

"Either he's very far away or he's a very small man. It can't be a child. Not out here. It's three miles into town, almost four."

In a few more minutes, they knew that it was a small boy who was coming. He marched across an open field that was filled with rusting irrigation pipes and coils of trellis wire. He stared almost defiantly into stinging whorls of mulch and sand. Without covering his face or eyes, he walked straight across the parking lot, then pushed open the door that the frenzied farmhands had just slammed shut. He stood in the doorway and in the epicenter of a pile of leaves and gravel. The boy seemed stunned by the sudden silence of the interior and by all of the startled, questioning faces staring at him. He closed the door behind him. Then in total silence he cast his eyes around the room before walking to an empty cot and putting his belongings on the mattress.

He was slight, with the usual brown skin and dark eyes of a Mexican. There were no laces on his shoes, and his big toes stuck through the leather. He was not wearing socks, and his filthy clothing was limp and threadbare. There were holes everywhere in his pants and shirt. He had pelo chino, curly hair, but it was filthy and stained with the oddest streaks of red. He peered again toward the dusty gaggle of braceros who were huddled together in the rear of the Quonset hut. They seemed suspicious, almost afraid of him. "Solo vino," they said warily, one to the other. "Solo vino." The one who comes alone.

Men who had been pouring water over their heads to wash away the dust that had lodged in every pore now stood staring at the boy as the liquid dripped down their shirtless bodies and onto the floor of the communal shower stall. Men who had made it to their bunks rose to their feet to stare at the newcomer. Men who had been speaking fell silent. The boy turned toward the old men who were still standing at the window.

"My name is Simon. Do you have work for me?" he asked softly. The two men looked at each other, then back at the boy. He was tall enough to reach the hanging grapes. They looked at each other again and nodded in unison. The Filipino cook walked to a nearby closet and found some blankets. The other man—the field foreman and cellar master—pulled a grape knife from his coat and tossed it onto the bed. The boy lifted the knife to his eyes, then cleaned the oxidized blade on his shirt. He dropped the tool into a tattered sack.

"Are you hungry?" asked the cook. "Tienes hambre?"

In the hours before the lady dropped from the sky, the boy had moved away from the salsa and fish sauce induced detonations and gas warfare of the bunks and cots, and made up his bed on a long wooden dining table. The table and its benches separated the unconscious babbling and foul stink of the sleeping area from the relative peace and quiet of the cook's tiny kitchen. When he abandoned his cot, he took the blankets with him, along with his most precious possessions: a dirty cloth bag packed to the top with comic books, a jar filled with tiny gears and springs, a filthy shoebox, and a few pieces of clothing.

For almost a full hour he slept fitfully, until he was awakened by a wrinkled pair of large-knuckled hands grabbing him by the shoulders and shaking him gently. There were tears running down the young boy's cheeks, and his heavily patched clothes were soaked with sweat.

"Simon! Simon, it's just a bad dream. Wake up, boy! A bad dream!"

The Filipino cook had come limping into his dark kitchen and, after putting away his hand-carved cane, had roused the trembling boy. Without moving his gaze from the child, the old Pinoy lit a single candle and began filling a five-gallon pot with water. He wet a dishrag and wiped the boy's scalding brow. Then, when he was assured that the boy had recovered from his nightmare, he fired up two burners on a huge five-burner stove that was covered with an impenetrable accumulation of soot and grease, and with the fossilized sediment of ten thousand spills of soy sauce and salsa El Tapatío.

It was his custom to brew tasteless, translucent coffee for breakfast that almost no one ever drank. He would always mix enough pancake batter to feed an army, although no one but the dogs and goats would ever eat those flapjacks. But it didn't matter. The field workers would pay him anyway. The Mexicans always honored the labor much more than the product.

But lunch and dinnertime were a completely different story. At those meals, for a single, magical hour, the old man would stop feeling like a lowly camp cookie and transform into a snooty, self-indulgent French chef at one of those white-tablecloth restaurants. The tired boys would trudge in from the fields and wolf down his steaming mounds of pork adobo and fried rice, and at dinner the cook would pour wine from a gallon jug of Mountain Red. The workers would devour his pancit baboy, dininguan, bitter melon, even his Filipino approximation of enchiladas—but Mexicans never, ever ate breakfast. It only slowed them down.

While the cook was shuffling back and forth from the stove to the icebox, the half-sleeping boy on the table sat up and turned toward him. After quickly getting his bearings, he jumped down from the table, stepped into the little kitchen, and dipped a tin cup into a small steaming pot still full of yesterday's coffee. He lifted up the frayed strip of electrician's tape covering a slot that had been cut into an old ammo box. But his hands were shaking so violently that it took three tries to get a penny to disappear into the slot. The lid of the container had been glued down, and the slot was taped shut every night for security. It was the cook's bank—where he kept his liquid assets.

On the last day of every month for the last twenty-some years, the old cook had used a butter knife to pry and tease most of the coins and paper money out of the slot. Then he would limp into a nearby town to buy a postal money order and an international stamp. Like clockwork, he would send the money off to Manila—to an address that he had tattooed into the skin of his left wrist. Number 3 Cabugao Street, upstairs apartment. He didn't know who lived there now, but he hoped that it was one of his relatives who had opened the three hundred envelopes he had already sent.

"That old coffee is for me. I'm making a new pot for you and the boys!" the cook shouted in the softest loud voice that he could manage. He didn't want to wake the men; they still had another hour of sleep coming. He tried to take the cup of stale coffee from the boy's small hands but wasn't fast enough. He glanced up at a small clock in order to time the coffee so that it would be ready just when the men woke up. He shrugged dejectedly, then asked, "What has happened to all of my clocks? I had three of them a few weeks ago. Now two are missing, and this one here has no hands." He shrugged and reached into an ancient paper bag.

"Here's some socks and shoes. I think they'll fit." He put them on the table.

"Thank you," said Simon excitedly.

The cook lifted the shoes that the young boy had been wearing and studied them. The leather was shredded, and the soles were hardly there at all. He shook his head, then dumped the old shoes into a bin. "How far did you walk?" he asked. As the boy was putting on his new socks, the cook noticed that his feet were covered with old calluses and some recent sores. "We should wash your feet. I have some salve. How far did you walk?"

Simon did not look up. As he put on his new shoes, he noticed a dead fruit fly floating belly-up in the rainbow-colored grease slick spreading on the surface of his coffee. The poor thing had probably flown into the noxious cloud of steam above the cup and been overcome by it, falling to its death. With trembling fingers, he finally managed to pluck the dead insect from the liquid without crushing it. He laid the tiny corpse belly-up on a nearby napkin. Grimacing, he put the cup to his lips and swallowed the awful potion in two gulps.

He bent down to inspect the deceased insect. Passing his still-quivering right hand slowly over the bug, he whispered, "Abracadabra," but nothing happened. "Simsalabim, simsalabim." Then he chanted, "Milagrosamente, milagrosamente." Still nothing happened. The little bug was stone-dead.

"Don't bother with that bug," said the cook angrily. "He's better off. There's no magic in this world. Why are you shaking?" he asked in a much gentler voice. "Tienes frio? Are you cold?"

"No, señor, that's not it. I'm not cold. In my dream I heard a woman's voice. I swear it's true," whispered Simon, whose lips were purple and trembling. His lifted his eyes from the napkin and the final resting place of the deceased insect. They were wide with residual fear from the wistful, doleful sounds that he had heard during his sleep.

"I was so scared. She could barely whisper, and her skin was as white as paper. " He shut his eyes to compose himself for a moment. "She was in so much pain. She looked at me and said something to me. At first I thought she was real scary, but then I saw how scared she was . . . she had tears in her eyes. But it wasn't death that made her afraid. The sleeping men over there are all having the same dream, just like me. They're saying it was her sobs that drove them from the vineyard," said Simon with a nod toward the bunks. He listened to the groans and mumbling of the men and translated.

"Now they say that she's coming soon."

The cook glanced at the fifteen Mexicans jammed into the sleeping area. None of them was awake. Aside from all of the snoring and farting and the occasional ecstatic moan of a wet dream, he hadn't heard a thing from any of the work crew.

"She's trying to break out of heaven!" said the boy with a look of profound wonder on his face. "She's been held prisoner up there, and she wants to break out. She hates heaven! She just hates heaven!" He had babbled that sentence over and over again in his sleep. Now the words came to his lips as he drank his cold, bitter coffee.

"She hates heaven."

The old cook emptied an entire can of Maxwell House coffee into the boiling water, then turned off the burner below. Next he cracked some eggs and scrambled them briskly. In precisely three minutes, he would pour the egg mixture along with all of the shells over the surface of the hot water. It would coagulate and cook and drag the grounds down to the bottom of the pot.

"This was how the GIs made coffee at Corregidor before it fell. The Americans called it cowboy coffee." The cook remembered the GIs smoking their Lucky Strikes and Camels and swilling cowboy coffee and arguing endlessly over which of their states back home was the best place of all.

"When I get outta here, I want to go back to sweet Oklahoma."

"To hell with Oklahoma," yelled another voice. "It's so goddamn full of Okies! Arkansas is the best state."

"Hell, Arkansas's got nothin' but Arkies in it! California is heaven."

"If this is heaven," said the Filipino cook with a sneer, "then I hate heaven, too."

He wiped his hands on his dingy gray apron. Reaching under the sink, he pulled out a large, discolored canvas pouch that had once been painted an elegant shade of red and stitched with thick black string. He opened the two buckles on the pouch and removed a stack of artillery maps and some yellowed topographical charts of the Philippine Islands. As a young man, and a promising bantamweight, he had proudly carried the pouch from one boxing match to the next.

When the war broke out, he had lugged it through jungles and swamps for over two years before being captured by a Japanese patrol. Before he could destroy the contents, the Japanese soldiers seized the maps he was carrying, looked at them for a minute or two, then tossed them back to him with a laugh. He had protected a stack of worthless papers for two years, guarding them with his life. Now he had been carrying those same maps for twenty years. He shrugged to himself, then dropped them into a trash can.

"Here," he said to Simon while setting the bag down next to the boy. "That sack of yours won't protect your comic books much longer. It's got rips at every seam and a big hole on this side."

The boy studied the sturdy bag and beamed from ear to ear. He immediately began transferring his collection of comic books to the indestructible map pouch, which bore the word BOXEO on one side.

"They were trying to form an Olympic boxing team in the Philippines," the cook explained. "Everyone who made the team got one of these bags and a beautiful pair of boxing gloves. I made the team," he said with a groan. "Then they go and bomb Pearl Harbor," he whispered with a sadness that could not be measured. His shoulders sagged in exactly the same way they had sagged that day long ago. "They go and bomb Pearl Harbor."

The cook picked up one of the books and surveyed the cover as Simon hopped off the table and walked to the trash can. The boy pulled the maps back out of the can, folded each one carefully, and put them all back into the pouch along with the comics.

"Mandrake the Magician?" said the old Pinoy. There was a look of concern on his face. He picked up a second book. "Doctor Strange? What's wrong with Batman and Superman? What's wrong with Captain America?"

"Batman is just a big muscleman," answered the boy as he admired his sturdy new bag. "And even a kid knows that you can't lift a skyscraper by one tiny corner of the building. The corner would crumble away. The sidewalk would collapse under Superman's feet. Those three guys just beat people up," he said as he carefully placed the remaining books, one by one, into their new protective vault. "Batman and Superman and Captain America can't see why people are the way they are. They can't see why people do the things they do. They can't change a person's thoughts the way Mandrake can."

The cook noticed a small Mason jar that had been hastily wrapped in a dirty T-shirt. He lifted it up to eye level and peered through the dirty glass. He nodded to himself. Now he knew for certain what had happened to his three clocks. He smiled as he watched the peculiar boy close the bag and buckle it shut. "I hate heaven," he repeated to himself as he reached for a pack of cigarettes. He nodded with satisfaction as he watched the boy put on maroon boxing shoes and purple socks. Both were emblazoned with the Philippine flag. He laughed, then wandered outside to look for his Portuguese friend and have a quiet cigarette somewhere out there near the limestone caves.

Still groggy and shivering, Simon reached into his pocket for another penny. His gaze happened to fall upon the center of the napkin: the corpse was gone! The boy searched the napkin frantically. The tiny deceased had dragged itself to the very edge of the paper and was slowly flexing its miniature cellophane wings. Simon's jaw dropped wide open. The magic had worked! As the dumbfounded boy lifted his arm into a ray of light to closely inspect his powerful and mysterious right hand, the fruit fly lifted off and flew away.

In every vineyard in California, the foreman was known simply as the old Portogee—the grimy, growling viejito who loved grapes much more than he loved people; the man who talked endlessly to himself and usually slept alone, buried deep in the dank coolness of the wine caves.

But this morning he was still lying on a cot that he had picked up at the storage rooms and, after trying five or six unsatisfactory locations, had plopped down smack dab in the middle of the arroyo seco vineyard. It had taken him almost three hours to accomplish this important task, but he had finally succeeded in positioning his small bed at the exact spot where three separate winds came together after dancing and skimming separately across hundreds of acres of vines and down three steep gullies.

A precise placement of the cot had been absolutely critical. From this spot and from this spot only, he could lie in his bed and catch a whiff of the crotch and armpit of every single branch of Pinot noir. He laughed to himself at a memory that always came to him when he slept with the grapes. A middle-school chum back home in Lisbon had once run up to him out of breath and exclaiming excitedly that he had just watched a local Spanish pervert smelling the benches and the bath towels in the girls' gymnasium.

"I have become a Spanish pervert," he announced to no one at all. He preferred to think of himself as a mentalist, a mind reader who could understand the thoughts of every individual vine, every single leaf and hanging grape. In his heart, he understood that he was merely a panhandler—a beggar to the breezes, pleading with them to stop by for a moment, to dally and gossip and whisper some small tidbit about the vintage—tell him anything they pleased about this insect, that fungus, or about some wild, ravaging yeast.

He always slept out in the vineyard in the critical three weeks before the harvest. His secret trick was that he slept without breathing through his mouth, so that even the tiniest wind currents passed over the enormous pores and burst capillaries of his bulbous nose and flowed directly into his hairy and flared Portuguese nostrils. With his hand covering his mouth, the old man could smell must, mildew, and crotch rot two weeks before the most trained eye could see it—ten days before even those snot-nosed university boys at Davis with all of their chemicals and test tubes could detect it.

On this particular morning, his supernatural nose informed him that the greedy gaggle of ambitious gringos who now owned the wine label had really botched things up. He shook his head angrily. He had only himself to blame. He'd left a good job with a family winery in Lodi because of the money that these people had offered him—more than he had ever made before. The people in the three-piece suits had told him that he was going to make the juice from this shady hillside vineyard into the best wine in the state, even better than the vintages in Napa or Sonoma. That's what all of those grinning faces had explained to him when he signed the last page of that tall stack of papers. He shook his head again. Whatever happened to a good old handshake between men?

"Best money I have ever made," he said sadly. "What the fuck do I need to buy?"

Now he understood the real reason why these people had brought him in. Now he understood that he was supposed to step aside and stay out of the way, but stand by just in case their modern high-yield methods ruined the vintage. This was the new world, and he was glad that he wouldn't have to live in it for long. He shook his head in disgust. These weren't wine people at all. These people were bankers. These were wingtips and cufflinks people. These people flossed their teeth, tweezed their nose hairs, and played golf. There was no dirt under their fingernails.

This very morning, his nose had discovered two distinct and

disturbing scents. The first odor had been hiding behind the second. His nose had sniffed the acidic distress of young, colicky grapes and the hard, regretful breath of a nameless woman. He knew immediately that both were suffering, and he knew that the wind was bringing them here to this place.

The old wine master flared his encrusted nostrils again and drew in a bellyful of air. All at once he recoiled violently when he detected the alarming scent of evaporating water hovering in the air above the Quonset hut and around his precious vines. The thing he feared most was about to descend upon his fragile purple children.

The cool onshore breeze that had swaddled the grapes for weeks had been driven back to the Farallon Islands sometime around midnight, taking with it the protective blanket of fog and the bouquet of saltwater. A harsh offshore wind that threatened to dry and crack the skin of the fruit had taken its place. It was an accursed wind that would have only one positive attribute: it would blow away the reek of cologne and aftershave that always filled the tasting room after it had been invaded by those weekend wine connoisseurs from the suburbs. He noticed with glee that there wasn't a single Cadillac or European sedan to be seen in the parking lot near the tasting rooms—only a few battered jalopies; Dodge Darts and two or three Bondo-encrusted Plymouth Valiants; Mexican limousines and Tijuana town cars complete with recapped tires and shirt hangers for radio antennas.

The old Portogee shook his head and chuckled to himself. The Mexican workers reminded him of the black gypsies of long ago who came up from Morocco to pick grapes in Portugal. Those people had seemed so exotic, so mysterious, to him, but these braceros were stranger still. He glanced again at their battered, dented cars. These Mexican laborers were single-handedly keeping the Grand Auto and Western Auto stores in business.

If they had to, any one of the braceros could drop and disassemble a Hydra-Matic transmission using only a pair of pliers and a butter knife. But to a man, each of them preferred another method. In the garbage heap behind the main parking lot of the winery were hundreds of cans of Mighty Motor Magic and Uncanny Tranny Wizard, Magic Barsleeks, Mandrake's Wonder Grease, Flat Tire Hex, Radiator Genie, and a can or two of Black Magic Motor Honey.

There were bottles of Gypsy Mystery Oil, Mystic Octane Booster, and Dr. Camshaft's Supernatural Valve Unguent. Put the word "magic" on a can full of viscous fluid, and the Mexicans would snap it up by the case. The old man's musing ended suddenly when he heard a soft rustling nearby. He threw off his blankets, pulled on his old boots, and stood up without tying the laces.

"Cookie, is that you? Simon, is that you?" He fumbled under the bed covers until his hand found his weapon. He lifted a baseball bat over his head as he imagined the she-lion out there in the blackness, hugging the dirt and ready to launch her lightning strike. He had recently spotted the mountain lion on a hill above the caves. "I know it's you, Simon," he said bravely. "Where is the moon? I woke up two hours ago, and the moon was full. Now it's gone away. I can't see anything. Something's not right. Is that you, Simon? There should be a moon."

"Señor," said a small, high voice, "it's only me. I couldn't sleep. There's been almost nothing to do for almost a week now, and the men have started drinking and fighting. There was trouble."

The old Portogee finally spotted the boy's faint outline and turned to face it. Drinking? Fighting? Trouble? This meant trouble for everybody. He dropped the bat next to the cot.

"Tell me what happened!"

"Somebody got stabbed last night. Epiphanio got drunk and used his grape knife on Germán. He almost took off his whole left ear. Blood was everywhere."

"Did the cook take care of it?" implored the old man. Now he was really worried. So that was the fresh blood he had smelled. His round, inquisitive eyes narrowed to slits. "The cops, do they know? How about the big bosses?"

"Don't worry. The cook sewed him up real good," said Simon with a grimace. "Now he looks just like Frankenstein in the movies. Shit, there was blood all over the place! Cookie gave Germán a whole cup of mezcal. Then a bunch of guys held him down while he put in eleven stitches with that thirty-pound line he uses for catfishing. Now those two idiotas are best buddies again.

"It's so crazy. If what they do is grown-up, I'm gonna stay a kid. The men are laughing at them. They say they're fighting over a woman down in Los Mochis who doesn't even know they're alive. The other guys are saying that she's already had five kids and is as big as a house. They're saying that these days she has titties like waterbags. What does that mean, señor?" The old Portogee shrugged in the blackness. An unseen gesture for a question best left unanswered.

"Come next year, Germán will stab Epiphanio over the same fat woman," said Simon. "You don't need to worry. No one will call the cops, señor. We don't have a telephone. Besides, the cops are too scared to come out here. Nobody out here talks about anything but how broke they are after they send their money home. All we need is some hard work, that's all. Then everything will be the way it's supposed to be. They came here to work, señor, but the grapes are late this year."

"Yeah," said the old man. If the bean counters in the front office had listened to him two months ago, this delay and now this extra step wouldn't have been necessary.

"I told those greedy idiots they left too many buds on the vines!" he grumbled as he walked away from his cot with the boy at his side. "Twenty buds per cane is plenty good enough! Twenty-five is still OK! But what do they want, Simon? Forty, fifty! What else could so many buds mean but a big, fuckin' overcrop?" The old Portogee's hands and arms were flying angrily in the darkness as he lectured first the boy, then the hills, and, finally, the hard-of-hearing heavens.

"Grapes with no sugar, that's what you get! Then they pour water on the field like they were putting out a house fire! What do these fools expect? You can treat Syrah like shit, and it'll make a big fist and smack you in the face!" he said as he clenched his right hand and threw a punch at the night. "You can push Zinfandel around—beat it to death, and it will come back at you for one more round. But . . . Pinot? Shit no! Pinot is a pimply mama's boy. Pinot is a spoiled rotten brat. Too goddamn much work for the money you get back. It loves the fog but hates to be wet. Pinot needs the sun, but then she blisters like a Spanish nun at the beach."

He snorted his aggravation. Then it occurred to him that the finely tuned instrument in the center of his face needed calibration. The old man sealed his right nostril by pressing a craggy, crooked finger against half of his nose. He blew one or two ounces of wet detritus from the left tunnel and grinned with deep satisfaction. "Not bad." Then he remembered a question he had been meaning to ask the boy for weeks. "Where are your mama and daddy, Simon?" he said in a soft, almost apologetic voice. The boy stopped walking, shrugged his shoulders, and said nothing. The old man could not see that young Simon had begun to tremble in the darkness.

"Do you ever go to school?" The shivering boy shrugged again. "You can't be like me. Look at me. I don't live anywhere. I've got nobody. I've got nothin'. I've always been nobody. You've got to go to school—learn something more than making wine and doing hard work that will only break your back. Where is your family?"

The boy was silent. His eyes were closed, and his teeth were chattering as though he were standing knee deep in snow. He stuttered and huffed and finally began to hum a fractured tune through shivering lips. The old man recognized the melody. He had heard the boy humming it many times since that day when the wind had swept him into camp. The song seemed to comfort the child. It was an English tune, or maybe Irish. Whatever it was, it meant that Simon was not listening, that he could not be spoken to. It meant that the strange boy was in another world—a world of his own.

"Well, boy," said the old Portogee in an awkward, almost brusque manner, "as soon as they're awake and ready to go, get the men together over by the tractors—between the John Deere and the big D-8, so I can tell them what we're going to do today."

Simon stood as still as a statue when the man put a hand on his shoulder. The pain in the old master's heart traveled down the length of his worn, sinewy arm and through his callused fingers, passing directly into the boy's young flesh at the base of his neck. In an instant Simon felt every minute, every year, of the old man's age and the vast, impassable barrier blocking his way back to his family and his homeland in Portugal. Then he sensed something else, something urgent. The old man was about to say something that was welling up from the depths of his soul.

"You need a low yield. That's what you need. You need to hand-pick each grape—no machines. You need one vineyard to make one wine. You can't mix this wine with that one except when you make table wine for workers. To hell with the French! You need wood barrels—new oak. You make wine like raising a boy into an honest man, a young girl into a fine woman. All of those are things we don't have here."

"You taste the soil and the sun when you drink the wine, Simon," whispered the old man as he took a few halting steps forward. "You're supposed to taste a year that is dry and a year that is wet. It means something, Simon, that a suffering grape has better flavor than some fat, happy grape. Suffering's got flavor."

The old man stopped moving. He lifted his hand from Simon's shoulder and stared straight ahead for a long minute, then began walking once more, his ancient muscles struggling against the dragging weight of a memory. The whole vintage was hanging in the balance and could be lost in the next few hours, and he knew it. He'd seen it happen before, in Tuscany and Argentina.

He stepped back and squinted his eyes to focus on various aspects of the strange boy's face. No, he wasn't a midget. He was a boy, all right—a healthy, handsome boy. But how could a nine- or ten-year-old be living and working in these vineyards all alone? Where was he from? "Who takes care of you? You need someone to take care of you."

"La verde?" asked the boy excitedly, ignoring the question for the second time. He smiled, knowing now that it would never be asked again. "In a week the grapes will be turning purple. Maybe they'll turn in five days with the hot wind that's coming. Not enough sugar for so many grapes. I tasted one today and it's as bitter as a lemon. La verde?"

The old man spat on the ground, ending forever the discussion about Simon's family. He didn't bother to answer the boy's question. He didn't need to. Shit, the kid already knew what was going to happen next. Simon was an odd little boy, to be sure. A child his age should be playing with sticks and balls and watching baseball games. He should be daydreaming and seeing strange shapes in the clouds overhead. He should be going to school and learning about Henry the Navigator. The old man shook his head and grinned at the mysterious kid. Was he an orphan?

"Go get the men together," he said quietly. As Simon ran off on his newest mission, the wine maker walked the hundred or so yards to the breakfast table. There, as he did every morning, he would have pancakes and terrible coffee with only the Filipino cook to keep him company. The two old bachelors would worry and discuss little Simon as they had every day since he came into camp.

"He's got fifty, maybe sixty comic books—maybe more," the

cook told him this morning. "They're all about magic people; not one Superman or Batman in the whole bag!"

"No Dick Tracy?" asked the old Portogee. "I like Dick Tracy."

The cook shook his head despairingly. "And he's got a little magician's cape. I saw it. He's a dreamer. The boy wants things to happen that can't happen. And there's something else. He was having a bad dream—when I woke him up, I saw these numbers cut into his skin—on his ribcage. He didn't use a needle to do it. He used a grape knife!" The cook winced as he spoke. "He must've broken open an ink pen and put the black color into his wounds. The numbers were upside down. They weren't there a week ago. I'm sure of it. I saw his belly when I gave him a better shirt to wear. And here's something else," he said as he lifted the gutted, empty shells of three alarm clocks.

"These were good clocks!" exclaimed the cook. "One Timex and two Rexalls. He's taken all the parts out of these clocks, and several others by the look of it. He's taken out all the gears, screws, and springs. He's added them to his jar, which was already half full. It looks like he's done this before. Some of the pieces were tied together with a thin wire."

"Did something happen to his family?" asked the wine maker. "Where is his family?"

"Something real bad happened," said the cook as he smothered a rubbery pancake with butter and syrup. He stuffed a piece of it into his mouth and talked as he chewed. "I don't know what it was, but it was real bad. One of the Mexicans from Arizona knows something about it, but he's not saying much more than that. He's real spooked. He said that all the men think the boy is cursed. He said he didn't even want to think about it. I beg him to tell me what happened, but he just shakes his head and says the boy got all twisted up inside when something bad happened to his mama and papa and sisters. That's right. He said that Simon had sisters. The man won't say any more than that, but the look in his eyes told me that it was something awful."

"Do the men think he's touched—that the boy is loco?" the old Portogee asked while tapping his own temple with an index finger.

"Yeah, but a special kind of loco. He doesn't babble or bump into things. He doesn't hurt anybody, but they're real scared of him just the same. But he does do something really strange: he picks up every dead animal in the fields. Have you seen that?" His old friend nodded as a chill ran down his spine. He had seen it.

"He picks them up and carries them in that cardboard box of his. On some nights he takes the little bodies out and lines them all up behind the tasting room. He's got rabbits, rats, and two or three wild kittens. He's got fifteen of those little bodies out there— always fifteen. I've watched him. Last week when the tractor ran over that family of rabbits, the boy cried for hours. Wouldn't let anybody come near him. They're over there right now." He nodded to a large stump. "They're right over there covered with a cloth like they're only taking a nap. He just gets right up next to them, looks at them, and talks to them while he makes these crazy hand movements. I'm real worried about that boy. Real worried. The Mexicans say something else. They say he tries to fly. At night when he thinks nobody can see him, he climbs up on the eucalyptus stumps behind the bunkhouse and jumps off over and over again. He wants to fly."

"No," said the foreman and chief wine maker, "he wants more than that. Pobrecito wants more than that," he said in a whisper. He picked up one of the eviscerated alarm clocks. Every piece of the clockwork mechanism had been removed. "He wants uma máquina," he said, lapsing into Portuguese. "He wants a machine."

The cook said nothing for five long minutes before asking, "What is that song he always sings?"

"I don't know," the wine maker said, "but it sure gives me the shivers inside."

The cook filled two cups with oily coffee.

"I gave him my boxing bag," said Cookie softly, trying to downplay the importance of the gesture. He had carried that bag with him everywhere he went for over twenty years. "I gave him those shoes that I only put on twice. I won both matches."

"I sure hope there's still some fight left in that bag and those shoes," said the old Portogee, "because the boy is going to have to fight. I can't tell if he is weak or strong, if one more hurt will break him—push him over the edge. He's got nobody. He's by himself all the time, and that isn't too good for a kid. Not too good."

"All those dead animals—one more sad thing could snap his mind in two," added the cook.

After these conversations, they would say goodbye for the day. Then the wine master would leave six bits on the table for his friend. He would rinse his face at an outdoor sink. He would dry his cheeks and forehead with his shirt and comb his hair with his fingers. He would blow his nose into a filthy blue rag, then walk a hundred yards to the spot between the skinny green tractor and the fat yellow one, wipe his brow with the filthy hanky, then shout out a long list of instructions to fifteen men and a boy who didn't need any of them.

Just minutes after the instructions had been given on this particular morning, the boy saw the skydiver fall. A corner of the dawning sky had stretched open, just a tiny curved slit of light in the spreading black and indigo mesh—a small circular slot just barely large enough for a set of forceps or a vacuum extractor to go in and pull her from one world and into the next. Simon was running his grape knife across the throat of a shaded bunch of green Pinot noir grapes when yet another sharp wind came up. The woman's sudden appearance in a momentary space between the grape leaves and in the deepest part of the sky above made him lose his grip on the grapes, and he let the fruit go tumbling to the ground.

His face seized with fear as a terrible realization struck him like a sharp rock between his eyes: she was falling down because he had let go of her! After all, she had begun to fall the very instant his fingers had slid the cold edge of the grape knife across the neck of a living bunch—the moment he had done the unthinkable: he had caused living things to die before their time. The boy told himself that it couldn't be his fault. He was only doing what he had been told to do, but now she was careening helplessly down to earth.

"It's my fault!"

Simon dropped to his knees and frantically picked up the cluster of suffocating and abandoned grapes. He imagined them choking. He imagined their tiny lungs gasping for breath. He lifted them off the ground, desperately picking up three or four loose grapes and pressing them back into the strangling bunch. Then he used his other hand to clumsily spread the vines open for another view of her. The magic wasn't working. He shouted "abracadabra" seven times, but it was no good. He could see that she was still coming down.

As a last resort, he lifted up the severed bunch and hastily hung it across a bare limb—a pale pantomime of life. It was then that he saw the billowing canopies of eight parachutes snapping open, one after the other, in the sky above her. He breathed a deep sigh of relief, then began giggling at his own foolishness. He reached out once more for the ineptly resurrected grapes and brazenly let them tumble to their deaths for a second time. This act of ritual sacrifice was what the French called *une vendange verte*. Simon and the other workers were supposed to cut selected stems with their grape knives and drop the living fruit to the ground. The death of these grapes was designed to drive the sugar into the surviving bunches— the lucky ones that would live on to become wine, then have to hold their breath for years, perhaps decades, before they were allowed to breathe again.

The boy glanced at the sky once more and gasped at what he

saw. He held his breath and stopped moving; every muscle in his body was as rigid as stone. He didn't feel the tears flooding his eyes or the warm stream of pee as it ran down his leg and filled his new left shoe. He stared with growing horror as a trail of smoke coming from a highway flare that was taped to her left ankle inscribed a wrinkled and blurred line downward from the ragged-edged morning sky through the dimly visible cusp of an emerging moon, and down to an oddly shaped nimbus cloud that had formed high above the vineyard. Because of some sudden cross-currents, she was moving from his right to his left almost faster than she was moving downward.

Using all of his power to break through the sudden paralysis that had gripped him, Simon tried to cross himself, but he couldn't remember how to do it or even what the gesture was supposed to mean, so he gave up. Instead he remembered the fruit fly and slowly raised his right hand, mimicking the famous gesture of Mandrake the Magician. He moved it back and forth across her falling image while his trembling lips launched a mad flurry of "abracadabras" and a "milagrosamente" or two. Beads of sweat began to collect on his reddening cheeks and forehead as he focused all of his astral energy on slowing her fall. She was so much heavier than a small insect. Somehow everyone down on the ground knew she was a woman.

Then he turned to the strength of Dr. Strange, the power of mental telepathy to call out to someone—anyone who would tell him that this skydiver was just braver or more experienced than the rest of the jumpers, that she was just one of those crazy gringa daredevils, waiting until the very last second to pull her ripcord and settle softly onto the tilled earth between the vines. He inhaled sharply when her smoke trail reached the purplish horizon, and he lost sight of her momentarily in the rounded peaks of the hills that surrounded the vineyard.

No parachute ever popped open. The woman slammed into the

ground at the center of the vineyard. Only one person moved forward immediately to kneel by her side, and that person was a small boy in boxing shoes. No one who saw it could tell if the child was whispering into her bloody, leaden ear or merely leaning over to gently kiss her eyebrow. Perhaps the little stoop laborer was trying to pick a few words from her fruitless tongue.

Suddenly an enormous red-faced man in a green jumpsuit rushed out of the circle of onlookers that had formed in the minutes after the impact. He stormed toward Simon and grabbed him violently by the head, wrenching him aside like a useless rag. The grape knife flew from the boy's right hand and landed a dozen feet away. "What the hell were you doin' to her?" the man screamed. "Keep your filthy hands off of my wife!" The boy was terrified: there were so many gnats around the man's face that his breath was filled with them. He had fallen through a thermal, and his clothes were covered with flies. The man then turned toward the group of dark men standing quietly nearby and roared, "Keep your greaser hands off of her!" He raised a huge fist at them. "This here is none of your fuckin' business!"

A smaller man moved forward tentatively. He, too, was dressed in a green jumpsuit, and he was carrying a limp, formless parachute in his arms. "Did she pull the ripcord?" he asked. "See, her hand isn't on it! Don't make these guys mad, Pete, they've got knives. The ripcord ain't moved! I told you! She didn't even try to pull it."

The first man glared at the field workers standing around him, then leaned toward the second man and whispered through his teeth, "This morning there was this weird-lookin' guy hanging around the riggin' shack over by the hangar. I think he moved her parachute—only hers and nobody else's—away from the wood pallet where the rest of them was stacked up. He only moved hers—nobody else's. Do you get what I'm sayin'? Last night I put 'em there myself, all neat and tidy. Her chute had been dragged a good ten feet away from the riggin' shack. I caught a glimpse of some guy. Anyway, I put the chute back, but I noticed that her name tag had been torn all the way off like some mad dog had got to it."

The smaller man at his side was distracted, mesmerized by the sight of scores of tiny dying insects under the taller man's chin and around his mouth. The tall man licked his lips, then spat a small graveyard. "I told her that I'd give her chute the once-over, to see if it was A-OK and all, but she got all flustered and flighty and told me to mind my own goddamn business. I tell you, that man did something to her chute. He cut a riser or somethin'. Whoever he was, he killed her, just as sure as I'm standin' here."

"But . . . Sophia didn't pull the cord, Pete," protested the second man. "It ain't moved a quarter-inch." He watched as the big man turned toward Simon. "Leave the boy alone," warned the smaller man. "There's fifteen of them and only two of us."

"What was that Mexican boy doin' to her, anyway?" shouted the big man. "The little bastard was right in her face," he said warily while glancing around at the brown men surrounding him. "I saw his knife and I saw him kneelin' down there, right in her face, and look there! Her ear is bleeding! Both of them are! Wait! Did he cut her ears?"

The tall man frantically ripped his gaze away from his wife's face as her entire belly, then her breasts and lungs, collapsed. The front of her jumpsuit was suddenly black with blood that had oozed through a zipper. The savage force of her body slamming into the soft dirt of the heavily irrigated vineyard at 175 feet per second had created a small crater, like a concave aura made of uprooted grass and crushed clods around her entire silhouette. It was almost a foot and a half deep. There was a hazy corona of dust curling in the eddy currents that were dancing above her corpse. It had been blasted up into the air by the impact of flesh and blood on soil.

Only her face was level with the surrounding terroir. Her intestines had burst. Her limbs were shattered, but her face was completely untouched. Her flaming red hair framed her head in a perfect fan, as if she were on a soft divan posing for a painter.

Her features, her makeup and ruby lipstick, were flawless—as though the last drop of her life's blood was spent making certain that her pretty face and dimming eyes would remain intact and looking straight up into the endless, wind-filled blue—so that the very last thing of this bitter world that she would ever see was a curly-haired boy kneeling by her side. There were tears in his eyes.

—

Long after the grapes were picked, after the crush, the fermentation, and the bottling, the camp had emptied out for the year. The workers had all gone on to other jobs. The Filipino cook and the old Portogee reunited at a Zinfandel vineyard in Lake County.

"I always feel like someone is watching us. I can't help it," said the cook. Glancing around, he sat down on a battered stool. "Have you seen the boy?" he asked his friend.

"No, have you? I worry a lot, you know," said the old Portogee. "First he has no family, then he sees the woman fall. I worry."

"I ask around all the time," said the cook. "I hear he's holdin' up," he said quietly. "Maybe he'll grow up OK. Maybe. One of the men saw him in Napa. He said he seems to be doin' all right. He said something else, too. He said there was this guy—a young gringo guy—a scary, suspicious-looking guy. Not one of the workers, but a stranger who came out to that vineyard just after the woman died. He was around twenty years old. He said that he had heard the wail of the sirens and pulled his pickup behind all of the police cars and the ambulance just to see what was going on. No one believed him.

"He started moving from person to person asking about Simon—what is the boy's name, where does he live, and those kinds of things. Never asked a thing about the poor lady. As far as I know, nobody said anything to him. Nobody said a word. I told them all to shut up, but I didn't need to. The braceros said he looked like an autómata—a zombie. Who could that stranger be?" wondered the cook out loud. There was worry in his voice, which was suddenly marked by dark notes of despondency and uncertainty.

"The newspaper said that the woman skydiver died instantly. It said that her parachute got tangled by the storm. Those things aren't true! I saw the ripcord. I saw her say something to Simon. Why did the newspapers lie?"

The cook took a deep breath. With a look of painful resignation, he said, "Do you remember Germán? Do you remember the one who almost lost his ear? I sewed it back on." The old Portogee nodded. He remembered. "Well," said the cook softly, "somebody told me that the ear turned green and fell off in Lodi or Paso Robles. Anyways," he said through halting, trembling lips, "I ran into Germán over in Silverado. I saw that my stitches didn't hold up so good. These days he only has one ear. He looks pretty funny, so he grows his hair real long." The cook's face stiffened. He looked as though he was about to burst into tears.

"He told me it wasn't Epiphanio who cut his ear off," he whispered, his voice breaking in midsentence. "It wasn't Epiphanio. Germán told me that he had drunk way too much wine that night, and he had staggered outside to take a piss." A single heavy tear ran down the cook's cheek. "He saw the boy out there in the darkness near the tree stump. Simon had lit a candle and laid out all those gears and screws. Remember those?"

The wine master nodded gravely. His eyes were swollen with dread. His mind had gone back to the story that Simon had told him about the fight between Germán and Epiphanio, a fight over a woman from Morelia. The boy's explanation had seemed so believable. He looked around to see if anyone was watching them, then reached out with a wrinkled right hand. His friend extended his own left hand until their fingers clasped. Each thumb softly rubbed solace into the knuckles of the other.

"Simon was saying some of his strange words over the bodies of some of his dead animals. You know how he does. Germán said they were a bunch of dead kittens . . . fifteen of them."

"Oh, no!" exclaimed the old Portogee, now certain that something terrible was coming.

"Germán got spooked. He thought the boy was doing some kind of devil stuff—thought he was acting sick and crazy, so he crossed himself twice and stumbled over to the boy. With one swipe, he shoved all of those clock parts and all of those kittens' bodies off the eucalyptus stump—scattered them everywhere. At first the boy started to cry, and then he screamed and pulled out his grape knife . . ." Now the cook was shivering uncontrollably as he spoke. "He pulled out his knife, and he was on Germán like a wild animal."

"Oh, no!" sighed the old Portogee. "Oh, no." His hands had flown together to a position in front of his face, disinterring a long-dead posture of prayer. Now both of the old men were crying, each man holding the other in his arms. "He called our little boy un monstruo."

A monster.

2

THOSE TOPLESS TOWERS

In the present time.

She wobbled to the window to close it against the stiff, icy breeze that was blowing in from San Francisco Bay. She cursed herself as she moved. If she had remembered to shut the window last night, she would still be asleep, snug in her warm bed with her baby-to-be curled up happily beneath her ribs. She would still be groping, searching in her sleep for that childhood dream. So many times in the last few years she had almost dreamed it. It was a forgotten dream, but it was there. She was sure of it.

It was there like a word perched eternally on the tip of her tongue, like a vague scent that gives pause again and again—an aroma that almost stirs up feelings that almost exist—like a fragrant breeze faintly recalled by a shiver on the nape of the neck. She had almost dreamed it for years, confusing her nightly disquiet with anxieties about money, confusing her fitful tossing and her abuse of her pillow with red wine or acid indigestion. She had become a stutterer, struggling to enunciate in her sleep—to break the rock-hard shell of a dream impediment. No psychiatrist and no guru had ever been able to help her.

Then one day something amazing happened. In fact, it was the same day her bizarre husband and his peculiar friend installed a new high-current, high-voltage circuit and a bank of battery chargers in the garage. On that very day, her lost dream began to return to her in scattered bits and pieces—a fragment drifting into her mind while she was bathing, another while she was standing in line at the grocery. Then small but blazingly bright little scenes had begun to flutter downward onto her consciousness like solitary flakes of snow.

The light snowfall of recollections seemed to commence when Simon abruptly began skipping dinner and started sleeping in the garage. The blizzard began with full force when he started ignoring all those term papers that were stacking up in his office, when he suddenly locked himself in the basement and began working obsessively on a strange-looking contraption. The eerie whine of an antique oscilloscope and a homemade signal generator down in the garage beneath their bedroom had heralded the return of her childhood dream in brilliant color and sounds that were as vivid as life.

But the sound of singing transformers and clashing frequencies had brought something else, something more than the dulcet dreams she had once had as a girl. Now her nights were filled with indescribable sounds—explosions and whispers, curses and prayers, squalls of tears and torrents of laughter. They were flooded with inexpressible images—too terrible for words, too wonderful for words. Had Simon's mysterious work in the garage brought these on?

Her eyes scanned the enormous fog bank that had closed in beneath their hillside home. Then her gaze fell downward to the driveway, and she saw him. He was standing alone near the street. He was wearing a light shirt and was shoeless in weather that was close to freezing. His dress shoes were on the roof of the car, and there was a suit bag on top of the trunk. His curly reddish-gray hair was shaking wildly in the snapping, whipping winds. She smiled wistfully. Her own hair was beginning to gray. The twelve-year difference in their ages was becoming less obvious by the day.

"There he is . . . ," she said to no one, "a Mexican gone mad: Simon Vegas, father-to-be, and completely convinced that he is the last man on earth who should have a daughter."

There he is, she mused—the man she married, and she still

knew almost nothing about his life in the years before they met. "Even after ten years of marriage," she said to the closing window. She laughed a bittersweet laugh. Then she remembered the first time she had ever read his writing. A dozen of his poems had been published in a local magazine, and she had read them over coffee. Those poems were why she had married him.

After five minutes, he was still standing like a statue in the driveway—turned to stone by the nightmarish, tangled workings of his own mind. The doctors had called his condition post-traumatic stress disorder. Elena had studied several books about PTSD and soon realized that with one exception, Simon suffered from every symptom listed: he was super-vigilant and overly protective, of course, but oddly enough, he was never depressed.

Since leaving the military, her husband had manifested every comorbid condition in the books and had taken and rejected every medication and therapy. The bathroom cabinet upstairs was filled with unused bottles of sertraline, paroxetine, and risperidone. "He has every symptom but classical depression," his current doctor had told her. "It's weird. He's quite saddened but never depressed. Never. He freezes up for a few moments each day, then starts moving . . . and he keeps moving. There's something at his core that keeps him hopeful. It's amazing, really. It's no wonder he never takes the medication."

Elena had always wondered how Simon could not be depressed. In every other way he resembled other men who suffered from *melancholia de guerre,* shellshock, nostalgia. He was eternally troubled and had endless episodes of anxiety, and he, like many, had become a substance abuser. She laughed to herself. His drug of choice was a 1986 Château Palmer. At $250 a bottle, he had chosen it precisely because he couldn't afford more than a bottle a month.

After ten years of watching him thrash in his sleep, she had given up on the idea that some clue from his past, some small tidbit from his youth, might miraculously leap forward and explain every-thing—his opaque past and his dark, impenetrable present. He had never spoken a single word about the war, and after a decade of silence, she had come to the conclusion that he never would.

And there was something else. She had always suspected that his soul had been seriously wounded long before he ever went to Vietnam. Where was his family? Simon had no parents to call on the phone; no sisters or brothers ever sent postcards; no relatives came to dinner. There were no cousins or nephews. There were no boxes of photographs and no stories about childhood.

She reached down and rubbed her huge, distended belly. That statue in the driveway was about to become a daddy. The possibil-ity of it had unsettled her for years. Then, seven months ago—for her own happiness, if not his—she had stopped taking the pill. The clock was ticking—the alarm about to go off. She smiled at the idea of him as a papa. Just a few weeks ago, the impossible, the unimaginable, had happened. Her life—her entire world—had been upended, altered forever.

She smiled. In the last two months, a few rays of light had bro-ken through the obscurities of her life with him. After years of frus-tration, she had finally made up her mind to find out who Simon Vegas really was. The time had come to stop asking and start look-ing. She had begun by snooping—by going through his notebooks in the library. She had pored over reams of his poetry but never found any of his earlier poems. She had read and reread the only book of poems he ever published but could find nothing.

"Even as a poet, he never speaks about himself." She thought about what she had just said aloud and added, "Of course he does. But he has camouflaged himself with symbol and metaphor." In his latest poems, her husband had hidden himself in tercets and quatrains—verse that is anything but free. She had examined his wallet and inspected every page of his old passports. She had dug through his boxes of notes from his classes and lectures, all to no avail. After giving up on the obvious, she had turned her attention to the garage. While pretending to clean it, she had moved some of Simon's wine racks and tools and stumbled upon a dusty old canvas bag. The word BOXEO was stitched in white thread on one side.

Simon had concealed the bag in a dark, musty nook. It had been shoved into a cardboard box and hidden beneath a stack of *Scientific American* magazines in exactly the same way that other men hid their collections of pornography from their wives. When she finally built up enough courage to open the bag, she somehow sensed the enormity of what might be inside it. Her hands were shaking as she undid the buckles that had sealed it.

Could her husband be a pervert—a closet pedophile? Was he a porn addict? Did this old bag contain the dark secret that he had kept hidden from the world—from his wife? When her fingers found the first book, she shut her eyes, then carefully pulled it from the bag. When she opened her eyes, she fell to her knees and gasped with shock and confusion. Then she began laughing hysterically. In her hands was a fragile, yellowed first edition of *Mandrake the Magician*. She tenderly turned the cover page and began to read.

It was this very comic book that had explained to her at last the origin, if not the true meaning, of those ridiculous movements that he made every morning in front of the bathroom mirror. She had always wondered why he stood there, wrapped in a bath towel, his eyes narrowed to slits while he pointed all five fingers of his mangled right hand at the looking glass. Now she knew that he had been gesturing hypnotically just like Mandrake.

That morning in the garage, she had also discovered scores of copies of *The Phantom* and *Dr. Strange*. It was evident from the condition of the comics that every page had been devoured hundreds, if not thousands, of times over the years. It was also clear that these books had been cherished and protected, first by a small boy, then by a soldier, then by a grown man. She found a jar crammed to the lid with tiny gears and springs. In other boxes she found hundreds of maps and countless ledgers filled with incomprehensible codes—page after page of scribbled and scrawled numbers.

She had laughed out loud at the absurdity of it all. She discovered from these comics that Simon's mind didn't always kidnap his soul and drag it back to Vietnam as she had always suspected. Now she understood for the first time that there were other places to which he might be taken. She imagined her husband's ethereal presence gliding through space on the other side of the galaxy while waging psychic warfare against a lizard-skinned Venusian warlord.

Or he might be in some faraway European capital fighting side by side with the Phantom, projecting his astral Mexican essence against the prodigious synthetic brain of a six-eyed alien menace from the planet Zothrax. After reading a third comic book, she felt a wave of deep sadness traversing her soul. Vietnam was insane, but at least it was real.

One morning just four weeks ago, Elena had called Simon's good friend Zeke and asked him to come to the house. Ezekiel Zacharias Stein, a private investigator for several attorneys in San Francisco, was a man whose spirit was forever locked in a struggle between Zen archery, Carl Jung, and rabbinical school. After begging him not to reveal anything that she was about to show him, Elena had led him down the wooden stairs and past the wine racks. After several minutes of soul-searching and hesitation, she showed him the secret trove that she had discovered in the garage.

When she pulled the buckles at the top of the bag, a hundred comic books spilled out onto the workbench. Elena had told him about the satchel over the phone, but Zeke had imagined the usual Aquaman, Captain America, or Daredevil comics. To his astonishment, there was not a single flying, acrobatic, muscleman hero in the entire bag of colorful books—only fantastical bearded magicians draped in majestic robes.

She shoved a small table saw to one side, moved a drill press back toward a wall, and showed him a box that had been invisible behind all of the tools. It was jammed with ledgers. She opened one, then two, for him to see. Each one was filled with dizzying sets of numbers. Zeke noticed that many of the ledgers predated the Vietnam War. Finally she showed him a wooden box that had been carefully crammed with folded maps—hundreds of maps, including a few that were of museum quality. When she lifted the box, the bottom fell out, spilling the contents everywhere. She turned on several overhead lights, then stood there, her mouth gaping.

She and Zeke found themselves wading ankle deep in maps—grid maps, topographical maps, military and street maps. There were maps of Germany, Cambodia, and France. There were maps that her own father had loved: the Hereford Mappa Mundi, the Piri Reis map, and the *Fragmenta tabulae antiquae*. She immediately recognized the Catal Huyuk map, the Pavlov map, and the reconstruction of the Madaba Mosaic by Eratosthanes of Cyrene. There were maps of pre–Civil War Atlanta and haunted Gorée Island, a diagram of Sing Sing Prison lying on top of a map of Auschwitz and one of the Bastille. There were wind charts, maps of ocean currents, and a map of the little village of My Lai. Then she saw it: a beautiful copy of her father's most cherished map, the *Tabula Peutingeriana*.

She knelt down in the mass of papers. Behind the box she had discovered a battered leather binder. She opened it and found hundreds of photographs and hand-drawn diagrams of a strange mechanical device. She turned the pages, perusing each one, and found blueprints, electrical diagrams, and three-dimensional drawings, all in Simon's hand. She found decades of correspondence with the curator of a museum, with an archaeologist at Yale, and with an antique electronic supply house in Tempe, Arizona. She found four pages from a *National Geographic* magazine that described an ancient machine that had been pulled from the sea. The pages almost disintegrated in her hands as she handed them to Zeke.

"I've seen this machine," she whispered excitedly. "He recently started working on it down here with an odd little man named Hephaestus Segundo. The little man walks with a limp," she added. "Is that a real name?"

"Maybe, but probably not," said Zeke thoughtfully. "Hephaestus was a cunning blacksmith to the gods. He was a god of fire and of artisans, but he suffered a demotion. I think he was replaced by Hermes. His city, Hephaestia, is on the island of Lemnos. In the most archaic iconography, his feet face backward. Hephaestus has always been associated with alchemy."

"Who is this man who's working with Simon?" wondered Elena aloud.

"I'll find out," said Zeke with a comforting smile.

When she stood up again, she was clutching a dirty, moth-eaten piece of folded cloth that had also been in the binder. She carefully opened it and stood staring at it for a small eternity. It was a tiny magician's cape that had been sewn by hand to fit the neck of a small boy. It was black with silver piping. It was covered with hand-sewn crescent moons and stars. Someone had stitched the initials S.V. into the lining with great love and an equal amount of care. She traced the stitches with her finger. She sensed the work of a woman. Long ago, someone had loved Simon Vegas.

"He has some maps that my father would have coveted. Museums and experts all over the world have been searching for decades for a glimpse at some of these. There is a map here"—she lifted a small tube and pulled out a tiny roll of brittle yellowed paper—"that was mentioned in Aristotle's comedies. This one over here is said to have survived the final fire at the Alexandrian Library."

Elena carefully replaced the tiny maps, then pulled out another. She began to tremble as she unfolded it and showed it to Zeke. Every square inch of this chart was covered with Simon's rambling, enigmatic notes, all in pencil. Some of the notations were done in a child's primitive cursive. "He really is unhinged, isn't he? He isn't well. He isn't going to get better, is he?" she asked no one in particular. It was less a question than a realization. A few of the letters had even been written backward. Simon had been at this for a long time—for most of his life.

Almost as an afterthought, she told Zeke that there was a fading, spreading tattoo on Simon's belly, a line of numbers written one above the next. "Each number is upside down," she said. "It's crudely done, like a prison tattoo." The indistinct green constellation she described had obviously been done long ago using a penknife and some India ink. Like the universe, the individual cuts had spread apart and away from each other as his body grew from childhood to adulthood. Elena said that sometimes at night she would gently touch those numbers or place an ear next to the pulsating, living list. She had always known that if those unusual markings ever spoke to her, it would be with a small boy's voice.

After their discovery of the binder in the garage that day, Elena had given Zeke a piece of paper on which she had written down the numbers in a vertical list. They were the same size and in the same order as those on Simon's stomach. Each of the twelve numbers would be right side up for young Simon but upside down to an external viewer. It was a mysterious code that neither the wife nor the investigator had been able to crack. After a week of trying, Zeke decided to go ask a god. He took a trip to the outskirts of nearby Emeryville and asked a man named Hephaestus Segundo about the enigmatic numbers.

"What are they?" he inquired while turning the pages of a dusty little book that he had found on Hephaestus's cluttered workbench. It was *The Book of Abraham the Jew*.

"No," the eccentric man answered without even bothering to lift his eye from the lens of a handmade Minoan microscope. "Wrong question, señor. Where are those numbers? That's the true question. That's the question. Dónde están? Now, put that book down and get out of here. I have plenty of work to do." Then he added: "Please, put it down carefully. It's over eight hundred years old. Isaac Newton once owned it."

"Professor Roberto Cantú," Zeke had explained to Elena later. "His family says that he went off his rocker about five years ago. One morning he drove off to the university as usual. He was supposed to give a lecture on the poetry of Octavio Paz, but he never made it to class and he never came back home. He left behind everything he owned, everything he loved, and moved up to Emeryville. They found his abandoned car at a bus depot in Oxnard. His suit and briefcase were left on the front seat. The keys were in the ignition switch. He left a wife and three kids in San Gabriel.

"His little girl told me on the phone that he shows up on their front doorstep twice a year and hands his wife a large leather pouch containing two ten-pound bricks of pure gold. The little girl claims that her papa has found a way to make gold out of bullet casings and aluminum lawn chairs. The family has moved to a larger house in Calimesa, and they've put in a half-acre playground and a swimming pool, but their hearts are still broken, and they still want their papa back."

While she was in the garage with Zeke, Elena had noticed that one map had not been in the box with all the rest but was on the workbench near Simon's arc welder. It had been unfolded and spread out. It must have been placed there within the last two days. She sensed that it had been singled out and set aside for a reason. There were pencil marks on its surface, and a large X had been drawn near the center of the small town. Next to the X the initials J.W. were written in and underlined. She picked the map up carefully and studied it for a minute or two. It was a very old map of Waco, Texas.

3

STRANGE FRUIT

Elena's dream was a timeless and edgeless cocoon that had been meticulously hand-spun, thread by slender thread, during the three thousand days of her childhood. When her hands were as small as a kitten's paws, she had woven into the weft the tender white filaments of an infant's vague and endless appetites. Then she had interleaved fragile blue threads of childish longing that would all too soon be overpowered by thick strands stained a reddish menstrual hue—by a new warp of desires—a confusing, compelling, all-encompassing web of design that had been waiting at the very center of her chrysalis.

The clatter and chatter of the two men working in the garage had been the signal for her inner self to come out of hiding. It had brought forth the small child who had been secreted within her soul—the girl who had once endlessly dreamed of being abducted by a gallant prince who would take her to a faraway throne that was surrounded by the topless towers of Troy. Heralded by a fanfare of harmonics and by the induction fields of power tools, the reunion of Elena and her childhood memories had been spectacular.

Now that her dreams were no longer mute and buried, the grown woman could once again recall them. There she was, brusquely shooing away the minstrels with a blasé glance, waving them away with a buoyant, unconscious flutter of a single finger while half-plucked notes and their myriad echoes and overtones still hung in the air. Even before they were gone, she saw herself brazenly dropping her gown and sashes to her feet as if she were simply beyond common human modesty—disrobing like an impatient ethereal being that was finally able to shed the dull, dead weight of a useless mortal torso.

She heard a muted incantation sung by minstrels who only pretended to be eunuchs, who only acted at averting their eyes as she passed by in the nude. Could that soft disturbance in the air be the sound of Simon's electronic equipment, or was it the coy whispering of her virginal maidservants as they busily reapplied waxed lids to jars of perfumed oils?

It was all an exotic invention, first conjured up within the four corners of a small bedroom in Brooklyn, where her bed had been crowded with stuffed animals and the walls had been covered with copies of her father's precious maps. Her papa had been a professor of ancient cartography at NYU, and every night of her childhood was spent on his lap in a fat chair that was stationed beneath a copy of the *Tabula Peutingeriana*, the most famous map of all. Night after night was passed beneath that map, listening to her papa's grand tales about the edges of the earth and the shining walls of Troy.

Three times over the course of several years, her father had read the entire epic poem to her. In her callow yet agile mind, the splendid vision had been endlessly reworked and re-polished during the dreamy incubus of childhood and through the awkward years of adolescence. Then one day she had awakened to that disquieting, dolorous morning when the secret life of the growing girl must come face to face with the wanton wishes and cruel disappointments of the woman. Why had her beloved father set those useless romantic dreams in her heart just a few years before his own weak heart gave out?

For years she hadn't known what her bearings should be. Now she was about to be a mother, and she was married to a disturbed and singular man. Within his brain was an alternate vision of the universe that coexisted only tenuously with the one that he was forced to share with everyone else on the planet, including his wife. She sighed quietly. Simon often seemed lost and foundering—and she was lost in her own life, with no map that could tell her which way to go.

She walked across the living room and pushed the curtains to either side. Her eyes were greeted by the thin rosy fingers of dawn touching the Oakland hills and stretching all the way from Point Richmond to Hayward. Elena leaned toward the window until she felt the cool dampness of the glass pane against her forehead and fingers. Then she suddenly jerked her hand away and glanced down at herself with a look of amazement on her face. For an instant she had not recognized the contours of her own amply distorted and inflated temple.

She stared in shock at her own nakedness, at what looked like three flesh-colored balloons tied to a single tether. There were two swollen, naked breasts below her chin and a massive mound centered just beneath them. Then, at the very top of the distended tummy, she saw something that almost caused her to break out in laughter. It was the unmistakable outline of an unborn child's tiny right hand pressing upward against a mother's taut skin.

The area just above the belly button had lifted up slightly, and the pressure of the unborn's touch had dislodged the blood at the surface, forming the perfect image of a small palm and five little fingers. In another instant the miniature imprint had vanished, the fingers behind it receding backward into the ancient briny deep. The mother-to-be nodded her head in stupefied acknowledgment. The semaphore had been sent and received, if not fully understood.

Elena's thoughts returned to the man in the driveway. She could see that he was still there, but not really present at all. Even from this distance, she could see the ugly scar on the back of his right hand. He never spoke about it, but recently he had flippantly referred to it as his magic hand. She had asked him about it, but as with everything else, he would never explain how the injury happened or when. She had seen him spend hour after hour looking at one side of the hand, then turning it over to carefully inspect the other side. He had wasted hundreds of hours of his life studying two scars—a small, almost invisible one on the palm and a large, obscene gnarl of waxy flesh on the opposite side.

The back of his hand looked like a frozen whirlpool made of brown wax. When they had first married, his hand had given her solace and comfort. Whenever she felt troubled or had a moment of disquiet, she wouldn't wring her own hands; she used to twist and rub his, following the veins as though they were streams of calm, trickling water moving through a troubled landscape.

The form of Simon's odd friend appeared suddenly in the driveway. He had spent the night in the garage and was walking home to Emeryville. He passed Simon but said nothing. She wasn't sure when Hephaestus Segundo had first begun coming by the house. He would appear at the back door in the early morning and wait patiently until Simon woke up and let him in. Then the two of them would disappear into the garage for whole days and nights, doing whatever they did down there.

Only recently had Elena discovered that each time Hephaestus came to the house to work, the bag of comics, the maps, and the ledgers would be spread out across the floor as though the two men were using them as some of sort of template or diagram. She had managed to catch a glimpse of them at work while pretending to take out the garbage. At the end of their workday, everything would be carefully picked up and hidden from view once again.

Sometimes while they were working in the garage, Elena would sneak down the stairs and spy on the two men as they mumbled, laughed, and cursed at their mysterious tools and their secret project. On several occasions she had witnessed a blinding arc flashing across their workbench. Those indoor lightning strikes had blown every fuse in the house. Once, a few months ago, the entire building had begun to shake, and a transformer across the street erupted into flame. At first she thought that an earthquake had rumbled through the fault line in the Oakland hills, but no other home on the block had been affected. Simon and Hephaestus had both suffered first-degree burns on their hands and forearms that day.

Finally, just one week ago, Elena had decided that the time for cowardly snooping was over. She brazenly waddled down the stairs and was about to confront her husband and his weird friend when she was overwhelmed by savage waves of vertigo and nausea. She nearly fell from the last step, but Hephaestus rushed across the garage and caught her just in time. He carefully placed a chair behind her and eased her down into it.

"Close your eyes," he said softly. "Try to relax. The dizziness won't last long. You see, we can't just turn it off. Every time we do, there's a lightning storm in this room. It has to be powered down slowly. It's all my fault. The device hates alternating current. I've got to build better batteries," he added in a rising, impatient voice. "I must scale down the power supply and find a way to shrink the power cells. Please don't be alarmed by any of what you see or feel, señora. This is the first test run of this version of la máquina, the machine."

Elena had done as she was told, but despite her tightly closed eyes, her optic nerves were pelted with images. First a billion photons bombarded her eyelashes. Next she felt the gravity and the space around her body twisting and flexing. Then all at once she saw it, unfolding like the brightest dream she had ever experienced—brighter even than the walls of Troy. It wasn't possible! She looked in every direction. The garage was gone! The walls and ceiling had disappeared! Her own dreams had never been like this. Whose dream was she having?

She found herself in a wheat field under a cloudy sky. Simon and Hephaestus were nowhere to be seen. The sweet scent of flowers and the pungent odor of dried grass flooded her nostrils. This was more than a dream. She looked around, and what she saw took her breath away. There, no more than five feet away from where she sat, was Vincent, looking wild and otherworldly, precisely like his self-portrait of 1889. She saw his eyes, and he looked directly into hers. She shivered violently. His intentions were clear.

Van Gogh, the great artist, had reached the point—the minute and the split second—when a singular piercing vision, an incomparable slant on the world, had been irreversibly transmuted into hopelessness, into a deafening solitude. She had reached out for him, but in the end he had plummeted away from her, free-falling into his illness. Elena clutched desperately at Vincent's arm—at the arm of her chair. As a girl she had always longed to help him, to save him. She shook her head wildly to clear it of the stark, unsettling images.

It had happened to Spinoza, too. It had happened to Hemingway, thought Elena. She recoiled violently at the booming report of the shotgun and all those words that were being sprayed across the porch in Idaho. It was as if she had been there—at all three places! She closed her eyes even tighter and inhaled deeply, clearly recalling Vincent's final breath—the turpentine scent of desperation and dementia—the polar opposites of inspiration. Spinoza's breath had exuded the same piercing, pungent smell, but the man could barely exhale at all. She could smell the cloying odor of world-weariness clinging to the wallpaper of his little rooms. His lungs had been clotted with bits of glass. Hemingway had held his breath.

Elena felt as if she had been drugged. She was wobbly—saddened and incongruously giddy at the same time. In the same instant she felt as though she had just been cut free of some tight, unrecognized restraints. She felt invisible fetters falling away. The walls of the garage reappeared and began to bend around her like the mirrors of a fun house. Then, as if in a dream, she heard her husband's voice: "We have no choice. She's got to come with us."

"Where are we going?" asked Elena weakly. "Where?"

"I've waited most of my life for this," said Simon as he lifted the jerry-rigged machine from the workbench and strapped it around his upper body, using a pair of antique leather bandoliers that formed an X across his chest. He looked just like the Mexican bandido Pancho Villa. Three motorcycle batteries had been taped together and were in a small pack that he slung over his left shoulder. A folded map was stuffed beneath one of the bandoliers.

"Julius Rosenberg," whispered Simon to Hephaestus and Elena, "probably died before the blue current burned its way through the core of his body. He expired in just a few seconds. On the other hand, his wife took three full-power jolts and over fifteen minutes to die. The stench and smoke from Ethel's living, baking corpse billowed through the execution chamber and drove out the gagging priest and the coughing, red-eyed executioner."

Simon pulled a wire from the battery pack and plugged it into the apparatus on his chest. He flipped a switch and began turning various knobs. Elena tried to look around and determine where in the universe she was, but she could learn nothing from her sense of sight. She could see only darkness. Her ears dimly heard her husband's voice, but she had no idea where he was or if he was actually speaking to her. She seemed to be weightless and high up in the air. The sensation of it frightened her. She swooned, and her stomach churned. Her baby's feet were tapping against her ribs—*a tinker shuffle picked up in the street.*

"It was over half an hour," shouted Simon over a noisy wind, "before the doctor could be forced to lurch blindly into the chamber. He stumbled back out just a few seconds later. He went in covering his nose and mouth with a handkerchief and called the death without even touching her peeling, smoking skin or feeling for a pulse. And Ethel Rosenberg was innocent of the charges against her. Here come the other winds!" he warned in a fierce voice. "Don't back away. Punch them as hard as you can."

In a slice of a split second, Simon Vegas and Hephaestus were shielding Elena while bobbing and weaving and throwing quick jabs at an aggressive onshore gust. Then, just as suddenly, all three were shooting through the clouds and soaring high above San Francisco Bay while simultaneously flashing backward in time to the 19th day of June in the year 1953.

"What happened to the pyramid?" shouted Elena above the blowing winds. "Look, all of the cars on the bridge are painted black and have whitewall tires."

They turned eastward and streaked across the country at almost the speed of light, arriving in Ossining, New York, at the stroke of midnight. Simon instantly realized that the machine on his chest had made an error. He and Hephaestus began to recalibrate it in order to travel back even farther in time to a point just before sundown. After making some careful adjustments to the peculiar-looking instrument, the three plunged through the ether and the black clouds above Ossining, then dove downward, passing like ghosts through the stone walls of the penitentiary.

They penetrated three tiers of cells before materializing at the ceiling of the Sing Sing death chamber. Simon spun around quickly and finally spotted tiny Ethel down below. Her head was already on fire. Smoke was billowing out from beneath a black hood that was covering her quaking face and shoulders. When Hephaestus and Elena turned away from what they saw, Simon told them to cover their eyes and move to the far side of the room.

Simon gestured hypnotically with his right hand and uttered a string of mystical words. In the blink of an eye, he materialized directly in front of the electric chair and immediately mesmerized the three guards who were standing in the room. Each one of them was instantly hypnotized into believing that the person who had just appeared in the center of the death chamber was none other than Miss Bette Davis, resplendent in a tight-fitting black dress that was covered in sequins and pearls. Her right hand was perched seductively on her hip, while her upraised left hand clutched an ivory cigarette holder that was tipped with a smoking Lucky Strike. In a pocket of her gown was a small golden statuette, an Oscar.

The electrician and the medical staff, men who were younger than the guards, never saw Bette Davis at all. Instead they saw a steamy, blonde-haired Lauren Bacall. The ravishing young star of the silver screen was dressed in a tan skirt and a revealingly tight white sweater. Each one of the staff members instantly stopped what he was doing and stared in dumbfounded awe at the famous star moving in their midst.

"Why are they looking at him like that?" asked Elena. Hephaestus shrugged.

None of them noticed that Bette was busily fiddling with a strange contraption that was strapped around her midsection just below her bosom. None of them realized that she was magically turning the clock back even farther—some forty-five seconds, to a point in time before Ethel's eyes bulged in their steaming sockets, then thirty seconds even farther back, to a moment just before her skin began to sizzle and spit.

The guards, the doctors, the electrician, and the prison priest all stood with stupid smiles on their gawking faces and watched in mute fascination as the billowing smoke folded inward, curling back into Ethel's head and returning every precious memory to its proper place in her mind. Then her singed twigs of hair swelled back into lustrous auburn locks, and her body temperature dropped precipitously from 140 to 98 degrees. Then lovely Lauren Bacall—or perhaps Bette Davis—tore away the leather and metal manacles and put an end to all of that horrid pain once and for all.

The movie star lifted Ethel, living and breathing, from the chair and flew her body through the ceiling of the death chamber and through the stone walls. Then she and Elena, Hephaestus, and Ethel flew far, far away from that dreadful expression of the public will, and far from that ghastly, unspeakable room.

During the trip down to the southlands, the small woman in Simon's arms never once stopped talking. High over the island of Manhattan, she began her motherly harangue by bragging about her fabulous recipe for brisket, and she was still lavishing herself with praise as they soared over the islands just off the coast of Georgia.

"Trim the fat, sure, but not all of it. Not all of it. Not even half of it. If you do, your whole family will be sitting around the table gnawing on shoe leather. You gotta have marbling. Besides, it's tradition. Everyone ate fat in the shtetl. What else did we have? Of course, the butchers in Florida are nothing like the ones in New York. Why am I talking like Fanny Brice? Now listen carefully. First you braise the meat until it is brown everywhere. Open all the windows! You have to use really high, scorching heat and a good, heavy pan."

She fell silent a few seconds after the words "scorching heat" left her lips. She closed her eyes, then nearly fainted at the thought of burning meat. She gagged when she remembered the smell of her own flesh catching fire. Ethel reached up and fearfully placed a hand on the top of her own head. She smiled when her fingers locked onto a thousand strands of dark, healthy hair. It was all there. No one had come into the room to shave her scalp. Now no one ever would.

"You brown a dozen chopped onions," she said quietly, as though finally able to tear her attention away from some small distraction, "and pour them over the meat. Then you add two or three cans of onion soup. Cover it all with tin foil and cook it for a day. Presto! That's brisket, Mr. Vegas. That's brisket!"

Over the city of Atlanta she finally changed the subject, complaining endlessly about the corns on her toes, caused by the cheap shoes the prison guards had forced her to wear on her last walk.

"The shoes were horrid! What's with those cardboard soles! The panties were even worse. I think they were made out of sandpaper. My rash you should see."

The quartet finally descended through a noisy squadron of seagulls and down toward endless rows of identical streets of cookie-cutter front porches and lawns in an outer suburb of Boca Raton, just as the sun was emerging from behind a cloud bank.

"My god, this place is enormous," she exclaimed. "Retirement homes from one horizon to the other! That's the unit, over there! No, that's not it! I've seen pictures of it. Oy gevalt! Is that Rebbe Elias's house? You know, back in the neighborhood, he had such a thing for me. Such a beheyme, David Elias. I did better with Julius. Well, at least I did for a while. There it is over there! No, that's not it, either," she shouted anxiously, unable to contain her excitement at the mere possibility of seeing her cousin's home once again.

Sadie's face was one of the millions of images that had flashed through her mind after the electrodes were attached to her scalp and her wrists and the hood was pulled down over her face.

"I seem to remember," she said with a look of sad confusion, "that Sadie died at Bergen-Belsen as a young woman, but that can't be right, can it? She wasn't in that awful tent camp! No, that can't be right. I've seen her all grown up. I've seen her, Mr. Vegas! She sends me letters. She survived Bergen-Belsen! She tells me that she wears two brassieres every single day! Can you imagine? A white one for housecleaning and cooking, and a frilly black one for the evening.

"I mean—what cooking does she do? Water the woman couldn't boil! She washes both of her size double D *Büstenhalter* in gobs of Woolite every night, then hangs them out on a line in the front yard. They would dry just fine over the shower curtain, but no—in the front yard for the world to see! She's trying to get a man, you know. Her dear Herschel passed, six years now. No, wait a minute. I'm confused. Did Herschel die a lifelong bachelor? He's a distant cousin of mine—a lifelong bachelor?"

The woman closed her eyes and tried to rearrange the jumble of thoughts rushing through her mind. Then she shook her head from side to side. Sadie had survived Bergen-Belsen. That would be a better world. She had married Herschel. That would be the best world. She is alive and living in one of those units down below.

"She's had her eye on the guys who just moved in next door," she continued with almost the same rapidity as before. "She's lucky. She wrote me a letter and told me that her neighborhood is very strange, in a good sort of way. She'd never seen anything like it. A few streets over there are nothing but Japanese people. She told me they are living on Fat Man Avenue and Little Boy Street. Such odd names! On the next street over, everyone seems to be from Armenia. There are lots of men. There are people everywhere, but the place is never crowded—and each and every one of them is dressed in a flowery Hawaiian shirt, no less!

"She sent me a photo of these two rather handsome-looking Italian men living just across the fence, and a wallet-sized picture of another one living right next door to her. Sadie says that the guy next door is a solitary fellow, always staring up at the night sky . . . and he used to wear the strangest old robes. Now he wears Hawaiian shirts like everyone else."

"His name is Giordano Bruno," said Simon. "He was burned at the stake for teaching astronomy and science."

"Whatever," said Ethel with a shrug. "Live and let live, I always say. There's a lovely little French girl on the other side of her, and there are hundreds of dark African people across the street. The funny thing is that they all have Jewish names. I guess they are all from one of the lost tribes. Oh, my. This community is enormous.

Look around, Mr. Vegas; it seems to go on forever.

"She says the French girl is very pretty, but she has this dreadful Prince Valiant haircut, and not an ounce of makeup. Sadie says she never smiles except when she looks at her son. In her picture she seems so very sad, like someone hurt her really badly. Sadie told me that the French girl almost never leaves her apartment. She has her adopted son living with her. He's five years old, from one of those countries in Asia that no one has ever heard of . . . and all he ever eats is chocolate candy! Now that I think about it, Sadie says that everybody here stays close to home. They go out to their social centers and play canasta and horseshoes and such, but they never go into town. I wonder why that is."

"I see the bras!" shouted Simon with enthusiasm. "They're hanging on a clothesline two streets over, and you're right, they're enormous. They look like shopping bags. I can see a two-tone white and green Rambler Ambassador with fender skirts and a continental kit parked out front. It has a Star of David hood ornament. It's parked next to a fish pond."

"That's it! That's Herschel's precious land yacht. Nothing was too good for that car of his. Oh my god, Sadie is going to faint when she sees me! She'll pee in her pajamas and fall flat on her fat tuchis. Serves her right! She wouldn't come to my execution—she said she couldn't bear it. But I know better. She never gets out of the house, Mr. Vegas, unless someone drags her out kicking and screaming. How does she ever expect to meet a man? But now that I'll be living here, we can go to bingo night and play canasta until all hours . . . until eleven-thirty at night!"

"Now that you're here, you don't have to be careful anymore," said Simon as he banked around a stand of palm trees and came in for a soft landing near a small artificial pond at the edge of a well-worn putting green. Hephaestus and Elena were only a few feet behind. Every hole was festooned with a tiny Israeli flag.

"You can talk about the trial or about the atomic bomb if you wish. After you've been here for a while, the past won't matter so much. People here live for each other. They do things they've always wanted to do. You could change your hairdo and maybe even dye your hair. I think strawberry-blonde hair would be good. You can even change your name if you wish."

"You're right!" said Ethel with an eager, animated smile. "I do have the skin for it!" She snapped her fingers with exhilaration. "A new name . . . I know just the name for me! When I was a girl, I once met a woman—a real darling—at a train station near Trenton. Her name was Ruth Malcah Edelstein. Such an impression she made! She was a lawyer from San Francisco out here on the East Coast visiting her family. She seemed so imposing to a little ketzellah like me—so inspiring with that big briefcase and all. Even then I wanted her name. Ruth Malcah Edelstein," she said while carefully pronouncing each delicious consonant and syllable." Did you know that Malcah means queen in Yiddish, Mr. Vegas? Now all of my friends here in Boca Raton can call me Queenie."

"Well, Queenie," said Simon as his feet touched down in a small sand trap, "I hope to see you again." He released his hold on her legs and let her feet touch the ground and green grass for the first time since her arrest almost three years before. Then he took his left arm from her shoulder and stepped back from the small shivering woman, who began rubbing her wrists, then the top of her head. A look of dazed distress had suddenly dislodged her recent burst of excitement over her new name.

She reached down and grabbed a handful of sand, then let it dribble out from between her fingers. She fell deathly silent as she stared intently at the falling grains. Her once-elated face had been transformed into an ashen and weary mask. When she spoke again, her voice was solemn and funereal—muted and muffled, as though she were speaking from within a coffin—from beneath a layer of soil.

"Did you see me, Mr. Vegas?" she asked without looking at her rescuer. "Please be truthful. Did you see me?"

"Yes," answered Simon in a somber whisper. "I saw you."

"Was I burning? Did all of it happen? Did that awfulness happen to me?"

She turned to look in Simon's direction, but her eyes were seeing right through him.

"I seem to remember coming to a precipice—up to a place of total blackness, then a pain beyond description. Is that all that we are, Mr. Vegas? Are we just bodies this far from pain or that far from suffering? Are we like those shiny steel balls in that plinky-plinky pinball machine that my two boys would so dearly love to play eight hours a day? Are we battered and beaten, sent on journeys short and long—all to keep from falling into that hole? Did I fall into the hole, Mr. Vegas? Did that awfulness happen to me?"

Simon averted his eyes and said nothing. He slowly began to levitate, lifting his feet just inches from the ground and balancing carefully with his outstretched arms. With all of his inner strength, he pushed away the chilling image in his mind of a small mother of two boys being seared from the spinal cord outward. He turned his face away from her as his mind's eye clung to its revolting view of three wispy columns of acrid smoke rising from her wrists and her naked scalp. He shook his head as he rose to an altitude of three feet above the ground.

"What is that machine you have buckled to your chest? What are those blinking lights? Did you see Julius, too?"

"It's a very special kind of gadget," said Simon. "No, I haven't seen Julius. Not yet," he said with a reassuring smile. "I have to go back to Sing Sing, but an hour or so before I saw you. I'll do that in a day or two—after we've adjusted this machine."

Then a terrible thought seemed to surge through her body and creased her face into a new mask of grief. "Where are my babies? Do you know where my babies are? Can I see them? Can you tell them where I am, Mr. Vegas? Can't you at least tell them that I'm alive?" She grabbed Simon's pant leg and tried to drag him back down to the ground.

"Your boys will soon be living with Abel Meeropol and his wife, Anne. They'll grow up healthy and strong, Queenie. They will always remember you and their father. They will always love you both. Abel wrote a famous song called 'Strange Fruit.' It's about the lynchings of blacks in the South. Billie Holiday made it famous. I think I'll get Julius next Friday."

"Don't let him suffer," said Queenie as she walked down the sidewalk toward her cousin's apartment. She turned to watch Simon Vegas rise slowly to the level of the rooftops. "We died together, Julius and I. We said our goodbyes. Somehow I'm beginning to feel that my old life is going away now . . . fading away."

At that moment, the two men who lived next door to Sadie arrived home from a trip to the grocery store. They were handsome men with dark hair and mustaches. They were wearing Hawaiian shirts and flip-flops, in accordance with a strict dress code. Their features and their animated hands were clearly Italian. Both men smiled at Queenie, put down their groceries, and shook her hand with great enthusiasm. Then they bowed in the Continental manner and introduced themselves in accents that were as thick as melted mozzarella.

"Mi chiamo Moishe," said the first. "Moishe Vanzetti."

"Mi chiamo Shalom," said the second in a much softer voice. "Shalom ben Sacco." Queenie was beaming and blushing coyly as the second man bent at the waist and gently kissed her hand. Then all three waved at Simon as he continued to levitate above their heads.

"Can you see me?" he shouted as he flew in a small circle above Queenie's new home.

"Yes, I can," she shouted with a confused shrug at her new-found friends. "Of course I can see you. I see all three of you. We all can." Moishe and Shalom both nodded in agreement. They could see Simon and his companions, too.

"Tell me, am I Mexican or am I Persian?" he called out in a louder voice as he reached the level of a flock of circling pelicans.

"Persians-Smersians. Who knows from Persians," answered Queenie as she tapped excitedly on Sadie's door. "You're a sorrowful person, Mr. Vegas. That much I can see, even with my bad eyes. Something has imprisoned you. That much I can see. Your little daughter is coming soon, Mr. Vegas. You can't give your sadness to her. I had two beautiful children. I stole the secret of the atomic bomb? What did I care from bombs? Zilch! Bupkis! But here's something I can't understand—you have a man's voice, and I know in my mind that you're a Latin male with an Irishman in the woodpile . . . but to me you look just like Bette Davis."

Moishe and Shalom shook their dark heads in disagreement with their new friend.

"Not Bette Davis," said Moishe. "We see Lauren Bacall, a true goddess of the silver screen."

"She's beautiful!" said Shalom, who had lifted his sunglasses above his eyebrows for a better look.

"Keyn eynhore," said Queenie as the door closed behind her.

"Keine ayin Har Ra," said Moise. "Kineahora," echoed Shalom. It was all the same word.

It was the phrase that balances out the entire universe—the phrase upon which the cosmos pivots. "Your baby is beautiful," a Jewish mother says, then "keyn eynhore." No evil eye. Let no one hold it against this sweet child that it is beautiful and someone has dared to enunciate that loving truth. Keyn eynhore. The small prayer under the breath, whispered by an ancient people who have come to know the twists of fate with an unrivaled intimacy—people who have learned to fear cruel irony and to laugh at it, all in the same breath.

4

EVERY GOAT ON EARTH

"What just happened to us, Simon?" asked Elena breathlessly, her chest heaving as she gasped for air. "It wasn't real, was it? It couldn't have been." She wiped a face full of tears away with her trembling palms. She tried to rise from her chair but didn't have the strength to free herself. She slumped against the chair, still too dizzy from the flight—too shaken by the sight of a woman on fire. But within mere seconds, she was no longer crying. He body had stopped shaking. Strangely enough, she was smiling. Her face was beaming. She felt some pressure on her belly and lifted her blouse to see what was happening. This time both of the infant's hands and feet were pressing upward, signaling mama. The baby inside of her was elated.

"Simon, you've been hiding from me—from everyone—for years," she said as she rose easily from her chair. "We haven't had a talk in a long time, and we don't go on walks or dates anymore. This is the first time you've taken me out in over a year, and where do we go? Sing Sing Prison! If that isn't bad enough, we go there over half a century ago! You made me witness an execution! It was horrible, Simon! Then, like magic, we reversed it, and we carried a living, breathing Ethel Rosenberg down to a retirement community in Florida where everyone wears Hawaiian shirts! It was ridiculous—insane. It was sublime—astonishing. Was it a tragic dream? Did I just witness Vincent's last moment on earth? How long have you been doing this?"

"Most of my life," answered Simon softly. "I started when I was nine years old. I started in a vineyard full of Pinot noir grapes."

"Have you always gone alone?"

"Yes," he answered in a whisper. "Before I got this machine and finally made it work, it took me months—years—to do what we did today in a few seconds. Long ago it took me years to go and get fifteen people. That's the best I could do with my old tools."

"I want in, Simon. Do you hear me? After this baby is born, I'm going with you. You can't go alone anymore. I know that you talk to winds, Simon. I've heard you. You've tried your best to hide that from me, too, but I've heard quite a few of your conversations."

He turned his head to meet his wife's intense gaze. "As you saw today, we don't really talk, but we do throw a lot of punches at each other," he said with a smile. She hadn't seen him smile like this in months. "You've never told me how you got this injury," she said as she reached for his right hand. Questions that had been on her mind for years were finally being asked—perhaps they might even be answered. "What does that incredible machine do?"

"This machine helps me look for lines and for the intersections of lines," he said.

"What happened to your hand? What do you do when you find a line?" Elena asked anxiously.

"I step out of it," Simon answered with a self-conscious smile. He lifted a bottle of wine that had been decanting on the workbench. He had decided to splurge if this test run of the machine was even a moderate success. This would be his second bottle of Château Palmer this month. He poured it equally into three glasses. Picking up his own glass, he swirled the wine for a moment, then sniffed at the edge of the crystal. The wine was finally breaking free. It was precisely like a reclusive life being released into rhyme—a life like the one lived by that poet from Amherst. He remembered how light her thin body had been—how brittle her bones had felt as he lifted her. For weeks afterward, he had discovered thunderously quiet little poems that had been rolled up into tiny scrolls and stuffed into every bullet loop of his bandoliers and every pocket of his suit.

"I step out of it," he repeated as he lifted the glass in a toast. Only Hephaestus Segundo touched his wineglass to Simon's. Following her pediatrician's orders, Elena declined to drink.

"You have to tell me everything about that machine," insisted Elena. Then she spoke in a much quieter, strangely modulated voice. "Why am I haunted by maps? Is that my father's doing, or yours? When you would take naps on the couch, I'd lie down next to you and wake up with vertigo. Why did that happen, Simon? Did I experience the answer to that question this morning—in New York—in this garage?

"A few months ago, I saw that famous picture of Archimedes about to be killed by a Roman soldier, and I just knew, beyond any doubt, that the picture was completely inaccurate. That's not how he looked!" Elena shouted at Simon and Hephaestus. "Archimedes had a sharp chin and a mole near his left eye! There was a scar on his forehead, and he had a missing tooth in front. He kissed me right here," she said as she touched a finger to her cheek.

Simon closed his eyes and laughed inwardly. Hephaestus was grinning.

"This year, on the anniversary of Malcolm X's death, I suddenly found myself sitting in the second row at the Audubon Ballroom. I recognized the seats, the furniture, and the flooring. I saw the mural on the wall behind him. I saw that overturned chair on the stage. I remembered the color of the drapes—and I saw the blood-stains everywhere and the faces of those men. I heard the shotgun, Simon! My ears rang for days. Those memories felt like they were my memories, even though they couldn't have been. Now they *are* my memories. I can see the assassins' faces as clearly as I remember my prom dress.

"Things like that have happened to me again and again"—her voice dropped down to a place below a murmur—"since you started working on that machine in our house." She was silent for a long moment, then began once again. "Those memories should have driven me mad—and yet every one of them makes me strangely happy. I can't help but think that someone paid a price for that happiness. It was you, wasn't it? Who are you, Simon? The time has come to tell me. Who are you? Who were you?"

"I was a monster," he said quietly. "When I was a boy, a Mexican man with one ear described me as a monster. He was right," he said as he emptied his glass of wine.

Elena reached for the third glass. "A little sip won't hurt the baby," she said. "Are you still a monster? I think I've figured out why you're sad but never depressed," she said excitedly. "Now, please tell me about the machine."

There was no other machine like this one in the entire world. In 1901 the original Antikythera device had been pulled out of an ancient shipwreck by Greek sponge divers who had decided to move their area of operations to the sea just northwest of Crete. The device had been designed and constructed in 100 BC, probably by the great Archimedes himself, and contained precision parts—finely tuned wheels and gears, shafts, bearings, splines, and sprockets, the complexity of which would not be approached, much less duplicated, for almost two millennia.

The amazing machine had languished silently beneath the silt and salt water of the Aegean Sea between the islands of Kythera and Antikythera from the time of the ancient Greek states through the rise and collapse of the Roman Empire. It had witnessed the search for the elixir of life, the Third Punic War, the sacking of Carthage, and the invasion of Russia by the Huns. It had watched the Crusades—the original Final Solution—and the centuries of pious bloodletting that followed. Only the light of the Renaissance brought with it a tiny glimmer of hope that the machine might be found on the ocean bottom, and that someday someone would look upon it without fear, but with curiosity and perhaps with awe.

For over thirty years, it had been used as a doorstop at the entrance to a small hotel in the town of Kalámai. One of the guests at that establishment became curious about the strange-looking object on the floor near the reception desk and bought it for the price of a she-goat. That guest eventually gave the device to his son, a young student of archaeology who conducted the first serious investigation into its arcane mysteries. When the young scholar realized that he was incapable of delving into the deepest inner workings of the machine, he reluctantly turned it over to his mentor, a world-renowned authority on such things at the University of Athens.

The famous expert studied the object for no more than thirty seconds, turning it brusquely, theatrically, in his hands while squinting at it through sleek sunglasses that he had recently purchased on a skiing trip to Chamonix. Standing before a crowd of adoring students, he moved the chic glasses to the top of his tanned head before wrongly proclaiming it to be the world's first mechanical clock. He then put the "primitive but provocative piece" up for sale on the international black market for antiquities, and promptly sold it for the price of a very large herd of goats.

The item was purchased at the secret auction by a man named Marco Nicco, an Italian auto magnate who planned to keep it as a conversation piece. He gave it a place of honor on the mantle above the fireplace in his famous yet intimate pied-à-terre in the Swiss Alps. Two years after his death, his ever-widening pool of rapacious heirs and their teams of carnivorous lawyers were packed into a high school auditorium on the outskirts of Zurich.

The local probate court was simply too small to hold the army of claimants who sat snarling at each other while listening to the reading of the Nicco will. Halfway through the reading, the contentious proceedings were abruptly interrupted by a dour trio of identically coiffed American generals who had come to make an offer to all of the potential heirs. They had not come to bid on the automotive factories, the oil wells in Nigeria and Iraq, or the lucrative brothel above a small bar in the North Beach section of San Francisco. The only thing they were interested in was a small clump of petrified mud and blackened bronze.

The Antikythera mechanism was purchased sometime after World War II by the U.S. Army for the price of every goat on earth. The three humorless generals and their bodyguards carefully wrapped the little machine in wads of sterile padding before gingerly lowering it into the bowels of an insulated metal box that was secured by three bulletproof locks. Each general had a single key that could open only one of the locks.

When the device was secured, the somber trio and their faceless guards sped out of Switzerland to an air force base in Germany, and from there disappeared to parts unknown. For years the rumors had swirled around Washington and Moscow that the American military had taken the ancient machine to an underground laboratory somewhere in the mountains of Colorado or the hills of South Dakota.

There the Antikythera device is said to have been modified for use as a control mechanism in several exotic weapons of mass destruction. The exact nature of these doomsday weapons and the modifications that were performed on the machine have been classified as top secret for decades and are still considered highly sensitive by the Pentagon.

There have always been unconfirmed rumors swirling like dust devils around the five-sided building. It was whispered that the device not only could control a weapon but could transport it anywhere on earth instantaneously. Even more miraculously, it could move any payload backward and forward in time. Some say that pipe dreams began flying around the coffee room in the Command Center at the Pentagon. Brigadier and major generals began having dreams about going back in time and blowing up the young girl who was to become Osama Bin Laden's mother, dreams about the four grandparents of Martin Luther King, the father of Abraham Lincoln, the mother of Howard Zinn.

The chiefs of staff at the Pentagon had swooned over the possibility of "clean massacres" that left no evidence whatsoever of the perpetrators. It was said that one of those weapons had actually been deployed on a field of battle. For years there had been snide gossips at the Lawrence Livermore Radiation Laboratory who insisted that the U.S. Army had become impatient—that the only completed and fully operational device had been clumsily lost somewhere in Southeast Asia during the Vietnam War.

"Heads rolled on that one," a tipsy major general told several brigadier generals and a reporter from the *Washington Post* at a picnic that was hosted jointly by Sandia Laboratories, British Petroleum, and the Bank of America. "That was the real reason General Westmoreland lost his job. That's why Lyndon Johnson couldn't run for a second term. Waiter, can I get another scotch?" Within a month, that major general had been demoted to lieutenant colonel and retired to run a coffee shop in Sitka, Alaska.

As it turned out, the remarkable journey of the small machine was not over. After twenty-one centuries beneath the waves and after years of mysterious and clandestine travels, the machine somehow fell into the hands of a lowly private first class named Simon Vegas, a reluctant draftee into the U.S. Army. For some unknowable reason and in some unfathomable way, a nobody—a rank foot soldier—had managed to detach the diminutive device from a much larger top secret payload while it was being deployed in combat for the first time. The soldier had hidden the device under his flak vest, protecting it with his life. Then he had lugged it with him when he was finally rotated out of the field.

The lowly draftee had hidden the device in his duffel bag and carried it out of the country when his miserable tour of duty in Vietnam finally came to a merciful end. At the lowest point in his sad life as a soldier, when useless, pointless death was everywhere, he had reached out from the depths of terror to tenderly touch the controls of this otherworldly apparatus. The strange machine had spoken directly to him—and to him alone.

The blinking lights on its face had somehow told the young soldier that the machine had another purpose, that it had never been intended for use in a weapon—that it had been built by Archimedes to bring comfort, not pain; enlightenment, not callousness. When the entire weapon was about to be shoved from the belly of a helicopter, the soldier had reached out and loosened the titanium wing nuts that secured the device to the main body of the multi-million-dollar payload. When it was free, he ripped it away.

Somehow Simon had stumbled upon a tiny morsel of solace—a small parcel of peace in a world of hurt. The machine had traveled in his duffel bag on an air force plane from Saigon to a base twenty miles outside of Paris. Simon had hidden the instrument beneath his bed in a tiny, cramped room three stories below street level on the Rue Ste. Germaine.

It had been kept in the refrigerator of his studio apartment on Euclid Street, two blocks from the Berkeley campus; in the attic of a cottage in San Francisco; and finally in the garage of his home in the East Bay hills. He had spent long months, then years, carefully, painstakingly, prying it apart, piece by infinitesimal piece, using a microscope, dental picks, watchmaking tools, and thousands of soft bristle brushes.

He had diagrammed, photographed, and catalogued every minute detail of it. It took him two years to wash away the chemicals that the military had applied to the brass wheels. It took over a year to remove the maze of wires that had been spliced in by scientists in Colorado or South Dakota. It took two more years to remove the robotically milled stainless steel gears that had been shoved into it to replace the originals, which had been cracked and eroded by salt and sand.

After he had succeeded in reconstructing the mechanism to

the best of his abilities, he drove down the hill to Emeryville and asked around at the local artists' lofts and coffee shops until he was directed to the grimy, smoke-filled studio of a reclusive artist who in another life may have been known as Professor Roberto Cantú. The members of the art community knew the grizzled, clubfooted man only as Hephaestus Segundo, an odd, painstaking genius in the art of metallurgy.

That strange name was scrawled in black paint above the entryway of a chaotic workplace that was packed from floor to ceiling with arc welders, oxyacetylene tanks, and hundreds of his bizarre creations, all in various states of completion. Hephaestus Segundo worked exclusively in metal. The wild-looking, shaggy-haired artist had crammed the grounds around his sprawling workshop with a forest of outlandish creations of every size and shape.

They were freakish, nightmarish installations, hulking iron and steel forms that had been endowed with pneumatic and electric muscles that were controlled by intricate interconnected clockwork mechanisms, all of which had been motorized. These delicate yet formidable pieces seemed to have been spawned out of some mad, irresistible compulsion.

Each elaborate clinking, clanking, hissing, and halting piece of kinetic art contained an unknowable number of parts that worked to assist other components in the performance of some indefinable act, while other parts acted only to hinder, delay, or even destroy that performance. Simon noticed that the pieces that moved well as a whole seemed very machine-like, while those that shuddered and shivered with indecision and internal conflict seemed eerily human.

Simon had commissioned the strange, gruff man to fabricate by hand dozens of new gears, springs, and wheels according to the specifications that he had so carefully compiled. He had unrolled the blueprints of the Antikythera device on the flat surface of a custom-made anvil. When the old artist bent over the plans for a closer look, he abruptly staggered backward, moaning and covering his heart with both of his hands. He closed his eyes for a moment and took several deep breaths. After he had calmed down a bit, he crept forward and stared quietly at the lines on the paper for ten long minutes, lovingly touching the surface of the blueprint with a single blackened finger. There was a profound look of recognition in his eyes—a look of remembrance.

Then Hephaestus Segundo had washed his hands in vain, fumbled through a box of clutter, and found some extra-thick reading glasses, which he rinsed under a faucet. After a halfhearted attempt to dry them with his filthy shirt, he put the spectacles on, then bent over the anvil to carefully study the blueprints in minute detail. After a few moments, he turned away from Simon and began to cry silently, his shoulders heaving.

"I will do this work! I must do this work! If you offer to pay me, I will be insulted beyond words!"

He danced wildly from one installation to the next, flipping switches and turning knobs until every piece of art in his grotto was in motion. Then he ran back to Simon.

"Archimedes! Definitely Archimedes!" he shouted over the metallic maelstrom of sound while pointing at the precisely detailed diagrams. "No one else could do this. Pobrecito, he must have been so alone in his time—lucky, unlucky man. As you can see," he said as he turned in a full circle in the center of his studio, "I've been trying to build something like it for years. What a fool I've been!" he shouted in a voice that could be heard a mile away. "I've always imagined it so much larger! I thought that the piece the men found on the ocean floor could only be a small fragment of a much larger device. Now I see that I was wrong. Please," he begged, "may I see it when it's completed?"

Simon had already pulled out all of the integrated circuits that had been so ham-fistedly crammed into the small box by military scientists. Now Hephaestus Segundo began fashioning replacements for the modern components, using miniature vacuum tubes, antique oil-filled capacitors, and hand-formed wire-wound resistors and coils. Three months later, he limped impatiently up the hill from the flats of Emeryville to deliver his work in person.

He stood quietly next to Simon as his custom-made parts were carefully placed into the machine. Hephaestus had fashioned dozens of tiny but perfectly formed pinions, fusees, pallets, and pallet arbors. There were barrel arbors made of platinum, ratchet pawls and tension springs made of brass. But his proudest accomplishments lay at the bottom of his sack. He reached his hand deep into the bag and pulled out three finial pieces: two bearings and a tiny spigot made of purest gold. The spigot had been created by a heresy—by a multiplication of metals.

"Be my guest," Simon had said with a bow. "You may also put in the spigot."

After Hephaestus spent three ecstatic hours putting his handiwork into various sections of the machine, the two men stepped back from the workbench as the strange object blinked and whirred to life. Simon laughed like a young boy, slapped his thigh, then disappeared for a moment. When he returned, he had two hand-carved wooden bowls and a Greek jar filled with mead.

Elena had watched as her husband took the two dusty old bowls and a crusty jar down into his cloister. Curious to see what other denizen from the outer fringes of sanity might be down there with him, she crept down the stairs until she reached a point where she could peek between the railings without being seen. She saw Simon standing next to a disheveled man with crooked feet who hadn't bothered to comb his hair in years. That was her first sighting of Hephaestus Segundo.

On the workbench between them, she saw an odd-looking lump of stone and metal that had been stuffed into a tin box. It was her initial encounter with the machine. Hanging from the box were a few light bulbs that had been loosely attached with wires and metal clips. On one corner of the box, a small spigot had been inserted.

She watched as Simon carefully tilted the machine to one side while Hephaestus held a small clay vial beneath what looked like a tiny faucet. She watched as a copper-colored liquid dripped into the miniature vessel. Simon tilted the vial and allowed two drops of the liquid to fall into the mead. Then the two of them raised their drinks in a toast.

"Válgame dios! I knew that expensive turbine lubricant wouldn't work!" shouted Hephaestus Segundo. "I've tried every exotic oil under the sun in my own machines. Then one day, about a month ago, I went down to the auto parts store on San Pablo Avenue and stood in front of the octane boosters, radiator sealers, and engine additives. I was immediately drawn to this black and red can." He held up a can of Marvel Mystery Oil.

"Yes, the Antikythera device seems to love it," said Simon with a sigh. When the two wooden bowls finally touched, the filthy man said: "A toast, un brindis—to Albertus Magnus and to Isaac Newton. It was Newton who first surmised that once this device was working properly, it might secrete a potent liquid from its coils and gears."

"To Archimedes and to Spinoza," said Simon as he gulped down the tangy mead.

Back then, all that Elena had been able to see was a hairy, unkempt man standing next to her brown-skinned husband. It was her nascent child, the tiny fetus suspended inside her pelvis—swaddled in salt water and wet bone—who, with her eyesight still forming, had looked out and seen two desperate alchemists struggling to coax a miraculous liquid from a jumble of metal and wires. She had seen them straining with all of their might, and finally succeeding—finally distilling just a few crystalline drops of the ever-elusive *aurum potabile*, the only known antidote to human cruelty.

5

THE GREEK TRANSLATION

The waters down below were not lapping at the eastern edge of Sicily or the southern coast of Turkey. It was only the San Francisco Bay. Nevertheless, Simon could see that Scylla was still out there doing her treacherous work, and she was doing it without the help of Charybdis. She was all alone now, devouring men on her own since 1959, when the ugly gray island in the middle of the bay was shut down and abandoned. Once upon a time Alcatraz had been the rock, but San Quentin Prison was still the hard place.

His brown face stared downward from the hill, his eyes only seeming to countenance the bridges and the deep fog that stretched across the dark waters. Far below his vantage point, a thousand asphalt arteries were funneling traffic into three giant stents made of concrete and steel. The graceful span straight ahead was world famous and was painted a dull orange, though everyone called it "golden." The groaning span to his left was the dull gray workhorse of the Bay Area, while the third structure, at the extreme right edge of his peripheral vision, was the bridge that went there—to that awful place that stands as a monument to our primal urges, to mindless male physicality.

At the western tip of that metal span was the hard place where thousands of men did their time, and some seven hundred of them waited in sterilized little rooms to die painless, civilized deaths. Simon Vegas felt his wife's eyes staring down at him from above. He knew that the baby who was four months away from descending through the birth canal was watching him, too. Then he remembered

Queenie's final words to him: "You can't give your sadness to her." Queenie was right. He clenched his fists, slamming the knuckles of his left hand into his right.

Simon grimaced yet again. Today was the day he had come to hate most of all the days of the month, and there were eleven other days just like it in every year of the calendar. There were so many better things to do with a day like this one. He could be reading Finneran's notes on Yeats or his favorite book by Thom Gunn. There was a new translation of the *Iliad* in his library, and yet another translation of Rilke.

But those things were not for this day. Today was the first Friday of the month. Today a bill had come due, an onerous obligation that had to be met. Today was the day when he kept that promise—that stupid, misguided promise to Lenny Hudson. The memory of that first unfortunate conversation still reverberated in his mind months later.

─────

"I'll come . . . I'll come . . ."

"You gotta come, man! Promise me! Shit, man, I'm lookin' at the Big One—the Big Jab! Three chemicals in the arm, then the big nothing! Nada—until the end of time. You gotta come. Give me your word."

"I'll come once every two months—the last Friday of every other month."

"No! The first Friday! Once a month—to the end, one way or the other. No matter how it goes. You won't have to come for long, man. As soon as they start up the executions again, I'm next up, after the Jamaican dude across the hall. My date's comin' up in four months—five months tops. The moratorium ain't gonna last, and you know it! You know damn well what the Supreme Court's gonna do. Thomas and Scalia want my head on a spit. I ain't askin' too much, am I? Will you come? To the fuckin' end?"

"I can't do it, man. My wife's pregnant. I'm about to have a kid. I've been told that I won't get a good night's sleep for two years! Once every other month, that's the best I can do."

"Hey, man, I'm a dead man. What about that don't you get? I'm a dog at the city pound about to get the gas, and you won't even come around to see me off? You won't throw me a scrap? You'd go see a dog, wouldn't you?"

"I have classes to teach at Berkeley and San Francisco State. I have papers to grade. What do you deserve, Lenny?" Simon had asked in a new, colder voice. "The two young boys you killed will never get a visit from anyone ever again. They didn't get a trial. They didn't get to say goodbye to their mothers . . ."

"Fuck their mother!" screamed Lenny. His yellowed teeth were bared, and the sinews and blotchy skin of his neck and face were suddenly raised and twisted into a dreadful, nightmarish mask. It dawned on Simon that he was finally seeing the private, unexpurgated face of Lenny Hudson—the last face that two boys working at a roadside fruit stand in Tracy had ever seen. There was no reasoning with that face. There was no mercy at all in those eyes, not one drop. This was his true demeanor. It was the congenial good-old-boy persona that was the mask.

Lenny seemed to understand that he had just inadvertently let down his guard and revealed himself to someone. Then, like a chameleon or a cuttlefish, his vicious face had flashed to an indeterminate neutral before slowly assuming tints and aspects that were a perfect complement to his immediate surroundings. Like a seasoned actor, Lenny had wrenched his entire being back into character.

"You hate me, eh? Do you really think I killed them two boys? You hate me 'cause I'm a monster, but that's why you've come here, ain't it? Hell, I know it's true. You ain't here doin' Kevin no favors. What did Kevin tell you, that I'm insane and I need someone to talk to? Fuck that! Well, you know what? I trust you. I trust you because you hate me and because you would believe that someone like me is still a human. If I woke up tomorrow and killed one of these worthless dumb fuckers here on the Row, you'd get me a lawyer, wouldn't you? I know you would. But that's not why you're here. You don't care about none of that. You want somethin' else, don't you?

"When I first seen you, my first hit on you was that you was one of them that craves the taste of death—you need a smidge of it on your tongue so you can figure out what's in it—the recipe, the exact ingredients. Yeah, that's the word, ingredients! I thought you were kinda like a chef. Then I began to see that you don't want to know what goes into death. In fact, I believe you hate death." He snapped his fingers and laughed. "No -death ain't it. Death is too common. You want to know what goes into cruelty. That's it! You want to know about all the wires and gears—how cruelty really works. Do you think that kind of shit would make a good poem?"

Simon turned away from him. Lenny was silent for a moment, then his eyes widened.

"That's it! I got it, don't I? It ain't murder that floats your boat, it's cruelty. I think that makes you kinda sick—kinda psychotic like me. Listen, man, I got nobody. I mean nobody. All these years in stir, and I ain't never got a single visit or even a letter. I really don't give a shit why you come, just come. Give me your word. Every first Friday. Besides," he said with a mischievous grin, "you may not know it, but you and me go way back. Hell, you and me are practically family. Do you know why I asked Kevin to get a hold of you and get you to come see me?"

"No," answered Simon. "Why?"

"I ain't gonna tell you," spat Lenny. "Not even gonna say!"

Simon looked into Lenny's eyes and saw them dancing with excitement. He was smiling at Simon's look of frustration.

"Look, I'm here because I'm taking over Kevin's poetry class next month. But my class is going to be a little different than his was. I'll come see you just after class, once a month. Do you like poetry? I could give you a few to read, and you could write down what they mean to you."

Lenny scowled and shrieked, "What the fuck do I care about poetry? No one in here gives a shit about it! Poetry's for fags!" The two guards talking at the end of the row of interview rooms glanced toward the prisoner, then resumed their conversation.

"Then there's no deal."

After a minute of silence Lenny said, "I'll read your fuckin' poems. I guess it won't kill me. But I ain't writin' nothin'. Look! You gotta realize one thing—I'm a dead man. If I get one new privilege in here, it means that I lose an old one, and I ain't got that many privileges to begin with."

Lenny leaned forward and looked closely at Simon's face. That was when he noticed that something odd was happening on the surface of his skin: his lips and cheeks were quivering, and his eyelids were fluttering. Simon stood up slowly and slammed his fist with all of his strength against the top of the metal table. A giant pot-bellied guard undulated up to the door, sized up the situation, then gladly went back to his box of pizza.

"I can't come every first Friday, goddamn it! Why not the last Friday?"

"Cause Phillipsborn comes on the last Friday."

"If John comes once a month, then why do you need to see me? He's the lawyer. He's the one challenging lethal injection. I can't do anything for you."

"Phillipsborn's a scientist," said the prisoner with a wide grin. "He's one of them pocket protector, mechanical pencil types that files every motion and hires every possible expert, but you—you're somethin' else again. I can't put my finger on it, but I have read some of your poems. I admit it. I'm not proud of it, but I admit it. Kevin gave them to me. Tell the truth, I didn't understand a goddamn word. Maybe it's because you're kind of a sick, twisted little puppy—something like me. No, that's close, but not exactly it—not exactly. But I'll figure it out soon enough. One of these days, if you're a real good boy," Lenny said smugly, "I'll give you what you're lookin' for. I'll tell you exactly who you are."

"He's an asshole!" cried a voice from the next interview room. It was another death row prisoner waiting for his good-for-nothing lawyer to appear. "That's who he is—an asshole."

"And you're not?" screamed Lenny at the top of his lungs. He turned back toward Simon and whispered in a voice that could be heard a hundred feet away, "That walking hemorrhoid over there likes to kill babies! How many did you burn to death? Five?"

"Hey, Lenny, do you know who you're talkin' to in that room?" demanded another voice from down the hall.

"He with Simon Magus Vegas!" shouted an ancient black trustee who was effortlessly mopping the hallway for the ten thousand and twelfth time. Years ago the mindless, menial chore had been nothing more than a chance for a few hours outside his cell. Sometime in the mid-eighties, this death row trustee had been given a highly detailed manual on the proper care and maintenance of linoleum floors. The old man had memorized every page in the book and was soon requisitioning hypoallergenic strippers, exotic sealers, and organic adhesives from all around the globe. He had even convinced three consecutive wardens to order hand-mixed cleaners and waxes from Switzerland, the country with the cleanest floors on earth.

By the late nineties, the California Department of Corrections was sending dozens of novices every year to learn at the feet of the man who had come to be known as the Floor Master—the "Flo-

Massa" to the black inmates. After only one hour this morning, the Flo-Massa had already done the sides of the hall next to the prisoners' doors in East Condemned Row. Now he was moving down the middle of the corridor inscribing one sign for infinity upon the next and the next, a thousand reclining figure eights lying one upon the other like geological strata laid down only to be buffed away.

Like an old elephant trapped forever in a cage at the zoo, his mop swayed like a trunk from side to side, ever slower and slower until it matched perfectly the rhythm of his aging heart. The instant that concurrence took place—the moment his aorta and ventricles began to pump in lockstep with his titanium and Kevlar mop handle fitted with a lamb's wool mop head imported from New Zealand—the old man was no longer a prisoner.

"Yep, he with Simon Magus Vegas. An' this here is my ten thousand and twelfth trip down this hallway. A strange name, ain't it? He with Simon Magus Vegas," repeated the Flo-Massa in a dreamy, almost ecstatic voice.

"Simon Magus Vegas?" asked Simon with a frown.

"Yeah, that's what they call you in here, my man," said Lenny with a smirk. "Simon Magus Vegas. I don't know who came up with it, but everybody in here started calling you that. Kinda catchy, don't you think? Some people say you got some kinda weird mojo power. They say you're kinda loco like the rest of us."

"Do you have any idea who Simon Magus was?" asked Simon, whose cheeks had reddened. He wanted desperately to end this conversation.

"No, man, and I don't give a flyin' shit who he was. I still ain't heard you promise."

After three full minutes of silence, Simon whispered: "I promise." The words scorched his vocal cords and burned his tongue on their way toward his clenched teeth. "Why did you tell Kevin that you wanted to see me and only me? You asked for me by name. Why?

How did you get my name?" Lenny had only shrugged. "Because you and me go way back," was all the prisoner would say.

The promise was now just four months old. After his first visit, the distasteful task had swelled from a nagging inconvenience into an insufferable drudgery. Each first Friday followed on the heels of the last one as though there were no days in between. But Simon could not see a way out of it. Once again first Friday had arrived, and he would have to sit with a maniac and smell the thick, cloying odor of his desperation and suppressed rage. He would have to sit and nod patiently at endless ravings about incompetent lawyers, preju-diced judges, and mindless juries. The raving and ranting seemed so contrived, so theatrical, that Simon began to wonder about the real motive behind Lenny's insistence that Simon come to see him.

For years the murders of the two young boys in Tracy had been relegated to a dusty file cabinet in the basement of the San Joaquin County Prosecutor's Office. There had not been a single witness to the shootings. There had been no fingerprints left at the scene, and DNA typing was still unheard of when the fatal shots were fired. All of the physical evidence, including the boys' clothing, had been lost.

There had never been a single suspect until years later, when Lenny Hudson was arrested in his cell for the murder of a fellow inmate at Corcoran Prison. Lenny had been sent to the facility after being convicted of a clumsy, amateurish burglary. Not counting his initial statement to a known jailhouse informant at Corcoran, he had promptly confessed twice to the forgotten double homicide in Tracy. He confessed to police inspectors in Sacramento and again to an inspector in Stockton. No one knew why he had decided to come clean after so many years in the clear. He was someone who had gotten away with murder.

He had viciously attacked his lawyers at the first trial—the double homicide—and had to be shackled for every subsequent interview and court appearance. He had been represented by a succession of attorneys for his second trial, but he had fought them all at every turn. He never cooperated with his investigators and refused to answer any questions about his past. After two years of investigation, no one knew a thing about Lenny's childhood or about his family history.

There had been almost no mitigating evidence to present during the penalty phase of his second trial. His life story went no farther back than a juvenile arrest for car theft in McComb, Illinois. Before he turned thirteen years old, Lenny Hudson simply did not exist on any birth certificate or hospital form or church registry. His name had to be an alias, but no one knew what his original name had been.

When the two boys were killed, the death penalty was unconstitutional in the state of California, but that was not the case when the murder at Corcoran took place. At the second trial the state had charged him with murder with two prior convictions of murder and had asked that he be put to death. The stabbing at Corcoran had been witnessed by five guards and recorded by three separate video cameras. Lenny had made no attempt whatsoever to hide his identity or disguise his actions.

A conviction at the guilt phase of his trial was a certainty, and Lenny had done everything he could to sabotage his lawyer's efforts to mount an effective defense during the penalty phase. It seemed clear to everyone that the prisoner wanted a room on Condemned Row and a date with the doctor and his chemicals. Still, Simon would have to hear over and over again how an innocent, misunderstood man was about to be killed by the state and by the cold-blooded citizens of California.

Simon pulled the keys from his pocket. It was a simple act that he would have sworn took no more than a second or two. Elena, watching from the window above the driveway, knew better. What would have taken a normal man one second to accomplish took

Simon ten absent-minded minutes—five minutes searching for the key, then five more minutes moving the key across the twelve-inch chasm between his pocket and the door handle.

The immobile statue of Simon Vegas suddenly sprang to life. He grabbed his shoes and retrieved his suit bag from the top of the trunk. He tossed the bag into the back seat and plunged the key into the ignition switch. He backed out of the driveway, then drove down the hill toward the freeway and the bridge—to San Quentin and to death row.

Simon drove past the hillside village of Point Richmond, down the incline portion of the San Rafael Bridge, where his eyes reluctantly caught their first sight of the prison. It was an ugly, rambling metal and stone structure that marred the atrociously expensive Marin County landscape around it—as one of his friends had once said—like a slice of shit stuck in the middle of an avocado sandwich. A dull pain formed in the pit of his stomach before moving inexorably downward to his bowels and into his lower limbs as he neared the front gate of that enormous pedazo de mierda.

Ten years ago, when prisons in California were still pretending at rehabilitation, Kevin Hughes, Simon's good friend from the faculty at Berkeley, had begun teaching a poetry class at San Quentin. Kevin had dreamed up the ambitious class. He had written the proposal, formulated the entire curriculum, and sold it all to a then wealthy Department of Corrections.

Once the plan had been accepted, he managed to convince the previous warden to allow him to use Prisoner Notification Frequency Yoyo, also known as radio channel PNFY. Channels X-ray, Yoyo, and Zulu were the last three working channels of twenty-six antiquated emergency radio bands designed to communicate with the prisoners in the event of a riot, an earthquake or fire, or a hostage situation on one of the cell blocks. The rest of the Prisoner Notification system had been replaced some years ago by a computerized intercom system. Any prisoners who wanted to hear Kevin read poems or play music on PNFY could do so on secure see-through pocket radios that could be purchased at the commissary. The cases of the little radios were made of transparent plastic so that no sharpened shards of steel or joints of marijuana could be hidden inside.

Kevin had used the radio channel to supplement his poetry class and to broadcast classical music, ethnic music, and jazz to the prisoners. But after only eleven months of a struggling existence, the station was shut down by the warden, who cited a universal lack of interest on the part of the prison population. Kevin had been the first and only announcer and disc jockey at station PNFY, and he had been the only teacher in the prison poetry class for ten agonizing years before he finally threw up his hands in full surrender and gave up on that idea, too. The warden had advertised for a replacement in five Bay Area newspapers, but not a single person had applied for either job.

A few days after making his regrettable promise to Lenny, Simon had strolled into Kevin's office at the prison just in time to see him packing away his precious first edition of Robinson Jeffers's *Collected Poetry*. There had been papers and envelopes stacked and scattered everywhere in the office. Some of the papers were wet and steaming, and a small brown puddle was growing on the floor. A cup of coffee had been thrown with savage force against the blackboard, and the brown liquid was still dripping down from the chalk tray.

"There's no such thing as subtlety or silence in this place," Kevin had muttered angrily, as much to himself as to Simon, as he stuffed as many books as possible into a battered cardboard box. Kevin's Irish eyes were flashing, and his cheeks were as red as sugar beets.

"These brutes would have robbed Yeats at gunpoint. They would have burglarized Jeffers's home at Tor House and buggered Ezra Pound. These fools would have dragged Emily Dickinson from her room, forced her into fishnet stockings, and put her on the streets!"

Books by those four writers had been carefully set to one side. It was obvious to Simon that Kevin detested each angry word, even as it gushed from his own mouth. After ten years of superhuman effort, he considered himself a complete failure.

"There's just too much noise in here," he said with the impeccable precision and resonance of an Irish gentleman who has read poetry out loud every evening of his life. "Their heads are stuffed with blather and cant. There is never a peaceful private moment in here. Noise drowns everything out: the night, the moon, the entire universe."

"The men out there on the yard are terrified of silence," countered Simon. "If they have any thoughts of their own, they don't want to hear them. The noise protects them from that. In exchange for a prefabricated identity as a gang member, these guys have relinquished the right to choose for themselves. Do you know what the Greek word is that means 'choice'?" he asked.

"You know that you're describing most of the modern world, don't you, Simon?" Kevin carefully put the four books into a box. He picked up a fifth volume and turned to the very first page. Of course he knew the Greek word that meant choice.

"Do these men disturb you because of what they've done to others, or are you more disturbed by the lives they've wasted—what they've done to themselves?"

"I hate cruelty," said Simon, his voice now barely audible, ". . . in every form."

"How is your sweet Elena?" said Kevin softly, trying to change the subject. "Such a beautiful woman. What is she now, six months pregnant?"

"She's five months pregnant," said Simon, turning away from his friend's gaze. "She's doing well. The ultrasound technician says that the baby is a girl." Then he turned back toward Kevin. There was no use lying to him. Some lies are necessary, even mandatory, but Simon had found that lying to his good friend was always difficult and uncomfortable.

"I'm not very good at marriage. I should never have dragged Elena into this—and now there's going to be a baby. I'm not sure I'm ready for a family—for any of this. From the look of things, I might never be ready. Sometimes I feel completely disconnected from myself, and from everything and everyone around me. Sometimes all I want is to be detached."

"Do you love her?" asked Kevin.

"I think so. I don't know," said Simon.

"I'd give you some sage marital advice," said Kevin, "but I can already hear my two ex-wives laughing hysterically at me. Both of them are sure that I'm crazy. I've spent more time in this prison than I ever did at home."

Kevin lifted a book to his nose and savored the musk of paper, glue, ink, and a hint of mold. "You know that this class is going to break your heart," he said as he reached out to shake his friend's hand and say goodbye. "I'm glad you're going to try to make it work. I know you're doing this for me. I really appreciate it. But I have to warn you, Simon, it's going to break your heart."

"Did you know that I'm going to revive your radio station?"

When he heard those words, Kevin stopped shaking his friend's hand, but he did not let it go. He held it for an endless minute and then for two. The station had been his pride and joy—his one great hope. It had once had the potential to reach everyone in the prison.

"I hear that you met with Lenny Hudson like I asked you to. Thank you for that, too. I don't know where he got your name, but he really wanted to speak with you and only you. He pestered me about it for months. He claims to want to talk with you about Walt Whitman's poetry, but I don't believe a word of it. Except for a few of your works that I lent him, that man has never read a poem in his life. You know, nothing we've said so far about any of these prisoners applies to Lenny Hudson and some of the others on the Row. He's in a different category, you know. Be careful, Simon. He's a monster. He's the one on the Row that really scares me. They're all scary over there, but he is something else. If there is evil in this world, it has found a home in those cold, dead eyes of his."

Kevin was silent for a moment. He had always wondered if what he sometimes glimpsed in the eyes of the men on Condemned Row was the actual presence of evil—flashing, evanescent sightings of wicked things moving in and out of sight like the dim silver bodies of fish darting back and forth at the bottom of a deep, murky pond. Was he seeing fragmentary glimpses of Auschwitz, Rwanda, and Wounded Knee—the look in the eye of a Hutu male when he first realizes that he is completely free to slaughter the Tutsi family next door, completely free to do whatever he wants with their budding and beautiful thirteen-year-old daughter?

He had always wondered if the men on death row were only sad, itinerant free agents—tawdry knights-errant who had missed their golden chances to maim, rape, and kill human beings under the flag of the Holy Crusades or the Spanish Inquisition or the Final Solution, and were now reduced to committing lonely, random atrocities without the benefit of a religious or political sponsor. Perhaps for every thousand human beings on the planet, there will always be one who would relish lighting the bonfire under Giordano Bruno or Joan of Arc or the little girl next door . . . and hundreds more who would gladly watch—or, worse, look the other way while it happened.

"Lenny's probably just a psychopath," Kevin finally said almost under his breath. It was obvious to Simon that his old friend was present now only in the flesh. His soul was already miles outside these high walls and was checking his bags at the San Francisco Airport. "Give them words, Simon." From the tone of his voice, Simon knew that Kevin's spirit had made a temporary return.

"Give them words."

"Words?" asked Simon.

Kevin suddenly snapped his fingers. He walked briskly to a nearby closet, threw open the door, and reached deep into the dark shelves within. He pulled out three more volumes and put them in the cardboard box. Simon recognized books of poetry by John Straley and Ed Pavlić. Kevin hefted the heavy box in both arms and turned toward his friend.

"You told me once, Simon, that you lived in Paris for almost two years. You left Vietnam and went to Paris because you couldn't bear to come back to this country. How many French words did you know when you first stepped onto French soil?"

"Just a few," said Simon. "Cigarette, omelet, au revoir, comment allez-vous?—not much more than that."

"And a few months later?"

"A few hundred words. Fifteen or twenty full sentences."

"Who were you in Paris after a few months?" asked Kevin. "When people spoke with you, did they hear your peculiar brand of humor, your biting sarcasm, and your sense of irony? Could they hear the poetry in your speech? Who were you?"

"I was no one—more invisible than the local street beggars. It was very difficult at first."

"Did the French ever glimpse the real Simon Vegas?"

"No. That would've taken ten years, maybe twenty."

"Did you know," said Kevin with an almost frightening intensity, "that several studies have shown that most of the guys in this prison get by, day after day, using a vocabulary of fewer than two hundred and fifty words?" He gestured toward the prison yard. "Their minds were imprisoned long before they ever got here. Their imaginations have been held prisoner by our vacuous culture and by their tiny ghetto and barrio lives since the day they were born. They have nothing to say. They are all overweight and have big biceps, but their dreams are famished and stunted. All of their expectations have been reduced to skin and bone. If one could photograph their souls, those men would look like victims of a famine.

"If they can't express themselves with language, all that's left to them is physicality: pushing, shoving, hitting, and shooting. They can only be angry. They can only lash out, like I'm doing right now!"

He took a deep breath, and then another. When he spoke again, it was in a quieter, more controlled voice.

"When kids from Hunter's Point, Richmond, East Oakland, and the Mission District leave their neighborhoods, they're in France. They're dumped onto the Rue de Rivoli and onto the Champs-Élysées. Imagine the Third Street bus pulling over and disgorging twenty or thirty black and Chicano juveniles onto la Place de la Concorde. They might as well be on Mars.

"Affluent, educated parents shower their children with words. Their children luxuriate in words every day—a thousand times more words than the children of the poor ever hear."

"The alternate reading of Genesis," said Simon with a smile.

"What?" asked Kevin with a look of mild confusion on his face.

"One of the Nag Hammadi texts that were hidden for safekeeping sometime in the second century is called the Testament of Truth. It was one of many alternate visions of Christianity that were violently suppressed as heretical. It was written by a woman. It was translated from the original Greek into Coptic. In that story, it's the snake in the Garden of Eden who speaks to the reader. It's the serpent who gives the gift of knowledge to the first couple—it hands them words and thoughts, urging them to get out, to escape from their mute, mindless paradise and run away from a life sentence as unthinking beasts—as prisoners. It's very interesting reading."

"You know, I've always suspected that you were a Gnostic," said Kevin with a smile. "Actually, it's more than a suspicion. You have an obsession with cruelty. You're not really sure that evil exists. If it does, it exists in all of us. Maybe you're here because you think you belong in here, Simon. These men are your brethren. As long as I've known you, you've been imprisoned by something. Are you still seeing that army psychiatrist?"

"So you're the one!" said Simon with a knowing laugh. "You're the one who's got these guys calling me Simon Magus Vegas. It was you! Do any of these fools even know who he was or who the Gnostics were?"

Even as Simon enunciated the sentence, he realized that he was speaking to himself in an empty room. His laughing Irish friend was already long gone—heading down Highway 101 South, heading off to India, where history is written in a language of dance; to China, where the people were drawing in the blackness of the void, creating their pictograms in the darkness, long before some say the world was even created. Then he was off to his homeland, to Ireland, where history is sung in meter and verse on breaths of tobacco and homemade whiskey.

⌒

"What are those?" bellowed the guard in the small shack where every visitor to the prison was searched, then ushered through a ridiculously insensitive magnetometer. "What is that?" he asked.

"It's an ancient machine," said Simon. "I use it in my class. It was built by Archimedes himself."

"Arky . . . who?" asked the guard as he placed the machine into a magnetometer. After it had been cleared, a second guard put it through a scanner that visually probed the interior workings of the device. Finally, a beagle hound sniffed the object and went back to her little mattress, where she curled up and fell asleep.

"Ruby says it's OK, so it's OK," said the second guard.

"What are those?" asked the guard again, this time while prodding the interior of Simon's briefcase with a black wooden baton.

"Those are books of poetry," Simon answered.

"Poetry in this shithole?" said the guard disdainfully as he waved a metal-sensitive wand over each book. "Show me every book, and rifle through the pages so I can check for contraband."

"That one is Dickinson, and this one is Theodore Roethke. This one is Octavio Paz, and this one is the Duino Elegies," Simon said while hefting a small volume with thirty or forty dog-eared pages. "And this is a book of haiku. Its pages are filled with silence," he said, holding up a small leather-bound book. He reached to the bottom of his briefcase, pulled out four more volumes, and held them up for the guard to inspect.

"This is Miłosz, and that one is Robert Hass. This one is Sappho, and this last one is Wisława Szymborska. Every word in these books is contraband."

After ten or eleven hard staccato chews on a wad of Wrigley's spearmint gum the size of a ping-pong ball, the guard finally muttered, "Whatever. It's all the same happy horse shit to me. If it ain't on cable TV, I couldn't give a flying shit about it." He abruptly fell silent and looked Simon up and down carefully. "Wait a minute, are you the one all the prisoners are callin' Simon Magus Vegas? Yeah, you're that guy. Don't deny it. Them poetry books is a dead giveaway. What the hell does that name mean, anyway? Simon Magus Vegas?"

Simon shrugged impatiently and walked through the full-body magnetometer.

"You gonna try and teach poetry to these useless assholes? Shit! And here I thought Kevin Hughes was as dumb as a bull with a set of tits. Dumb as a bucket of hair. But he comes here twice a week out of his own free will. I can see as plain as day that you ain't none too happy to be here. At least Kevin comes here by his own choice. You can put your books and your gadget back into your bag."

"Choice?" answered Simon without turning back to look at the guard. "Do you happen to know the Greek word for choice?"

"Greek! You think I'm some kind of faggot? I got your Greek right here!" Feeling insulted, the bewildered guard had found himself at a loss for words, so he had lowered his right hand and grabbed at his own crotch. "Choose this! I got your Greek right here!"

By that time Simon was already thirty yards away, repeating to himself alone the answer to his own question.

"Heresy."

6

THELONIOUS

The heavy antique microphone positioned on the table in front of him had been purchased by some long-retired prison staff member the same week the "Red Light Bandit," Caryl Whittier Chessman, was executed in the gas chamber—way back in 1960. The formidable instrument was a Telefunken U-49, a model manufactured in 1947 that was the instrument of choice for the recording industry in the fifties and sixties. It still had "Property of Columbia Studios, N.Y.C." stamped into its base.

Simon stared at the machine, imagining that tiny molecules of Tony Bennett's breath were still trapped in the windscreen, and that a scientific analysis of the fine mesh covering would find trace particles of Chianti and white clam sauce. The image of a youthful Miles Davis flashed into his mind. The twenty-year-old jazz giant had once aimed his muted trumpet at this very mike's receptive innards.

An hour earlier, he had been furiously polishing and buffing this same yoke, using the cuff of his shirt and moisture from his own breath, when his eyes were suddenly trapped—ensnared by a chance reflection in the gleaming metal. His gaze had fastened upon a disturbing glimpse of a monstrous, distended face stretching from the center outward in every direction on the curved silvery surface—a face with dull, almost vacant eyes dancing unsteadily at the epicenter of a black and brown miasma. The unsteady image resembled the gigantic stone heads that had once been sculpted by the Olmecs, the ancient magicians of Mexico.

How many thousands of times had he washed this face or

shaved the stubble from these same cheeks and chin? How many times had he bemoaned the gray hairs that were flaring up on the edge of that hairline and were now spreading relentlessly across his once reddish-black crown? Yet even after so many years of inhabiting these bones, he had been caught off guard, astonished yet again by the fact that his haunted soul had, at some unknowable point, been wedded for all time to the corporeal form of a Mexican male from the mountains of southeastern Arizona.

This moment of amazement had happened to Simon countless times—every time he passed by a reflective store window or caught a sideways glance of himself in a mirror in the airport men's room. On every single morning of their marriage, Elena had covered her ears with two pillows, knowing full well that at six-thirty on the dot, the same ridiculous exclamation would emanate from the bathroom and rattle the windows of the house: "Well, I'll be goddamned! I'm a Mexican!"

When had the choice of a "temple" for his soul been made? Simon imagined a game show in outer space featuring a noisy studio audience and a smiling leggy blonde in high heels and a one-piece bathing suit. She was striding unnaturally, each new step crossing over the last—each stiletto heel stabbing into the carpet as she bounced. When she reached center stage, she extended her arms and used all of her strength to give the zoetrope, the heavy wheel of life, an enthusiastic spin.

Had the pointer clicked and snapped through ninety wooden pegs before slowing down perceptibly somewhere between Lithuanian and Peruvian? Had the heavy wheel begun turning agonizingly slowly through Polish and Maori? Had the limber pointer flipped wearily through spaces marked Nigerian and Sri Lankan? Had the audience members held their breath, recoiling in horror, as destiny's arrow barely limped past Pygmy? Had there been a collective sigh of relief when it became clear that the finger of fate would come to rest at Flemish?

Had the wild applause of the studio audience grown unbearably raucous as a master of ceremonies with blindingly white teeth leaped forward, grabbed the mike, and was about to announce the blessed event that would soon be coming to the family of Jergin and Frederika Demeester, two newlyweds who were anxiously awaiting the glorious moment in a cozy thatched house just outside of Antwerp?

Had the roar of the crowd suddenly died away into a cold silence as inertia expended its last joule of energy in its battle against friction, nudging the tired pointer into an unnatural contortion until it snapped forward into the next category? Mexican—more specifically the Vegas family of Morenci, Arizona—a family of four, living in a small adobe house that was located in the foothills just outside of town.

When the call came in from the cosmic game show, Simon's mother, Siobhán, stopped washing dishes, dried her hands, and walked quietly down a rocky path and into a freezing outhouse. She knew that it would be empty because the frigid blasts of air that blew through its walls after sundown made using the room a form of torture. She used a dish towel to turn the frozen doorknob. Even after sunup, the small structure would remain frozen until midday.

The drafty little building had been built by her grandfather over forty years ago, after he had finished the main house. She locked the door behind her, lit a candle, and spent half an hour shivering and brushing her blazing red hair while she studied her face in a tiny mirror that had been tied above the sink with a leather shoestring. On the wall behind her head was a green and yellow flag, the Harp of Erin. Within the main house there was a second, identical flag that was being used as a bedspread.

Her great-grandfather had been an Irishman, a member of the famous Batallón de San Patricio—the Saint Patrick's Battalion, which had helped to defend Mexico against the onslaught of

Zachary Taylor and the gringo armies from El Norte. He had been captured by the gringos, and he and fourteen others were hanged on September the 10th in the year 1847. Bardán Ó Floinn had stubbornly refused a last meal and had turned away defiantly when the hangman attempted to cover his face with a hood. But he had demanded that his captors allow him to sing one song before the mules were whipped and the cart beneath his dusty boots was jerked away.

How many times had she sat on this same cold seat imagining his thin, high tenor voice and his shocks of flaming red hair? She imagined bruises and cuts on the skin of his face and forearms. At the crack of the whip, she could see his hair suddenly upright, stretching to touch the sky as his body beneath it plummeted downward. She saw his eyes rolling upward. Then she saw his hair piling up short, crashing down to his skull as the rope snapped to its full length. His long locks shivered, then draped to one side. She imagined herself as a wraith, curling around his body in the last moments—lifting him, lifting him, pulling the rope away from his windpipe. She imagined the song beginning again.

She had never even seen a photograph of the Irishman, but her grandfather Ciarón had always hummed his father's haunting gallows tune and had handed it down to his own son, Éamonn, her papa. The wistful Irish tune that had always been on her father's breath was now on hers as she wondered if she had the energy for another child—if there was enough food to feed a fifth hungry mouth. She had hummed the tune while braiding her sleek tresses, twisting and winding her long hair into the style of her youth—the style of courtship and la luna de miel. When she approached her husband, it was with a face filled with worry.

"You're humming that tune again, mi amor. Whenever you hum that tune, it means that something is troubling you," said Augusto, her husband.

"Lo siento. I'm so sorry, Viejo—so sorry," she said while strangling the forgotten towel in her quivering hands. She used it to dry a tear at the edge of her eye, then inhaled deeply. "I missed my period. I missed it last month, too, but I had to be sure before I told you."

Her old man's response had been the response of every poor Mexican Catholic of the time: "Don't worry, mi amor. Cada niño nace con un taco en la mano y una enchilada en la otra": Every baby is born with a taco in one hand and an enchilada in the other. "We'll have enough food to feed this one, too. What do you want to name him?"

"Him?" Simon's mother had asked.

"Well, we do have two girls. I'm outnumbered three to one. I've been hoping for a boy."

"You've been hoping? Then I've been worried over nothing!" She tossed the dishrag at her husband, hitting him playfully. "We'll name him after my little brother. Simónn," she whispered pensively while remembering the scent of that newborn baby. "But the Spanish spelling will do. Simón."

"The one who died?" asked her husband. He had almost forgotten about the little boy. He shook his head at the sadness of it.

"Yes," she said quietly. "Now he'll live again. Simón Ó Floinn Vegas."

For most Irishmen in the New World with the family name Ó Floinn, the spelling had changed to Flynn sometime around the turn of the century in order to conform to an American penchant for simplification—for cultural leveling, but leveling done as an act of dominion and derision, and never as an act of acceptance. The pronunciation had remained almost the same. The literal meaning of the name had been lost overboard somewhere on the Atlantic Ocean. In Ireland it still means a dazzling, bright red.

"You know that Americanos don't believe in accents," said Augusto. "He'll wind up being just plain Simon."

Seeing the weariness in his wife's eyes, the father-to-be rose from his seat and hugged her tightly.

"This year, I promise," he whispered into her ear. "This year you'll finally have your indoor toilet. I promise. Next week your father and I will go into town and get the lumber for the frame and walls. No more adobe. We'll get sheetrock and tape, and we'll buy pipes for the indoor plumbing. Señor Zarigüeya and I have already dug all the ditches. This baño will have a linoleum floor and a flush toilet. Señor Zarigüeya has his water piped in from the town. I helped him dig the trenches. He's said that he'll let us connect up to his service. He's already offered us his old septic tank. It's been sitting in his yard for ten years. At first he tried to sell it, then he tried to give it away. He'll be so happy just to get rid of it."

"I'll cook him the biggest bowl of menudo," sang Siobhán. "But we can't make him too happy," she warned her husband. "Be sure he's sitting down when you give him the good news and the food. That possum disease he has is such a terrible curse. Did he really get it from a possum's bite?"

"No, mi amor," said Augusto with a smile, "he was born with the illness. It's called narcolepsia. I'll make sure he's sitting down when I ask for the tank. We can't have Señor Zarigüeya breaking any more bones. After your papa and I bury that tank, we can start on your new toilet."

"And heat, too?" she asked with a sigh. "We've been freezing in here for years. This is the only town in Arizona, besides Flagstaff, that has icicles in the winter. No one ever told me that we could freeze in a desert. Besides," she said with a beaming smile, "when it's done, I want to celebrate." She smiled at her husband, knowing full well that "this year" could mean ten years from now.

"You want heat, too," he said with a laugh, "but promise me you won't breastfeed for so long this time. The old man needs some, too," he said with a wink. He squeezed her left breast as he kissed her on the mouth.

Siobhán pushed him away, laughing almost hysterically. It was at these moments that he could clearly see the Irish in his wife. Her hair was fiery red with flecks of silver as she danced in and out of a shaft of sunlight. She had a bright, easy laugh that had been bequeathed to her by ancestors who had tasted years of starvation yet still managed to sing and smile.

"I have a name for the new toilet!" she shouted. "And I'm going to paint the name on the door as soon as it's done!"

"You're going to name a toilet?" asked her husband with a laugh. He was relieved to see that her earlier concerns had vanished completely from her face and from her tongue. That sad song was gone from her lips. "Tell me what you're going to paint on the door."

"You'll see," she said with a sly giggle. "You'll see. And when everything is done, I want to have a big party—a theme party about living where it's warm and there's sand between our toes. I'll invite the whole family. And . . . I know! We'll all wear shorts and festive luau shirts!"

Simon pushed the memories away and shrugged. Perhaps fortune had not been so unkind to him. After all, hot and red chuletas de puerco and a steaming bowl of menudo for Sunday breakfast were a hell of a lot better than boiled potatoes, haggis, or cloudy jars of gray lutefisk. Where else could he possibly live but in the brown body of a Mexican? The only other viable possibility would have been the body of a Persian magician. Persians had been one category past Mexican—the very last peg on the wheel of life.

Arrayed on the table in front of the Mexican were tall stacks of vinyl records. At his right elbow was a forty-year-old Thorens turntable that had once been Kevin's pride and joy. Behind his chair was a pair of vacuum tube amplifiers. The squat Russian 7199s and a tall quartet of British KT88s were radiating a pleasing amber glow. Inside each tube, a thin stream of electrons was ebbing and flowing as he breathed into the mike.

Under the table, sequestered within a leather briefcase, was the latest iteration of the precious machine. He reached down and carefully pressed a button and twisted two of its control knobs. The external battery pack was gone. Hephaestus had perfected an amazing battery. It was the size of a stick of butter. The lights on the Antikythera device began winking sequentially. Then all five of them lit up simultaneously. As they did so, the lights throughout the entire prison dimmed for a moment. He closed the briefcase. The device was now on standby mode and ready for takeoff.

Simon squeezed his eyes tightly shut and pressed the palms of his hands against them in an attempt to quell the maddening shiver of his eyelids. He clenched his teeth and forced his lips together until he had temporarily stifled the never-ending string of seemingly unconnected syllables that began spewing from his psyche every time the machine was energized. His mother's sad Irish tune was demanding a place on his tongue. His lips grew colorless from the exertion required to keep from singing the song out loud—and into the microphone.

He placed his right elbow gently against the copper toggle switch that would connect the output of the amplifiers directly to the prison transmitters. Showtime was at noon sharp. He rubbed the back of his right hand with the fingers of his left hand. Then his elbow pushed the switch of the amplifier and his lips parted.

"Good afternoon. This is radio station PNFY, with fifty pulsating watts of power serving the city of Tamal, San Quentin Prison, the entire parking lot, and the rifle range on the northeastern side of the facility. If the wind is blowing just right, our signal will occasionally reach the Richmond District in San Francisco. Today this station will be heard by thousands of people. In fact, we'll have a captive audience. And two weeks from this date, no more than ten or eleven listeners will even bother to tune in to my show.

"We are located at the high end of your AM radio dial at 1515 kilohertz, and we are thrilled to have this opportunity to serve this grand institution where the tuition is absolutely free, where the entrance exam is a breeze, where anybody—and I mean anybody with so much as a heartbeat in his chest and a pulse in his veins— can gain admission. And even if you're doing a life sentence—a "kickstand" in the local parlance—or languishing forever on Condemned Row, you're guaranteed to graduate from this institution . . . eventually. Isn't that incredible? Stanford or Harvard couldn't make that promise to you.

"After you've attended this institute for your allotted period of time and fulfilled all of your requirements, this hallowed establishment will give you two hundred dollars walkin' money and a bus ticket home. But here's the beauty part: you will always be welcomed back for an advanced degree—as many as you want. And it won't cost you one thin dime!

"Once again, greetings and salutations to my dear golem, my brethren. Good evening to all of you acolytes, coprolites, Areopagites, and Luddites! You don't have the foggiest notion of what those words mean, do you? Well, my friends, that's why you're in state prison! And all this time you thought you were in here for detracting from the good of the whole, for breaching the general peace of the community! If you happen to believe that, you might fancy yourself a neo-Platonist, but of course you would never do that. Why not? Because none of you has ever read Plato."

Simon flicked another switch, then turned up the volume on the echo reverberation. His next sentence sounded like it had been bellowed from a foghorn on one of those hulking Chinese freighters anchored in the bay.

"And that, my esteemed audience, is why YOU'RE IN STATE PRISON!" He turned off the echo-reverb.

"And now, friends, you should know that you can't read the Declaration of Independence or the New Testament without reading Plato. And all this time you thought that the Bible was just something you carry with you into parole hearings.

"Well, my lumpen brothers, have I got a deal for you. Send me a kite telling me something about Plato's life or his works, and I'll have Warden Harris put twenty-five bucks on your books so that you can gorge yourself on Vienna sausages and clog your arteries with ramen noodles. The warden thinks it's a safe bet, but I actually believe there might be someone out there who has burglarized a house and accidentally grabbed a copy of the *Symposium* or the *Republic* along with all that fake jewelry and loose change. And if one of you knows what the word 'golem' means, I'll make Warden Harris put thirty dollars on your books. The first correct answer wins."

There was a soft tapping on the glass in front of Simon, and he turned to see the cherubic pink face of Warden Victor Harris grinning at him from the metal stairway on the other side of the glass. The warden was a handsome man with thinning blonde hair and shocking blue eyes. As usual, his office staff had exiled him to the outside of the building, where he could indulge in his hourly cigarette without killing everyone else. He raised a hand and pressed it against the glass. The index finger and thumb were joined at the tips, forming a zero. That was how much money he expected to put on any prisoner's books.

Before stepping down to the grass below the staircase, he showed Simon the earphone in his left ear, pointed around the studio, then drew the same index finger across his neck from ear to ear. It was his rather blunt prediction about the radio show's longevity. Simon smiled at the former general contractor and prison psychologist who was now a warden at the oldest prison in California, then moved his lips even closer to the microphone.

"As you know, the call letters for this old radio station are PNFY. A lot of you lifers and old-timers believe that those letters stand for Prisoner Notification Frequency Yoyo, the middle band between frequencies X-ray and Zebra, and a lot of you, including the staff and guards of this illustrious prison—and that includes the warden—would be absolutely wrong. More on that in a few minutes. First let me inform you that this radio station, which my saintly Irish friend Kevin Hughes somehow managed to keep on the air for eleven months, is now under new but far less competent management. As I'm sure you already know, my name used to be Simon Vegas. Not anymore. It seems that my prison name is Simon Magus Vegas.

"If you remember, and I doubt that you will, Kevin played Borodin, Liszt, and Dvořák for all you knuckle-dragging lowbrows. He read Wallace Stevens and Adrienne Rich, and of course his show eventually went belly-up. I tried my best to warn him. You can't do anything that requires these guys to think, I told him. If they were capable of thinking for themselves, they wouldn't be here (he flipped the reverb button) . . . in STATE PRISON. But he wouldn't listen to me. For some reason, Kevin believed in one or two of you out there. Actually, he swore to me that there were five or six hundred semi-authentic humans out there among you six thousand—a tiny handful of you who are, at this moment, capable of some independent thought. Not that you are thinking independently, but you're capable of it.

"Well, personally I didn't believe it until I realized that if you adjust for the high percentage of psychopaths and pedophiles in here, the percentage of potential freethinkers in this lockup is only slightly lower than it is outside these walls. So . . . in honor of my friend, I've decided to give it a go. But I've also decided to do something a little differently. Two weeks from tonight—if I'm still on the air—we're going to have a night of Pachuco Boogie with music by Don Tosti, Las Hermanas Mendoza, Flaco Jiménez, Ry Cooder y su familia, and many others from Tejas, East Los . . . and Santa Monica.

"If I'm still here in a month, I will present a program planned especially for you white supremacists. I have to say that I don't blame you Aryan guys for picking skin color as the only criterion required for supremacy. What else have you got? It's all so dreadfully, desperately dumb. But then . . . that's why you're in STATE PRISON! God, I love that reverb! But now it's time for a bit of political commentary from yours truly."

Simon pressed a button on a small tape deck and played thirty seconds of a brass and drum fanfare written by Aaron Copland.

"Now, I know there are experts out there in the yard who know everything there is to know about illicit drugs. There are dope fiends in my distinguished audience who have been addicted for decades. There are tweekers listening in who have poured everything into their arteries, from PCP carefully handcrafted in a grease trap in Union City, to crack cocaine that was cooked up in a broken toilet in Hunter's Point. There are folks out there who have used black tar heroin that was whipped up in a dumpster in Tijuana and methamphetamine made with the best Drano and Clorox that money can buy.

"Some of you enjoy the dull, drooling stupor, the minor death that some of these drugs can give you, but most of you go in for the high and that rush of endorphins. Well, has Simon Magus Vegas got some fabulous news for you. That rush is a trickle from a leaky faucet compared to the Niagara Falls of endorphins that you can get from a dose of peptide hormones.

"I know you're out there looking at one another and shrugging in confusion. You're perplexed and confounded—by the way, the warden will put ten dollars on your books for the definition of each of those words, 'perplexed' and 'confounded.' Peptide hormones? What the fuck are those things? You're asking yourselves: Is that the new shit they're cooking up in the sewers of Belize? Is that the new large animal tranquilizer coming out of Borneo? Could it be that narcoleptic cocktail coming out of Thailand?

"Well, my captive brothers, it's none of those wonderful things. In fact, it's far more potent than anything you've ever snorted, injected, or smoked. Have you ever tried oxytocin or vasopressin? Never heard of them? Do you mean to tell me you've never shared a filthy, microbe-encrusted needle in some dingy, rat-infested slum basement with two or three toothless emaciates when one of them suddenly regained semiconsciousness and said, "Anyone wanna do some vasopressin?"

Simon turned up the level of the Copland fanfare, then began to reduce the volume.

"These two peptide hormones will give you the best high you've ever had. Ah, but there is a downside to oxy and vaso. There's always a downside, isn't there? You see, in a recent experiment some behavioral scientists sprayed a group of male prairie dogs with the stuff. In case you don't know—and I'm sure you don't—male prairie dogs are world famous for being shiftless philanderers. Some of them can impregnate up to a dozen females in a single day, and none of them ever stick around to help with the kids. Sound familiar? Well, after the animals were sprayed with vasopressin, guess what happened? Every one of those prairie dogs fell head over heels in love with their kids. And here was the worst part of it—they actually began mating for life!

"Imagine what would happen if Warden Harris requisitioned a helicopter and sprayed fifty gallons of this stuff out on the prison population tomorrow morning. Those studs out there who didn't immediately fall in love with the guy in the next bunk would suddenly have an overpowering desire to get a job and send all those kids they haven't seen in years to private school and to college. They . . . you would have an irrepressible need to change your kids' diapers and read to them and tell them about the idiotic, vacuous life you once led. It sounds pretty goddamn scary, doesn't it? Setting an alarm clock and going off to a job sounds a hell of a lot tougher than nodding off behind a portable toilet in the Tenderloin District. I have a word of advice for you."

Simon Magus Vegas hit the reverb button.

"BETTER STICK TO CRACK AND HEROIN."

He switched the reverb off, but the phrase seemed to bounce endlessly from every wall in the prison. "Better stick to crack and heroin . . . crack and heroin . . . heroin."

"At the end of tonight's show, I'm going to read two poems aloud to you. The first was written by Countee Cullen, and the second one will be by Langston Hughes. If you black dudes don't know who these guys are, you should call the parole board right now and cancel your upcoming hearings, because you deserve to stay right where you are. Any black dude who knows anything at all about these two poets, drop me a line explaining what you know, and if the answer demonstrates even a modicum of lucidity, Warden Harris will put enough on your books for a month's supply of corn chips and orange sodas. And now we're going back to November 27th, 1957. The location is Carnegie Hall in New York City. On the stage are Thelonious Monk, John Coltrane, Ahmed Abdul-Malik, and Shadow Wilson."

He lowered the phonograph needle into the first groove of the album. Leaning back in his chair, he listened to side two of the record. "Epistrophy" came to a close, and the applause died away. "If art doesn't move you," said Simon softly, "you will always be a prisoner, immobile until it does. Once again, this is Simon Magus Vegas, and this is radio station PNFY, and if you think that owning a noisy motorcycle gives you an identity, then this station is Probably Not For You.

"If you think that speeding on the freeway, weaving in and out of lanes, racing against soccer moms and schoolteachers, is the adventure of a lifetime, then this radio station is Probably Not For You. If you think that car of yours—the one waiting for you back home—is the uniquely perfect expression of your dominant masculine personality, just remember (he flipped on the reverb) THAT

THE AUTO MANUFACTURER MADE TWO HUNDRED AND SEV-
ENTY-FIVE THOUSAND JUST LIKE IT!"

Simon glanced up and saw the face of Victor Harris staring at
him once again from the other side of the glass partition. The warden's eyes were huge, and his mouth was wide open in an expression
of mock horror. There was smoke curling upward from the breast
pocket of his Brooks Brothers suit. His cigarette had fallen from his
lips and was about to set his kerchief and his coat on fire. The astonished warden had a see-through transistor radio pressed against his
left ear. The earphone had been tossed aside. He walked to the door
and stepped inside the small makeshift studio. As he drew closer,
Simon hit the toggle switch, muting the microphone.

"Simon Magus Vegas!" howled the warden, shaking his head in
disbelief. "What the hell kind of stage name is that? Wasn't Simon
Magus some kind of wild-eyed biblical heretic? I thought you might
make it to a second show, but let me revise that estimate, my friend.
What are you trying to do, Simon? If these men don't have their
bullshit belief systems, they've got nothing. And if they've got nothing, they've got nothing to lose! We'll have a riot on our hands in no
time flat."

The warden grimaced through the glass, then turned and
walked away.

"In no time flat."

7

AMADOU

The next morning, Simon had driven back to the prison to teach his poetry class and to see Lenny Hudson again. He muttered to himself as he waited for the fourth scheduled meeting with the condemned man. He looked around furtively, inspecting the room and the adjacent halls. There was no one else in the interview area. None of the guards seemed to be in any hurry to do anything. It might be fifteen minutes before Lenny appeared. Simon rose from his seat in the waiting room and walked into an interview booth.

He closed the door and looked around, then reached into his briefcase. He fiddled with the device hidden inside it. He glanced around again. He could do it—he could be gone and back before anyone even noticed. He had awakened this morning aching to stretch his wings. There was something he desperately needed to do.

An instant later, the lights in San Quentin dimmed to a dull yellow, and the Mexican Flyboy lifted off unnoticed and shot over the Sierras, gaining speed over Nevada before flaring like a meteorite across the skies of Colorado and into the Midwest. He increased his speed and did not slow down until he got his first glimpse of the Hudson River and the dark ocean beyond. He dropped down from the clouds and in another instant found himself hovering over Soundview in the Bronx.

The dials on the Antikythera device had been set for February 4th, 1999. Simon glided silently down a quiet street and stopped at 1157 Wheeler Avenue. He probed the darkness with his eyes and finally spotted the Ford Taurus just pulling to a stop. Beads of sweat were dripping from his brow as he watched the officers exiting the vehicle. There below his feet were those familiar cement steps that he had seen in a dozen newspaper articles. The porch light was out, and the vestibule was dimly lit. His stomach began to churn with anxiety as he watched a young man leave the sidewalk and climb the stairs. It had happened again. He had arrived too late.

Simon winced when he heard the hard crack of guns firing, and he witnessed the body of Amadou Diallo collapsing downward—the lethal, life-threatening wallet flying from his hand. Simon moaned as he watched the last of nineteen rounds entering Amadou's shaking, jerking body. One bullet severed his spine, while another entered his leg and traveled upward toward his belly. The final bullet entered the sole of his right shoe and exited through his toe. He had been shot while flat on his back. As the Flyboy swooped down to sidewalk level, trying frantically to turn the seconds dial backward, he suddenly heard another noise emanating from a time in the future and from a place three thousand miles away. He had to go. There wouldn't be enough time! He glided past the cops and upward into the vestibule.

"I have to go, Amadou," he wailed tearfully as he lifted the young man's head and whispered into his cooling earlobe. Amadou's sweat and blood were smeared on Simon's hands. "I have to go. I'm sorry." As he said it, Amadou's eyes rolled back, and his body sagged as life abandoned him. Simon inhaled deeply, then carefully blew air across the young man's eyes. A second later his eyelashes were inert. "But I'll be back even before I've left. I promise. I promise. No mistakes next time. I promise!" Down below the porch, the cops were pointing up at them and reloading their guns again.

"There's someone else up there with him. I can see her!" cried one of the police officers. "She's armed! I see a gun."

"No," said a second cop. "There's only one up there, and he's down."

"I'll be back before the first shot is fired—before the pain," said Simon. "I promise you that."

He heard another loud noise. He put the Antikythera device into a holding pattern and closed his briefcase. His hands were shivering uncontrollably. Amadou's dying face was still in his mind's eye. He turned his head and saw Lenny alternately dragging his heels and lunging toward the interview booth. He was wearing full shackles and hobbles, and there was a bulky, beefy guard on either side of him. The three men together had assumed a peculiar, ungainly pace, like inept Siamese triplets who were completely at odds about their foot speed and constantly at loggerheads regarding their direction of travel.

The two outer triplets were in no hurry to go anywhere, while the scrawny one in the middle was straining with all of his strength to reach his destination. Once again Simon noticed what was called the death row tan. From the lack of sunlight, Lenny's skin was bleached as deathly white as the underside of a catfish. The flesh of his arms resembled unbaked pizza dough. Each of the guards had a fat hand on one of his bony elbows. The ungainly trio were talking and laughing at high volume as they stumbled toward the booth.

"Four weeks?" said one of the guards while laughing hysterically. "Shit, you ain't gonna be back for a second show! I'm telling you, Vegas, the next time you come in here, you'd better be wearing body armor. Did you cut yourself, professor? Your hands are bleeding real bad. Man, you look awful—like you seen a ghost."

"I never heard anything like it," said the second guard. "And I've heard it all in the last seventeen years. We've had bleeding hearts, tree huggers, and televangelists with expensive teeth and cheap wigs palaverin' at these guys, but never anything like you. I didn't understand half of the shit you said, but I think you've got a death wish going for you. You're trying to take a fall."

"This afternoon the entire mainline was cursing your name,"

said the first guard as he pulled a handkerchief from somewhere and gave it to Simon. "At least a dozen radios was thrown against the walls and smashed to smithereens. There's guys in here who killed their mothers; what do you think they'll do to you? If I were you, Mr. Magus Vegas, I wouldn't show my face around these parts for a while. This place is Probably Not For You," he said, then began laughing fitfully. His enormous, fat-infused body was shifting beneath his Teflon vest like landfill during an earthquake.

"Yep," agreed the second guard. "A couple dozen of these crazies in here would love nothing better than to slide a shiv between your ribs and twist it real good. Did you know the lights are blinking on that machine of yours? Do you want him unhooked?"

Simon nodded as he used the handkerchief to wipe Amadou's blood from his hands. The shaking was finally subsiding. The second guard pulled out a key and unlocked Lenny's hands. The foot shackles stayed on. This was special treatment for a man who had murdered a fellow inmate. When Lenny sat down, the two guards locked the interview room, then lumbered to a nearby pod that had a bank of video monitors on one wall. There they could pretend to be keeping their eyes on the interview rooms while they sipped cups of tepid coffee. The large white guard smiled as his black partner switched the center screen to a local TV channel. Both men groaned at what they saw. The Giants were already five runs behind the Yankees, and it was only the second inning.

"Did you hear what the Supreme Court did?" asked Lenny quietly. There was a cold heat in his eyes and a hard tension in his voice. He hadn't spoken the question so much as he had taken aim and launched it. He had been repeating the sentence to himself all day—saying it silently over and over since before sunup. Now he was finally able to spit the words into the Mexican poet's face. "Did you read what those fuckers went and did?"

"Are you talking about the Kentucky case?" said Simon calmly.

He had heard about the case in the administrative lounge the previous morning. Some of the staff members had been talking about it.

"Justice Roberts—no, Just-ass Roberts doesn't give a flying shit if it's painful or not," said Lenny. There were flecks of frenzy moving in clusters across the crags of his pasty white face, like a platoon of army ants swarming toward a fallen grub. The only completely immobile features of his seething demeanor were twin clots of white spittle, one lodged at each corner of his mouth. As he spoke, Lenny's eyes scanned every inch of the interview room but never settled on any part of it. He had what medieval jailers once called "dungeon eyes." He looked everywhere, his gaze casting into the shadows, then into the light. But no matter where he looked, all he saw was himself.

"All he cares about is a 'substantial risk of harm,' whatever the fuck that means!"

Lenny raised his hands. He used his index and middle fingers to stab the air, supplying the quotation marks for "substantial risk."

"He doesn't give a shit about what I'm actually gonna feel when the potassium chloride starts rooting out my veins like drain cleaner. Fuck, I'll be paralyzed. I'll be lying there paralyzed like some fuckin' quadriplegic waitin' on the street corner for a special bus—and I'll be trying to scream at them deaf, heartless bastards that I can feel every goddamned thing!" He pushed away from the table and stood up.

"What if the sodium thiopental don't put me to sleep? What if I'm feeling the beginning of cardiac arrest? What if the potassium chloride just kills off half my ticker, and one of them doctors with tickets to the ballgame burnin' a hole in his pocket calls my death while I'm still alive? What if they bury me that way? What if I wake up kicking and screaming six feet underground over there in that prison cemetery?"

Lenny had begun to scream. There was a thick, unnatural

sheen covering his entire face. Simon looked at it closely and realized that it wasn't sweat at all. Something more than perspiration was squeezing from the follicles of his stubbled chin—something more viscous than mere salt water painting his features. There was a layer of gesso, a cloying ooze of inner plasma that had bubbled up through his pores and had thickened until it was too dense to run.

"Have you ever seen a play?" asked Simon. Lenny shook his head angrily, resenting this obvious waste of his time. His wild eyes were still darting around the room, snagging nothing. The weird question had caused him to lose his balance. The topic of conversation was always whatever Lenny Hudson chose to talk about. The subject of any conversation was always Lenny Hudson.

"Have you ever looked in the newspaper to find out what the local playhouses are presenting? Have you ever picked up the phone and bought a ticket for yourself, something right down in front? Have you seen any kind of stage play—a high school play, even a community production? Some of the best actors are in small theaters, you know."

"What the fuck?" screamed Lenny as he sat down in the chair and angrily crossed his arms. He had never seen a movie that wasn't on television. Why the fuck would he pay good money to see some local idiots in some stupid play? This was some kind of trick. His fists were clenched, and the veins on the backs of his hands were swollen and purple. His exasperation was quickly turning into rage.

"For me, the most pleasurable thing about a play is the part that comes after the last act: the curtain call. I love it when the dead soldiers get up and pull the bayonets out of their bellies. They drop the blood-soaked bandages from their bodies, then take their bows while holding hands with the enemy soldiers who ran them through just minutes before. I love to see the gentleman caller take little Laura's hand and, with a wide smile, walk with her through the parting curtains to accept their bouquets together. The sight of

Tosca's shattered body, now whole and unbroken, dashing out from behind the parapets to receive her standing ovation always sends shivers down my spine. A frail and wounded Blanche DuBois . . ."

"Fuck all of this shit!" shouted Lenny as he rose from his chair again and slammed his hand against the window. Faces turned from fifty yards away as the plexiglass flexed, then oscillated back and forth for five or ten seconds. The two guards put their coffees down and turned to investigate, but happily resumed their positions behind home plate when Simon waved them back.

"It ain't gonna work," said Lenny as he eased himself back into the white plastic chair. His rage had vanished in an unnatural instant, but the layer of shellac and sweat had returned to his face. He forced the twin spots of spittle upward into a stilted smile and said, "I can see what you're doin', and it ain't gonna work. I can see right through it. You got all this fuckin' education and you think it means somethin'? You read a few fuckin' poems on the radio and you think it means somethin'? It ain't gonna work with me or with them." He tossed his head toward the yard, where a few hundred prisoners were getting their allotment of cold wind and fog.

Simon turned away from Lenny and looked out into the exercise yard.

"When Blanche DuBois comes out to center stage and takes her curtain call with a wide smile on her face, that's as close as I can ever seem to get to a feeling of real justice in this life. I love it when Stella's broken sister walks offstage in triumph, then goes off to a candlelight dinner with a gaggle of admirers and fellow actors."

Lenny clenched his fist and moved closer to Simon Magus Vegas. For the first time, Simon noticed what a small, wiry man the prisoner was. He seemed muscular and powerful despite being so scrawny. Lenny had the skin of an albino and eyes like pieces of black obsidian—like chunks of wet coal.

"Why the fuck are you here, man?" asked Lenny, who was

standing up again, this time with his fists and arms trembling. "You don't like us. You don't respect us. You are one fucked-up teacher, Mr. Magus."

"Maybe what you need is a messed-up teacher to teach messed-up people. You confessed three times, Lenny," said Simon who was standing once again. He took a step toward the prisoner. Their faces were now just a few inches apart.

"You're the one who wanted to be here. I don't know why you wanted the world to know that those killings in Tracy were yours, but for some reason you did. When you killed those boys, there was no such thing as DNA testing. No one was hunting you. Everyone who worked on those murders is retired or dead. You were completely in the clear. Then years later, you killed a prisoner in front of a dozen witnesses and spilled your guts to anyone who would listen. You wanted to be right where you are."

Simon sat down in his chair and signaled Lenny to do the same. The prisoner complied, though with hesitation and a look of utter confusion on his face.

"You're only a small part of what's out there," said Simon, gesturing with one hand toward the ceiling and the universe beyond it. "It's been out there forever."

"Oh, I get it," shouted Lenny, almost triumphantly. "You wanna know if there's evil in this world. You wanna know what evil looks like. That's why you told Kevin you'd come see me. You wanna study me—put me in a test tube like some fungus and take a real close look at me! Now I can see it all! Now I see everything! You think if you study Lenny Hudson and find out what made him go off, you'll know if there is something real extra-special about me—something extreme that keeps me from being any face in a crowd, any boy growing up next door. You're wondering if you and me could be the same."

"Do you ever think about those two boys in Tracy or that prisoner down in Corcoran?" asked Simon. "Have you ever felt remorse for those two kids? Do you ever wake up in the middle of the night and apologize to them? Do you ever wish that you could go back in time and stop yourself from doing those terrible things?"

Lenny looked stunned for a moment before something approximating a smile began to grow on his lips. In less than a minute, the perpetually twisted muscles at his temple and hairline had relaxed and gone slack. The green veins in his neck and arms had submerged into his flesh, leaving behind a canvas of pallid white skin. Even the dark blackness of his pupils had softened to a brownish-gray. Simon was shocked by what he was witnessing. This man could not possibly be Lenny Hudson. He looked like a distant relative of the triple murderer. The man sitting opposite him could almost get up and walk out of Condemned Row without being recognized by any of the prisoners or guards.

"Do you know how it is when you've had too much to drink?" asked Lenny with a suspiciously wide grin. "You know you shouldn't do it, but you go ahead and have one more drink anyway. At one of your fancy professor dinner parties, you eat way too much—you're full as a son of a bitch. But you go ahead and reach out with your fork and stick it into that slice of roast beef that you really shouldn't have. You take it anyway, don't you?

"You really shouldn't shoot that boy, but you do it. You see his eyes get real wide, and you do it. It ain't no big thing like buyin' a car or eatin' too many donuts. I tell you what, Mr. Magus, I think about the look in their eyes, and that's about it. I think about how scared they were, and it's better than forcin' a woman to her knees. And you know what? Here's the real kicker. I'm scared to die! That's right! I'm scared to die. Do you know why?"

Simon shook his head.

"Because I don't give one single shit about your rules, your logic, and your moralities, or whatever the fuck you call them. It blows my mind that a killer who don't wanna die is something that messes with everybody's head. I ain't tit for tat. Fairness ain't my thing! I ain't found Jesus; hell, I ain't lookin' for him. I ain't found Muhammad or Confucius or anybody else, either. I just don't wanna die because I don't want to. It's as simple as that. I don't feel like it. Hell, every guy on death row thinks he should be out there walkin' the streets right now." He lifted his right arm and pointed a finger at Simon. "I ain't justice! I ain't fairness! Justice is what people like you do to people like me! It's that simple!

"But there's somethin' else I just figured out, Simon Magus Vegas. It hit me a minute ago, just like one of them silver bullets that kills a werewolf. I know a little somethin' about you," he said in a mocking sing-song voice. "I know a little somethin' about you, Mr. Professional Man!" He rose from his chair and moved his arms and legs rhythmically in something that might be called a victory dance. The look on his face was gleeful, triumphant. He pointed an accusing finger at the poetry teacher.

"You killed somebody—just like me. Nobody else knows that. It's true, ain't it? Your wife don't know it, does she?"

Simon was stunned by a hard recoil against his right shoulder. He smelled gunpowder, and he felt his stomach filling with acid. The prisoner's words had been like a punch to the temple. How could Lenny know?

"You killed somebody, too, and you think I can take that off your conscience by showin' you that I ain't a monster through and through—that I'm just some poor guy who got all twisted up by his life. You think I can bleach it all away for you, don't you? That's why you're here—to learn from one of your own kind. You can deny that, but I know better. I ain't stupid," the condemned prisoner shouted as two burly guards walked up to the interview room and knocked on the glass. One of them held his hand up and pointed to his enormous military-style watch. Using his fingers, Simon asked for ten more minutes. The two men shrugged and walked away.

"You don't care if I die, do you? Did you see what happened last week in Ohio? Let's get down to the nitty-gritty," shouted Lenny. "Did you hear what happened yesterday in the federal court in San Jose?" His face was covered in sweat, and his crazed intensity was at the highest level that Simon had ever seen. Lenny screamed so loudly that Simon had to cover his ears with his hands in order to stop the intense pain.

"Them bastards took thirty minutes to find a vein! They kept stickin' him like he was a voodoo doll or somethin'. Like he was a pincushion. What the shit is a pincushion, anyways? Did you see what happened over in Ohio last week? Man, are you even here? You're sittin' right here, but I don't get the feelin' that you're here with me. You're somewheres else! Did you even hear what I just said? They want me to die in pain."

"Yes, I heard you," said Simon in a distant, distracted voice. He had reached down and touched the machine in his briefcase. In another moment, Lenny's voice faded into a muted whisper as Simon pushed the door open and ceremoniously led Amadou Diallo into an apartment that was only a ten-minute walk from the ocean. The smell of the sea was everywhere around them. The large picture window to the left of the entrance revealed the beginning of a seemingly endless expanse of beach that was just fifty yards away. Simon called out, and a group of voices answered back from somewhere in the rear of the house.

"Are we in Guinea?" asked Amadou.

"No," said Simon. "We're somewhere near Boca Raton."

He and Amadou followed a stone path and found her reading out on the patio. She was the inventor of the plane astrolabe, and she was the daughter of Theon the philosopher. She held a book in her hands that was a discourse on quantum mechanics. She had been deep in thought and had not heard them come in. There had been at least a dozen scrolls on this subject in her beautiful museum in Alexandria. The Mexican Flyboy touched Hypatia on the shoulder, and the lovely woman with long black hair and beautiful ceramic skin looked up from her reading and smiled.

Her eyes met Simon's, and for half an instant he was streaking over Lusitania, past Taraco and ancient Sicilia and down to the moon gate on the shore of Alexandria at the beginning of the fifth century. He banked right and passed between the enormous red granite obelisks that stood at the entrance of the Caesareum. He flew through the towering portals and caught them in the act; he saw the angry, frothing mob of Christian clerics smashing tiles against the floor and preparing to use the shards to cut her skin away from her living muscle and bone. He had lifted her away from all of that.

Hypatia pushed the same memory from her own mind, then looked at Simon's companion, rose from her divan, and walked silently toward him. Simon lifted Amadou's hand, then extended it to Hypatia, who smiled shyly before extending her own.

"Eratosthenes is going to love that book," she said with a smile as she dropped the volume onto a nearby lounge chair. The two Africans strolled off hand in hand, down a narrow sandy path toward the swimming pool. Simon watched Amadou as he kicked off his shoes and tossed his wallet and his bullet-riddled clothing into a garbage can. He watched as the Lindbergh baby, laughing and smiling, toddled up to the newcomer and gave him some baggy shorts and a flowery black and lavender shirt. A small Vietnamese boy picked up Amadou's bloody shoes and socks, washed his feet, and handed him a brand-new pair of orange flip-flops.

"Yes, I read the article about the prisoner in Ohio," said Simon softly. There was a smile on his face.

"That's all you got to say? That's it? You read the fuckin' article?" asked Lenny. "Did you see what they did to that guy over in

Lucasville, Ohio? They killed him without usin' the three-shot cock-tail! They killed him by injectin' him with nothin' but a single dose of sodium thiopental. That's it—just one lousy chemical! Goddamn it, I want the cocktail! I demand the cocktail!"

Simon jerked upright in his seat. He was shocked by the words he had just heard coming from Lenny Hudson's mouth.

"You want the cocktail? I thought you didn't want to die."

"They're gonna kill me. You know that. I just don't want sodium pentothal along with nothin' else! Ain't they supposed to paralyze me first?"

"Isn't it thiopental?" asked Simon.

"Thiopental and pentothal are the same goddamned thing! Don't you know none of this shit?"

"A couple of drops of that stuff in the vein," Simon mused aloud, "and even the toughest secret agent spills his guts. Isn't that the same drug you see in all those spy movies—the truth serum?" he asked. That question silenced Lenny immediately. For thirty or forty seconds, the once raving maniac sat staring at the wall next to his chair. The words "truth serum" had stunned him like a sucker punch to his temple.

"And yesterday some federal judge in San Jose goes and lifts the moratorium on lethal injections. Albert, the serial killer three cells down from me, is gonna be the first to go—then it's my turn. Now the same guy . . . the very same guy," began Lenny, in a ghostly, almost disembodied tone, ". . . that same guy that give that sodium pentothal to kill Kenneth Biros over in Ohio is right here in this prison—right now—this very fuckin' minute!"

In another split second, the old Lenny was back. His entire personality was animated by rage—his flaccid body suddenly inflated by it.

"The son of a bitch has been flyin' all the way out here to give lectures to these local idiots on how to kill Lenny Hudson! He's the one who rebuilt the San Quentin death chamber! He designed everything! All that horseshit about havin' two infusion rooms and the gurney bein' light green—those are his ideas. He's the one who first ran the intravenous tubes through the wall! He leans over and blows air across a prisoner's face to make sure he's dead. Somethin' about the eyelashes flickerin' or somethin'. Can you believe that? All of those bullshit rules about how to place the pillow just so—he wrote them!"

"He's here?" asked Simon, suddenly interested in Lenny's ranting. "What's his name?"

"Shit, it's in the article, didn't you read it? I thought you said you read it!"

"What's his name?" asked Simon again, impatiently. "When is the next lecture?"

"Therage," said Lenny, almost spitting the name. "Jeffrey Therage," he said, pronouncing the last name like "the rage." "He used to be some kind of medical doctor, but the article said he gave up his patients and his big-money practice to go out and do these executions all over the country. He don't give the shots himself. He just tells people how to do it and how to upgrade their death chambers.

"I guess he's too all-fired good to do it himself—doesn't want to get his filthy hands dirty. His last lecture is tomorrow afternoon, but he's already here visitin' the staff . . . and his shiny new death chamber. The warden is going to give him the grand tour. But first the doctor is going to attend that meeting of the committee. He'll be here when you're on the air."

Simon had been dumbfounded by the mention of the doctor's name—Therage. It was a French name. It was pronounced more like *garage*. He had heard that name before. Where? When had he heard it? Then he thought he remembered something: Had it been centuries before? Had it been somewhere in France? Had it been in Poland? No, he had heard that name in France—six or seven hundred dred years ago.

Simon stood up. Without uttering a word, he signaled the nearest guard that the interview was over. As he closed the door to the glass-enclosed room, Lenny stood up and shouted at him.

"When you see Therage, ask him if Biros said anything!" pleaded Lenny. "Ask him if he said anything—anything at all! Ask him if Biros babbled on and on like an idiot about this and that—like he couldn't stop talkin'." The prisoner fell to his knees and clasped his hands together. He began sobbing. "Did he say shit that didn't make no sense? Real personal shit that didn't make no sense? Please. Please!" he pleaded. " Do that for me, please!"

Simon turned around to look at this newest version of Lenny Hudson. In all of his visits, he had never heard the man use that tone of voice. Lenny was terrified and begging. There were tears in his eyes, and he was pleading! For the first time since he had begun talking with the condemned prisoner, Simon could almost glimpse the boy that Lenny had once been. But it wasn't death that was scaring Lenny. All of the trustees and guards outside the room and down the hall turned their heads away from the television monitors and toward the interview booth when they heard that plaintive voice. It was a voice that had never been heard from Lenny during his long years on death row.

Down the hall, the Flo-Massa abruptly stopped his mopping and said, "Lenny Hudson ain't never say the word 'please' to nobody—'bout nothin'. Never. No time! Somethin' funny goin' on in here. Somethin' real funny. Lenny is all-fired scared of that truth serum. That's what he scared of. Worse than the grave. Lenny done gone and found somethin' worse than the grave . . . worse than livin' in here . . . if you can call this livin'."

Simon inhaled deeply, then exhaled slowly, pensively. He'd had enough of this for today. He had something to do—there was someone he had to meet. At that moment the two colossal guards returned. As the guard on the left moved, twin tsunamis of fat undulated across his back in opposite directions, flowing like a chain wave toward his ribs and belly. Lenny was about to speak when the other guard kneed him in the thigh.

"Interview's over," he said gruffly. "You've got nothing to say, dead man. The State of California is only getting one body out of this deal, and you got three. Don't seem fair to me. Richard over there has thirteen, and that other one has nine. Don't seem like a fair trade to me."

"What would you do?" asked Simon. His face was a portrait of disbelief at the guard's callous words. "What would you do to Lenny if it was up to you?" The black guard stopped moving for a moment, then looked up at the poetry teacher.

"Hell, I don't know. A nice, slow bath in battery acid might be a good choice. Or maybe I'd cover him head to toe with honey and let a family of rats gnaw on him for a month. No, no, I've got it! What was that thing they used to use in them dark ages days? I seen pictures of this contraption in that book the captain has in his desk."

"The rack?" said the second guard with a giggle. "They used to take a whole day to pop one bone clean outta the socket."

The ungainly Siamese triplets reappeared, then shoved and lumbered awkwardly to the sound of clanking chains and jingling handcuffs, finally arranging their six legs so that three bodies could squeeze through the narrow door of the interview booth.

"That's it?" said Lenny despite another savage knee to his side. "You fat faggots would put me on the rack. What about you, Mr. Magus Vegas? There's blood on your hands, too. I can see it from here."

Simon offered the bloody handkerchief to its owner. The guard glowered and waved it away.

"Shut up," said the second guard. "Somebody's got to pay for them three people."

"The rack ain't shit!" exclaimed the other guard. "Tie him to a pole and set fire to a hundred bags of charcoal briquettes piled around his bare feet. We could do it at a tailgate party at the Oakland Coliseum."

As the stumbling trio reached a metal security door leading into Condemned Row, Lenny turned back and winked at Simon Magus Vegas and shouted with a cold, high laugh, "What makes you think I only killed three? I know who you are, Mr. Poetry Man. Like I said, we go back. Way back. What makes you think I only killed three?"

8

FIFTEEN MEXICANS

While sucking through chattering teeth the last few gusts of air that he will ever breathe, every old gringo, no matter what his station in life once was—from predatory banker all the way up to street corner beggar—finds himself in an unexpected place. He isn't lying under the white sheet that has just been pulled over his senseless, motionless face. He isn't belted down in that whirring, clicking robotic hospital bed. Nor does he find himself slouching downward from that saggy green leatherette couch in a ranch-style convalescent home sixty miles from his third ex-wife and grown children—but in a place much, much farther away.

In fact, in the final flickering moments of his life, every old gringo is horrified to discover that his feeble, failing remains have sprouted a pair of forelegs where his arms once were, and the entire surface of his skin has been completely covered with coarse brown fur that is capped by a shaggy black mane down the ridge of his back. Even worse, this new version of his corporeal self has somehow been deposited in an open field where there isn't a single tree to keep the merciless equatorial sun from scorching his dappled hide.

Desperate to know how he got to this place, he dimly recollects what he thought was the last moment of his life. In his muddled memory there is a vague intuition of a musical flourish, of the wave of a magic wand and the sheet being pulled away with a theatrical flair to reveal to an invisible audience that his corpse has mysteriously vanished into thin air and has been miraculously transported to Africa. He might remember a distant hypnotic voice saying: "Now, Mr. Keyes, on the count of three I am going to snap my fingers. One, two, three. You are now a wildebeest."

Trying desperately to get his bearings and to comprehend what is happening to him, he ignores the insane pounding of his own heart. He listens carefully, and he hears not the dull, anesthetic drone of the wall-mounted television or some simplistic patter between two bored, underpaid orderlies, but the cavernous, guttural roar of lions. He glances around frantically and suddenly sees every person he has ever known in his entire life: his coworkers, his grammar school buddies, his legitimate sons and his daughters out of wedlock—he sees his fellow wildebeest, high shouldered and huddling, grinding their wet cud and staring at him in silence as he lies there helpless to move in the brown savannah grass.

The herd that once counted him as a member moves as one to a spot a hundred yards away, leaving him all alone—out there on the farthest fringe. He watches as they lift their curved horns and fly-ridden heads to frantically scan every corner of the field around him for what they know is coming. Their doe eyes suddenly grow wide with terror at the first fleeting glimpse of three circling lionesses. Then those sharpened gazes dull and go dim, and scores of bearded muzzles quickly give their full attention to the tasty shoots of grass just beneath their hooves.

They have nothing at all to worry about. In fact, the entire herd is slowly put at ease by the deliberate and precise—almost hypnotic—movements of the fearsome tawny cats. The three powerful females have their cold green eyes tightly fastened on the one they came for. For now they'll be satisfied with him. They'll eat some of him, then drag the rest of the carcass away. At the abrupt muffled sound of the actual kill and the ensuing death rattle, the entire herd of wildebeest fidgets, their dusty withers shivering for a moment or two.

Then all of the bulls, cows, and calves slowly settle in at a new stand of grass just thirty yards farther away, secure in the knowledge that it was those cigarettes that did Uncle Peter in—those extra fifty pounds. It was karma. He should have swallowed two ginkgo biloba and one aspirin a day. He should have dyed his hair, gotten a jowl lift, and signed up for that yoga class. Just look at his second ex-wife! She got a boob job and liposuction and—*shazzamm,* a brand-new husband!

Old Mexicans, on the other hand, die a very different death than the gringos. South of the border, everyone rips and tears at la muerte daily with their fingernails and their teeth. On el Día de los Muertos they consume death—roll it in sugar and flour, shape it into tiny comedic horrors, slosh it in egg wash, and bake it until its crust is golden brown. Then they bite off monstrous morsels that must be washed down with sloppy, drooling mouthfuls of home-made pulque or cloudy, unfiltered mezcal. Death is swilled into their gullets—into their gizzards, giblets, and guts. If they stay on this diet long enough, their blood and skin will become so bitter, so acrid, that death himself can barely stand the taste of it.

When he comes to take an old man in Mexico, the Grim Reaper comes pouting and cussing and oddly standoffish. Where's the fun in taking the life of someone who has been dying as long as he has been alive—and alive as long as he has been dying? Using all of his magical powers of misdirection, terror, and hypnosis, death has never been able to draw an audience south of the border. Even worse, he has never been able to mesmerize a single old Mexicano into believing that his expiring body and soul are stretched out helplessly on the burning Serengeti Plain.

The Famous Wildebeest Trick positively slays 'em, knocks 'em dead in countless venues in El Norte and in most places in Western Europe. But the Great Illusion doesn't play at all at a deathbed in Morenci, Arizona, where three generations of a family all lived in the same small house—where the newest member of the family slid from his mother's womb onto the same tattered mattress that held his grandfather when he first saw the light of day.

Death—positively mortified by ennui—merely gestured half-heartedly, and Éamonn Ó Floinn, el abuelo, the grandfather of Simón Ó Floinn Vegas, nodded his head proudly, defiantly, and complied without question. In point of fact, everyone in the family did that—both of Simon's sisters, his father and mother, aunts and uncles, they all did that. No trap doors, no curtains or hidden contraptions are of any use whatsoever with people like that. How stultifying! How incredibly boring! Everywhere else, the magic trick comes off beautifully—without a hitch every nine or ten seconds, around the clock—around the world.

⌁

Simon turned onto Bryant Street and began circling the block in search of a parking space. He finally found one two blocks away from the Café Roma. When he walked in, Ezekiel Stein was sitting alone in a chair in the center of the café. His graying head was bent over a steaming cup of tea and a large leather-bound volume. As he got closer, Simon could see that Zeke was reading the *Biographia Antiqua,* and that the book was open to the section on Hermes Trismegistus.

"Still resisting the Talmud," said Simon as he sat down next to his old friend. Zeke looked up from his book and smiled.

"My mother says that the Talmud is the inevitable destination for me. She may be right, but I've decided to take the long road from the proto-Christian myths of Mithras through the crucifixion of Quetzalcoatl. It's not in my nature to choose a meal without reading the entire menu."

"What happened to your obsession with Zoroaster and Carl

Jung? How long have you been looking over the menu, thirty years?" asked Simon. "Why are you limiting yourself to that? I know it's frustrating that there's nothing in the entrées and desserts but the so-called five great religions and all of their variants. Why don't you invent a religion of your own?"

"It's too late—and too soon for that," answered Zeke. "The patriarchs and the prophets knew that they had to hurry up and write those chapters and verses and get them out there before anyone brought in an investigative team to start looking for independent witnesses at the site of an alleged miracle. Can you imagine a team of nosy scientists checking Methuselah's teeth or examining Lazarus for a pulse?

"Can't you just see a team of archaeologists informing a blonde, blue-eyed Adam and Eve that they are actually a pair of dark-skinned Negroes and that the entire garden scene has to be knocked down and moved, lock, stock, and barrel, to Kenya—not to mention back in time a couple of million years? That sort of scrutiny could put quite a damper on a budding religion. So I missed that early opportunity to invent Steinism, but it looks like another chance is right around the corner. If real journalism keeps dying off, we'll soon be ripe for another age of miracles.

"I've been meaning to tell you that last week I caught your first show on PNFY. Where my house is situated, on the Panhandle of Golden Gate Park, I can pick up all of those little pirate stations that are operating out on the water in Sausalito and Tiburon. It's some pretty interesting stuff, I'll tell you. One guy claims that he can prove the Confederates won the Civil War."

"They did," said Simon.

"Every week I listen to this one guy who broadcasts from Richardson Bay. He lectures for hours on the Qutb Minar, the famous Masonic structure. One week ago, right in the middle of his talk, a new, stronger signal broke in on his frequency and completely buried his show. I recognized your voice immediately. Oh, man, I didn't know you had that kind of *tsuris* in you. At first I thought it came from anger, but after two or three minutes I knew there was something else coursing beneath all of that intensity. When's the next broadcast?"

"Tonight," said Simon. "This time they want me to go on at five o'clock. The administration wants everyone locked down in their cells when the show airs. Not even trustees and administrative workers will be allowed out, and all visiting hours are canceled. I guess Warden Harris is afraid of a riot. I think the future of my show is in grave doubt," he said with a wide smile.

"So now it's Simon Magus Vegas," said Zeke with a laugh.

"I think Kevin Hughes had something to do with that name," said Simon. "It's the only thing the prisoners will call me now. The funny thing is that I like it. It seems to fit me."

"Do any of them know what it means?" asked Zeke while reopening his heavy volume. He went through the index, then turned to a page. "Here it is, that worn-out old Vatican news bulletin about the Magus locked in spiritual battle with Saint Peter in Rome. Of course, it was written six hundred years later. According to this, Simon Magus told Peter that he could fly without the help of Peter's god . . . and he did!

"He lifted off from the cobblestone street and soared high above the avenue in front of hundreds of the usual unnamed witnesses. So Peter got down on his knees and prayed to his god to command the winds and demons of the air to let Simon fall to his death, which also happened. Of course, this act of deliberate, premeditated murder proved to everyone that Peter's god was superior to any feminine Gnostic deity and her inferior female apostles."

Zeke closed the book.

"Modern research has proven almost conclusively that Peter was never in Rome. If he was actually crucified upside down, it happened somewhere else. There are at least seven other versions of

Simon Magus's death. There is even one very interesting tradition that claims that he landed safely and lived to be a hundred and ten years old. Another story relates that he married the ghost of Helen of Troy. As you know, Helen, the alleged daughter of Zeus and Leda the swan, married Menelaus, then betrayed him by running off to Troy with her lover Paris. Some say that after the Trojan War, she took as her second husband the only man in history ever to fly without the aid of machines."

"Or of gods," said Simon softly but with great intensity. "The point is that he flew . . . with no one's help, he flew. He got free of it—all of it."

Zeke looked up and stared at his friend's face for a moment. He realized that it was the face of someone he had never really seen. Of course he knew Simón Ó Floinn Vegas. He had been his friend for years. But there was something profoundly different about the person sitting next to him this morning. Suddenly, Zeke knew exactly what it was. For the first time in what seemed like a decade or two, he was able to fix his eyes on the surface of Simon's face and skin. In the past his lips and cheeks and hands had always seemed to be in constant, frenzied motion. And sometimes when Simon was speaking, Zeke thought that he could hear a faint tune, a hauntingly familiar melody modulating every word that came from his friend's mouth.

Everyone who knew Simon understood that he had been an unwilling participant of some sort in one of America's holy crusades. No one knew much more than that. Simon had always been an accepted outsider. He was a lonely homeless person who happened to have many friends, a fine home, and a beautiful wife. Often he could be seen acting just like a punch-drunk street person, someone who ducked invisible punches and constantly muttered to himself—a stream of incomprehensible words.

A frantic Elena had called Zeke a number of times in the past because her husband would sometimes walk out of the house in his sleep. Zeke had arrived early one morning to find Simon in the middle of the street swinging his fists at the wind and sparring with a nonexistent opponent. On another early morning it had taken Zeke two hours to talk Simon out of jumping from a tall eucalyptus tree. The Mexican had become convinced that he could fly. Despite all of this, he showered and shaved every morning. He put on a suit and tie, and prepared his classes with care and imagination. His students loved him.

There was almost certainly a deep-seated reason, a ground zero, for Simon's malaise, his case of walking, high-functioning lunacy—perhaps more than one ground zero, but Zeke had never been able to put his finger on anything concrete. Simon suffered from something beyond soldier's sickness, that so-called *melancholia de guerre* that untold millions have endured since the beginning of humankind. Zeke knew something about Vietnam but had always suspected that something even more primal and even more painful was hiding underneath the crippling terrors of combat—something that had fossilized in Simon's soul long before he reached draft age—something that had nearly derailed him early in life. Elena had sensed the same thing.

Whatever it was, Zeke guessed that it had also strengthened him, annealed him. It had actually helped him to survive the war, and it kept him working and going to classes all the way through graduate school. Simon could have turned to crime or heroin or homelessness, like some veterans. Or, even worse, he could have built a perfectly acceptable life in the American church of automotive worship or by losing himself in television situation comedies. The arc of his life could have risen and fallen quite acceptably with the fortunes of the local football team.

Somewhere in all of those dark rooms behind Simon's eyes was that one room—ground zero—where no light had ever been allowed to shine. The contents of that single room punished Simon. It scourged his spirit every day—yet somehow what was in there kept him alive and gave him hope. Still, there were storms inside his skull—tornadoes that were continually touching down. The proof was there, sequestered in his eyes and his obscure aeronautical poems. It seemed to Zeke that every one of Simon's stanzas of poetry dealt with flight.

"You said on the phone that there was something you wanted me to do. At least I think you said that." The investigator slumped visibly in his seat as Simon removed four oversized playing cards from his briefcase and laid them face up on the table: the four kings. Zeke shrugged, then smiled wearily. He had been through this a hundred times or more. Still, he reached out and pulled the cards toward his chest, turning them face down.

Maybe this time he would finally figure out how this tiresome yet intriguing trick was done. He watched Simon, looking carefully for any hasty or unnatural move that might give him a clue. He wondered if the appearance of these cards at this point in their conversation meant that Simon was diverting attention away from something. Was this trick a minor act of misdirection that was meant to conceal a second, more significant act of misdirection?

"The four armed kings," said Zeke as he lifted the corner of each card to make doubly sure they were still there. "The Egyptian Ammonite architects. This quartet gouged out the center and the four corners of the universe with their knives."

He hunkered down to study his friend's every move. Simon took off his jacket and pulled the sleeves of his dress shirt up past his elbows. He removed his wristwatch and spread his fingers to show Zeke both sides of his hands. They were empty. Zeke stared at the cards and at Simon without blinking. He refused to let his eyes follow along as Simon put the watch on the table because it might be a strategic move, a trivial yet critical act that was meant to pull his attention away for a hundredth of a second.

"Are you ever going to tell me how you got that hole in your right hand?" asked Zeke as he pushed at the edges of the four cards until they formed a small congruent stack. He peeked once again and saw that the kings were still there. Without answering, Simon reached across the table and tapped the deck with the index finger of his wounded hand. He then withdrew his hand to a point half-way between himself and his friend and moved it back and forth in front of Zeke's face. Simon muttered some words; then, with a flourish, he invited Zeke to turn the cards over. When he did so, Zeke laughed to see four aces in place of the kings, one of each suit.

"It's the only card trick I can do," said Simon. "My right hand is a mess." He lifted his hand to inspect the old injury and to massage the palm. "A mess."

"I don't think I'll ever figure out how you do that. Except for the tap at the end, you never touch the cards. I must say, you sounded pretty weird on the phone this morning, Simon—nothing like your usual eccentric self. This is something you've wanted me to do for a long time, isn't it? I can only remember four or five times in the last few years when you were as intense and as disturbed as you were on the phone. I've always felt that there was some investigation you wanted me to do—something you wanted me to help you with. For some reason you couldn't—or wouldn't—ask me before now. Today's the day, isn't it?"

The smile disappeared from Simon's face. He took a sip of his coffee, then sat up straight in his chair while wondering why he had waited so long to do this—over forty years. Why was he doing it now? He considered retreating into silence once again, but managed to shove that nagging impulse away for the last time. He inhaled deeply and tried to imagine the unimaginable: a little girl's face—the face of his unborn daughter.

The time had come. His buzzing lips repeated and repeated the phrase: "the time has come." The words began to echo and re-echo in his mind, the sound from his lips building with each repetition. His eyes rolled backward into his head, and in a sliver of an instant he was lifting a man out of a hideous contraption made of metal, wood, and leather straps. He smiled into the face of Ethel's husband, Julius Rosenberg, just before setting him down safely on a stretch of warm Florida sand.

"It was a marvelous flying taxi ride, Mr. Simon," said Julius, "but I'm afraid I have no money for the fare. None at all! I can't pay you. I'm so embarrassed. You see, I've been in prison for a while. They took my money and my watch and put it all in a brown envelope . . ."

Simon's cyclonic maze of whirling thoughts stopped dead in their tracks when he felt a firm hand on his neck and a familiar voice speaking forcefully. What he heard was not the sad, confused voice of Julius Rosenberg, but a voice asking, "Who was more alone than Giordano Bruno as he was burning to death in the Campo de' Fiori? Who was more alone than beautiful Hypatia?"

"Aristarchus was more alone than Giordano," answered Simon as if he were emerging from a trance. Zeke had long ago discovered the way to pull his friend out of his waking dreams. It required a firm grasp of his neck while asking a particular kind of question.

"Aristarchus was more alone," whispered Simon. His eyes were still closed. "When the nomadic Hebrews were stoning young girls to death for being flirtatious, and the Egyptians were busy believing that the sun was a disc the size of a wagon wheel circling the earth at an altitude of fifty yards, Aristarchus alone knew that the stars were very far away. He was writing about parallax when everyone else on earth was washing their clothes in goats' piss. He had no one to talk to. No one at all."

"Where did you go just now?" asked Zeke when his friend

opened his eyes. "You blanked out for almost a minute. I've seen it before. Tell me, where did you go?" He had never dared to ask these questions before.

"I went to a vineyard somewhere in California; then I went to Sing Sing Prison," said Simon with a shrug, as though Zeke should have known the obvious answers to his own question. "I went back to 1953 and got to Julius just in time to save him from enough electricity to light Times Square. It was a perfect flight, Zeke, not like with Ethel. I had to readjust my temporal target three times to get to her . . ."

"Ethel and Julius Rosenberg?" asked Zeke, his eyes growing larger by the second. "The Jewish couple who stole the secret to the atomic bomb? Temporal target?"

"The machine is working better every day," continued Simon. "It was strong enough to take Elena and Hephaestus with me when I got Ethel. This time I was in and out of there in thirty seconds flat. Those guards at Sing Sing probably lived their lives and died believing that they had seen Mae West's cleavage and gotten her autograph."

Now it was clear to Zeke that his friend was hallucinating. His mind was awash with twisted, highly complex delusions. Before he could react to these disturbing pieces of information, Simon began to speak softly.

"When I was a boy . . . ," he began almost inaudibly. He knew that Zeke had not heard him, so he cleared his throat and began again. "When I was a boy, I watched a woman fall to her death." He could barely force the words past his tongue. Zeke was completely unnerved by the sound of Simon's voice and the pallor of his face. His voice was high and thin, like the voice of a prepubescent boy. His face was almost white.

"She fell from heaven. Well, that's what I thought at the time. I watched her as she fell from what must have been a mile up or more. It seemed like an eternity. She jumped from an airplane just as the first rays of light were peeking over the hilltops. She jumped with eight other people. Then, somewhere between the dark edge of the troposphere and the hard ground, she made the decision not to pull the ripcord. She made the decision to die. I know it. Other than a single sentence from a man's mouth, I don't have any evidence for it, but it has been something I've felt inside for over forty years."

Simon's voice began to fall in pitch. Zeke heard the adult voice speaking the next sentence.

"Honestly, I can't prove that she killed herself, but she fell from the sky and slammed into the earth right at my feet. The sound of her back striking the earth was deafening. I watched that woman die, Zeke. I knelt over her and watched her body liquefy inside her jumpsuit. I tried to stop her fall, but I couldn't—at least I couldn't back then. I looked into her eyes and saw that she was seconds away from what she wanted most of all—peace.

"She said something to me—three words, and I'm still not certain what they were or if I heard them right. Sometimes I'm not sure she said anything at all." He turned his eyes away from his friend. "I have witnessed her death through the eyes of a child ten times a day, every day of my life, since then. But—I should begin at the beginning," he said. Simon's breathing had become labored. There was a thick sheen of sweat building on his forehead and cheeks.

He told Zeke about the old Portogee with the miraculous nostrils, and about the lonely Pinoy cook who had fought the Japanese and spent the remainder of his days in labor camps in America. He carefully and painstakingly explained how imperious and demanding Pinot noir grapes can be. He told Zeke about the blistering harbinger wind that had arrived at the vineyards just days before the woman fell. He described in detail the *vendange verte*—the green sacrifice. With each word, he felt more and more like a traitor to his wife. He had never told any of this to Elena.

"I don't know where it happened, but there aren't that many places in California where Pinot noir is grown on a large scale—Napa, Sonoma, Mendocino, Santa Barbara, and some parts of Monterey and the Livermore Valley. There has to be an airport nearby, probably a small community airfield. Her husband was a big guy—a red-faced fellow named Keyes. I saw the name tag on his jumpsuit. I will never forget that name. One of his skydiving companions called him Pete."

"Peter Keyes," said Zeke as he made a notation.

Simon reached into a pocket of his suit and pulled out two small photographs. Each had been carefully sealed in plastic. Zeke noticed that one of the photos had ragged yellow edges, while the other looked fairly new. Simon looked at them, then hurriedly put them both back into his pocket. After a moment of visible inner turmoil, he took the newer photo out again and handed it to Zeke.

"It's a picture of a section of the wall, the Vietnam War Memorial in Washington."

"A name has been circled," said Zeke, who reached for his reading glasses and read the inscription out loud. "Fulgencio Garza."

"Pronounce the 'g' in Fulgencio like an 'h,'" said Simon.

"Full-hen-sio Garza," repeated Zeke, proud of his Spanish accent. "You want me to find him? You want me to find his family? Do you want me to find the Rosenbergs, too?"

"No," said Simon, finally understanding that Zeke was not at all certain of his friend's sanity. "No. I know where Ethel and Julius are. The skydiver and Fulgencio are different—very different. I want you to find the soldier's son. He has his father's name."

"Fulgencio Garza Junior," said Zeke yet again. It was an assertion rather than a question. It was an attempt to communicate to Simon that he understood—even if he didn't.

Simon nodded. He was visibly shaken by the sound of Garza's name as it came from a source other than his own tempestuous mind.

"It shouldn't be difficult for you with all those illegal databases of yours. There's an electronic registry for the names on the wall. They're listed according to the date of their death and the hour of the day. The soldier's hometown is included. I think he came from Port Arthur. I'm not certain about that. I only had two real conversations with Fulgencio, one before he died and one after. When I visited the wall, I was shaking so hard that I couldn't locate his name. What am I saying? Hell, I couldn't get closer than fifty feet from that wall. Someone else had to walk up to it and photograph his name for me." After a moment of obvious inner struggle, he pulled out the older photo and handed it face down to Zeke.

"Don't let me see it," said Simon. "I can't stand looking at it anymore."

"It's a boy—just a toddler," said Zeke, who put both of the pictures into his pocket before turning to face his friend. "You got this during the war? That would put him in his late thirties or early forties today. Something's going on with you, man, something substantial. You've always been wound kinda tight—kinda like the Gordian knot. Anyone close to you knows that. Is something making you unravel? Did something happen?"

"It's going to happen," whispered Simon, almost to himself. "A little girl is going to come into this world and find out that she's got me for a papa. They spun the wheel, and the pointer clicked and clicked from one peg to the next, and she wound up with a basket case—a Mexican flyboy. A million possible fathers, and she gets me—a mediocre poet who suffers from shell shock. I've tried to deal with this problem for decades. The madness abated for a while, but it's back and getting worse."

"Because of the baby?" asked Zeke, almost under his breath. "It started again when Elena got pregnant?" Simon acted as though he had not heard the question.

"I thought I could wait this out, but I'm just kidding myself.

Hell, it's been forty years and a half-dozen army psychiatrists. Do you know how many multipurpose rooms I've sat in with guys even sicker than I am—guys with no arms, guys with no legs or faces—and talked on and on with them, listening to them trying to describe indescribable things? But here's the kicker: I couldn't bear to tell those wounded veterans my real secret—that I was suffering from this even before I went to Vietnam. It's never going to end, Zeke. It won't ever end for me until I catch that woman in my arms—until I find young Fulgencio. Maybe it'll never end."

"I'm no shrink, but in my humble Yiddish opinion, you're not *quite* insane," said Zeke, who had been overwhelmed by Simon's sudden and wholly uncharacteristic barrage of words. "Now, my uncle Louie Stein was clinically insane. You are certainly a strange duck, but not a solid-gold nut case like Louie. I know that there's a horror film playing in your head in full Technicolor and in 3-D. You're not quite like my grandmother Goldie. You remind me of someone or something else that I can't seem to put my finger on."

Zeke sipped his tea thoughtfully, then began again.

"My Grandma Goldie would be sitting alone after dinner. After the plates were cleared, she would turn her chair away from the dining table and keep turning it until she was facing the wall. She would stare at that wall for hours. I knew that the projector in her brain was starting up again and the reels were spinning. I could see the lights of a horror film flickering in her eyes. She spent three years in the concentration camp at Treblinka. Funny thing was that she seemed to get a little happier with every day that passed. I could never figure that out."

"One person at a time," said Simon softly. Zeke snapped his fingers. He had just remembered something.

"I remember when I was a kid," said Zeke, who had heard what Simon said but brushed it off as just another incomprehensible sentence from a strange man. "My mother and father separated for a while, and Mom took me to live in a small flat in Brooklyn. It was on York Street, just a few blocks from Gleason's Gym down on Front Street. You know the place; it's famous, right? They've got posters of champions all over the place—Ali, Foreman, Tyson. Well, it was so famous that they wouldn't let me in.

"I had to hang out at Sal's Gym on the back side of the block from Gleason's. Sal's wasn't slick and clean and prosperous like Gleason's Gym. In fact, it was a dump. There were no champs there, only losers—sweaty, swollen, gimpy dreamers who were long past their moment . . . if they ever had one. This was where all of the has-beens hung out all day, looking for any job—you know, clean the urinals, wash the sweaty jockstraps. Sometimes there would be a dozen guys out there, shadowboxing and reminiscing about this fight or that injury or that split decision. The ring doctor there had a name for it. He called it dementia pugilistica. You remind me of those guys! I think you've got a touch of that, Simon, your own variant of dementia pugilistica. More than a touch. That's my Yiddish-Zen diagnosis."

Simon said nothing. Ezekiel Stein stared at his friend for a full minute, then shrugged his shoulders before asking: "After all of these years, you want me to find Garza's boy . . . and you want me to find the woman, too." He closed his notepad and stuck a pencil into his frizzy hair. "I assume you want me to find his whole family?" Simon did not answer.

"You need to name her, don't you—that woman who fell, her full name. That's it, isn't it? You need to name her to put an end to your own pain. But what was that one thing—that thing about catching her? You mentioned saving Julius Rosenberg a minute ago. You said that Elena and your friend Hephaestus went with you to get Ethel. Do you think you can fly, Simon? Are you saying that you want to fly like the Magus? And what was this thing about Mae West? Are you cross-dressing, too? It seems that Kevin Hughes knows something about you that none of the rest of us has even suspected."

"The skydiver who was there with Peter Keyes called her Sophia," said Simon. "His friend said that Sophia didn't even pull the ripcord. I see the field where she fell every day, Zeke, but I worked in so many vineyards that I don't know where she was geographically, and that means that I can't get to her. I can only get near her—in her proximity, and that's all. I need to know her exact longitude and latitude and the precise moment that it happened—Greenwich Mean Time. If I don't know her full name, I can't lift her." Simon's tone was approaching panic. "I can't take her away from that awful hole in the ground."

"Take her away?" asked a confused Zeke. His level of concern for the well-being of his friend was rising by the second. "Take her where? You said something about not being able to catch her—to stop her fall. Then you said 'not yet.' I'm having trouble putting all of this together conceptually. Can you give me a hand over here? What on earth does all of that mean? Who is, or was, Fulgencio?"

Still Simon said nothing. He collected the four cards from the surface of the table and put them into his briefcase. Zeke caught a momentary glimpse of the cards as they disappeared into the bag. He saw the face of the king of diamonds. Then he got a peek at something else: a metal box with several controls and some small lights on its face. He had glimpsed the object before, but only for a split second or two.

Was this the machine that Elena had seen in the garage? Had this bizarre contraption been built according to the diagrams and schematics that he'd looked at with her? Where did all of those comic books and maps fit in? The first time that Zeke had seen the machine, Simon had angrily slammed his briefcase shut. The second time, he had thrown an overcoat over the device and refused to talk about it.

"What is that thing?" asked Zeke. "Tell me about that machine."

Simon closed the lid of his briefcase and pulled his sleeves down. He put on his watch and buttoned the cuffs. When he turned back to Zeke, the investigator saw fear in his friend's eyes.

"Just find Sophia," Simon said. "Then look for Fulgencio. Find both of them. The time has come. I'll pay you for your travel and your time."

"Sophia, the second queen of heaven after Isis and before Mary," said Zeke after ten seconds of silence. "She was the eternal virgin of wisdom, the heavenly woman who fell into the material world. She is the one whom the philosophers have wooed since time began." Simon still said nothing. Zeke understood that the subject was now closed.

"Did you know, Zeke," said Simon as he put a finger to his own lips and leaned toward his perplexed friend, "that Simon Wiesenthal and his team of researchers and investigators discovered, to their supreme astonishment, that fifteen Mexican citizens were imprisoned in Auschwitz? The Nazis called it the Mexikan Camp. All of them went to the gas chamber on the same day."

"You're kidding," said Zeke, who was still not sure if his friend really needed the help of an investigator at this moment of his life. Maybe he needed a cut man at ringside or yet another army shrink, but not an investigator. "I knew there were gypsies and homosexuals and even one or two Hindus in the camps, but fifteen Mexicans? How on earth did that happen?"

"A lot of historians of the Holocaust have asked that question: How do such things happen?" said Simon in a soft whisper. "How did fifteen Mexicans find themselves in Auschwitz? How did fifteen Mexicans come to be naked and huddled together holding their breath with hundreds of other breath-holders waiting for that awful cyclonic wind—for Zyklon B canisters to pop open and spew out their gaseous cruelty? No one has ever come up with a satisfactory answer."

"When you told me about the woman in the vineyard, you said that you were beginning at the beginning, but that wasn't true, was it?" said Zeke in a cautious, controlled tone. He had never dared to ask his friend a question about his childhood and family. "In all the years that I've known you, I have never heard you mention your family, your parents and your siblings."

"Don't ever ask me about them!" seethed Simon in a menacing voice. Then he fell silent. His body seemed to be paralyzed. He began humming his familiar tune, but at a level that anyone within ten feet could hear. Zeke instantly recognized the melody as an old Irish song, but he couldn't remember its name or its lyrics. After a full minute of Simon's deathlike immobility, Zeke put his hand on his friend's neck and asked: "Who was more alone than fifteen Mexican breath-holders in Auschwitz?"

After another minute, he asked the question again.

"Who was more alone than fifteen Mexicans in Auschwitz in 1944?" Zeke was trying to calm his friend while simultaneously attempting to imagine the improbable—the impossible route from some small towns in Oaxaca and Michoacán to a small town in Poland where in four short years men had almost out-slaughtered all of the Holy Crusades. They had surely surpassed the crass, smug cruelty of the Holy Inquisition and even preempted their own god himself by designing and building, in their own time and on their own world, a working replica of hell.

9

PEN STATE

"Good evening, San Quentin Prison! This is your smiling host Simon Magus Vegas, graciously welcoming you to this evening's feature presentation on fabulous radio station PNFY. Ain't it great to be from California? This is the state with more penitentiaries than any other state in the country—and they're still building them! You guys out there are the new cash crop of Califas. Forget about lettuce, cauliflower, and marijuana. In the Golden State, guys like you are a commodity like pork bellies and coal. People with big money are betting that vacuous, vacant lives like yours will continue to result in acts of mindless cruelty and fits of self-destruction through the next ten fiscal quarters and far beyond. If and when you guys leave this glorious institution, you will be able to brag that you went to Pen State.

"This is radio station PNFY, and before I tell you again why this station is Probably Not For You, I'm going to read some letters that were sent to me in response to my first show. Here's a letter from Larry over in Badger Block. He says, 'Dear Mr. Magus: You can't insult us like that! Keep it up and you'll find yourself getting plasma and oxygen in the back of an ambulance. Mr. Magus, you are an asshole.' That's all he has to say. I must say he has a nice vocabulary. Well, let's do a little checking on the computer. Bingo! There's only one Larry in Badger. Now let's scroll down and see what he was convicted of.

"Oh, my, Larry—we're doing a double life sentence, aren't we? What an insider like you would call a 'bowlegged kickstand.' You've parked your bike for good. I'll bet you tell the guys in your bay that you're a bank robber—one of those dashing, romantic Machine Gun Kelly, Baby Face Nelson kind of guys. You probably tell them that you were a real Robin Hood of the urban forest. With charges like yours, what other option do you have? Well . . . would you like me to tell everybody in this radio audience what you're really in here for? I'll bet you wouldn't, and—don't worry, Larry, I won't let your little secret out.

"But I'm just amazed at your hubris. (Thirty dollars on the books of the first person to send in a definition of hubris!) I'm astounded that someone with your record thinks that I'm the asshole! Well, Larry, keep running out to your mailbox, because radio station PNFY is sending you—now hold on to your seat"—Simon turned on the reverb and cranked the volume all the way to the right—"a gift certificate good for one full-body immersion in a fifty-gallon drum of Preparation H. Take my advice, Larry. Don't shrink from this unique, once-in-a-lifetime—or should I say once-in-two-lifetimes?—opportunity.

"Felipe Castillo over in D Block sent in an answer to the question 'Who is Plato?' His answer is lifted straight from the *Oxford Classical Dictionary*, but the prison librarian was beside herself with excitement when she told me that it's the first time that book has been opened in twelve years. The woman almost fell over when she saw Felipe pulling the dusty volume down from the stacks. Congratulations, Señor Castillo, Warden Harris will be putting twenty-five dollars on your books tonight. Angelo Butler sent in a very cogent definition for 'golem.' Congratulations to you, Angelo. Warden Harris is going to put the same amount on your books."

At that instant Warden Harris sauntered into the radio booth. Simon nodded at his friend, then pulled out a copy of Ry Cooder's *Chicken Skin Music* and slid it into the player.

"Well, what do you know?" he said into the microphone. "Our

beloved warden has just come into the booth. Well, my dear brothers, this could be the end for yours truly and my ill-considered foray into radio broadcasting. I've got an ugly feeling that Victor Harris is going to axe this station. So . . . for all of you vatos out there, here is some music featuring Ry Cooder and Flaco Jiménez. We'll start with 'The Bourgeois Blues,' written by Huddie Ledbetter, also known as Leadbelly. If you don't know who Leadbelly is, it's no wonder you're in state prison."

He started the music, then turned toward his friend.

"Well?" said Simon cautiously.

"Well, you've only cost me fifty-five bucks so far. Now I guess I've got to look in the budget for money to pay for a vat of hemorrhoid cream. To be honest, I didn't think this show of yours would cost me a dime. I didn't think anyone was going to listen to you after that first program. I gotta tell you, that thing with the prairie dogs was beautiful. My wife says I could use some of that vasopressin myself. There's a buzz out on the yard, Simon. The staff is telling me there's definitely a buzz out there. Some of them hate your guts—big surprise, eh? Some of these guys hate Winnie the Pooh. They spend their nights plotting how to murder him and sodomize Tigger."

The warden reached into his pocket and pulled out a cigarette. It was one of those cheap generic brands. His wife, Liz, had won a round.

"Most of the mainliners aren't sure what to make of you, and one or two dozen of them even admit to liking you a little bit. At least that's what they say when their friends aren't around. I'll tell you this: they're all listening. I'm on your side, Simon. You know that. But the rest of the board isn't quite so sure. They believe that an unstimulated prisoner is an unaggressive prisoner. You know, we had to stop using saltpeter years ago. All the committee wants is peace in the yard, Simon—no riots, no lawsuits, no complaints to the courts. We're going to discuss it at our meeting this evening."

He glanced at his watch. "Actually, the meeting is in about ten minutes. We didn't quite have a quorum at five-thirty. I'd better get going. We'll see . . . we'll see," he mumbled as he walked out of the room and into the hallway. When he was out of sight, he shook his head dejectedly as he lit his cigarette. The decision had already been made. The vote would be little more than a formality.

Simon turned back to the microphone and interrupted the music after the second song. His voice was measured, almost solemn.

"Well, my golem, it looks like this truly is my last broadcast. It's too bad, because I was really looking forward to that white supremacist show that I promised to do. This also means that I have to get going on tonight's show. This evening I'm going to tell you about the death of Jesse Washington. You've seen those pictures of him, I'm sure of it. Every one of us has glanced at the sepia-toned photographs of that lynching. You've seen them, but you probably turned your eyes away or dismissed the pictures as remnants of a bygone era. Here, with a little help from Margie, the warden's personal assistant, are some photographs of the lynching of Jesse Washington in Waco, Texas, in 1916."

The televisions in each of the cell blocks blinked on. Three black-and-white photographs were displayed on their large screens.

"I came across them years ago in a used bookstore in Berkeley. I found them while turning the pages of a book—*Under Milk Wood*, I believe. The photos fell out onto the floor. I had seen them before but had never studied them closely. The warden was kind enough to let me show them to you. If you've never seen them before, it's no wonder you're in state prison. As you can see, in the first photo of the triptych the young man is still alive. Can you see his eyes? He doesn't have long."

Simon waited while the hand-held camera moved in closer to the first photo.

"His black body is shining and radiantly serpentine at the base of a tree. His skin is glistening, and his musculature is as chiseled and as defined as an athlete's. People who knew him said that he was a slow-witted and gentle young man. He is surrounded by hundreds of white men in white suits and white hats, but he is all alone in the universe. There is nowhere for him to go, no one who can help him. Who could be more alone than Jesse Washington? Someone who was standing near the tree wrote later in a letter that Jesse was praying as he lay there, but to which god? What good would prayer do when there were ten or eleven ministers in the audience along with dozens of their parishioners?

"If you look closely into the faces in the crowd, you can see smiles and you can almost hear the laughter. You can see hugs and back slaps—handshakes, brisk tips of the hat, and friends greeting friends. You see men fresh from the perfumed talc and lively jabber and banter of the barbershop. You see men who are tired and sweaty after hours of walking in the furrows behind two gray mules. At the top of the photo, you can just make out some men who are giggling and tipsy from a couple of beers at the local saloon.

"Look in the lower left corner. Right there! You will see a young red-haired Irish boy in a linen cap. He is lighting a cigarette. You can't see it in his freckled face or his white skin, but he is half Mexican, and he is about to do something awful. Look around in the picture. You see men who have just hugged their haggard wives and mussed their children's hair. In the second picture you see Jesse dangling above their heads like a bag of clay. In a circle around his black feet, some freckle-faced children are leering and laughing.

"In the third photo . . . Margie!" shouted Simon. The warden's personal secretary shouted back from the next room, then hastily moved the camera toward the third photograph.

"In the third photo, Jesse Washington's arms are now only stumps, and his legs are stubs of charcoal above the knees. Someone has poured kerosene on his body. Someone else has tossed a flaring matchstick. By most accounts he was alive when the flames began to enrage all of his nerve endings. A fourth photo—not part of the triptych—is found on a picture postcard. As you can see, someone has written the words 'This is the barbeque we had last night.' To the right of the handwriting is a square containing the words 'Place stamp here.'"

"How does this happen?" asked Simon in a quiet, measured voice. "How does something like this happen? How can loving parents let their kids push and shove to be in the picture with the charred, smoking body of a man who was alive not ten minutes ago? The town of Waco turned it into a holiday. How could Roman families prepare picnic lunches and bring blankets to spread on the ground so they could watch in comfort as Spartacus and his fellow slaves were crucified by the hundreds?

"I, Simon Magus Vegas, on this, his second and final show that is Probably Not For You, will tell you how these things happen." He poured himself a cup of coffee from a thermos, then inhaled deeply before beginning to speak his next sentence.

"You've all seen paintings by the impressionists, by the post-impressionists and expressionists. I know you have . . . even you here in state prison have seen the paintings of Van Gogh, Edouard Manet, and Paul Gauguin. Everyone loves their work today, but in their own time no one loved them—and I mean no one. There was a special venue for many of these artists. It was called the Salon des Refusés—the salon of the rejects. Vincent Van Gogh never sold a painting while he lived. Only one or two people out of the millions living in Paris could see the beauty and power of their work.

"Those one or two Parisians were derided as absurd, ridiculous—they were branded as tasteless radicals. In fact, they were the lucky ones. History shows that they were right. What were those other millions of Parisians thinking and doing at that time?

Nothing unusual. They were doing what everybody everywhere does—even today. They were marinating in the culture of their day, happily mouthing the clichés and the jargon of their time and place, thinking the current thoughts, following the current fads, and eating and drinking the current foods of their time and place. Like you, they selected their music from the few choices that were placed in front of them.

"Black prisoners play black music out in the yard, brown inmates play brown music, twelve-year-old girls all love the same little boy bands—it's so stultifying, so damned predictable. When you've been simmering in your own cultural broth all of your life, your flesh and your soul soon begin to take on the common color and flavor. In time you lose the power to taste your own individual life on its own separate terms.

"Nowadays everybody loves Van Gogh. People line up at exhibitions of his art and pay millions for his paintings. But it's a cheap love. Vincent climbed all the way out of the mundane and painted what he saw through his own wild bipolar mind. He had to escape the tepid broth, and he paid everything he owned to attain his unique vantage point—for his art. We pay nothing for it.

"If you'd lived in Paris during Van Gogh's life, would you have stepped forward to champion his work? You can only answer 'yes' if in your present life you have stepped forward to defend someone or something against the opinions of everyone around you—against your entire era and against your whole culture. If you were that kind of courageous visionary, you wouldn't be in here counting the days until your next parole hearing.

"The ones who loved Vincent when no one else did were his true lovers. They were the geniuses—like those few lonely people who picket outside the walls of this prison in the cold hours before every execution. Do you want to know if you're one of those people who came into Waco by train to see the spectacle of Jesse's death? Do you want to know if your love is cheap? The question you have to ask yourself is this: What is it that I believe that no one else does? What cause do I espouse that is hopeless—radical? What salon of rejected artists or thinkers have I stepped into lately?

"I hear a telling silence out there in my radio audience. Do you know what that means? It means that you and I were in that crowd when Jesse Washington's neck snapped. You and I were there hooting and hollering when someone tossed kerosene on his still-twitching body. It was us. We were fastidiously unfolding and spreading out our picnic blankets alongside the Appian Way. It was you and I who debated endlessly whether women had the mental power to vote. It was you and I who devoutly believed that Negroes and Apaches were a lowly form of life that no god could love. You and I made ready to move into that Cherokee home the minute the cavalry was done with its former occupants.

"What would your life be like if you could fly out of your time and place, go into the future, and look back at your own era? You would see how tragic and laughable the beliefs that separate us from one another have been and continue to be. The people who wanted to slaughter the Cathars in southern France were the same ones who believed that the earth was flat and went on to believe that gays should not be allowed to marry.

"Well . . . Simon Magus Vegas has had it. I'm trying as hard as I can to fly out of this smelly broth that we're all drowning in. The effort has driven me into madness. I want all of you to lie in your beds tonight when everything is quiet. I want you to use your imaginations to melt away your tattoos—let all of that murky ink dribble down your fingertips and drip onto the floor. Use what's left of your imaginations to tear away your gang language—all two hundred dull, insipid words of it. Pull all of those tired clichés out of your mouth and spit them onto the linoleum tiles. Rip away every facile obscenity. Then peel all of that deadening television culture away from your gray matter.

"After you do all that, ask yourself: What's left? Where am I? Who am I? It might seem like there's nothing left of you inside that body. You all look like prison and smell like the street. But take my word for it, there is something there. Each of you possesses things that you've never seen, never even sensed. You have the power to fly away from this awful place."

Simon pushed the button on the player and selected another piece of music. He leaned back in his chair and closed his eyes. When the final note of the recording sounded, he turned his microphone back on and leaned toward the perforated metal of the windscreen.

"That was 'Goodnight, Irene,' also written by Leadbelly. You should know that he was a prisoner when he wrote this song. He was locked up, just like you, but in a prison far worse than this one."

In her house in the Oakland hills, Elena moved to the side of the bed. She dropped the freshly laundered maternity dresses and underwear that she had been putting away and sat down on the bed. She turned to her left and adjusted the dial on her ancient Remler radio. She loved its beautiful Bakelite body and the Scotty dog above the dial. It had belonged to her father and had been falling apart until her husband decided to restore it.

The mother that Elena had never known had used it in her dorm room at college. She had been an exchange student from Spain, and she had abandoned the little radio three days after the birth of her daughter. Elena's father never knew where she had gone—probably back to Spain. There had been a casual reference by her to a home in the Azores, but nothing more. She was somewhere on one of his maps, but he had never looked for her. Elena knew her name: Margarita Oropeza. She had never looked for her, and she had seldom thought about her. Elena's father had filled every gap.

Now the radio had a new transformer and all new capacitors in the power supply and the signal path. All of the old tubes—whatever those were—had been replaced by new ones from Russia. Elena had no idea what any of that meant. She only knew that her father's radio was alive again and that the voice of her husband was coming out of its small speaker. Somehow she knew that he was speaking directly to her. Then she shrieked; she jumped up and raised her blouse just in time to see a small mound on her belly slowly receding and regaining its color. This time the baby girl inside of her had used her foot.

"He's going to Waco tonight!" Elena explained to her unborn baby. "I found the map on his workbench, and I knew what he was going to do—but I didn't imagine that he would do it on his radio show!" She rubbed her belly and whispered, "After you're born, I'll put together some matching flight suits, a big one for me and a tiny one for you. I'll get out my grandmother's old sewing machine. We'll have to go shopping and pick out the perfect fabrics. It'll be so much fun. We'll need warm, windproof flight pajamas and a strong carrier. Best of all, my airline will serve hot food. No peanuts! You can breastfeed in midair."

A single hand appeared on her belly . . . and then another.

10

GOD OF A SMALL HOTEL

Warden Harris twisted and shifted uncomfortably in his coal-black Brooks Brothers suit as he minced and moped his way down the hall. He stopped dead in his tracks when something dawned on him. What he was feeling at that very moment was something that he had not felt in fifty years. He felt diminished. He felt precisely the way he had as a boy whenever he bought candy with money that he had stolen from his hardworking mother's unguarded purse. Chocolates and peppermints that should have tasted heavenly to a ten-year-old had somehow been transmuted into flavorless chunks of lead and solder.

Tonight he felt like an impostor, like a traitor. He shuffled his Italian loafers down the long hallway, unconsciously aiming his downcast eyes and dejected face in the general direction of the main office, where his loyal staff of workers were busy cleaning their desks after a long day. Several hours of overtime had been necessitated by this unscheduled meeting of the full board. As he walked, he could hear Simon's voice issuing from every corner of the prison and the administration building. He smiled to himself. The prisoners were listening despite themselves.

Then he remembered why he felt like a traitor. A radio had been brought into the conference room, and Simon's voice could be heard by everyone during the meeting. Dr. Silver had insisted on it. In the end the warden had given in—he had capitulated. He had been a coward and cast his vote against his close friend Simon. He had voted against what he thought were his own beliefs. He had sided with Eric Safire and Marvin Rous and the rest of the bean counters on the board.

Worst of all, he had aligned himself with Dr. Silver. The resolution to end Simon's show had been the last item on the agenda, and it had carried unanimously. He grimaced and ran his tongue over his teeth. His mouth tasted like tin. As he walked through the doorway of the main office, he saw four female faces in the room—two black and two white. Each of the women turned to look up at him. As soon as he shut the door behind him, he felt his posture, his entire demeanor, being prodded and probed by their anxious, questioning stares. The warden had always been a fastidious and dapper man, but at this moment his expensive clothing was hanging on his frame like a canvas tarpaulin.

In the distance, the voice of Simon Magus Vegas could be heard coming from somewhere on Margie's desk. She loved Probably Not For You. She had recorded all three hours of the first show and played it every day during her lunch hour. Now she was recording the second show—the last one. When her boss went out and closed the door behind him, she quickly grabbed her handbag and reached inside to turn the radio off and hide a tiny recorder. It was against office rules to play music or listen to any broadcast show during work hours.

"No, that's fine. You can leave the volume up, Margie," squeaked the warden. His voice, uncharacteristically timid, was barely audible. He reached into his coat pocket for a cigarette, then lit it on his way across the room to the nearby door of his own small office. For the first time in years, none of the ladies said a word about the miniature roiling hell of nicotine and sulfur fumes that was spewing from his mouth. Now they knew for certain that the rumors that had been swirling through the hallways of the administration building were true. They were listening to the last broadcast on radio station Probably Not For You.

"The board is a bunch of cowards," said Margie angrily. She didn't see the warden wince. "I wouldn't give you a nickel for none of them, but Safire and Rous used to be good guys. And what in heaven's name is wrong with that man Dr. Silver?"

"My son is doing time in here," whispered one of the other women, but only to herself. Then she said it again for her coworkers to hear. "My son is in here. You all know that. So is his good-for-nothin' father. They need to hear stuff like this. Somebody needs to get in their faces. Somebody needs to pay attention. Now my littlest boy at home is dressin' like a prisoner. He's swimmin' in them pants and snarlin' at everything. He walks around the house gruntin' like an ape.

"All the kids are doin' it. I don't understand half of what that man Simon Magus Vegas is saying, but he cares about these men, and I want my men to hear it. Hell, nothing else has worked. How long am I gonna have to wait to have my family back together?" She broke into sobs that twisted and deformed her pretty face. The other three rose from their chairs to console her.

"Almost everybody who gets released this month will be back again inside of three years—six out of ten of them can't stay away. Somebody's got to break the awful spell that's been cast on our children and on this place," said a second woman. "Somebody's got to do it," said a third voice. It was Margie.

"Sometimes I just hate this country," Margie said as she dabbed at her friend's teary eyes with a hanky. "In this country, if you've got a car you've got a life. The car makers, the banks, and the gas stations dangled that bait in front of us seventy-five years ago, and we still got that hook stuck in our mouths."

She walked to the water cooler and filled a glass. "I saw this nature show on television a few weeks ago," she said to the warden as she handed the water to her coworker and friend. "And now I can't get it out of my mind. I know this sounds crazy, but the show was all about hermit crabs. They are these ugly, drab little creatures. They are naked, helpless little bottom feeders that crawl around in the muck and murky salt water looking for a special kind of seashell that has been abandoned by an animal that has grown out of it and moved on—probably gone off to college. When they find one, they climb into these shiny shells—these Cadillac and Mercedes-Benz shells—and drive around the ocean bottom pretending that the big, pretty casing and the little worm hiding inside it are the same thing."

Warden Harris took off his jacket and tie and slumped heavily into his leather chair. Twenty years ago, his personal secretary's only child and a high school buddy had jumped into the car of their dreams as it was parking in a lot at the El Cerrito Mall. They had forced the driver from the car at knifepoint, then pointed their prize toward San Lorenzo and a triumphal tour of their old high school in their shiny new Mercedes seashell. They couldn't have known that the owner of the car was an off-duty police officer. It hadn't occurred to them to disguise themselves or change the license plates on the car.

They were still in the parking lot when they heard the first sirens, but the two boys never considered pulling over. After all, no hero in any movie quietly pulls over when the pursuing cops appear in his rearview mirror. So they led the police on a high-speed chase across Oakland and into San Leandro. The exhilarating pursuit seemed like a scene straight out of an adventure film, and the two boys imagined themselves to be the handsome, invulnerable stars of the show. Somewhere out there, an imaginary audience was sitting on the edge of their seats—watching the boys' every move. The two began singing at the tops of their lungs, providing their own sound effects and a rousing musical soundtrack.

The chase scene came to a sudden and dreadful end when Margie's boy and the precious car ran three stoplights, then plowed into a family from Laos who were crossing Estudillo Avenue. But no cameras had been rolling. No director had yelled "cut!" into the small end of a megaphone. The three Laotian actors never got up when the scene was over. They never brushed themselves off and got ready for another take. Two days before his nineteenth birthday, Margie's son and the other boy each entered a plea of guilty to one count of felony murder and received a sentence of twenty-five years to life. As part of the plea bargain, two counts of murder were dismissed.

The warden leaned back in his chair and reconsidered tonight's meeting. The entire board had listened to excerpts of Simon's first show and to the second show as it aired. They had concluded that Simon might be clinically unstable, perhaps even deranged. In-house counsel had written a lengthy memo predicting that his "disrespectful" language and excessive harassment of the inmates would inevitably subject this institution to a lawsuit. Dr. Silver, the prison psychiatrist, openly questioned Simon's competence to teach anyone, much less highly dangerous inmates.

"Listen to him!" said Dr. Silver as he pointed toward the radio. "He's having a manic episode right now! He could start a riot. House counsel is right about Vegas. We need to cut him off as soon as possible. I assume he'll sue us, but he doesn't have a leg to stand on, not one leg to stand on! He seems to be functioning satisfactorily as a teacher, but he's no psychiatrist and shouldn't try to be one. I spoke with him at length one day, just after his poetry class. He said the strangest things, and he looked at me as though I was some sort of sideshow freak. He just kept staring at me in the oddest way.

"So I did a little investigation. I pulled out his original application to work here. It contains the psychological evaluation that I did on him six months ago, and it also contains several evaluations done by the U.S. Army. How on earth did he ever get hired? He has the classic symptoms of mania: pressured speech, flurries and flights of ideas, and highly florid delusions. He seems to have developed some kind of highly complex and fanciful compensation mechanisms—really strange ideations that allow him to live with some remote pain that may or may not even exist. I say he's too unstable and aggressive, and he has some abnormal ideations about flying that just might give rise to a rash of escape attempts. I vote to truncate this problem here and now. I say we cut our losses and chop this fellow off at the knees."

The warden snorted his disgust while exhaling a cloud of purple and gray smoke. Dr. Silver was a real piece of work in his own right. How on earth had someone like him managed to pass the battery of tests and the psychological screening that were required for a job with the California Department of Corrections? Whatever happened to background checks? Dr. John Silver wasn't even the man's real name, and everyone on the prison board knew it. He had worked in several German and Austrian prisons using the name Christopher Frederick Gauger.

Five years ago, the warden had ordered a secret independent investigation into the professional qualifications of the doctor. It seemed that the man had also worked in prisons in several countries in Latin America, but under a different pseudonym. While working at an infamous Peruvian prison, he had changed his name to Juan Largo Argento, Spanish for Long John Silver—the same name he had used at a prison in Brasilia and another in Lima.

But Dr. Silver's expensive suits covered something even more sinister than a long list of aliases. The doctor had suffered for years with a condition that had come to be called "body integrity identity disorder. "Another psychiatrist who reviewed the results of the warden's investigation concluded that Dr. Silver had somehow been stricken at an early age with apotemnophilia, an erotic desire to have a limb amputated. But those who had shared more than a few drinks at an office party with a talkative and tipsy Dr. Silver soon came to realize that it was not a genuine desire to lose a limb, but only a pseudo-desire—a demi-desire. There is no Latin phrase to describe someone who only wishes that he truly wanted to have his leg lopped off, so the second psychiatrist coined the now fashionable term *Apotemnophilia dilettantis silverus* after interviewing the bizarre man at length.

The warden quietly unlocked and then pulled open the bottom drawer on the right side of his desk: the secret drawer that everyone in the building joked about behind his back. He pulled out a water glass and a large blue bottle of genuine absinthe. He had purchased a case of the illegal liqueur in Paris over twenty years ago. This was his last bottle.

For a moment the warden considered sharing a drink with his bizarre next-door neighbor. He knew that at this very same moment, Dr. Silver was in his own office reaching into his own bottom right drawer. But there was no alcoholic beverage there. His secret compartment contained a much more exotic—more *outré*— form of diversion.

He laughed to himself as he recalled the late evening last summer when the janitor had rushed into his office screaming that she had stumbled across some sort of torture device while cleaning Dr. Silver's office. The warden had summoned an armed guard, and the three of them had crept stealthily into the office to investigate the situation. That was when he had discovered the object of Dr. Silver's adoration. Hanging from a rack in the doctor's private shower was a prosthetic limb that had been lovingly washed, rinsed, and left to air-dry. It was no modern flesh-colored device made of titanium and plastic that the trio found, but one that was over a century old, hewn from whale bone and then meticulously hand-carved by a master scrimshander from New Bedford.

On every square inch of the prosthetic leg were scenes from *Typee* and *Moby-Dick*. What began as a ten-inch stub cup culminated in a tip no wider than a gold doubloon. There was a nest of leather straps with brass buckles screwed into the top of the stub cup. A leg like this one was precisely what the terrified men of the *Pequod* heard every night thumping ominously across the deck boards just over their heads.

The warden lit another cigarette and blew a perfect smoke ring across the room. Two more followed the first one. The administrative board had been immovable. The original vote had been six to one against Simon's radio show. The minutes would reflect that the six board members had recorded seven "ayes" because the clerk had erroneously recorded Dr. Silver-Argento's vehement "aye-aye" as two votes. Although his vote didn't count, Dr. Therage, the visiting expert on the chemical termination of life, had voted "aye" from his car phone. He had gotten stuck in traffic on his way up from San Francisco and had missed the meeting.

Warden Harris wondered why he had felt compelled to change his vote and make the final tally unanimous. His vote hadn't been necessary for passage. He could have voted against the motion and told Simon that he had been outvoted. Had he been worried about his résumé? Did he secretly, subconsciously agree with his colleagues? He shrugged. Now he knew for sure that the sixties were dead.

He reached for his transparent radio and turned it on. He turned out the only lamp in the room, then grinned into the darkness as a familiar thump-thumping sound from Dr. Silver's office penetrated the thin wall between their workspaces. He turned up the volume on the radio and smiled as the notes of one of his favorite tunes reached his ears. He poured himself a drink before leaning back in the chair. He sighed aloud: the fermented, distilled eau de wormwood that should have burned his throat so sweetly tasted inert and disappointing—like base metal. He turned the volume up again. He loved this music.

"Of course, none of you androids, incubi, and automatons out there recognized that tune or the transcendent quartet playing it. Do you know how I know this? Because no one who ever listened to this music and loved this quartet ever woke up to find himself in this place. None of you knows this, but one of the ironclad requirements of high art is virtuosity—something you just don't find in the testosterone-drenched dreck that you guys flush into your ears every day. What does that big word mean? Virtuosity means learned or skilled, from the Latin *virtuosus*. It means hard work and supreme dedication. It means discipline. Of course, that was the Thelonious Monk Quartet. I played the other side of the record for you on my first show.

"Once again, this is radio station Probably Not For You, coming to you from the most beautiful piece of real estate in Marin County. You guys out there don't know how good you've got it. On the outside of these walls, only the richest gringos can afford to live in a gated community like yours. And at no extra cost to you, there is full-time assisted living and twenty-four-hour security! This next and final tune that I will play tonight is called 'Sweet and Lovely.' It is nine minutes and thirty-four seconds in duration. I chose to finish with the longest tune of the concert because that will give me just enough time to take care of some business that simply can't wait any longer.

"Ordinarily I would never tell anyone what I'm about to tell you, but this is my last show, and I can't keep hiding my secret any longer. In those nine minutes I'm going to Waco, Texas, to get someone who was more alone than anyone on earth. Earlier this evening I filled you in a little about the lynching of Jesse Washington. I wanted all of you to see something of who we really are. In the next five hundred and seventy seconds, I'm going to travel back to 1916 and carry him away from all of that cruelty. If Elena is listening, she can come with me—if she feels up to it."

Warden Harris groaned and poured another drink. There it was, the last nail in the coffin. He had always known that Simon Vegas was a strange man, an eccentric, but what he was saying into the microphone now was completely delusional and profoundly disturbing. The board was probably right. He heard Dr. Silver next door whooping a string of nautical terms with extreme delight. "Avast! Belay! We cut the scoundrel off at the knees!" He was listening, too.

"While I'm gone, please close your eyes and listen by yourself to what these four men have to say to you. The men that you're hearing tonight formed a quartet, but first each one had to be a free agent, a soloist in his own right. Coltrane was in danger of being a journeyman horn player until the day he met Monk. He was verging on being a lifelong sideman, always playing someone else's music and sitting in with someone else's band. He was invited to go to Monk's small apartment in Harlem, and when he got there in the early morning—in the crepuscule—he found Thelonious in his underwear, already working at the piano.

"On the piano bench at the great man's side was a quart of vanilla ice cream that his wife, Nellie, had packed into his favorite bowl. Stuck in the middle of that mound of ice cream was the pianist's favorite spoon. That meeting lit a spark in John Coltrane that sent the man on a journey straight up into the stratosphere. In this great recording you can hear him almost fully fledged and ready to go soaring on his own.

"All of you probably know who Lenny Hudson is. He's housed in the Adjustment Center on Condemned Row. He's been called a monster—the worst of the worst. You also know that he's probably first or second in line to be executed. Not long ago Lenny told me something. He said it was obvious to him that I was a murderer, too. 'It takes one to know one,' he said. He told me that he could see it written all over my face. He told me that I'm a killer just like he is. Well, Lenny Hudson is right: I am a killer. I'm a monster. I've lived with it a long time. It's time to come clean."

The cigarette leapt from the warden's gaping mouth and found its way into a crease between his expensive pinstriped pants and his even more expensive reclining chair. A shaken Victor Harris instinctively tossed his glass full of absinthe at the base of the smoke rising from the hand-stitched leather seat, and the resulting green and orange seat cushion flambé brought Margie sprinting into the room with a fire extinguisher under her right arm. Right on her heels was Dr. Silver, who was covering his mouth with a handkerchief and waving the fumes away from his eyes with his other hand.

"He's a killer! Did you hear what he said? It came from his own guilty lips! He should be locked up with the rest of them!" shouted Dr. Silver excitedly from the smoke-filled doorway. "I knew there was something very wrong with that man!"

The agitated doctor froze in place when he noticed that Margie and the warden were staring down at his knees. In all the commotion, he had forgotten to remove his prosthetic limb. The right pant leg of his suit had been rolled up to his crotch, and the ivory stub had been lashed to his hairy thigh with a pair of heavy red straps. His naked right foot was pulled up behind his right leg and lashed to it with slashes of duct tape. The blood instantly drained from his face. He smiled sheepishly and began hobbling backward until he disappeared into his own office and quickly slammed the door behind him.

Simon switched on the music, then, far under his breath, began murmuring and mumbling a string of odd, mystical words. His voice grew louder and louder as he moved his misshapen right hand back and forth, gesturing hypnotically in front of the microphone. His eyelids began to vibrate, and his lips buzzed with the vowels of a thousand comic book obscurities all shrouded by an Irish tune. But in his haste to fly away, he had forgotten to switch off the desk microphone.

"*Zauberspruch—simsalabim. In vovo legem magicarium y Collegium Magikos.* I first set my eyes on sweet Molly Malone," he chanted as he opened his briefcase, reached inside, and removed his machine. The entire prison and parts of three counties heard the opening notes of "Sweet and Lovely," with Simon's eerie flow of words superimposed right over the music. When she heard the stream of incantations, an astonished Elena in her bedroom across the bay rushed to turn the volume up even higher. She had heard these sounds from her husband's lips so many times before, but never so clearly.

"*Brimborium. Brimborium. Through the eye of Agamotto as written in the Book of Vishanti. Tontus Talantus and Muchos Milagros.* In Dublin's fair city where the girls are so pretty." The entire prison population then heard the sound of a hurricane.

In a flash, Elena knew exactly where those words had come from. Now she fully understood that they were feverish boyhood words from his dark, distant youth—incantations voraciously sucked from a tattered satchel that was filled with magicians—and, more importantly, filled with longings and dreams, enough of them to fight off Simon's demons of the air, or whatever his demons were.

An instant later, Simon was rising from his chair and hovering as silently as an albatross just below the overhead lights. He made some last-minute adjustments to the machine that he had strapped across his chest. Then he passed like a smoky wraith through the bars, ceiling tiles, stone walls, and concertina wire and shot past the eastern guard towers of the prison. He tussled with a weak offshore breeze, then gained speed over the Ferry Landing, banked twice around the north tower of the Golden Gate Bridge, and within a split second was flaring like a blazing meteor through a bank of clouds over Santa Fe and preparing to begin his descent while cruising above Sterling City, Texas.

Using the sensitive dials at his fingertips, he checked the power supply and calibrated his direction finder, pressing a button that could add or remove tiny lodestone particles that adhered to a minuscule metal grid at the heart of the machine. Archimedes himself had painstakingly removed these microscopic iron grains from the brains of homing pigeons. Simon turned the clock back almost a century, then cut his airspeed in half over Brownwood. He bumped and shook downward through dozens of scalding thermals.

As he slowed, he watched as one by one, power lines disappeared from the countryside, the wooden poles and long wires simply flashing out of existence. He saw strips of asphalt retreating into the distance and buildings and houses stripping themselves of their clapboards, their skeletons dismantled in seconds flat, and their naked foundations vanishing to reveal miles of lush, virginal forest.

When he finally arrived on the outskirts of Waco, there was no one in sight. He followed a narrow dirt and gravel street until he saw them all, a large, animated crowd of people jammed into the town center. He sighed mournfully when he saw a bright flash of light in the distance followed by rolling, boiling puffs of black smoke that were piling upward—one towering billow climbing on top of the next. Then Elena, Simon, and a thousand prisoners heard a clap of thunder, which lagged far behind the stabbing instant of white light. Simon's heart sank when he realized that it was not thunder at all, but a spontaneous round of appreciative applause from the crowd. He knew immediately that he had miscalculated yet again and arrived ten minutes too late.

He flew in a large circle above the town while readjusting the device. Unlike most lynchings, this one had been photographed from beginning to end, but no one had bothered to record the exact time. By studying the photographs and the few historical documents that were available, he had determined that the hanging of Jesse Washington took place at two o'clock in the afternoon. Now he knew that one-fifty was the correct time. He carefully began turning the adjustment knobs on the face of Archimedes's machine.

The Antikythera device, modified and sporting the newest batteries that Hephaestus could create, was now a bit larger than a two-slice toaster. There were four tabs, one on each corner of the mechanism. Each tab featured a slot, suggesting that the device had once been attached to a much larger machine with four bolts. Without touching the brass knobs that controlled the year, the day, and the hour, he turned the minute controller until he saw the cloud of black smoke shrinking backward and folding inward on itself, leaving the sky above a clear, crystalline blue. Simon flew to a point just above the hanging pole. He shuddered at what he saw, but forced himself to concentrate on the task at hand.

When a small amber bulb lit up on the face of the instrument, he teased the minute dial counterclockwise until he saw Jesse's charred, smoking arms rise up from the ground like two black fish breaching water, then leap straight up from flaming waves of heat to simultaneously reattach themselves to his jagged, smoldering shoulders. He moved to the dial that was in command of seconds and half-seconds and watched as purple fluids flowed back into Jesse's pores and a body of cracked, desiccated rubble reassembled, swelled with fluids, and smoothed over until the shiny salamander skin in the first grainy photograph was visible once again.

The stretched skin, the ripped, disjointed jaw and charred teeth of the death mask were gone. Simon watched as horse-drawn carriages moved in reverse. He saw dogs swallowing their barks, horses bending down to fill a water trough with the contents of their bellies. He saw smug puffs of white smoke returning to the tips of self-satisfied cigars.

The Mexican Flyboy surveyed the scene from a hundred feet above the mob as four men in white suit pants, vests, and skimmers walked backward, converged on Jesse, then turned around to face him. A boy ran up and put back a bar stool that tipped upward and lifted Jesse's feet. The four men hefted Jesse upward until the rope went slack. They pulled the noose from his neck, then laid him down roughly by the side of the tree as the white stool disappeared into the crowd. Then they used his ankles to push him away from the base of the trunk. Simon searched through every corner of the crowd until he spotted the tripod and field camera and the photographer bending down behind them. The man was smiling. His eyes and skin were glowing with excitement as he waited to consecrate the event.

Simon looked to his left and watched a stream of kerosene as it leapt upward from the spout of a gallon tin and back into the spigot of a fifty-gallon drum—a chaos of spillage and randomly flung drops from the original pour were coalescing into a tight stream, then returning to the quiescent darkness of the large container. He saw the earnest faces of the two people who would soon toss the liquid. They were the same face—father and son joined together in a hallowed, blessed endeavor. He carefully studied the red hair and the conflicted face of the young man who would soon strike a match and start the conflagration.

(*A hundred years into the future, every convict in San Quentin Prison listened to John Coltrane's sweet solo and simultaneously heard Simon's voice and the noise of the excited crowd. Warden Harris desperately tried to fine-tune his prison radio in order to get rid of some maddening interference: the sound of barking dogs and whinnying horses.*)

When the Flyboy settled at an altitude of just one foot off the ground, a man on his right dropped his mug of beer and pointed excitedly at him. In an instant the entire throng fell eerily silent. Everyone turned to look at Simon Magus Vegas as he glided toward the base of the hanging pole in the town center and knelt down beside Jesse Washington. The stunned populace of Waco began to buzz with frenzied excitement. The whispers began at one side of the square and swept across it in seconds flat. Astonished murmurs moved from person to person before turning into full-throated whoops and shouts of glee. Could it be true? An internationally famous movie star was in their midst!

Everyone in Waco had seen her picture. Some had even seen one or two of her movies while visiting Houston or Dallas. She had snow-white skin and large, beseeching brown eyes. Her head was covered with auburn and blonde curls of hair that tumbled to her shoulders. She was dressed like a hungry little street urchin. It was none other than Miss Mary Pickford, America's sweetheart, who had gestured hypnotically and parted the crowd as she walked toward the creature who was lying face down and shaking like a wounded fawn.

The local women oohed and aahed at her perfect white skin. The men sighed at the sight of her rosy red lips. The crowd stood hushed as tiny Miss Pickford somehow managed to heft Jesse's muscular body up to her waist. Against his skin, her small white hands shone like diamonds against a setting of obsidian. She rose from the ground and levitated with him at a level just above the wooden pole.

Then she rose another ten feet and circled the crowd, flying overhead until she found what she had hoped she would find: three faces huddled together in a distant window. A mother and her two children were crying at the horrid scene below their room. Jesse, who had been shivering like a tethered and splayed calf about to be butchered, slowly regained his senses as they gained altitude. He studied Mary Pickford's face for two or three minutes before glancing downward at Waco and the awful scene below.

"You know, Mr. Vegas," he said softly, "if I squints my eyes, you look jes' like a Bible angel. Is you guardin' the tree at the center o' paradise?"

"That wooden pole down there is far from paradise," said the Flyboy, who was studying the faces of the men below. "And I am not an angel."

(One hundred years into the future, Margie rose to her feet. Carrying her radio, she walked to the doorway of the warden's office. She held the little radio up and pointed to it with her other hand. "How is he making all those sounds—all those voices and the sounds of the animals? I can even hear the voice of Jesse Washington—bless his poor tortured soul. I've never heard the like of it." The warden only shrugged. "Well," said Margie as she turned and walked back to her desk, "I hope my son is listening.")

"Right now you look jes' like a movie star," said Jesse, "although I ain't never seen no movie. I'm lookin' direct at you, and I knows you is a man, but I sees a real pretty woman. I don't understand, sir. How'd you do it? Is you a ju-ju man, a conjure man?" Then his voice dropped to below a whisper. "I ain't hurt nobody, Mr. Vegas. Why they do that terrible thing to me?"

"Because they're scared to death, Jesse," said Simon as the two men passed over the western edge of Louisiana and forward in time almost a hundred years. "They don't want to be left all alone. That's what it is. It's not the same kind of alone as a young boy who is lost in a dark, foreboding woods. It's the kind of alone that a spoiled only child might feel when he finds out that a new baby is coming into the family.

"One more person to love and give love back doesn't make that kind of child happy. It only makes him feel more alone than ever. He believes that a new baby brother or sister means there will be less love to go around—less love for him. This only child dreams of taking that new sister and putting her body into a shallow grave. He dreams of hanging his brother and setting his body on fire. There's no room for you in their little heaven, Jesse.

"They are a jealous people who have a jealous god. Those people back in Waco have turned a god of Alpha Centauri and the Crab Nebula, a god of Spinoza and Newton, into a small, penny-pinching absentee manager, and his heaven has had a rusted, buzzing "no vacancy" sign flashing in front of it for over two thousand years—the god of a small hotel."

Jesse reached up to rub his neck. Simon's words were big and alien to Jesse's limited life, but somehow he understood every one of them perfectly. With each word that was spoken, the terror in his eyes was abating and the tremors in his face were subsiding. The two men gained altitude in order to clear a small range of mountains.

"Where are we going, Mr. Vegas?"

"We're going to a place that some people call Florida, and we've got to hurry. I only have six minutes and twenty seconds before the last note of 'Sweet and Lovely.'"

"Where am I gonna live? I got no money. Where can I stay?" asked Jesse tearfully as he inspected his arms and the skin of his chest and stomach, touching the places where the flesh had bubbled and charred. They were all intact and perfect—oxygen and water were coursing beneath his purple skin. He studied each of his elbows. Despite his vague and disconcerting memory of being armless, it appeared as though they had never been burned. He felt his neck and throat and found that the vertebrae were no longer separated and the fatal kink in his windpipe was straight and clear.

"You're going to live in a corner of mi cielo Mexicano," answered Simon, "in a section of my Mexican heaven that's called Boca Raton. And there's someone special waiting for you there. You have marvelous next-door neighbors, a woman named Hypatia and her lover. I've already lined up a roommate for you. His name is Emmett. You'll love him. Everybody there loves him. He's such a nice kid," said the Mexican Flyboy as he and his passenger flew high over Athens, heading for the southern border of Georgia.

(Three thousand miles to the west, tears were streaming from Margie's eyes and dripping down onto her blouse. In her fondest fantasy, in her most precious daydream, she always materializes like a genie in that

parking lot in El Cerrito. She reaches her callow son just before the Mercedes sedan pulls into a parking space. Despite his anger and his resistance, she drags him away. She takes the knife from his pocket and drops it into the bay. In her dream she sells her home and moves the boy out into the country, where he rides a bicycle to school and learns to play the flute.)

"The mailbox out on the sidewalk already has your name printed on it," said Simon. "I can't wait until you see it. It reads WASHINGTON and TILL in giant letters. You'll have a garden with benches and a little pond that is filled with fat koi of every color. You're going to discover just how much you love tea and the poetry of Baudelaire in the original French."

"I ain't never . . . I've never had no tea. I've seen the fine ladies having tea."

"You'll have tea—all the tea you want. You've never seen a Hawaiian shirt, either, but your closet is already filled with them."

"I saw this young man in the crowd, Mr. Vegas. I saw the man who threw the match at me. He had red hair and a handsome face, but I saw something else . . ."

"The beginning of a life of regret," said Simon.

"Yes, that's what it was," said Jesse thoughtfully. "Do you know the young man?"

"Yes," said Simon. "I know him. He is mi abuelito—my grandfather. Fifty years after what happened to you down there, he would tell me stories in bed. Every night when the stories ended and the lights went out, I saw him bury his face in his pillow, and I heard him scream your name into it. Every night. 'Jesse Washington! Jesse Washington!'" shouted the Flyboy. His voice broke, and tears flooded his eyes. "Soon," he said softly, "my grandfather will be coming to live with you."

"Do I have to talk to Emmett about what happened to me? I don't know if I could do that. It might scare him away."

"You won't need to," said the Flyboy. "Emmett will understand everything."

"Shouldn't my name come second on the mailbox, Mr. Vegas? Doesn't W follow T? Doesn't Washington follow Till?"

The Mexican Flyboy stopped scanning the sky for airplanes and looked directly into the eyes of his passenger.

"No," said Simon softly, "you died first."

11

ERSATZ WINDS

1968—somewhere in Southeast Asia.

At nine or ten years of age, the boy had escaped that vineyard of Pinot noir. He had fled headlong from the falling woman and from Germán, the man with the bleeding ear. He had escaped the rows of finicky clones for the toughness of Zinfandel and Syrah. He had carried his dead along with him—fifteen tiny fetid carcasses reposing in a small cardboard coffin. He had practiced takeoffs and landings for five years before he finally flew, but it had been so hard, so taxing on his young body. After each trip, he would have to sleep for an entire day just to regain his strength. He had to use all of his comic books, his tiny cape, every one of his incantations and spells, and every ounce of his imagination just to levitate a few inches above the ground.

It had taken him almost five exhausting years to make his first round-trip flights out to the high desert—fifteen flights in total—all to the same tiny home. After each trip he had taken one of his tiny animals from the box and buried it in the soil of a vineyard. Each burial had given him immeasurable relief and a small bit of peace. Still, there had to be a better way to do what he needed to do—and there was so much more to do. The flights were wearing him out. Then one day a truancy officer spotted Simon driving a tractor in a field near Healdsburg. The officer registered the young man for school and for the Selective Service. The next day, Simon spent his first awkward hours in a foster home and in a classroom. Ten months later, he was armed to the teeth and sitting in the dark, deafening innards of a helicopter.

He was seventeen years old when he landed in Vietnam. He had gone from the stifling heat of Bien Hoa Air Base to a holding area somewhere on the outskirts of Saigon that was even hotter. It was a vast, sprawling complex filled with thousands of sweating boys nervously waiting for their assignments and wondering what an ominous, exciting thing called war would bring to their lives. There were slick-sleeved privates and rosy-cheeked second lieutenants everywhere earnestly lugging duffel bags, bumbling around and stumbling over each other amid small flurries of apologies and awkward salutes. There were endless rows of cots, on which sat countless young soldiers busily writing letters back home.

Simon found a cot and tossed his duffel bag onto it. He saw a lanky second lieutenant sitting on the bunk next to his. He seemed lost and terribly homesick. Simon could tell that he wanted to talk to him . . . to anyone at all, but wasn't sure of the proper protocol, as the Mexican soldier was a private first class and he was an officer fresh from ROTC at a little college somewhere in Indiana. The lieutenant cleared his throat twice and practiced his words silently in his mind before working up the nerve to speak a sentence out loud.

"How long have you been in country, soldier?" he squeaked in a voice that was not long past puberty. Back in Indiana he had been given a one-hour block of instruction on the most effective use of the "command voice," but to no avail. He was so nervous that he asked the question again.

"My name is Officer Mitchell . . . Larry Mitchell. I'm from Indiana. How long have you been in country, soldier?" It was the ubiquitous question: "How long have you been in country?" was the only thing that new soldiers who were fresh off the airplane could ask one another. The soldiers who had been in Vietnam for some appreciable time never talked about being "in country." They only talked about how much time they had left to do: "Ninety-three days and a wakeup."

Simon looked at the officer's innocent, hairless face and said with a deadpan delivery: "You are mistaken, sir. I am not in country. However, I am incontinent."

He had told that corny joke a hundred times—no, a thousand times—while he was in Vietnam, and no one there had ever laughed—no one but a private named Fulgencio Garza, and English was not even Garza's first language. Still, he got the joke when no captain or colonel or general from Da Lat to Dong Ha had ever gotten it.

Just a few weeks after leaving Saigon for a post near the northern border, Simon found himself in the belly of a gray metal whale that was speeding along at a hundred miles an hour through the dark sky two hundred miles west of Quang Tri. No one had bothered to tell him the destination. No one had told him the direction of travel or how long the flight would take. It was three o'clock in the morning, and the old helicopter felt like it was about to shake itself to pieces. There was only one tiny light in the interior of the machine, and it was twenty feet away from where he was seated. Except for a candy bar and a cup of terrible coffee, his stomach was empty. He sat nervously spinning the top cartridge of a magazine that was strapped to the front of his vest.

Young Simon Vegas had found a seat on the starboard side sitting at the head of the row. The ground unit, the "grunt" who sat down on his left, was Fulgencio. There were seven troopers on one side of the chopper and eight on the other. They were all beyond silence. Each one of them was sitting there probing the profound blackness just in front of his own face—touching eternity with his fingers, looking for a sign, an omen—anything that would tell him that this was not going to be the last day of his life. Considerations and concerns about being maimed or crippled or worse—thoughts that eighty-year-old men try to avoid—were trampling through their teenaged minds.

Sergeant Ajax Carruthers, the most hated man in the Americal Division, was standing in the center of the chopper. He was six feet, five inches tall, and his skin was so black that it was almost blue. He was muscular and mean, and he'd had five wives and bragged that he had abused them all. He had five bullet wounds in his body, and the scuttlebutt was that not a single one of them had happened in combat. The gossip was that each of his wives had tried to shoot him dead before she filed for divorce. He loved to curse everything and everyone, but he had recently learned to distrust his own foul mouth because of the strange, otherworldly words that he had begun to spew with greater and greater frequency.

The sergeant was bilious and wretched every second of his life, and he did not have the slightest inkling why. If he had been born a white man and just twenty years later, his particular personality profile would have been coveted by every headhunter on Wall Street. With his cold blood and even colder heart, he would have been a perfect investment banker instead of an unhappy lifer in the army—instead of a squad leader in Korea and a platoon leader in Vietnam.

Before Ajax was born, he was exactly what everyone once was: gaseous, vaporous, and weightless. He was a soul waiting to descend into flesh, waiting for a body to be picked out—a culture to be chosen. Like everyone else, he flew in a holding pattern around and around the earth, waiting for his turn to descend. When the pretty assistant sashayed over to the zoetrope, the big wheel of life in that game show in the sky, she turned to face the audience, smiled at the camera showing a mouth full of blinding teeth, then spun the wheel with every ounce of force that was appropriate to a thin young model in a bathing suit, six-inch heels, and even higher aspirations. The pointer went round and round and finally came to an auspicious halt at the Carruthers family on Wall Street.

The studio audience went wild with joy. The Wall Street Car-ruthers! What on earth could be better than a life of leisure and wealth? They imagined a huge glass-walled penthouse overlooking Central Park and a grinning, cap-doffing, white-gloved Negro door-man down on the street level below. They all imagined a family of bluebloods whose ancestors had stepped directly from the decks of the *Mayflower* onto the paper-littered floor of the New York Stock Exchange. They cheered madly until they slowly came to the terrible realization that the pointer had actually come to a stop on a com-pletely different Wall Street, not the famous one in Manhattan.

In truth, there were three Carruthers families on the earth who met the qualifications: the one on the top floor of Number 10 Central Park West, the Carruthers family who currently lived on a ninety-foot yacht named *Wall Street* that was anchored in a small protected cove just south of Monaco—and then there was that last possibility.

Upon closer inspection by the master of ceremonies, it was soon painfully clear by the look of shock on his face that the next unformed soul to be shot down to the earth's surface would go to a poor black family living in an unpaved, unincorporated, nameless little shanty town in Louisiana just outside of a grand metropolis called Happy Jack—a town in Plaquemines Parish that had been dubbed Wall Street by the locals. The town was named after the sin-gle standing wall of a crumbling sanitarium that had once graced its only street. On this particular Wall Street—and there are dozens of them in America—there were only forty-one residents, living in six ramshackle wooden houses, behind which were six dilapidated outhouses.

There was a tiny grocery store, a small peanut farm, and the Madison Avenue pig ranch, which was owned by Cleophus Lee Mad-ison. Instead of wide boulevards alternately pulsing then choked with cars, smoking buses, and taxicabs that were being driven from one stoplight to the next at neurotic speeds by men in beards and turbans, this Wall Street had only one wooden sidewalk, which ran the entire length of the town. Made up of 131 slats of cypress wood, it had been built by slaves during the Civil War.

The pointer should have stopped on New York City or on Monaco. It was meant to stop at either one, but the wind resistance of the great wooden arrow on the wheel of life had been irrevocably altered by a gaggle of fruit flies that had landed on it for a short rest on their way down to earth. The flapping of their miniature wings had created tiny eddy currents and a slight drag on the pointer, slowing it just enough over a few dozen rotations to cause the awful, irreversible error. In the two other lives that Ajax Carruthers should have had, he would have outranked every general and every United States senator—even the president himself.

Standing twenty feet away from where Fulgencio and Simon were sitting, Sergeant Carruthers was completely misplaced in the world. He was surrounded by frightened young men when he should have been encircled by a natty gaggle of golf partners. Except for the single light that was bathing the sergeant in an eerie glow, it was almost pitch-black inside the flying machine. The roar of the engines was deafening.

One of the troopers on this flight was a mestizo. His father was a Nez Percé Indian from northeast Oregon, and his mother was a Mexican. He was sitting at the end of the starboard row laughing to himself at the crazy ironies of life. He knew that this helicopter was not a C'inúk, but merely a Chinook. The gringo name was abhorrent to him, and he knew in his heart that it was an omen, a message from his grandfathers telling him that he would not survive this war.

"C'inúk" is a Penutian word of the Salishan, Klamath, and Nez Percé, an incantatory word. On the other hand, "Chinook" names a synthetic wind stirred up by straining rotors, droop stops, and smelly turbines—a twin funnel cloud, a double twister touching down to disgorge the Long Knives who will slash into the children of Chief Joseph. A c'inúk is a wind. A Chinook is an abomination of breezes forced together under duress—compelled to spin madly by a foul mixture of combustion and fumes.

All that the fifteen soldiers on that Chinook knew was that it was around three-thirty or four in the morning, and they were sitting in the cold trough between two synthetic cyclones, and they would give everything they had—all of their hopes and their dreams—just to continue fanning the small ember of consciousness that burned nowhere else in all of the far-flung constellations but in the warm, soft tissue between their ears.

"All right, shitheads, listen up," shouted the sergeant. He was standing precariously in a half-open door, his right jungle boot perched on top of an M-41 gun mount. His voice was almost lost in the whine of the turbines and the howling of the winds that were swirling through the opening. "Even you fools have noticed that this here ain't no Huey. This here is a Chinook CH-47A twin rotor flyin' Greyhound bus. Now, we coulda had a Chinook ACH-47A— there was one on the tarmac not fifty feet away from this bucket of bolts, and it was loaded down with double mini-guns, a twin rack of two and three quarter-inch rockets, and a pair of M-60s.

"The other chopper has the T55-L-7C with two hundred more horsepower per engine. Now, that might not mean nothin' to them spooks sittin' just north of us," he sneered with disdain at a secretive group of five men who were huddled together near the front of the craft and poring over stacks of paper, "but it sure as shit means somethin' to the likes of you and me."

His voice was raspy with the exertion required to browbeat his men. "This aircraft can haul over thirty troops plus gear, but all we have are fifteen because those Army Security Agency spooks over there wanted more space for their precious, infernal machine. Plus we're haulin' them five effeminate noncombatants!" He glanced toward the front of the chopper.

"That thing over there weighs a half-ton all by itself. We're overweight, undergunned, and if we gotta di-di outta there in a hurry, we're gonna wish we had that extra horsepower."

The sergeant struck a match and tried to light a cigarette. The flaming Ohio Blue Tip lit up the central portion of his hardened, shining face before dying away prematurely in the windy interior of the chopper. He lit two, three more matches before striking three at the same time and pressing them directly against the tobacco. The white tube protruding from his heavy lips began to glow. The face in the doorway smiled as the hot sulfur found its way into his lungs. The sergeant pulled the portside door downward until it was almost shut. Then he turned toward the five officers.

"Or are you guys CIA? None of you guys even has a tan, not even that skinny high-yellow brother sittin' over there. Just look at you boys sweatin' like fat bankers in a steam bath. I'll bet you miss that air conditioning down in Da Nang. Well, this ain't Da Nang, and our troop strength has shrunk to nothin' because you sissies don't have to get out of this bucket when the feces and the ventilator come into close proximity.

"All you people have to do is run up like little pansies, then cut your precious cargo loose. When it rolls down that ramp into the darkness, one of you has got to go down and turn some knobs, while the rest of you huddle up close to the pilots like a bunch of fairy-faggots. While you are over there shiverin' like schoolgirls, I gotta put three men out front and four to each side of that thing when the ramp goes down."

Then he turned toward his troopers. Each one of them averted his eyes. "Then I got to have one trooper followin' up right behind this gizmo." He reached out and touched one corner of a hulking black cube that was strapped down in the center of the cargo bay.

When he bent down and lifted an edge of the canvas covering the box, one of the officers in the corner stood up and shook his head no. The sergeant grinned sheepishly and lifted the covering even higher. Then he let the canvas drop, but it did not cover the machine completely. A small control panel was left exposed.

None of the troops even looked up at the sergeant. In fact, they barely heard his rant. They were forcing their minds to be else-where—anywhere but where they actually were this morning. None of the men were moving now, not even a finger. They all sensed that the landing zone was close. Pre–rigor mortis was setting in. Each one of them felt his ties to home and family being stretched out thinner and thinner, then snapping altogether. Now no one back home would ever know the true circumstances of their deaths or the last moments of their lives. Next, the already tenuous connection with the U.S. Army snapped. There was no army out here. Out here no one was in control. They were going off the map and over the edge.

One of the five officers sitting in the area near the cockpit of the chopper stood up. He took five unsteady steps toward the sergeant, then reached up to a point above his left breast pocket and ripped away a flap of tape that had been stuck to the front of the shirt. Under the flap was the insignia of a full-bird colonel. The face of the young African American officer was bathed in a cold syrup of sweat, and his soft brown eyes were oscillating wildly in their sockets. He was clearly terrified and seething with anger at the same time.

"If you know anything about this mission or this classified device, sergeant," he shouted above the noise of the turbines, "you had better keep it to yourself, or I will personally see to it that you are thrown in the stockade in Saigon, then into a cell in Leaven-worth. You have already agreed on paper never to inquire as to the nature of this device or its use. You have already agreed never to speak of it again. Do you understand me, sergeant?"

The helicopter suddenly lurched and dropped thirty or forty feet before its rotors regained their grip on the air. The solitary piece of cargo in the Chinook shifted forward, then back violently, snapping one of its restraining straps. The colonel covered his badge of rank, turned quickly, and glanced at one of his colleagues. An even younger officer in a perfectly starched uniform jumped up smartly and ran to inspect the machine. He lifted the corner of the tarpaulin that was covering the broken strap. He nodded and smiled weakly at the colonel and returned to his seat.

Sergeant Carruthers's mouth and eyes were open wide. His face was screwed into a grotesque mask of mock bemused terror. The only two black men on the chopper were now standing three feet apart and glaring coldly at each other.

"Colonel, when you was still shittin' in your diapers, I was landin' at Inchon. Now, in case you didn't know it, that's Korea I'm talkin' about. That was a real land war, a company and battalion war—even whole regiments, not this platoon and fire team shit we got here now. All we do here in the Nam is ambush this or ambush that, or get ambushed ourselves. You didn't need no body counts in Korea. We measured the Chinese dead in acre feet. What do you tech people have planned for us next, a war with nothing' but booby traps and flyin' robots killin' people by remote control? It's you people who want to fight wars using expensive gadgets and widgets. I heard you fellas talkin' over there, using all them highfalutin fifty-cent words like 'disruption' and 'fifty-mile radius.' Even a fool knows that your machine is supposed to disable all their electronic equipment and kill every human from here to Laos."

The colonel gasped in surprise and took an involuntary step backward.

"Did you think that Sergeant Ajax Carruthers is stupid? Shit, I was born on Wall Street! I got my black finger on the pulse of America! And I've got even more news for you. Didn't no one ever tell you that Charlie ain't got no electronic equipment? He don't have radar. He don't even have radio! Hell, all he's got is whistles and these tiny little trumpets and these markers that they put on trees. You ain't never heard those whistles or trumpets, have you? That sound will send chills right down your spine, into the crack of your ass and straight into your nightmares. That machine of yours ain't gonna do shit to people like that. Besides, where you gonna find a concentration of gooks that's not gonna wipe out a solo Chinook as soon as we land?"

The anger in the sergeant's face subsided for an instant as he pondered his own question. His eyes flared up again as he snapped his fingers and shouted with glee, "You incompetent fools went and found the NVA's main underground hospital complex! Supposed to have five hundred beds in there. Hundreds of nurses and doctors. We've been lookin' for it for years. That's what this thing is for! This is your flamin' sword goin' before your sacred army—a god at the head of your columns to smite thine hospitalized, bedridden enemy!

"You paid some gook spy to get you in the general area, and now you tech boys are gonna test out your electronic baby! This gadget is for modern urban warfare, ain't it? It sniffs out computers and X-rays or somethin', then goes and gets 'em. This ain't for the Nam! Five'll get you ten this whole goddamn mission is a fuckin' demonstration! Did you think I didn't see them gunships trailing us? Two of them gunships behind us ain't loaded with weapons, are they? I'll bet they're loaded with Arabs, ragheads and Iraqi spectators— potential payin' clients! Who's footin' the bill for all this, General Motors or Haliburton?"

"I'd keep my mouth shut if I were you, sergeant," shouted the colonel. His sepia-toned face was turning blood-red.

"Well, I've got even more news for you, colonel. That spy of yours—whoever he was—is workin' for them, too. Shit, they all are. You think this landing zone is gonna be quiet . . . a walk in the park?

Read my lips. Nobody in the bush ever believes army intelligence! This is gonna be an ambush, colonel. That's what this is gonna be. We're only ninety miles out, and I can feel it from here. My hemorrhoids is curlin' up in my little pink panties . . . and my hemorrhoids never lie! That Vietnamese janitor who sweeps the floor in your laboratory got his doctorate in Paris. He's out there right now fixin' to jump up and take charge of this gizmo of yours as soon as we lift off, assuming that we can lift off."

The colonel shot a glance at his compatriots. Their faces mirrored his own outrage and disbelief.

"Shit, they're smarter than you are, colonel! They don't want to waste their time shuttin' off any X-ray machines and disruptin' intercoms. They know this thing is gold and you fools are givin' it away. When they get their hands on this contraption of yours, they ain't gonna use it to turn off a dentist's drill that don't even exist! They're gonna take it apart, go public with it, and sell futures on it. They're gonna monetize that thing and mortgage it piecemeal to the Chinese and the Palestinians. They'll bundle up those debts and sell 'em to the Germans and the Icelanders."

Even as he spoke, the sergeant knew that the outlandish language he was speaking did not yet exist—even on the real Wall Street. Throughout his barefooted childhood on Wall Street down in Louisiana and his entire adult life in the army, peculiar and anomalous phrases had had a way of streaming out of him like yards of ticker tape. It was as if the life that he would have lived if that pointer had clicked over to Manhattan or Monaco kept bleeding over into the miserable, menial life that he had actually been given.

It was crosstalk, but was it going both ways? Was there a prim and proper young socialite heiress named Madeleine "Muffy" Carruthers on a yacht anchored somewhere near Monaco who was holding her teacup demurely up to her mum and suddenly shouting, "Gimme some mo' tea, motherfucka"?

"Then," the sergeant said in a disembodied, almost ghostly voice, "they're gonna find people who will want to bet on whether those bundled-up debts go into default or not. Besides . . . ," he said quietly, almost in a whisper. He seemed completely dazed and befuddled by his own bizarre vocabulary. There was a faraway look in his eyes. Over the years the words had evolved, gaining more and more complexity with each passing day. Where was this arcane jargon coming from?

He merely opened his mouth, and out flew the words. He canted his head in order to hear his own voice with more objectivity, more detachment. The sergeant had never been to New York City, nor had he ever perused the business pages of a newspaper.

"Besides that . . ." His lips were moving of their own will. "Besides all that, tonight is the night when the options, the index futures and index options, all expire. This is the triple witching hour, the last hour of the third Friday in June. At least it is back in New York City, and that's what counts." The sergeant went still for a second or two while a changing of the guard took place in his cerebellum. Then his military soul returned to take charge of his lips and vocal cords. "I'm telling you people that Charlie is waitin' down there and he's gonna hit us hard."

"Consider yourself up on charges, sergeant," said the colonel, who had been completely stunned by the sergeant's strange words. "I'm going to ask for a full court-martial as soon as we get back to Da Nang. I think you've got mental problems, and I'm going to order a complete psychiatric evaluation."

The sergeant smiled at the young colonel. "My hemorrhoids just shot me an update. You ain't gettin' back to Da Nang, colonel— not alive and breathin'. And here's some more bad news for you: you ain't gettin' that promotion."

"Is that a threat?" shouted the colonel over the raging ersatz winds.

"Colonel, I know this shit better than you know electronics. I can see it in your face plain as day. You and that Walther P-38 on your hip don't belong out here. You're way out of your element. You're dead meat out here. You remember those three gunships, no, those two sightseeing buses and one gunship that are trailin' us, are four, maybe five miles behind us? Well, they're too far away! What Charlie's got planned for us is gonna be all over in ten seconds. As I said before, the shit and the fan are now in close proximity, my young black brother."

The sergeant's stream of verbiage abated for a moment as, deep in his psyche, a dark intuition was morphing into an even deeper thought.

"But ain't nothin' gonna happen to Ajax Carruthers," he said haltingly as the thought fought its way to the surface of his consciousness. Maybe there wasn't going to be a real ambush at all. It was the first faint flicker of awareness that perhaps the whole operation was a fraud.

"I got five bullet holes in me. I've got my share," he continued unconvincingly. "Ain't no more comin' my way. I'm fuckin' immortal."

"Intelligence assures me that the LZ is cold," shouted the colonel above the howl of the rotors.

While the colonel and the sergeant were screaming at each other, Fulgencio Garza reached beneath his flak vest and into the pocket of his field jacket and pulled out a tiny photograph. It was a picture of a small boy. He turned toward Simon Vegas and extended his shaking right hand, attempting to show him the picture.

"He's cute," said Simon, who didn't really know what to say. His terrified mind had been far away from the interior of the helicopter. His frantic thoughts had gone ahead to the landing zone, the place where his life might end. They had flown back to a field of grapes and to the cook and the old Portogee. They had flown back to her—

to the plummeting woman. "He's cute," he repeated as he tried to focus his eyes on the picture. Other than his own two sisters, he had no experience with children, and he certainly had no idea what to say to a father who was scared to death that he would never see his baby again. Simon fell back on a tired old cliché. "He must take after his mother, because you sure as hell ain't that cute. How old is he?"

"He's five years old—cinco años," said Fulgencio proudly. "He's living con his mama in Port Arthur, back home in Texas. I never married her," he said without looking up from the photo. A chill shot through Fulgencio, and he shivered as though he were freezing. It was over ninety degrees outside. "I should have married her. We only had sex that one time, and she goes and gets pregnant. Dios mío, I was awful! I just managed to get my thing inside of her when I lost control. My first and only time making love was over in thirty seconds, maybe less! What a pendejo I was! We were both just kids. I hardly knew her, but I stuck with her through the pregnancy. That part was easy.

"I bought her whatever food she wanted. I drove her to the doctor and visited her with flowers every day even though I could see that every bouquet I brought always ended up in the trash. Dios mío, her parents hated me for getting their little princess pregnant! How could I blame them? She was a kid having a kid! But I stuck with it. I got her medication for her when she had those days of morning sickness. I gave her back rubs when she could barely stand to have me touch her. And I bought her those special panties when she was incontinent for two months.

"But I don't think she ever liked me. I never saw her naked again until she gave birth to my little boy. Shit, I don't blame her. I had no dinero in my pockets and no futuro. I couldn't get a decent job to support my son, so I went and joined the army as soon as I could get my parents to write a letter. Then Magdalena—that's her name—then Magdalena found a boyfriend, some slick dude from El

Paso who drove a Coca-Cola truck. I sent her money anyway—every month.

"A funny thing happened, though. One day her boyfriend left her cold for a gringa with blonde hair, and we started writing to each other—every month at first, then every week. We started falling in love through the mail. I sent her letters from Fort Carson, from Berlin, and now from here. In a little while she and little Fulgencio became my family. I've got a bad feeling, Simon," he sputtered and grabbed Simon's arm. "I got this feeling that I'll never see either one of them again."

He stared at the photograph in his trembling hand, bringing it closer and closer to his sweaty face until it was only an inch or two from his right eye. He grabbed his right hand with his left in order to steady the image. In that moment he put his lips to the paper and kissed it.

"Ain't this some shit," he said with a disbelieving shake of the head. "Only one time in the sack with a woman, and then I go and buy the farm ten thousand miles away at three o'clock in the morning. That's not much of a life, is it? Ain't this some shit." Tears were dropping down onto his flak vest, and a line of snot was dribbling from his left nostril. "But I don't deserve better, do I? I don't deserve to see my little boy again. Did you see what happened on the perimeter the other day? Did you see that?" Private Garza's face was knotted with grief.

"Did you see what happened?"

12

DIOS X. MÁQUINA

"Did I see it?" asked Simon. There was dread and sorrow in his sagging face that paralleled the gloom in Fulgencio's features. "Don't you remember, Fulgencio?" he shouted into his new friend's ear while grabbing at his vest. "I was with you at that fucked-up outpost. I fired, too!" he screamed. "We both fired, but it was me that killed that poor little boy, not you. I'm sure it was me. I don't think I'll ever sleep again. I know that I'm never going to follow orders again. Never."

Private Vegas's lips were beginning to quiver. He had been trying so hard to suppress the awful memory. He had shoved at it and choked it with every positive thought that he could cull from his recollections, but the only thought that had the momentum and the gravity to shove the vision of the dying boy aside was the all too familiar image of a woman with red hair streaking downward to the ground. Private Simon Vegas was trapped at that place, caught between two awful memories and hovering above a landing zone filled with North Vietnamese regular troops. He felt like his body and soul were being torn into three pieces.

For seventy hours now, the two men had been ravaged by the same unspeakable memory as it played through their minds over and over again. Three days ago, just at sunrise, a little boy wearing bright orange flip-flops, tan shorts, and a dark jacket had appeared from out of nowhere and approached the western perimeter at Landing Zone Cherokee. The sounds he was making sounded like gibberish at first, like childish nonsense. But soon enough it was clear that the boy was singing. His chanting had the repetitive sing-song cadence of a children's song.

The child tugged playfully on the concertina wire, then bent down an inch or two and walked calmly underneath and between the rings of razor-edged metal. The perimeter had not been designed with a forty-pound boy in mind. The singing child walked forward but kept turning his head to his left and nodding slightly as though he were listening to someone who was hiding just out of sight. He took a step to his right, and then, in compliance with directions from that mysterious someone out there, took a step back and moved three steps to his left, just barely avoiding an anti-personnel mine. He walked forward seven steps, then moved to his right, missing another buried explosive by mere inches.

Someone in the brush abruptly shouted a few hard syllables and threw something high into the air. The boy began to run, quickly crossing an open area that was only lightly mined and reaching a second tier of concertina wire that had been strung parallel to the first row. He began hunting back and forth for something on the ground—for whatever had been thrown. Simon could see that the child was wearing a bulky jacket over bare skin. It had no buttons or zipper but was tied around his waist with a length of rope. Fulgencio picked up the radio handset. "Do you see that?" he said to some-one fifty yards to the rear who was poking his binoculars through an opening in a sandbag shelter. Then he groaned and turned to Simon.

"Dios mío, they say we have to shoot him. Shit! They think he's a sapper. What if he gets to the command post? They say his jacket is bulging with something. They think he's loaded down with C-4 *plastique* explosive. Shit, he's only four or five years old at the most! He's the same age as my boy!"

Simon grabbed the handset from Fulgencio and spoke to the man at the other end of the line.

"What about a warning shot?" he asked in a frantic half-whisper, half-scream.

After a short, heated discussion, Simon tossed the handset to the ground and took his rifle off safety. There were tears streaming down his face as he tried to move the bead of his gun sight toward the center of the young boy's chest. The spasms of sorrow that were convulsing his body made it almost impossible to aim with any degree of accuracy. The gun sight swept and swayed to the right, then over to the left.

"I hate this! I hate this fucking war and this fucking army! I didn't want to come here! I don't want to shoot babies! I don't want to shoot anybody! I hate this so much," said Simon between savage, heaving sobs. A voice in the radio was bellowing: "Shoot him! Shoot him! That's a fucking order!"

He closed his eyes and squeezed the trigger just as Fulgencio fired his own rifle. When Simon opened his eyes, he saw that Fulgencio had taken a step backward and slid down to the bottom of the hole. His arms were around his legs, and his hands were clasped. He was shivering uncontrollably. His teeth were chattering, and his tongue was bleeding. His lips and gums were purple and crimson. His rifle was still perched on top of the sandbags that circled their position. Simon slid down to join him. The two men stayed in the bottom of the hole for almost half an hour.

"I'm not getting home, am I?" sobbed Fulgencio as the chopper was momentarily slowed by a headwind, then lunged through it. "Now I know I'm not getting home. Please help me, Simon. I love her now—and I've always loved my son."

"I don't know if I can keep my mind together—in one piece," said Simon as he wiped the tears and mucus from his own face with the sleeve of his jacket. "That little boy was so alone, Fulgencio. I can't bear it. He was so alone, and I was such a fucking coward. I should have been with him, Fulgencio. I should have been with him, to pick him up and take him far away from all of this shit. I'm no soldier. I've never been a soldier. I can't help you! I can't help anybody."

"Then they'd kill you, too," said Fulgencio. "If you went out to talk with that boy, they'd kill you, too. Someone on that radio would order me to shoot you, and you know that's true. And if I refused to shoot you, someone else would shoot us both."

An hour later a squad was sent out to clear the perimeter, inspect the boy's body, and search for the person who had directed his movements so perfectly through the minefield. When the soldiers came back, they dumped the flimsy, floppy little body on a pile of sand near the command post. The left side of the boy's chest was open. His left lung and half of his ribcage were gone. A tiny purplish and green heart dangled into the gaping wound. The little jacket had been loaded down, packed tight, but not with plastic explosives. The pockets were filled with American candy bars.

There were precious Mars bars, Charleston Chews, and Milky Ways stuffed into the boy's jacket—enough sugar to stay alive in a defoliated wasteland for an entire month. Enough sugar to feed a family. The little waif had been paid handsomely to do what he did by someone who wanted some American soldier to be forced to shoot him down—by someone who wanted some poor grunt to suffer for the rest of his life—by a sadist who knew that there were things even worse than combat.

"Here's the entry wound. He's only got one hole in him," said a buck sergeant with a heavy drawl and a beaming smile. "One of you two bleedin' hearts still has a shot at goin' to heaven. The other one is a baby killer," he said with an uproarious guffaw. "I've seen this before, up in Dong Ha. It's a real mindfuck, ain't it? A week ago this jarhead from the Fifth Marines goes and shoots this little girl who was messin' with the wire. Teeny little thing. Two days later he puts his M-16 in his mouth. You know the rest of the story. If you ask me, these zips ain't worth it. They just ain't worth the grief."

He reached into his pocket and pulled out a small object in a brown and white wrapper.

"Anyone want a Milky Way? Someone threw four or five of these out there. A few more feet and the little boy would've found all of them. We thought they might be laced with poison, so we fed some to the zip who collects the honey buckets and burns the shit. He survived, so we figured they must be good. By the way, the kid's name was Hong Van Ha, not that anyone gives a shit. Someone pinned a death poem to the inside of his jacket. Too bad the kid couldn't read."

The Chinook lurched again as a sudden wind shear slammed into the starboard side.

"Back at Cherokee base I shot my own son," said Fulgencio with a howl of pain. "That's what I did, isn't it? It's the same thing, isn't it? But at the same time, my boy's alive back in Texas. I can be selfish, can't I? I can be a hypocrite, can't I? Isn't the world full of them? I can love the little boy in this picture and kill the little one in that minefield—on the same day—with the same breath!"

"I don't deserve to make it. But people who don't deserve still get ahead, don't they? Ain't that how it works? I can't go out there, Simon. I can't go out there. Not tonight! Please, not tonight!" He clawed at Simon's sleeve as he spoke. "Please, not tonight."

"Don't worry," Simon shouted directly into Fulgencio's ear. "If Carruthers sends you out front, I'll take it for you. Hell, he can't tell one Mexican from another one anyway." Simon took the picture of the Virgin Mary that Fulgencio wore on his helmet and placed it on his own.

Fulgencio smiled weakly, then slumped in his seat. He lifted his hand to his face and kissed the photograph of his baby son. The little boy had his father's face.

"You know something?" he said. "Something real strange happened to me when I shot that little boy, and it's happening again right now. Just before I hurt that little pobrecito, I thought I saw a Mexican man flying over the concertina wire. I know it's crazy. I've been keeping it inside 'cause I know it's crazy. He was wearing a suit and tie, and he had this machine—una máquina—on his chest. Right now, this very second, I can see him over there near the cargo doors. He's sitting in the shadows, and he has another man with him. The older man is in a suit, and he looks something like you! Only he's got gray hair. He's wearing a bandolier like Pancho Villa in all those old pictures. The younger man looks a little like me. He's staring at me. They both are. I'm going crazy, ain't I? Do they know I shot that little boy?"

Fulgencio began to sob.

"Oh, glory be!" shouted Carruthers while pointing at Simon and Fulgencio. "Are you two sissies still carryin' on about that little baby gook? Well, you'd best wake up an' smell the coffee, 'cause Ajax Carruthers ain't gonna bite the dust tonight because you two Mexicans can't keep your shit together." He pointed toward the row of troopers across from Simon and Fulgencio. You, Mendez and Lopez and Robriguez . . . Oh, glory be!" he shouted to everyone within earshot. "My troopers are all a bunch of Mexicans tonight, every goddamn one of 'em. Fifteen Mexicans in here. Can you beat that!"

"We've seen all this before, ain't we? America's done shipped in fifteen illegal aliens to do the dirtiest work there is . . . and at the lowest wage there is—somethin' just short of slave labor. What the fuck is America gonna do when it can't get no more Mexicans, send the jobs to Mongolia? We got fifteen grunts on this chopper, and three or four of them is about to get unlucky. Somebody's fixin' to die tonight! Somebody's fixin' to go all gray and cold. Somebody's mama is gonna jerk upright in her bed and feel her son's last moment on this earth.

"Right now some machine is sewing the flag that's gonna be folded up and placed in her hands. She gave one hundred and eighty pounds of life to the U.S. Army, and she gets back a five-pound wad of folded cloth stuffed into a polished wooden box. That's some bargain! But it ain't gonna be my sweet mama. My mama is gonna sleep the whole night through and wake up full of piss and vinegar!"

The sergeant was gesturing wildly with one arm as he assaulted his men with his usual caustic sermon. The single light behind his head gave his outsized form a demonic cast.

"Yep, I can hear that infernal machine back home gearin' up to make sure nobody ever thinks twice about what really happened to you out here. They got your local minister all lined up and ready at a moment's notice to preach your mama that sermon that says you're in a better place. They got the local rag ready to pull out that story about makin' lemon meringue pie and print a high school picture and a short paragraph on the front page about you dying for freedom. There's gonna be a moment of silence for you at the local ping-pong tournament. They're all ready to roll. But I can tell you one thing for sure. It ain't gonna be me," scowled Sergeant Carruthers. "They're not getting' my life. My mama is getting' her black boy back in one piece."

The sergeant took a deep breath and opened his mouth for another savage volley of words, but they never came. His eyes narrowed and began darting back and forth. Everyone felt it. The chopper had begun slowing and losing altitude. The abusive rotors above their heads had eased up on the atmosphere, taking smaller and smaller hacks into the thick, fleshy velvet that is the heat and humidity of South Vietnam. There was the heart-rending whirr of an electric motor somewhere in the dark, and the terrifying clicking and ticking of hydraulic hoses becoming turgid. There was the horrifying exhale of release valves, the thump of relays, and the wheeze of pneumatic arms getting ready to flex. The sounds of finality.

Simon and Fulgencio instantaneously forgot about the boy. Their mutual grief had been replaced by a sad, tense relief. Their stomachs became as tight as drums. Their skin tingled as adrenaline flooded their bodies. Their minds addled, cleared up, then addled again. Their arms and legs suddenly felt like lead weights had been strapped to them. Terror gripped their brown faces. How could they possibly get up and take their positions when their muscles had turned to jelly and their legs had hardened to stone?

Simon's desperate gaze flew wildly in every direction. His tortured eyes darted everywhere—scouring the interior of the chopper for something, anything, any small, insignificant distraction that might grab his attention and hold it for a few seconds of peace. He desperately tried to focus a mind and control a body that were in full rebellion against this unnatural moment—this true crime against nature.

"Do you feel it, troopers?" barked the sergeant. "Do you feel the army's big green weenie goin' straight up your ass?"

Simon's flailing, fluttering eyes unexpectedly landed upon the enormous bomb that was strapped down in the center of the bay. One of the corners of the tarp had been left open. He could see a small control panel that was lit by a few tiny yellow bulbs. It was no more than two feet from his face. There were five hexagons etched onto the panel. At the center of each hexagon was a single knob. All five were machined of bright, shining brass. Each one was encircled by incremental markings and numbers. In the next instant, Simon's frantic mind had been seized, wholly captured and enraptured by the small rectangular device.

He studied the control box and began to see something much more than a weapon of war. In a second heartbeat, he had divined the machine's true purpose. In a flash of insight and of memory, he understood precisely what his eyes beheld. He had once found a photograph of this very device in a scientific journal! He had been sitting in a barber shop in a town somewhere in Sonoma or Napa. This was the same object! He was certain of it. The army had stolen it from the archaeologists! They had imprisoned it, butchered it, and attached it to a weapon of war! There, not two feet from where he was sitting, right there in front of his face and within arm's reach, was the world-famous Antikythera device!

For decades, no one—no physicist or historian—had been able to discern its precise purpose or function, and now the U.S. Army was trying to use it as the control mechanism of a weapon! They wanted to disable and doom a five-hundred-bed hospital full of wounded and dying men. They wanted to kill all of the doctors and nurses while preserving all of their equipment. The military didn't really understand its true purpose, but this Mexican draftee knew.

Simon closed his eyes and imagined himself reaching out his hand and touching the first control knob. He saw himself twisting it backward, then turning every other knob until the machine was set to a point in time exactly one year before this horrid night—back to a time just before that terrible day in July when he had received his draft notice. He would go back in time and pack his bags. Then, when the mailman put the notice into the mail slot, he would tear that letter up—rip the accursed thing to shreds.

He would move to Morelia or Toronto. He would make this helicopter and this madness disappear—vanish like steam. He would keep his country from murdering him without witnesses, and then burying him six feet deep in syrupy mythologies. The soldier reached out. When his trembling fingers touched the first control knob, he began to twist it, but he pulled his hand back abruptly when someone standing next to him shrieked at the top of his lungs.

"Can you feel it, my friends?" shouted Sergeant Carruthers. "Can you feel it? This here is gonna be somebody's last minute as a whole, intact person. There's only one way out of this, you know. You got to get some. The only way you can get through this is to make sure that the mama who cries tonight is some gook's mama up in Hanoi waitin' up for her boy."

There was a loud clank as the locks for the cargo ramp partially released their hold. Everyone in the Chinook tightened their shoulders and puckered their anal pores as their bodies flooded with chemicals—their guts sloshed with acid, and their brains were clogged with gallons of viscous fear and half a teaspoon of hope. Safeties clicked off. Two men on the port side crossed themselves with their hands.

Fulgencio lifted a cross from the depths of his shirt and placed it on top of his son's little face. He kissed them both. His lungs heaved. His lips were babbling quietly, and drops of urine dribbled down the inside of his pant leg. His healthy organs and pristine eighteen-year-old body were just ninety seconds away from traumatic dysfunction caused by a blind, mad intrusion of metal. His head was seconds away from almost complete decapitation. His young brown face was a mass of grief.

The heavy door began to grind open. There was only silence and blackness outside as the chopper danced and dipped, spinning slowly a few feet above the ground, probing here, then prying over there for a particular piece of level ground. One of the spooks had gone up to the cockpit with the warrant officers and was directing them while talking to someone on a radio-telephone. The excited faces of his companions were lit up by the dim orange display of a portable electronic screen.

When the Chinook finally squatted onto the ground, the sergeant moved quickly down the port side and then up the starboard side, touching helmets as he moved. He tapped Fulgencio's helmet and said, "You got point position. You go down with that black box and position yourself five meters in front as it rolls to a stop. And don't go worryin' your pretty little head about nothin,' mi hombre, because your Mexican ass is dyin' for freedom . . . and a free market economy!"

Everyone had already been given his assignment, but the sergeant had been performing this same ritual through three tours in Vietnam and two in Korea, and he wasn't about to change it now. He moved on immediately, touching each trooper as he passed, walking toward the back, then up the other side toward the front. He had to scream at the top of his lungs now because three doors were open, and the winds pounding downward from above the craft were howling and yowling as the blades hacked them, then carved them again. The wounded winds outside were spilling their innards everywhere.

"You and you and you got portside, five meters out and three-meter spread. As soon as that thing rolls to a stop, one of those spooks over there is gonna make sure it's armed. When he runs like a scared rabbit back to his bunny friends, I want you to di-di the fuck out of there and get back in here. You got that? If we take fire, shout out the direction of fire for the door gunners, then kill as many as you can. If you spot Charlie movin,' hold your position and call out which way he's goin'. You know the drill. If you die out there, it's for freedom—my freedom to stay inside this chopper and survive this piece-of-shit mission.

"You over there, you got door gun as usual. They know we're coming, so nobody's gonna be any farther out than a hundred meters. The tracer rounds are gonna be right on the money. I need suppression! They won't want to damage that thing, so there's only gonna be small arms. You got that? " In that instant the intuition that had evolved into a submerged thought some minutes before suddenly broke through the surface of his consciousness and emerged as a vague idea.

"Maybe . . . we don't need any troops outside at all," he said in an inaudible voice. "Wait one goddamn minute. Maybe we don't need to fire a single goddamn round. It's the machine they want, not us. And for some reason we want them to have it." His voice had started to rise, and the intelligence officers near the front of the chopper stared at him with a look of amazement on their faces.

"Maybe none of those gunships followin' us is armed. Maybe all the ships are carryin' camera crews and observers—window shoppers from Pakistan and Libya! Maybe that's why the brass wouldn't give me the extra troops. This is a dog and pony show for the cartels and the Arabs—and America and Vietnam are co-hosting it! That means . . ."

"You'll never get out of Leavenworth, sergeant!" thundered the young colonel. If I'm not alive to bring charges, one of my officers will. I've already radioed Da Nang about you."

Carruthers scowled at the young colonel. He shook the strange thoughts from his mind and tapped another helmet.

"You follow that thing down and position yourself behind it. If I'm right, Vegas, they want this chopper and those spooks to leave here and go back to Da Nang in one piece—it's all part of a plan, a big business deal. Their fire will all be for show, so as to make this entire enterprise look like the real thing. There's only two safe places in this deal: on this chopper or on top of that machine. Sure, they'll have to kill a few people to make it look good—but wait a minute . . . you ain't Vegas!"

He turned to see Private Vegas at the front of the black box, preparing to move down the ramp. The sergeant tore the tiny photograph from Fulgencio's hand and threw it to the floor. He grabbed the soldier by the front of his flak vest and began dragging him toward the ramp just as it slammed into the ground.

"You fuckin' coward!" the sergeant screamed as he dragged a resisting Fulgencio forward and onto the ramp. "Goddamn coward! You wanna get me killed?" When the two men struggled past him, Simon reached out for Fulgencio with his right hand, seizing him by his shirt collar and yanking him back to the foot of the ramp while the sergeant cursed and pulled back. At that instant the blackness behind the chopper became a blaze of lights as scores of tracer rounds began flashing past the open door.

The men moving on either side of the black box were engulfed by a tempest, by a copulation of metals—iron, brass, aluminum, and steel—that were madly mating with canvas, cloth, and human fluids. In half a microsecond, the heavy black box came to rest about ten feet behind the Chinook. In another slice of time, the young men who were on their bellies outside began firing frantically and screaming that there were hundreds of them—too many of them— all on the starboard side.

"They're dug in! They dug those spider holes yesterday! We've got wounded! Let's get the fuck outta here! Why aren't they coming after us? They're holding back!"

Someone called for the medic, who was busy feeding the door gun. Two frantic troopers tumbled back inside, their clumsy movements inaudible in the din. It was all they could do to hold each other up. Both were bleeding profusely from their upper bodies. The sergeant tugged savagely on Fulgencio's arm, dragging him off the ramp while screaming into his ear.

"Fuckin' coward! Still mopin' about some dead gook baby! Now get over there and kill his big brother. Maybe you can get his father, too."

Summoning every ounce of his strength, Simon braced himself, then grabbed Fulgencio by the shirt collar and flak vest and jerked him out of the tall sergeant's grasp, kicking savagely at the officer's left kneecap. Sergeant Carruthers instantly collapsed to the base of the ramp and groaned. Then Simon watched in slow motion as the bullet that ended Fulgencio's life tore through his own right hand, bringing pieces of his friend's neck and spine with it. He felt Fulgencio's entire body quake and stiffen as though fifty thousand volts of electricity were shooting through him. Simon's face and shoulders were coated with flecks and fragments of Fulgencio. Simon's own flak vest was soaked with his friend's lifeblood.

Fulgencio's bewildered face tottered for a second, then fell to the left and dangled from his shoulders at an odd, impossible angle. It was hanging by the thinnest slice of white gristle and a length of pink windpipe. In another fraction of a moment, the dead soldier crumpled, his head slamming insensibly against the base of the ramp two seconds before the rest of his body. Simon watched him as he fell. He cursed the horror inside his brain that had paralyzed him, that had kept him from reaching out and catching Fulgencio before she slammed into the rich soil of the vineyard. He knelt down by his friend's side for only an instant. When he stood up again, his nostrils were filled with the stench of Fulgencio's desolate sadness and with the distant sweet scent of Pinot noir.

The young junior officer who had been assigned the job of starting the machine once it was stabilized on the ground dashed past Simon. As soon as he came within five feet of the weapon, he jerked violently, then fell over mortally wounded. The young colonel followed the first officer. He was hit by three bullets just six feet from the end of the ramp. Someone pulled their bodies back into the chopper. No one else tried to start the machine.

Simon released his hold on Fulgencio's shirt. He ran to the far side of the machine and began firing at the tree line to his left. "Get the wounded, you son of a bitch," he screamed at the sergeant. It was only then that he realized that Sergeant Carruthers had crawled from the end of the ramp and was sitting completely unprotected on top of the black box. His arms were folded defiantly in front of him, and his holster was empty. His pistol had been tossed to the ground.

"I've finally got this figured out! This is the last thing they're gonna fire at," said Ajax Carruthers with a wide grin. He crawled down and untied one corner of the tarp that was covering the machine, flipped over onto his backside, and began to slither under it, feet first. The Mexican private swung his rifle in an arc to his right and stopped the muzzle at a point just two inches from the sergeant's nose. The two men glared at each other for what seemed like an eternity before Simon eased the pressure of his trigger finger.

Simon tossed away his rifle and lifted the tarp. He wrapped his thumbs and fingers around the sergeant's neck, squeezing with every ounce of his strength. He strangled Ajax Carruthers as the larger man threw desperate savage punches at his chest and stomach. The sergeant grimaced in pain each time the knuckles of his hands pounded against a sharp-edged object made of metal.

"What is that thing?" he wheezed. Then he glanced downward at the secret weapon and saw for the first time that the control box had been detached from it. A wiring harness was hanging down unconnected. PFC Vegas had stolen the box and shoved it inside his flak vest. The sergeant could see its blinking lights illuminating the grunt's neck and chin.

Simon slammed a fist into Carruthers's ear as two, then three bullets ripped into the ground at his feet and one projectile grazed his helmet. He wondered dimly how the enemy soldiers could possibly miss at point-blank range. Then he knew: The sergeant was right. They were not trying to cause any real damage. Their primary objective was the safety of the machine. But why had the two young officers been shot? Had they been left out of the military-industrial information loop? Had they died for verisimilitude? Hadn't they been informed that the machine was to be delivered as is, untouched and in mint condition? It came to Simon in a flash of insight: It wasn't the bomb that the North Vietnamese soldiers wanted, it was the Antikythera device. They weren't going to let anyone touch it.

He stopped moving and dropped his hands, then stood staring at the demon that was desperately clawing the air for oxygen. Carruthers stiffened, then slumped backward onto the tarp. His lungs were heaving for breath. Above the machine, three choppers circled slowly overhead. Simon could see that none of them was a gunship. The entire engagement had probably lasted thirty to forty seconds. They could have killed everyone. Instead, they had only killed the people who tried to touch the controls—controls that were no longer attached. The bullet that hit Fulgencio must have been a mistake, a panic shot or a ricochet.

Simon grabbed a grunt who was on his knees and attempting to aim his weapon with a shattered and useless arm, his face and eyes covered with dirt and blood. He dragged the soldier up the ramp, stopping only long enough to reach down and pick up a small black-and-white photograph. Someone had already dragged Fulgencio's body up into the belly of the chopper. Simon stared at the photo for a moment, then turned and went into the Chinook.

"Anybody else out there?" shouted the medic, immediately taking charge of the wounded soldier. "I don't get it, man. The Chinook stayed put, and not a single round hit us. Anybody else out there?"

Simon looked out into the morning light and saw that the perfect symmetry of the black box was marred on one side by the shape of a barely conscious man. At one edge of the tarp he could see the black waffled soles of a pair of combat boots.

"Anyone else out there?" shouted the medic again while preparing a morphine syrette.

"All accounted for," lied Simon. "All fifteen Mexicans are in here," he said truthfully as he looked down at the body of his friend.

At that instant the rear door of the chopper began to close, and the ship lifted off. Simon sat down. Raising his bleeding, mangled hand up to his face, he inspected the wound carefully. The back of his hand had exploded outward. He could see yellowish bones and purple ligaments. The blood had already clotted, and the pain was coming in stabbing pulses. The skin around the wound was hanging like the petals of some hellish flower. He knew that he would have these scars for the rest of his life. Until the day he died, he would have micro-chimeras, pieces of Fulgencio Garza living inside him.

Simon sat with Fulgencio, conversing with him until the chopper reached Da Nang. He had carried his friend's body from the top of the ramp and lowered it slowly into a canvas seat. Then he went back for the young soldier's face, cradling it against his chest. He placed the head carefully atop the gaping wound between its owner's shoulders, then sat down in front of his friend. Even as other soldiers looked on, the two men sat face to face finishing a conversation that would have been impossible an hour ago. Simon gestured and shrugged; he even laughed as he spoke with the unmoving body.

When they arrived at the air base, Simon walked up to the front of the Chinook and asked one of the surviving officers what their coordinates had been. The young first lieutenant smiled weakly and handed him a torn, crumpled grid map, then turned away to hide his tears. He was sitting at the side of the dead colonel. A captain across from them was cradling the body of the officer who had been shot while trying to reach for the controls on the machine. He had just died of his wounds.

"He asked me to go visit his mama," said the tearful captain. "Then he said the strangest thing just before he died. He said he heard lions. I think I heard him right. He said he heard lions—they were coming real close." The captain turned his face away for a private moment of grief. A few seconds later, having managed to control his sorrow, he turned back to Simon. "I didn't see anything," he said with a weak smile. "As far as I'm concerned, Sergeant Carruthers died for freedom."

As they all walked out onto the tarmac, the other two surviving officers walked up to him, each whispering the same thing into his ear.

"I didn't see anything."

"I didn't see anything, either. Fuck him."

Simon waited with Fulgencio until a team from the graves detail arrived to cart the bodies away. Every member of the five-man crew was dressed in rubber clothes, even in the stifling heat. When they got to the chopper, they put on heavy gloves and began hurriedly placing the three bodies into body bags.

"Put that head in there!" a specialist fifth class barked at a specialist fourth class. Covering his nose and mouth with the crook of his left arm, the spec-four grabbed Fulgencio's head with his right hand, holding it by the hair. He gagged twice as he hurried to the open bag and dropped the head into it. Then he tore off his rubber gloves and ran down the tarmac to an outhouse. Simon unzipped the bag. He knelt down beside Fulgencio, bending over his friend's body and studying his face carefully for the last time, memorizing the color of his eyes, the tiny hairs on his chin, and the curvature of his jaw.

The two friends would not speak again for many years. A pleasantry was passed and a solemn promise was made. Then Simon stepped back and watched as the soldiers lifted Fulgencio's body bag, pulling it away from the eucalyptus stump. The next time these two men would speak, the head, weighed down by an orchid lei around its neck, would casually answer back. The spec-five could see that the Mexican private was crying. He lit a cigarette and offered it to Simon, who shook his head.

"You better get that hand looked at. It looks like corned beef hash with ketchup. Are you guys friends?" asked the spec-five as he exhaled a thick plume of smoke. Simon nodded.

"How long you been in country?"

"I'm not in country," answered Simon, fighting back a new wave of tears. "I'm incontinent."

The spec-five look puzzled for a moment. He shrugged his shoulders and walked away muttering to himself.

"Fuckin' idiot. Vietnam ain't a continent. Some people don't know shit."

13

SAINT JOAN'S SON

Simon waved goodbye to Jesse Washington, who waved back from the front porch of his new home. The young man in the Hawaiian shirt watched as the Mexican Magus gained speed, then became a brown streak as he flashed across the horizon. Simon was on his way to San Francisco—back to San Quentin. An instant later, the radio host said farewell to his audience while lifting the stylus from the last groove of a spinning record. He removed the black disc from the platter and slid it into a sleeve. Then he flicked the toggle switches that shut down Kevin's beautiful amplifiers.

He walked to the staff lunchroom and bought a cup of their awful coffee, which he took to a small booth that was hidden behind a bank of vending machines. He surveyed the room, and when he was certain that no one was watching, he reached into his briefcase. The Antikythera device was still warm from the trip to Waco, then to Boca Raton and back. A minute later, every light from one end of the prison to the other dimmed perceptibly. Video monitors went black for several seconds, and alarm systems momentarily switched to battery backup.

Ten minutes later, Simon opened his eyes. He shook his head to clear his mind of the horrible, wondrous sights that he had just witnessed. Placing the Antikythera device back in his briefcase, he got up from the table and walked toward the administration building. There were tears in his eyes and a tight smile on his lips as he pulled open a heavy door. He brushed his lapels with his hand, watching as white ash and grimy soot from fifteenth-century France drifted to the ground. He then stepped into the reception area and the brightly lighted offices of the warden and his staff. One of the four women toiling in the room looked up and smiled at Simon before informing him that Warden Harris was due back in ten minutes.

"I'm really sorry to hear about your radio show," she said softly. "All of us here really enjoyed listenin' to it. Never heard nothin' like it. Sons never listen to their mothers, you know. I know my boy was listenin' to you 'cause he told me so. He said you insulted him. I told him that I'm the one that's insulted, havin' to come to work in this corner of hell just to see my baby boy walkin' by into the yard. I've done years in this prison, and I ain't never stole nothin' nor hurt nobody, not a single soul."

The other women nodded and smiled sadly. One of them waved at Simon. "The warden is with that consultant fellow from the East Coast—a doctor who's been here half a dozen times in the last few months. Something about that guy gives me the heebie-jeebies, Mr. Vegas," said Margie. The other women shivered and nodded their heads in enthusiastic agreement. "He is one strange man. Something about them eyes. Hoo-doo eyes."

"And that hand!" said another voice. "What's with that funky right hand?"

Simon unconsciously hid his own right hand in his jacket pocket and walked to a small waiting area. He sat down at a table that had recently been moved from the wall to the center of the room. He smiled to himself. Against the warden's halfhearted orders, these women were always rearranging and redecorating the office in an effort to make it homier. There were three vases of flowers in various locations and an emaciated cactus in a small window.

A few minutes later the door opened, and two loud, jovial men sauntered in. The first to enter was a laughing Warden Harris, who immediately waved at Simon. The second man walked into the room seconds after the warden. He was smiling and chuckling heartily until he glanced to his right and his gaze fell upon Simon Magus Vegas.

In another instant the laughter had vanished completely, and Jeffrey Therage was standing paralyzed in the doorway. There was a look of horror etched into every pore of his narrow face. He stared wide-eyed at Simon with his mouth agape, inspecting him slowly and carefully, from his footwear to his Mexican visage. The doctor tried to say something but could only stutter, his jaws moving spasmodically. He could only stammer and spit. His left hand shot up to his throat. He looked like a man who was suffocating—drowning in air and confusion.

"Do . . . do the of two you know each other?" asked Warden Harris tentatively and with obvious trepidation. The look on the doctor's face was alarming. No one answered the warden's question, so he moved self-consciously to one side and watched as Dr. Therage finally managed to regain some of his composure. The doctor walked unsteadily toward the center of the room and slowly circumnavigated the seated Simon Magus Vegas.

The women on the warden's staff had all dropped whatever task they were performing and were watching the bizarre pantomime that was playing out before them in the center of their workspace.

Dr. Jeffrey Therage was tall, and as gaunt as a longtime prisoner of war. He had long waves of graying hair that perfectly matched the subtle striping of his blue suit. He had a face that would always be described as darkly handsome despite his sunken cheeks and yellowed teeth. His diction and his enunciation of syllables were crisp and perfect. His pronunciation of words contained remnants of several foreign languages and artifacts from many different dialects.

Despite his professorial carriage and his Continental bearing, however, there was something fundamentally disturbing about him, something vulgar and crass. His eyes were cavernous. They were deeply set and seemed exhausted beyond description. It was as though someone had transplanted the world-weary eyes of a ninety-year-old insomniac into the face of a man in his forties.

Then there was that right hand. It was covered by a black leather glove that extended over the wrist and slid under the right sleeve of his coat. Every inch of skin beneath that glove was intended to be hidden from view, but a few stitches had come loose, and part of the hand was visible to everyone in the room. The skin under the sheathing was greenish and shot through with a web of capillaries that were almost jet-black. The back of the thumb looked mutilated and gangrenous.

Simon rose from his chair and walked toward the doctor, politely extending his scarred right hand. Instead of extending his own right hand in a proper greeting, the doctor gingerly placed his briefcase on the floor and extended the left hand. After an uncomfortable, awkward handshake, the briefcase returned to the left hand as the right hand disappeared into a coat pocket like a black mamba into a burrow.

"Do I know you?" asked the doctor in a trembling, timid squeak of a voice that could barely be heard. The urbane, educated bearing of the world's leading expert on the painless termination of human life had vanished. He repeated the question, this time sounding even more desperate. His antediluvian eyes were moist and pleading. They looked like the wet, weepy eyes of a chained elephant.

"Please, sir, do I know you?" he begged plaintively as his eyes welled up with tears. "Have we spoken before? Did you once have long red hair? Have we met, face to face, you and I? Have we met?"

"We have met," answered Simon brusquely. There was anger in his eyes. "Is Dr. Silver in his office?" he asked the warden and his staff without breaking eye contact with Dr. Therage.

"Yes," said Margie. "Shall I call him?" Simon nodded. "Dr. Therage, do you know someone named Juan Largo Argento or John Silver? He's had a variety of other names."

Dr. Therage shook his head no. The anxiety in his face was approaching a look of delirium. He was perspiring profusely and seemed unable even to breathe, let alone take in his immediate surroundings. At that moment Dr. Silver emerged from his office and stood in the doorway. He was wearing a dark full-length coat that almost covered a solitary shoe. He looked directly at Dr. Therage, who jerked his gaze away from Simon to focus on the man who had just emerged from a darkened room to his left.

The instant their eyes met, both men threw out their arms, flailing blindly, madly searching for a nearby chair or a wall—something, anything, to cling to. They fainted dead away at the same instant, crashing dumbly to the office floor like a narcoleptic pair of synchronized swimmers collapsing in perfect unison at poolside.

Dr. Therage's briefcase struck the floor and burst open, spilling its contents across the carpet. The black leather glove flew from his right hand. Silver's coat had flown open, and a prosthetic limb that had not been fully secured came free of his bent knee. All of the loose straps and belts that had not been properly fastened lay fanned out on the carpet like a beached giant squid made of metal, bone, and leather.

When they saw what had been concealed by the glove and, far worse, what had been hidden inside the briefcase, the women screamed at the tops of their lungs and covered their horrified eyes. When the third leg tumbled from Silver-Argento's clothing, Margie wailed like a banshee, climbing across her desk and scattering two weeks' worth of hard work. She then clambered to the top of a file cabinet to get as far away as she could from the hideous objects lying there on the floor.

A trio of guards burst into the room, kicking their way through the door with their guns drawn and leveled menacingly. When they saw what had been deposited on the carpet, two of them hastily retreated into the hallway and used their radios to call for reinforcements, while the third fell to his knees and vomited a pound of chicken wings and hot sauce into a nearby wastebasket.

The object from the briefcase had fallen to the carpet and clattered across the floor until it came to a stop at the warden's feet. One of the women in the office screamed and fainted at her desk. Her suddenly inanimate face slammed heavily against a computer keyboard as her body slumped to the floor. No one moved to help her. Now there were three people passed out on the floor of the office. Simon walked over to the warden, and the two men exchanged confused glances before bending down to inspect the hideous thing.

"Simon, who are these men?" asked a visibly shaken Warden Harris.

"This morning I had only a hazy recollection of them," answered Simon. "I've caught glimpses of them in gangs and mobs all over the world. I seemed to remember seeing them together in front of a cathedral in Western Europe—sometime in the fifteenth century. To be certain, I flew there just a few minutes ago—right after the show ended."

"A few minutes ago?" asked the warden, who was staring down at the object next to his feet. "What are you talking about? Is everyone on my staff stark raving mad?"

Simon did not answer. He got down on all fours and studied the metal form. It must have weighed twenty pounds. It was fashioned from two pieces of hammered iron that had been fastened together with hand-forged hinges. No modern tools had fabricated this horrid piece. Only muscle and sinew could have done this work. A thousand hammer blows at glowing iron by blacksmiths long dead had been required to beat this reluctant iron into the shape of a right hand. It was made in two pieces so that it could be opened and closed like a clam shell.

There was a riveted hinge in the curve between the thumb and index finger and an ominous pair of thumbscrews hanging from the opposite side. The screws had been loosened by the impact of the fall, and the internal workings of the metal hand lay exposed. A second woman fainted when she realized what it was that she was seeing. She, too, collapsed in a heap, joining her coworker on the rug.

The interior of both halves of the metal hand was studded with dozens of half-inch spikes that had been sharpened to ominous pinpoints. They were discolored to a muddy red by bits of dried blood and rotting organic matter still clinging to the tip. Slam the two halves together, then tighten down the thumbscrews, and the human flesh trapped between those spikes would experience paragraphs, pages, whole chapters of the most eloquent, inexpressible agony. The people who were still conscious and standing in the warden's office were staring at a miniature Iron Maiden that had been custom built for a single purpose: the ongoing mortification and mutilation of the flesh of Dr. Therage's right hand.

"The rivets are not the originals. They have all been replaced," Simon announced to no one in particular. "It looks like the changes were made in the late fifteenth century. This exquisite retrofit can only be the work of Giovan Battista from Urbino. Those particularly sharp pieces near the center of the palm had to have been honed a century later by Filippo Negroli. Look at the grooves made by the file here at the inner thumb. It has to be Negroli. No one else could fashion an edge like that. No machine and few men could do it today. The thumbscrews and the tiny rack that is used to stretch the index finger until the joints pop out of their sockets had to have been designed and fabricated by Konrad Seusenhofer of the Tirol."

The warden moaned and turned his face away.

"It's all true . . . every word of it . . . but how could you possibly know all of this? It isn't possible!" said a groggy, slurred voice. It was Dr. Therage, who had regained consciousness while Simon was examining the horrendous metal hand. Next to the doctor,

Christopher Gauger, whose name had been Kristof Gaugere in the fifteenth century, was blinking his eyes and groaning like a drunk. The women lying beside him on the carpet would not wake up for another fifteen minutes.

"Hand-hater," spat Gaugere as he picked up his artificial leg, brushed off his clothing with the back of his hand, then stormed angrily out of the office on his way to the parking lot. "Hand-hater," he growled again as he walked down the long hallway. He would never again return to San Quentin Prison.

"Limb-loather!" shouted Therage as his eternal associate stormed out of the room. He picked up the small Iron Maiden and put it back in his suitcase, and with a wave of his mangled hand, he was gone. The two men would climb into their cars and drive at blindingly high speeds for hours in opposite directions—one toward Juneau, the other toward Tijuana. Each man would assume a new name and a new identity. They would board planes, then ships, then rickshaws and oxcarts, then travel on foot in random directions for days, then months, one through India and the other across all of Africa.

They would run away from one another and toward the most impoverished, most violent places on earth. Each man would finally stop running when all of his money and almost all of his life energy was spent. Each man would collapse in a room in a cheap flophouse in Beirut or Baghdad or Tripoli.

After lying in a semiconscious state for days on the filthiest beds on earth, each man would finally awake and stumble bleary-eyed down the hall and behind the stairs to the only men's room in the four-story hotel whose outer walls were pocked with bullet holes. There they would discharge defeated, depleted, dejected streams of piss into one of a matched pair of filthy urinals, one eternally haunted man standing right beside the other—yet again.

As he flew, the Mexican Flyboy made an entry into logbook number ninety-one: just back from Waco, now back to France—for the second time. Haizebeltza, a pugnacious Basque wind, had ambushed him just west of Calais. The unruly gust had sent the Mexican Flyboy reeling and spinning. When he finally regained his balance, he found himself miles away from his intended flight path. Soaring at an altitude of fifteen thousand feet above the heave and swell of the frigid Atlantic whitecaps, Simon glanced down at the yellowed map that was unfolded in his left hand and flapping wildly in the wind. With a nod he confirmed to himself for the third time in twenty seconds that the correct coordinates had been entered into the machine.

He was nearing his destination. In the last few seconds he had flown past the dazzling artificial lights of the island of Manhattan in the early twentieth century and the pitch-black Azores in the seventeenth century, and he was now streaking over the English Channel. He could see Sainte-Mére-Église and a stretch of land that would someday be designated as Utah Beach. The next point of interest would be Le Havre as it was in the early 1600s.

Simon shook his head sadly. He had done all of this twice before, once on one of his first test flights of the device, and again this morning. But this morning he had not landed. There had not been enough time to set down, but he had confirmed his suspicions. He had spotted the man from a hundred feet above the cobblestones. Coming back to this particular time and this place was disturbing, unsettling to him. Lenny Hudson had mentioned a name. That name had been vaguely familiar. Now he knew that the man was down there. Simon had to see him, face to face. His first trip to these physical and temporal coordinates had made him sick to his stomach. He took a deep breath and steeled himself against what he was about to witness.

The small yellow bulb in the center of the device began to blink, first once a second, then once every tenth of a second, indicating that the temporal circuits were closing in on the designated year. When the yellow light was fully illuminated, the green light next to it began to blink, meaning that the circuitry responsible for acquiring the exact month was functioning. When the orange light began to glow, the target date was approaching.

When all six bulbs were on, Simon would be descending to a point just above the Place du Vieux-Marché in the center of Rouen, France. The date was May the 30th in the year 1431. If everything had gone perfectly, he would be touching down at least five minutes before the flames were lit, and he would not have to see her writhing in the center of that awful fire. He couldn't bear to see it again.

The Flyboy cursed loudly when he saw the leaping flames and, surrounding her, a thousand faces that had been illuminated by a combination of fascination and absolute certainty. He used the sleeve of his coat to cover his eyes and to wipe a flood of tears from his lips and cheeks. No matter how precise his calculations had been, no matter how many times the machine was recalibrated and readjusted, for some unknown reason the Antikythera device always forced him to be a witness to the suffering! Was windage the problem? Was it the constant ferocity of the winds that was disturbing the delicate mechanisms? The machine would never be perfect. He and Hephaestus Segundo could work on it forever and it would never be perfect.

"*Dulcet et decorum est. In vovo legem magicarium. Dulcet et decorum est,*" he chanted over and over while stifling his tears. He fumbled with the knobs, jerking them awkwardly counterclockwise, and watched as the red light dimmed and the fire finally began to recede from Joan's pretty face and hair. The retreating fire line continued downward toward her small breasts, pulling away patches of blackness as it crept toward her hips and then on to her tiny feet, reweaving and replacing every stitch in her garment and every cell in her skin as it moved backward toward her toes. Her blackened and scorched face, once striated with grisly char, was pink and vibrant once again. The Flyboy closed his eyes and sighed as Joan's coarse gown fully reappeared to cover her lovely body.

He twisted the knob to the left. When the savage fire had shriveled away to meek nothingness, he watched the area at the front of the pyre until he spotted the man he had come to meet—the man he had crossed heaving oceans of minutes and endless constellations of inches to see. That particular man was down there—walking backward, a prisoner of his time. He was walking away from the frightened, struggling girl, and away from the mountain of dried firewood stacked beneath her feet. Simon could see burning pieces of kindling in his right hand. The man walked backward until he reached a small fire that was leaping in a cauldron. He touched the burning sticks to the flame in the iron pot, and when he pulled the bundle of wood away from the fire, the kindling was whole again and unburned.

The man stood at attention between two expressionless English soldiers and awaited the solemn, reverential nods of the head from His Holiness Bishop Cauchon, from the English military, and from the churchmen of the inquisitorial court. The young woman whose prowess in battle had elevated Charles VII to the throne of France had been tried not as a prisoner of war but as a heretic in order to defame and depose the new king. It was the Burgundians, the pro-English faction in southern France, who had sought to burn her alive. The best seats were filled with military men and men of the Church Militant.

But the attention of the crowd was not on those men. All eyes were staring in awe at a figure that was descending from on high. There were no movie stars in the fifteenth century. There was no personality who would be instantly recognized by everyone in the stupefied crowd, so the Flyboy had come down from the sky disguised as the usual pre-Renaissance representation of an angel: a small, milk-white, ceramic-skinned androgyne with long, spatulate fingers, miniature feet, and undulations of reddish hair piled on its head. A tiny pair of ineffectual wings protruded from its shoulders, and a dull yellow aura surrounded its face.

He floated slowly to the ground, landing directly in front of the two English guards and the man with the kindling in his right hand. All three men were clearly petrified. Their eyes were wide, and their faces and hands trembled spasmodically.

In 1431, almost every peasant lived out his life and died within a ten-mile radius of his place of birth. In 1431, it was considered quite hygienic to bathe once each summer. There were no photographs or fan magazines anywhere on the flat earth, and no newspapers in most of the world. The only images that would be universally recognized were dour pious representations that had been heavily scrutinized by church censors. This authority extended its patronage only to those artists whose renditions of biblical figures conformed to the current canon of propriety. In one era artists were not allowed to depict the female breast, while in a later time the mammary glands were considered de rigueur, and new artists were then commissioned to add newly authorized breasts to old paintings.

That is why the nursing Madonna's breasts were often portrayed as jutting out from a shoulder or dangling awkwardly from an armpit. That is how the archangel Micha-el, once a mighty earth-fertilizing lightning snake to the Chaldeans, once part of Mercury's caduceus, then a terrible being with six wings and four faces, slowly transmuted into a girlish, white-skinned, red-haired twelve-year-old boy with perfect feet and pink cheeks. It was this version of Michael that the stunned crowd in the Place du Vieux-Marché saw descending from the clouds and settling to the ground just in front of the executioner and his two guards.

"What is your name?" Simon asked the man who was standing

between the two British soldiers. "Comment vous appellez vous?"

"Je m'appel . . . I am Geoffroy Therage," answered the man, his face contorted in abject fear at the sight of a heavenly being.

"Are you here to take me to hell? Am I going to hell for burning this girl?" asked the frightened executioner as the Flyboy's feet touched the ground. "Please tell me, am I going to hell for burning this girl!" he screamed.

The executioner attempted to place the kindling into the cloth sack that hung from his belt, but his arms and hands were shaking uncontrollably. The two guards at his side had turned their faces away from Simon, averting their eyes in stark terror. Simon noticed that Geoffroy Therage had been madly rubbing his right hand during their conversation. The fingers and palm on that hand were red and raw from the crazed flurries of friction. Drops of blood dripped from the fingernails and stained the cobblestones below.

"Why does it hurt so much, blessed angel?" implored Monsieur Therage. "The pain in my hand is terrible. I can't sleep anymore. My wife won't let me sleep in our bed because I scratch it constantly in my sleep. My blood is spattered all over my clothes and the bedsheets." He dropped to his knees and began to wail. Glancing around, he raised his arms to the heavens.

The Mexican Magus turned to look at the faces of the townspeople surrounding the pyre. To his surprise, they looked exactly like the crowd in Waco, Texas. Could they be the same people? There was a lifeless smugness in their faces, a dreary amalgam of fear, faith, and arousal in their eyes.

"I can tell you this, Monsieur Therage. You will botch this holy pyre of yours. Her left leg, her intestines, and her heart won't burn, and the Englishmen will be furious with you. The English generals will blame the church bishops, and the church will blame you. They demanded cinders with no possibility of a relic."

Therage shook his head in confusion. The youthfulness in his eyes seemed to be draining away with the blood that was dripping from his hand.

"You'll use that right hand of yours to rub oil and charcoal and raw sulfur into her chest cavity and onto her heart. You will rub the chemicals onto her legs, and you'll restart the fire twice in order to please your English overlords. But the chemicals won't work. Her heart and liver will discolor, but they won't burn. A young monk will later say that he found her heart in the smoldering rubble. He will tell everyone that it was still beating when he cupped it in his hands.

"A peasant will run through the blazing embers of the pyre in his bare feet and grab her charred left leg. He will run home with it and carefully hide it in the straw mattress of his own bed before tending to the third-degree burns on the soles of his feet. This guard standing to my left is named Kristof Gaugere."

Simon Magus Vegas moved to his left until he was looking directly into the eyes of the frightened, trembling guard.

"You, Monsieur Gaugere, will do exactly as your uniform demands. You will chase that poor peasant into his hovel and beat him to a bloody pulp in front of his cowering wife and children. You will proudly return the charred leg of that beautiful young woman to Monsieur Therage. The feel of her soft leg will never leave your dreams."

Then Simon muttered a magical incantation and reassumed his true form. The crowd gasped when the ethereal, iridescent form of Michael was suddenly replaced by a brown-skinned man with graying reddish hair. He rose ten feet from the ground and approached the maid, whose face was filled with a look of calm amazement that had completely displaced the terror that had possessed it for so many months.

He gently untied her hands and feet, put his arms around her, and lifted her away from the stake and the massive pile of unburned wood. He had done these same things before but had to do it all over again in order to meet Therage—to study his face and look into his eyes. The first time, he had paid no attention to him.

"It's Simon Magus!" shouted Bishop Cauchon, who had risen to his gout-ridden feet. He began gesticulating wildly and calling out to Saint Peter—demanding that he come down from on high and do battle with the brown Persian heretic.

"Shoot him down!" shouted the bishop at the English troops. "Shoot an arrow through the heretic! The longbowman who kills him will go to heaven! Where are the spirits of the air when you need them? Put an arrow through his head and you'll sit at the side of John the Baptist!"

A few people in the crowd began throwing rocks, but they all fell far short. The Flyboy raised a hand and uttered a few words as some of the soldiers shot arrows into the air, but none of them could reach him and his precious cargo. Their arcs ended abruptly, and the missiles all fell straight down to earth as though they had hit an invisible shield.

"I have to feed my family!" moaned the guard above the noise of an increasingly restless crowd. "We have to eat!"

"Is that all?" shouted a desperate Geoffroy Therage to the figures levitating above his head. "Is there more? Please tell me!"

Simon did not answer. In a few centuries, Therage would be in Paris using his right hand to pull the release on the fabulous death machine of Dr. Joseph-Ignace Guillotin, who had proclaimed to all of France that the condemned prisoner would feel nothing but a "refreshing coolness." In another century, Therage would appear in Milan. There the doctor would use that right hand to turn hundreds of poor young boys into castrati.

Years later he would be in the Belgian Congo using a thick metal blade to slice through the wrists of African slaves. He and his lackey Kristof Gaugere would load thousands of bleeding hands into woven baskets and send them back to King Leopold II for the monarch's own personal inspection. Then the two men would appear on the decks of various slave ships plying the infamous Middle Passage.

"What are they doing to me down there? What are they doing?" asked Joan of Arc without lifting her face from the Mexican Flyboy's chest. Her thin arms were wrapped tightly around his neck. She was still shivering, and her lovely skin seemed to fluoresce with portents of flame. She jerked and shuddered in his arms as harbingers of heat cut into her skin.

"You know what they're doing. Don't look down. Please don't look." The Flyboy hastily turned the controls to new settings. It was he who looked down and sighed inconsolably as he watched Geoffroy Therage reach out his wretched hand to light the small bundle once again. He cringed as the executioner turned to face the pyre and dutifully waited for the signal. Simon began fine-tuning the control knobs and watched as each of the lights began to flash wildly.

"Now you can look."

Joan looked down and laughed with astonishment when she saw a France that was somehow familiar, yet she could barely recognize what her eyes beheld. There were smooth black pathways leading everywhere, and metal objects with bright torches on their faces were moving at impossible speeds along those paths. She saw people getting in and out of those carriages but wondered why none of them was being pulled by horses or mules or oxen.

She saw soaring buildings from one horizon to the other. They all seemed to be made of transparent walls. She saw enormous boats speeding up and down the Seine. Not one of them had a mast or a sail. She saw wide boulevards and placid parks and marveled at a tall metal tower in the center of a Paris that had grown from a sleepy village into a city of unimaginable size. Everywhere she looked, there seemed to be lights that burned without fire—without flame.

"Where are we going?" she asked after a long silence. "Am I already there? Why do I seem to believe in my deepest heart that somewhere out there I have a little son? I have a son? Is there a little black-haired boy somewhere out there waiting for me to come home and care for him? I know there is. He's waiting for me. Memories seem to be coming to me now in droves, like the fluttering butterflies back home in my papa's meadow. They would see me and flutter to me in a cloud of color that would block out the sky overhead. Hundreds of them would land on my hair, on my eyelashes, on my shoulders . . . they were so weightless . . . so lovely. The sight of it would make my mama cry.

"I can still hear my papa's laughter. He called me his *petit papillon,* you know. That's what I've named my sweet little boy. I call him *petit papillon.*" Joan began to quietly sob, and the Flyboy's shirt was soon wet with tears.

"My son and I have breakfast together in the morning and spend the day going on long walks by the sea. We laugh all day long. Every day we go to the market and buy our food, but he eats so much chocolate candy! For some reason he never gets a cavity in his teeth! He won't wear good shoes, only these orange things he calls flip-flops. I have a next-door neighbor named Queenie. She is such a wonderful woman. Who is she? Did someone set her on fire, too? The house behind mine is empty, but they say a family is coming—a woman and her sons. I have all of these wonderful memories—but I'm not supposed to have them, am I? I love these memories, but are they really mine?"

The Flyboy did not answer. He could see that she was filled with questions, some of which she was too frightened to ask.

"Your mama and papa fought for you," said Simon. "They never gave up. They fought the church, the government of France . . . they fought everyone because of what was done to you. Do you know that you are a saint?"

"A saint?" said Joan without expression. "I would rather have one minute in my parents' arms."

She closed her eyes and remembered the warmth of the kitchen in their small home. She could see her family sitting down to *petit déjeuner*. Jacques and Isabelle, her three brothers, and her beloved sister are all waiting patiently as young Joan dawdles upstairs for a few minutes more before coming down from her bedroom.

"Are we all slaves—even me? Are you Michael? Are we enslaved by our own times, by our own stories? Are you Michael?" she whispered into his ear after a long silence. She asked the question in a meek, humbled voice as they passed over Iceland. "If you are radiant Michael, I saw you seven years ago in a field near my home. Do you remember me? I did everything you told me to do. Or were you only a butterfly? Are you Michael come to take me up to the heavenly gates?"

"No, I'm not Michael. I'm Simon, come to take you to Florida."

"Why did they do that to me, Simon? Wasn't I found innocent? No charge was sustained."

"You wore men's clothing," said Simon.

"Like Hypatia of Alexandria?" said Joan softly.

"You didn't know your place."

"I've seen you before, Monsieur Simon. I saw you once before in Rouen. We made this trip once before, didn't we? But that's not possible, is it? I was burned to death only once. Still . . . the last time we met, I could not understand a word you said. Your voice was like a noisy gong or a clanging cymbal. *Maintenant*, now it's almost as clear as a bell. Almost. Are you an angel?" she asked as they gained altitude high over Newfoundland. "Are you an angel, monsieur?"

"No," he answered. "I'm a Mexican."

14

AN IMITATION OF PRIVACY

Zeke walked into Simon's cluttered office on the Berkeley campus. Behind three tall stacks of paper on the desk was a Mexican professor who had been staring at them for over an hour. When he looked up and saw Zeke coming through the door, Simon's face lit up like a beacon. At last he had a legitimate excuse to ignore all those term papers.

"Glad to see me, eh? Well, I've been to Port Arthur," said Zeke as he walked toward the desk. He leaned over the piles of work and handed his friend a folded sheet of paper. Simon opened it and stared silently at the contents for three or four minutes before refolding it pensively and putting it into his jacket pocket. He exhaled wistfully.

"I've been running database searches every night since I got back from East Texas," continued Zeke, this time with an edge of excitement in his voice, "and I've found someone you'll want to meet right away. He's ninety miles away from where we are right now. I interviewed him just last week, but we could go see him tomorrow morning if you want. He's out in the suburbs of Sacramento. But you should see him soon, Simon. He doesn't look good. He's seventy-seven years old, and he's in a convalescent home. The old guy has to lug around an oxygen tank, and he still smokes like a chimney. He remembers you, Simon. He never learned your name, but he remembers you. He wants to talk to you. I've found the big skydiver who almost broke your neck when you were a boy. I found Peter Keyes."

"I hate this place. I can't take it here no more," the red-faced man said as he exhaled dolefully. He slumped forward on a green leather-ette couch, grunting and rolling his prodigious body in an effort to extricate himself from the deep, groaning cushions that had capit-ulated, surrendering completely after hours of suffocating beneath his enormous butt. In the air around and above his head was the shattering rattle and clatter of spoons and forks being spilled onto the floor, the repeated slide and thud of melamine trays being angrily stacked on a wheeled cart by a disgruntled kitchen worker who was on her third straight shift.

Below all of this was the gentle tinkle of soup spoons and the sibilant slurp of people sucking up creamed pea soup. There were leitmotifs: the clack-clack of butter knives stabbing at shivering multicolored cubes of gelatin, and the dull thumping of feet and soft slippers as they slowly transmuted into hooves. Soaring above it all was the mewling, saccharine, sycophantic blather of a game show announcer describing yet another new car to a dayroom full of people who no longer cared about such things.

"Come on, let's get outta here. I gotta go outside," grumbled Peter Keyes. "At least I can smoke out there. They filter all the god-damn air in here, and they've got humidifiers runnin' everywhere. When the heaters ain't on, the AC is runnin' full blast. Did you know that a man's mind and body starts gettin' weak if the tempera-ture around him never changes? I read that someplace. That's the plan here, you know. They sign you up to an ironclad, nonrefund-able twelve-month contract, then they kill you off in eight months. That way they get to double-bill your bed. Now they're selling these policies where investors can bet on whether or not you make your twelve months. A man can't even die the way he wants to."

He managed to rise unsteadily to his feet, swaying a bit until he regained his balance; then, with his oxygen tank in tow, he walked down a hallway toward a distant door. The battered dark green tank was mounted on a pair of wobbly, long-suffering rubber wheels, with a bent metal handle that he gripped with his left hand. There was a long, thin transparent tube connected to a red valve situated on the top of the tank, with the other end clipped to one of the man's enormous hair-clogged nostrils. He leaned on the tank handle with his left hand in order to maintain his balance while his right hand fished furiously through the pockets of his pajamas for a contraband cigarette and a pack of matches.

When he reached the exit door, he turned around and studied the interior of the large room that he had just abandoned. Some familiar denizens of the home had already minced and shuffled in from all directions to claim his coveted spot on the couch. One of them had spilled a plate of miniature waffles during this slow-motion melee and was frantically trying to get the attention of an orderly. There was thick brown syrup dripping from his muzzle and his pajama sleeve.

"They filter the water. They filter the air. They filter the food! The weather in here never changes," the big man said in a deep, breathy voice as he shuffled along in his pajamas and disposable slippers. "No one is ever too cold or too hot. It's always exactly seventy-one degrees in here. Do you know why?"

He didn't wait for an answer.

"Because temperatures above seventy-two degrees loosen the sphincter. That's a scientific fact. Samoans shit all the time; Eskimos never do. Have you ever seen an Eskimo shit? Keep the temperature just one degree lower than that, and the bedpans stay empty. The orderlies have less to do. That's how it goes in here.

"There ain't no fall, no winter, no sunburn, no frostbite. No one ever gets hungry. Nothin' ever happens in this place. There ain't no greed in here—no lust— nothin'. Reminds me of those old hymns that my mother always used to sing—somethin' about heavenly shores and never growin' old. I guess this is as close to heaven as anyone's ever getting, and I hate it—every inch of it.

"Hell, for the first two years in this place, I didn't have one chubby—not a single hard-on. I tell ya, my pecker had gone AWOL on me. They must be puttin' somethin' in the food. Come on out back," he said with a toss of his head in the general direction of the outdoors. "There's a table and some chairs out here on the patio. No one ever comes out here. The place is always empty.

"What's wrong with your friend?" he asked, nodding toward Zeke. "He looks like he's seen a ghost. Last time he was here, he couldn't stop talkin'. This time he ain't said a goddamn word."

⌐

The two-hour drive to Sacramento had been marked by a condition that was commonplace for Simon Magus Vegas but exceedingly rare for Zeke: complete silence. Between the two of them, they had uttered only eleven words as they passed through El Cerrito, Crockett, and across the bridge into Vallejo. Both men had been lost in their own private thoughts during a ninety-mile trip that seemed to take no more than ten or twenty minutes. Zeke had nodded brusquely, jerking his head every few seconds during the drive. He had muttered a dozen strings of curses and shrugged to himself as he watched the road ahead.

Tonight Zeke would be driving to the airport to pick up his mother. The cackling and cooing, the bittersweet assault on his life was about to begin anew. The mere thought of it made the muscles in his jaw tighten and ripple with anxiety. Then he smiled at the memory of how loving, steadfast, and headstrong his mother had always been. In just a few hours she would be standing empty-handed in front of one of the shelves in his library, and in a voice that could be heard in Marin County, she would shout down to her son, who would be lugging all three of her heavy suitcases up the front steps and in through the front door—one suitcase for each day of the visit.

"Carl Jung!" she would shout in her heavy Brooklyn Jewish accent. "Ruskin! Bertrand Russell! Can you believe Vivienne left T. S. Eliot for him? You know Spinoza was a Jew, don't you? *Maps of the Ancient World*? Where's Maimonides? So tell me again, what's wrong with the Talmud?"

Outside the small town of Rodeo, Simon had reached into his briefcase and casually pulled out the odd-looking contraption that Zeke knew was perpetually secreted there. He had never gotten a good look at the whole thing, but he had the impression that it looked like something out of a Flash Gordon comic book—futuristic, but in a quaint and antiquated sort of way. Shocked by what he was finally being allowed to see, Zeke drifted slowly across the broken white lines on the road as he looked down to inspect the mysterious gizmo.

When he got a good look at it, he almost smirked, but managed to restrain himself. The bandoliers were outlandish, made for Mexican bandidos. The jerry-rigged device in his friend's lap looked ridiculous, almost cartoonish. Zeke steered the car back into his lane, shuddering as he remembered a mysterious event that had taken place outside the Roma Café just a few weeks ago. While standing next to Simon, he had suddenly been seized by the talons of a waking dream. While the reverie unfolded in his brain, his entire body was paralyzed. It was the most powerful, lifelike hallucination he had ever had.

"It's May 13th," he had casually mentioned to Simon as they rose from their chairs to go outside. "The day that Chet Baker died," he said sadly. "He fell or was pushed from a second-story window in the Prins Hendrik Hotel in Amsterdam back in 1988. Every year on this day, I have three martinis and listen to every Chet Baker album that was ever cut. By the third drink I'm crying like a baby. The fall cracked his skull and spilled all that beautiful music out onto the pavement."

Simon had casually reached into his briefcase and done something with that machine of his, and suddenly Ezekiel Zacharias Stein had felt a savage dizziness and nausea. An instant later he saw himself materializing from out of the clouds and gliding down from a stormy sky onto a high window ledge somewhere in Amsterdam. It was a hotel. He realized a moment later that he was on the Prins Hendrikkade near Zeedijk.

Then, against every instinct, he felt himself following Simon—letting go and leaping headlong from the rooftop ledge, then swooping down from a black sky just in time to catch Chet and keep the once handsome trumpeter's ravaged face and famous embouchure from kissing the cold cement. When Zeke abruptly awakened from the dream, he found himself surrounded by pedestrians who were staring at him and pointing at him.

The sun was shining brightly, but the Yiddish investigator's body and clothing were drenched with water. It was as though Zeke had been there in the cold rain and darkness of Amsterdam. He had been there—lifting Gabriel. And there was something else. When Zeke had flown south from Amsterdam with Chet and Simon, he had caught a glimpse of Hephaestus following close behind. The odd-looking man had been carrying a battery pack and some electronic gear. Wrapped around his waist was that most ubiquitous of Mexican tools: a set of jumper cables.

Chet Baker had been in his dreams every night since that day. Each time he awakened from that dream, he felt strangely elated, almost giddy. He went to sleep each night now hoping to have the dream yet once more. Each time it was more real, more gratifying, than the time before. In last night's dream he had seen the puncture marks on Chet's arm. He had felt the scars. He had looked into his cloudy, yellowed eyes and smelled his frantic breath. They had spoken at length about Chet's childhood and about his love for the trumpet—about that album with Bill Evans. But Zeke had never allowed himself to believe for a moment that Simon's machine had anything to do with it. It had only been a dream—a wishful but very powerful reverie. Still, the sight of Chet with new teeth, clean-shaven and wearing shorts and a luau shirt, jamming with Buddy Bolden and Bix Beiderbecke, made Zeke feel an extraordinary sense of contentment. Not to mention the fact that the music was amazing.

Zeke snapped his fingers and slapped his forehead with the palm of his right hand. He had just been bowled over by a sudden recollection. He had once spent an entire rainy afternoon reading about the horn player Bix Beiderbecke, and he had stumbled across the strangest fact in chapter one of the *Encyclopedia of Jazz*. The fact had been so bizarre that he had never forgotten it. This odd detail had been documented and substantiated by no fewer than three witnesses, including the woman doctor who had examined Bix and pronounced him dead.

"When Leon Bismark Beiderbecke died in 1931," said Zeke, "a man named George Kraslow heard him screaming from his room that there were two Mexicans hiding under his bed. It actually happened, Simon! People heard it! It's in the encyclopedia, for shit's sake! Two Mexicans on 46th Street in the borough of Queens in 1931!" Zeke seemed dumbfounded. "It wasn't—you're not gonna tell me . . ."

"It was us," said Simon almost sheepishly. "It was Hephaestus and me. On that one we were so clumsy, and poor Bix was feverish. We tried to explain what we were doing, but just the sight of us was too much for him. A year ago the machine was still very unstable. We tried it again a month later. That time it worked quite well."

Simon smiled patiently at his friend as he loosened two thumbscrews and opened the left side of the contraption. He bent over the device in order to check the settings and make a few careful internal adjustments. Zeke shook his head in disbelief and in grudging admiration. If nothing else, Simon's ludicrous mental world was very highly evolved. It was multilayered, intricate, encrypted, and as indecipherable as the dreams of a shaman—or an educated lunatic.

It was shot through with arcane mythology, amateur sorcery, a thorough understanding of electronic circuitry, an obsession with history and with the occult. Zeke could see that his friend did not suffer episodes of lunacy that surfaced out of long periods of normalcy. In fact, the opposite was true: now and again, Simon would suffer from sudden attacks of normalcy. Zeke closed his eyes. Had Bix Beiderbecke actually looked under his bed and glimpsed Simon and his odd friend hiding there? It just wasn't possible. Had the two Mexicans botched their first attempt to save Bix? Zeke shook his head savagely.

"What am I thinking!" he shouted. "Now I'm going crazy, too. No one saved Bix! No one saved Chet Baker!"

"I had to reintroduce and reintegrate the Sothic Cycle," muttered Simon as he strained his eyes and forced his fingers to make the most minuscule movements possible. "The army blew it. They got the geocentric part right, but they used the Julian calendar! Can you believe that? What a blunder! They brought in physicists and engineers to work on it day and night, when they should have brought in some alchemists, a few historians, and a philosopher or two.

"Of course, I made my own mistakes. I tried to integrate a global positioning circuit that would have linked up with the satellites up there, but the Antikythera device kept rejecting it. It blew out a dozen house fuses, not to mention the transformer across the street. As far as I can tell, the machine was nauseated by that technology. It recoiled. It got sick and started puking electrons until I tore out the GPS wiring. Look here! Just look at the Moon mechanism—only Hephaestus Segundo could've rebuilt this elegant train of gears. It's beyond belief. Just look at the work that he did on the ancient section of this machine. My work looks so clumsy next to his."

Below the jammed circuit board was a dizzying maze of intricate springs, wheels, and gears, all quiescent and resting. Some of the pieces looked newly fabricated. These were polished and pristine, while others seemed dull and old beyond age—they were the color of coprolites, the hue of dunnage, or the mottled shades of the matted wrappings of an Incan mummy.

Zeke took several deep breaths to calm himself. He would need all of his strength to keep from being drawn into Simon's dementia. He could clearly see several tiny vacuum tubes positioned on a circuit board next to scores of resistors and diodes all stacked and stuffed together in cramped rows on a perforated platform. He gave the innards of the odd machine another skeptical cursory glance. In the next instant he began shaking his head forward and back and using one hand to rub his eyes furiously.

For some unknown reason, the sight of the tightly packed components had dimmed the overhead lights in Zeke's mind and was now projecting a distressing, disturbing image onto the surface of his hippocampus—an image that he had once seen in a museum—an off-white and sepia-toned drawing of hundreds of African slaves jammed together like cords of firewood in the darkest, dankest hold of a ship.

"The resistors are suffocating to death," he abruptly announced to no one. His throat tightened, and his vocal cords were now vibrating an octave above his last sentence. "They're terrified and they're suffocating. The diodes and thermistors are gasping for air and pissing all over themselves," he roared. "They've completely given up on personal hygiene and privacy. The adult capacitors have stopped caring for the children. Until this very moment," he said with a look of shock in his face, "I have never known the name of any electrical component—not a single one," he said breathlessly. "What do I know from resistors?

"Wait a minute! One resistor has located his secret wife," he slurred. He rubbed his eyes and forced himself to concentrate on the road ahead. "If the slavers find out that the man and woman are married, they will be separated forever," he moaned. "I can see them right there on that circuit board of yours. They are making love for the last time in their lives. They are mating in a painful imitation of privacy, hidden behind a shroud of despair. Somehow I know that she is dry in her breasts and thighs. He is thin and watery in his expression.

"They are diseased. That's it—diseased! They are nauseated and very dehydrated. I hear her sighs and his powerless grunts—the dull, muted, distorted echoes of the dulcet tones of their wedding night so long ago. Their eyes are squeezed shut. They are imagining Africa. In their minds they are jumping a broom. They are laughing and tearing off their clothes. Something is going to happen to them!" he screamed at the windshield. His face was growing more crimson by the second.

"Something is going to happen to them!"

They have a young son," said Simon. His voice seemed muffled, enveloped by a thick layer of fog. "Look closely, and you'll see that he is lying at their feet. He's in great pain, but he is still healthy."

Without saying another word, Simon closed the small door, unhooked his seatbelt, and attached the mechanism to the front of his body by looping the bandoliers around his neck and hooking the straps to metal rings on the machine. After pulling the straps tight, he turned the machine on and began to manipulate the dials, one at a time.

Zeke instantly felt a queasy sensation in the pit of his stomach just as the instrument flashed, blinked, and whirred to life. He grabbed the steering wheel with both hands. This was precisely how he had felt just before the dream about Amsterdam! His stomach began filling with a noxious tea of hot acid. When his vision blurred and his hearing dulled, he somehow came to the realization that the machine was not affecting just him; it seemed to be bending and distorting all of the space around it.

The speedometer needle on the dashboard of the car pegged itself at zero, then at 120 miles an hour and back down again, while the gas and temperature gauges jumped madly in their small cages. The odometer was spinning wildly in its tiny run, the numbers in each slot tumbling and trampling over each other to go nowhere, everywhere—anywhere.

"What's going on here, man? What the fuck is going on?" he shouted in desperation, slamming his thumb repeatedly against the button that controlled the window on the driver's door. The glass refused to come down, and Zeke began gagging and covering his mouth with one hand while frantically trying to control the car with the other.

"Don't worry. You've already done this once before. The nausea and vertigo are pretty unsettling at first, but you get used to it after a while. It's a lot like seasickness or a bad hangover. Take a couple of deep breaths. Hang on for a few more minutes and it'll pass."

Simon reached into a pocket and pulled out a battered leather-bound ledger. Zeke recognized it. It was from the collection of them that Elena had shown him. He leafed through it carefully until he located a particularly ragged, dog-eared page. Then he put the book down on the open door of the glove compartment in front of him. He dropped his hand from its place over his mouth, and a faint smile of relief appeared on his lips. The sickening waves of vertigo and nausea had finally subsided.

He glanced at the highway, then back down at the open book,

before turning his attention back to the road ahead. After performing this maneuver a dozen times, he was able to focus for a second and saw that the right-hand page had a dozen combinations of numbers and letters that had been written down and then scratched out, not carefully but in anger or in frustration, one after the other. He had studied one of the ledgers in Simon's garage. He had never been able to make any sense of the contents. There was a hand-drawn map hastily scrawled in an area just to the right of the numerals. He had seen all of this before.

Now he knew that he was going to see the purpose of those writings—if there really was a purpose. There was a new set of letters and numbers that had been written in below all the rest. It suddenly struck Zeke that what he and Elena had mistaken for numerical codes were actually coordinates—map coordinates. Simon had run the digits together without spaces or any modifying marks—no seconds, minutes, or degrees. Longitude ran into latitude. He could see that these numbers indicated a location at seventy-six degrees and nineteen minutes west longitude. A single group of numbers had never been scratched out, which led him to deduce that the latitude must be correct.

A set of dates had been given the same treatment. The 29th and 30th of November had been crossed out, as had December 1st in the year 1781. The only date left was the second day of December. A circle had been drawn incisively around that date in red ink. Zeke shook his head sadly. His friend's make-believe world was far more byzantine, far more warped and knotted, than he had ever dreamed possible. How could someone like this ever hope to function as a husband, a teacher—or as a father?

"Why, after hiding that thing from me for so long, are you letting me see it now—on our way to Sacramento at eighty-five miles an hour?

"You're going ninety-five miles an hour," said Simon without looking at the speedometer.

"Are you expecting me to validate this crazed invisible world of yours—this universe that you have all to yourself?" Zeke pleaded in a strained, distressed voice. "Is that why you're showing me this after all this time?"

The image of the two lonely black resistors—soldered together for the last time—making furious, desperate love abruptly seized control of his mind once again. This time he widened his field of vision and could clearly see a little boy lying at his parents' feet, sobbing hysterically while he watched them frantically, desperately mimicking the act that had created him. Zeke turned his face away from Simon for a moment while the unsettling vision dissipated. He took another deep breath and after a few seconds surrendered to his own burning curiosity.

"OK. All right," he said with a sigh of complete surrender. "I give up. What happened on the 3rd of December? Why isn't that date on the list?" His voice trailed off as the images quickly reinvaded his mind. The little boy's tear-filled eyes seemed to be staring upward from the bottom of the hold and directly into Zeke's eyes.

"The ship was docked on that date," answered Simon. He sounded nervous and anxious. "It pulled into port on the morning of the 3rd. All of the damage was already done by then. On the 29th of November, the ship's crew manacled together fifty-five living human beings and dumped them into the sea, chains and all. If the captives had died of their illnesses while on board, the insurance company would not have compensated the slavers for the loss.

"The next day a second chain of forty people were thrown overboard. On December 1st, twenty-six more people were drowned. Ten went overboard without being tied to the chain. I've gotten to every one of those people, one hundred and twenty-one of them, but I can't find the boy! I've looked and looked, but I couldn't find his final moment on any of those days. I know he never made it to port. I have to find him, Zeke," said Simon, his voice breaking with emotion.

Zeke's facial expression teetered somewhere between uproarious laughter and utter disgust. Now he knew for certain that his friend was insane—more insane than Uncle Louie.

"All that's left to try is December 2nd," said the Flyboy as he dried his eyes with his sleeve. "I've already tried seventy-six degrees plus twenty-two, twenty-one, twenty, and nineteen minutes west longitude on every other possible date. There's nothing left but seventy-six degrees, nineteen minutes and December 2nd. The reports say that it happened at daybreak. I know exactly when the sun rose on that morning. I've already programmed that into the machine. I have to locate the boy when he is up on the main deck."

Simon sounded frantic. His muscles were tensed. He had the look of a trooper about to step out of a chopper into a landing zone where the enemy was ready and waiting.

"What are you saying? What happened to those people?" asked a shaken, overwhelmed Zeke. The husband and wife had reappeared in his mind's eye and were kissing each other's face for the final time. They were saying goodbye forever. Two hatches had been rudely ripped open, and dim glories of harsh daylight were invading the black hold. Zeke rubbed his eyes and shook his head violently. He hadn't had a drug flashback in years. Even on his worst trips with LSD, he had never found himself in the hold of a slave ship. Now he could see the little boy rising defiantly to his feet.

"Are you saying that a hundred living, breathing people were chained together and thrown into the sea?"

Without answering his exasperated friend, Simon leaned forward while he slowly turned one knob, then a second, in strict accordance with the words and numbers that were scrawled on the map and in the notes to the left. He unwrapped a stick of gum and touched it lightly to a tiny spigot on the upper right corner of the machine. He gave the gum to Zeke, who hesitated, shrugged away his indecision, then put the stick into his mouth. Suddenly he could hear the sound of winds building up to gale force.

"About one hundred nautical miles due east of Morant Point in Jamaica is the only description given in the court records," shouted Simon above the wail of a vengeful westerly. His hair and jacket were flapping violently with the force of the winds. "It was a rough estimate back then, and it still is. The slavers who testified in court had no interest in being accurate. These numbers are the best that I've been able to do," he shouted into Zeke's ear.

Zeke disregarded the confusing sentence, abruptly changing his mind and refusing to participate any further in his friend's florid, intricate dementia. His hair was whipping into his face, and he wondered how it was possible for a cyclone to be whirling in the front seat of a four-door sedan.

The light of three lanterns lit up the hold as even more sailors entered. Zeke gasped at the horrid scene that the sunlight and lanterns had illuminated—at the sheer number of despondent human beings who had been stuffed into that small space below decks. White men with rum-soaked rags pressed over their noses and mouths came in and grabbed the husband and wife, unlocking their ankle chains, pulling them apart and out of their fetid, soiled slots.

The little boy got up and hugged the woman's leg, but a large man with red hair grabbed the child by the head and threw him aside like a rag doll. Zeke winced as his mind's eye followed the couple up to the deck, where they were beaten bloody, then chained to fifteen others who were also sick and sweating with fever or quaking with chills. Behind them there were ten more blinking, blinded Africans being dragged up from the hold.

On the starboard side, a stack of large metal weights and broken anchors had been cobbled together and wired to one end of a long chain. The weights were hoisted up to a location above the deck railings and swung out to a foreboding position over the cold waves. Zeke's head was swimming with the whimpers, the coughing, and the prayers of the doomed. He had seen their eyes, wide like those of terrified children.

Then the lights on the Antikythera device began to burn with greater and greater intensity. The mechanical humming within its casing became almost deafening. Zeke cried out in pain, then abruptly slashed across four lanes of traffic at a very high speed. He careened down an exit ramp without even trying to slow the car. Disregarding the stop sign at the end of the off-ramp, he wheeled the speeding, lurching vehicle into the parking lot of a gas station.

He skidded to a halt and sat behind the wheel with his eyes closed tight and his lungs heaving. His car was immediately enveloped in a swirling cloud of dust. He slumped against the wheel, alternately gasping for air and spewing mouthfuls of salt water and algae onto the tattered, greasy upholstery of his seat. This time Zeke could not hold back the tide. He puked the thick, bubbly brine onto the car's speedometer and instrument panel. It struck the dashboard with such ferocity that it rebounded, covering his shirt and pants. Behind him at the intersection were two stalled cars and a jackknifed truck that had driven off the road in order to avoid hitting him.

The moment that the machine on Simon's chest began to whine and flicker and explode with lights, the drone of the car's engine and transmission died away meekly, then vanished completely. Zeke was driving while blinded and deaf. The whine of wheels out on the interstate disappeared. For a split second there was nothing in his ears but the wind and that familiar Irish tune on Simon's breath, just before the weighty roar and the heavy heave and seething roll of massive ocean waves washed through the car again, almost drowning the Yiddish investigator.

As he sat behind the wheel, Zeke's cheeks and face were buffeted and deformed by savage gusts of an insolent, pugnacious norther. Even with his eyes closed, he began to perceive sights, as though he could see right through the skin of his eyelids—right through the headliner and the tin roof of his car—right across two centuries of time.

He saw the spanker mast, the staysails, and the jiggermast of a square-rigger looming over his head, its enormous bow threatening to crush his car beneath its weight. He saw deck planking, bulwarks, and scuppers. He saw flickering lanterns, bowsprits, and armies of flies hovering around the lids of battened hatches. He saw a ripped and resewn topsail and a flying jib sheet that had been torn in half by a recent gale. He heard the creak and snap of twisted, tormented sisal and the muffled complaints of tortured wood that was being smothered beneath a dozen layers of caulk and tar.

A surly white overseer was watching two emaciated black men dump the foul-smelling contents of a large barrel into the swelling sea below. "Empty them honey buckets!" he commanded. "Give them animals less food and they make even more shit!"

Zeke gagged as the odor of human waste reached his nostrils. He saw the long arm of a winch and crane swing outward, and he saw a rope being cut through, allowing the heavy cluster of metal weights to drop overboard, followed abruptly by a dozen weakened, coughing humans who plummeted helplessly downward into the swells. A few who resisted and wedged their feet against the railing were stabbed and prodded until they finally gave up hope and dove, bleeding and screaming, over the side.

He saw men throwing the bodies of sick babies overboard. Their little wrists and ankles were too small for the manacles. He saw that their small arms and legs were covered with boils, welts, rashes, and insect bites. A group of ten men who were yet to be tied to the rusted chain-link of humans had joined hands and were leaping over the side together in a last proud act of defiance. From the instant that they had decided to jump, they were free men. Why would free men do the bidding of slaves?

Then Zeke caught sight of the husband and wife. They were the last ones to be hooked onto the giant black charm bracelet at the end of a newly created jumble of rusted weights. He saw his gaze lost in hers and hers lost in his, and he saw them embrace as they stepped onto the railing seconds before the hard snatch of the chain. They watched together as each metal link shot overboard, scraping and scarring the railing and rudely jerking the next link down to oblivion, then the next link behind that one. The husband and wife shouted a single word, then followed the weight downward into the shadows below. Above them, standing on the observation deck at the stern, Zeke saw a man who must have been the captain. He was wearing a hideous metal glove on his right hand.

Zeke saw the sun rise, dash across the sky, and then settle onto the horizon with blinding speed, as though someone or something had learned how to accelerate time—even when that time was far in the past. Then, appearing from out of nowhere, he caught a glimpse of a moving shadow—he saw ankles flashing, then a naked black boy dashing like a sable gazelle across the wet boards. Two white men were chasing him, tripping here and bumping there—cursing angrily, trying again and again to grab him and hurt him for making them expend so much energy so early in the morning. One of the clumsy men was wearing an ill-fitting ivory peg leg.

The two black men looked up from their awful and endless chore and shouted something to the child. They would be whipped for their words—one lash for each uppity consonant, one for each insolent vowel. The boy made it to the main deck, then scrambled onto the railing, where he screamed two words into the waves below. Then, with a wide victorious smile, he tossed his small body into the air above the seething, beckoning sea.

In the same instant that the boy was arching above the railing, Zeke was callously battered, blindsided by a downdraft that had flown in from South Carolina just to shove him backward into his seat—to put him in his place. Knocked almost unconscious by the airy blow, he dimly heard Simon's voice calling to him from a dark distance, as if from behind a curtain.

"You have to fight back. Those winds are everywhere. They aren't the winds of change. They change nothing. That's their power. Beat them back, Zeke! Give them a clean shot at your jaw, then duck and counterpunch."

Zeke lifted his hands and made a pair of fists. He took a boxer's stance but could not hold it. A small cyclone landed a haymaker to his left ear. As he began to lose consciousness, he caught a glimpse of what looked to be a brown man in a three-piece suit. Wearing a tiny cape around his neck, the man swept down from the top of the mizzenmast and dove unswervingly toward the white foam and floating feces below—flying toward the drowning boy. He disappeared, and an instant later there emerged from beneath the waves a living boy, shining and flapping like a dark fifty-pound tuna in the wet arms of the Mexican Flyboy.

The flailing, dripping boy was carried high into the air, his mouth yawning open, then closing, longing for salt water. The two flying people gained speed, shedding sea-foam as they moved west toward the Mexican Gulf. They attained the speed of sound, then the velocity of light, the rapidity of neutrinos, and, finally, the speed of yearning.

1 5

THE GOOD SHIP *ZONG*

When he finally awoke from his sullen, windswept catatonia, Zeke was astonished to discover that he was no longer behind the wheel of his car. Instead he found himself walking down the center of a long white linoleum-floored hallway. Dizzy and disoriented, he seemed to be following an old man into the bright sunlight and onto a slab of pink cement behind the same convalescent home that he had visited just days before.

When his eyes adjusted to the light, he saw a small pond at the center of the patio, a hundred gallons of water that were surrounded by an artless array of plastic ferns and stands of rubber bamboo. A miniature pump at the bottom of the pool was feeding a weak stream of green water to a small angel that was dangling above the display. A dribble of muddy pee ran down one of its green patina thighs, then dripped back into the pond.

"How did we get here?" asked Zeke in an almost funereal tenor. He rubbed his eyes and shook his head violently yet again in an attempt to clear it. He was still in a state of shock, his mind still swamped with ocean sights and sounds. His nostrils were clotted with flecks of seaweed.

"You drove us here," answered Simon. "You're going to have to pay the bill for that special tow truck that came and straightened out that eighteen-wheeler back on the interstate. The driver says you owe him for lost time, too."

"I have some questions for you," said Zeke with a dark but controlled intensity. His voice broke. "You have to answer my questions, Simon. You have to. Now I'm going crazy, too. I'm seeing things. Something happened back there. Something really strange happened. It was a dream, but then it wasn't. Elena told me that the same kinds of things are happening to her. Those numbers on your chest are coordinates, too, aren't they? They're just like the numbers in your ledgers. Coordinates written vertically and upside down so no one but you will know what they mean.

"It was more than a dream, wasn't it? I don't know what it was, but when this interview is through, you're going to answer some questions. Somehow you've sucked me into your craziness . . . for the second time. I'm involved in it now, and I don't want to be. Seriously, you've got to answer my questions." He paused for a moment, then added, "What eighteen-wheeler?"

Simon nodded and smiled understandingly at his friend. He turned toward the interviewee and could see that Peter Keyes was still an imposing figure: massive across the beam of his chest, with hands that were almost inhumanly large—like speckled pink catchers' mitts. Simon recognized his body, but nothing about his face or the tone of his speech was familiar. In Simon's dreams, Keyes's voice boomed down from above his head and resonated from all directions like the voice of Zeus, Mithra, or Jehovah. There was only one seat at the table, so he and Zeke each lifted a metal chair from a nearby stack and carried it toward the big man.

"Looks like you finally woke up," Peter Keyes said to Zeke. "How come you got seagull shit on your shoulders? You're a hundred miles from the nearest ocean. It looks like you've gone and puked on yourself, too. Your hair's a mess. You look like somethin' the cat dragged in. I saw you just a few days ago. You looked fine last week. What the hell happened?"

Zeke looked down at his shirt and lap, then glanced toward first his left and then his right shoulder. He began searching around furiously for a towel or some napkins. He went behind a small tiki bar that was stationed near the pond and returned with a roll of paper towels. He dabbed his shoulders with a wet wad of paper while Simon took off his shoes and shook out two small piles of white sand.

"I can't say I remember you," said Peter Keyes in a deep voice that was oddly soothing. He was staring directly at the Mexican as he spoke. "But I can sure say that I've thought about you every day of my life. Every goddamned day. I do remember that curly hair of yours. In my memories, your hair was some kinda reddish color all those years ago." He lit a cigarette and inhaled deeply, almost ecstatically. "I've got one lung, four ex-wives, two young daughters, and three grown boys, and I'll be damned if I haven't thought about you more than any of them—all of them."

He exhaled a long, languorous plume.

"We're connected. We share a memory, you and me. Kind of an amazin' thing, ain't it. Somewhere up here," he said while touching an enormous pink finger to the silver hair at his temple, "somewhere underneath all this white hair and dandruff is this memory. Now, it ain't no bigger than a flea's egg or the eye of a fruit fly, but it's there and it ain't never goin' away. It's there in every thought I think. And you've got it, too," he said, pointing at Simon with a trembling index finger that was wedded to an unfiltered cigarette. "You've got it, too. I can see it."

He took another deep puff, then began to shake. His face reddened, and he squared his shoulders and covered up as if he were fighting off flurry after flurry of punishing jabs. His eyes filled with tears, and he began to sway in time to a subterranean rhythm, side to side like the Flo-Massa back at San Quentin, then like a tethered elephant, front to back in larger and larger swings.

"I've gone flyin' back up to that airplane every day since the day it happened," he said between sobs, wiping his eyes and nose with the sleeve of his pajamas. "Sometimes five or ten times a day.

Human beings like to think they're free, but they ain't really, are they? They're only free to hurt themselves—or someone else. I've gone up there, and I've tried with all my might to undo it all, to pay some attention to her and keep her from doin' what she done. But it never works. It never does. The same thing always happens, over and over. Do you know what I'm talkin' about? Do you know what I mean?"

Simon nodded again. He knew what Peter Keyes was talking about. He knew what he meant.

"I go flyin' up to that plane and try to talk to me. I shout into my own ear, trying to talk some sense to me—to tell me not to be so goddamned stupid, not to think with my pecker and balls, but it don't ever do no good." His face was turning beet-red as he spoke. "I look at me struttin' around that plane, squeezin' Veronica's ass, and I see someone who can't never listen to nobody. The fool never hears me . . . I never hear me." He smashed an enormous fist against his chest.

"Then I watch me jump from that plane just like before, and I see it all again—I have to comb through the dark sky to catch sight of Sophia, then I have to watch her flip her body over and slam into the dirt with her back. I have to see that spray of dust from when she hit. She hit so goddamned hard."

The big man stopped swaying and began to weep without restraint. "She turned her body around in midair just to look at me, didn't she?" he said between sobs. "She wanted to see me and cuss me out for disrespectin' her like that with Veronica. She wanted to see the look on my face when I realized she wasn't gonna pull that ripcord. Then after I landed, she wanted me to watch her body sink into that soil. I had to stand there with them fifteen mad Mexicans surroundin' me, ready to cut my throat for what I done to you. Did I hurt you, son? I been wantin' to ask you that question for so long now—for more than forty-five years. Did I hurt you?"

"I really didn't feel it, Mr. Keyes," said Simon. "I was afraid of you at the time, but all I could feel was Sophia's pain. I should've felt yours, too. I cut those grape stems with my pruning knife, and I saw her tumble down from a cloud. I thought it was my fault. Honestly, I never felt you touch me. All I could see was her beautiful face looking up from the ground. The only thing I felt was the suffering in those eyes. All she wanted was a moment of peace. Just some peace. She was so sad and so hopeless—and you were so angry. You feel responsible for her death, don't you? You didn't cause it, Mr. Keyes. It wasn't you. It wasn't me, either. For years I thought it was me."

At first it seemed that Peter Keyes had not heard what Simon had just said. Then the big man stood up and stretched to his full height.

"I shouldn't've hit you. How could I do that to a kid? What a coward I was." He sat down and closed his eyes before speaking again. "And I remember what you did. You told them angry pickers to leave me alone, to let me be. You didn't say nothin'. You just looked up and said somethin' with your eyes." He leaned toward Simon and touched him on the shoulder. The small gesture healed something inside of Peter Keyes. A fissure somewhere in his life was stitched shut; a torn piece of tissue was pressed together and allowed to mend.

"We was married just over two years, Sophia and me. We was real hot to trot when we first met down at Fort Benning. I tell you, when that little gal was happy, she was that turnin' light on top of one of them lighthouses. Twice every minute you could see her from a hundred miles away. Everybody was taken by her. She was the center of every party we ever went to. But when that light went out, she was lost in a real black place, and she didn't want nobody to find her. It went out a lot. Somethin' was eatin' her up. She always laughed too easy and too hard. When she went black like that, I couldn't even touch her for days."

"What was her name?" asked Simon anxiously.

"Sophia Keyes for a hot minute, but she changed it just one month after we was married. She'd been married lots of times, so she used a lot of names. Changed it all the time. I think she was hiding from something."

"What name was she using when she died?" asked Zeke.

"Hanson or Harper or somethin' like that," answered the old man. "At least I think that was the name she had on her name tag, the one that some fella ripped off her parachute. It sounded like it was Irish. I'd never seen or heard that name before, but it didn't surprise me none. She wrote it on the name tag with one of them big black markers. Big letters, too. She kept her past to herself, but on that day she was tryin' to say somethin' to somebody.

She had a baby real young—by somebody. She was just a kid when it happened. I know that much, but she would never talk about it. Except when she talked in her sleep. Once in a while she would give an entire church sermon in her sleep—real hellfire and brimstone stuff. It was the strangest thing. Later on she was married to this dark little Hindu fella from the valley, but she never, ever used his name. I don't know why—she used everybody else's name, why not his?

"I went into her purse once and saw some kinda foreign return address and his full name on a letter that she always kept with her. She hid it in the lining of the purse, but it wasn't hard to find. Every woman hides her drugs in that lining. That letter was real precious to her. I could see that right off. It was all wrinkled and folded up. I think she unfolded it and read it every day, whenever she thought no one was lookin'. I don't know what became of it. His name was Damodar Vimel Chabra. I wrote it down someplace. Crazy fuckin' foreign names." He shook his head, then found the bent, flattened remnants of another cigarette. It was torn at the center, and flecks of tobacco were leaking out. "Hanlon!" he shouted suddenly. "That was the name on her tag. Hanlon."

Zeke pulled out his notepad and scribbled the Indian name and Sophia Hanlon, the one that had been on her name tag. He reached back into his briefcase and retrieved a full unopened carton of cigarettes and a green plastic lighter. "You thought I'd forgotten, didn't you?" he said as he handed them to Peter Keyes. The old man smiled. He still had most of his teeth. His lips were chapped, but there were no gnats dying on them.

"No filters?" he asked hopefully.

"Not one," answered Zeke with a smile.

"Damodar Vimel Chabra," whispered Simon to himself. Then he whispered it again. He looked stunned. Something about the East Indian name was vaguely, dimly familiar to him. He strained at the thought for a moment, then let it go. The request had been lodged. The answer would come of its own accord. He knew his own obsessive, eternally perseverating brain. Some compulsive and dogged thing within the turmoil of his mind would not rest—would strive and toil maniacally until the answer was found and written down, then inserted into a bottle and allowed to drift up to the surface of his consciousness. Sometime in the next few seconds, hours, or days, it would wash ashore onto his tongue.

"Tell me about the man who tore off the name tag," said Simon, his lips and cheeks beginning to quiver. There was rising tension and anxious anticipation in his voice. Amazement gleamed in his eyes. In the last few minutes, ten thousand silent nightmares had suddenly, miraculously, been given a soundtrack. Actors had been named, and scripts had been handed out. There was a familiar hint of pain in Simon's face, but there were also intense notes of relief in his eyes. Finally, after more than forty years, he was talking to another soul who had lived through that same surreal and terrible moment in the vineyard. Someone else had heard the tree fall in the forest. "I heard you mention him to your friend—to another skydiver."

"Shit," said Keyes through a haze of smoke. "It really did happen, didn't it? Do you know how much alcohol I drank to wash it away? I ain't just a babblin' crazy man after all. You saw it, too. It ain't just me. It really did happen. You and me been damaged by it. We're the proof—you and me. It ain't just me." He inhaled deeply, pulling the hot nicotine and sulfurs down to the bottom of his lung. "That fella you're talkin' about, the one who took the name tag, I seen him for half a minute and not much more. Our eyes met, and he ran off like a snatch-thief. Never seen him again.

"He looked to be about eighteen or nineteen years old. You know, draft age. He was lanky, almost scrawny. He had dark hair and these cold, cold eyes. His hair looked awful—like a bad dye job. He looked like he was from another world, like he didn't live here in this one with the rest of us. Ten or fifteen years ago, I decided that he looked like one of them boys that was raised by wolves. You ever read about them?"

Simon closed his eyes and leaned back in his chair. The name of Sophia's East Indian husband—Damodar Vimel Chabra—and the description of the young man at the parachute rigging shack had struck several chords. These things meant something.

"He was too fast and too damn alert-lookin' to be human. He made these quick animal jerks when he moved his head. He looked like a hunter—or maybe he was bein' hunted. He looked like everything on this earth come hard to him. You see them plates and bowls over there?" He yanked the cigarette from his mouth and used it as a pointer. "There's a lady here who feeds all the wild homeless cats that we got livin' in these fields out here." He turned to look out beyond the cyclone fence at the edge of the yard. There were no buildings on the other side of the fence, only brown grass and softly rolling terrain that extended to the horizon. There was not a single tree to be seen. The senior home had been constructed at the very edge of the city.

"Nobody stops her because they come in here and take care of all the mice. And we got a lot of them, I'll tell you. Guess they haven't figured out a way to filter out the mice. Anyway, she says them cats are feral. I never heard that word before—or maybe I heard it and ignored it because it didn't mean nothin' to me. I do that a lot. I looked that word up—well, my girlfriend actually looked it up for me, and damned if that ain't the right word for that man! He was feral.

"He looked like he'd never had a home or he'd lost it a long time ago. I think he had a couple of freckles on his cheeks next to his nose. I saw him tear that name from that parachute like a wolf pullin' at a wad of gristle. He looked at me and growled like a starvin' dog. It sent a chill right down my spine. But I'll tell you one thing: he knew why he was there."

He exhaled a puff of white smoke that curled around his head and completely covered his face. Now Simon recognized him. The thick smoke had obscured the deep wrinkles around his eyes and softened the crow's-feet tearing at his temples. Like magic, the white wraith had stretched his cheeks tight, smoothed over the smoker's crevasses in his lips, and flattened out the loose folds beneath his chin. For a minute or two, the face of a thirty-year-old Peter Keyes was visible once again.

"Whoever he was, Sophia knew him. I described him to her, and she commenced to tremblin' and shakin' all over. For years I thought I saw terror in her eyes when she was up in that airplane, but now that I'm old and know what regret looks like, I know that's what I saw in her face—a powerful regret. That last night I tried to talk her out of jumpin', but she wouldn't listen to me. I don't know why I didn't want her to jump. But it didn't matter anyway. She wouldn't listen to me." His voice broke, and he turned his face away for a moment of privacy. "The minute she hit the ground, I started drinkin', and I didn't stop for twenty-five years." He wiped his eyes again.

"I tried to follow Veronica, but she went back to beauty school in Bakersfield and wouldn't have nothin' to do with me. The last time I ever saw her, we was havin' breakfast at a truck stop next to the freeway. She had shaved off them beautiful eyebrows of hers and penciled in these awful-lookin' arches. I know you've seen the kind I'm talkin' about. A lot of the Latin gals and the colored gals have 'em. For some reason she reminded me of a nun—one of them novice nuns. I couldn't tell you why. If she's alive right now, she's in pain just like me and you."

The big man pulled a new, perfectly formed cigarette from one of the packs. He lit it and inhaled a lungful of smoke. He exhaled as he spoke.

"I got remarried drunk—three more times. I had kids drunk. I put in a thousand swimming pools up and down the state of California, and I don't remember a single one. It's no wonder my three boys don't want nothin' to do with me. I had kids out of wedlock with two other women. Two girls. I never gave a damn about none of 'em. Now all I wanna do is go back and change him—change me into someone that don't hurt people, don't mess up their lives." The giant man began to cry. After a few moments, he dried his tears with the other pajama sleeve and lifted his head. There was the beginning of a smile on his lips.

"I've got a gal in here," he said almost sheepishly. "She's a Jewish gal named Shayna. I think it means beautiful. She's real booksmart. Her husband died some years ago, and she had no kids, so there's no one to look after her. Now she's got me. She's some kinda vegetarian—even apologizes to the carrots before she eats 'em. She's got a real nice shape." He used both hands to make an hourglass shape in the air.

"Even in this place we can sneak in a little whoopee every once in a while, if you know what I mean," he said with a sly giggle. When he smiled and thought about Shayna, the years seemed to drop away from his face.

"She used to be a lawyer. I guess she still is. She helped me adopt the two little girls. She helped me set up these trust funds for every one of my kids—all five of them. Every dollar went into it. That's why I'm in this cheesy place. Who coulda guessed I'd end up here in Serengeti Manor. Some name, ain't it? It's owned by some rich South Africans. They've built these things all over the world.

"She's in here 'cause she gave all her money away—to some museum in Washington, D.C. It went to pay for a special exhibit. I've seen pictures of it—a room full of shoes and a humongous pile of teeth. Shayna and I just kind of fell in love. It took a long time, but it was the right way to do it. Sometimes we sit together out here all night, especially when there's a bright moon.

"We smooch a little, then we cuddle up together with our right hands up in front of our faces. Of course, my left hand is somewhere else," he said with a naughty laugh. "Anybody walkin' by must think we're crazy. We're covered in blankets, all cozy and gigglin'. We look upward and hold the moon in that teeny space between our thumbs and our pointing fingers. You've done that, ain't you?"

Both Simon and Zeke nodded their heads.

"Shayna says to coddle the moon, to cradle it in your fingertips and never, ever crush it. She says there's this thing in the middle of everyone's mind that wants to squeeze the moon until its innards gush out—and then apologize when it's too late. She says to fight that thing and never squeeze, not even in play.

"She gets moody sometimes. She says that if the Third Reich—I guess that means Hitler and them folks—if they had dumped their propaganda campaign—she taught me them fancy words—if they had dropped their campaign and hired a New York advertising firm instead, they'd still be in business today. There would be these commercials everywhere with a sweet, friendly insurance-company voice sayin' that the moon ain't really being crushed; it only looks that way. Sometimes we cuddle out here for hours, talking and laughing and coddling the moon. She calls it 'repairing the world.'"

"Tikkun olam," said Zeke softly.

"I've heard her use those exact same words!" exclaimed an astonished Peter Keyes. "I'll be damned. The exact same words."

"Where was the vineyard?" asked Simon in an anxious whisper. He had waited over four decades to ask this question of someone who might know the answer.

"In the Livermore Valley," Peter Keyes answered, "in the foothills beyond the town. We jumped out of the small airport near the highway. That was some freak wind that hit us. Powerful. Almost a hurricane, the newspaper said. It didn't start blowin' until we left the plane. Some folks swore they saw a funnel cloud touchin' down. The pilot had to land the plane all the way over in Hayward. The local newspaper said that winds like that had never hit the valley before—not in recorded history. It almost collapsed our silk. That was my last time jumpin'. I've never been back there. Never strapped on another parachute."

Simon leaned back in his chair and closed his eyes. He had always imagined a vineyard near Santa Barbara or up north in Sonoma or Napa County. He had tried thousands of coordinates with no success. The most he had ever been able to do was hover helplessly as she fell and be forced to watch her from a vague, indistinct perch as she plunged downward—but nothing more.

"I've got a question for you, Mr. Vegas," said Peter Keyes. "I seen you bendin' over her body when I run up to where she fell. I seen your face real close to hers. Back then it made me real mad—I don't even know why. Her ears was bleedin', but I knew you wasn't hurtin' her. I knew that." He slammed a hammy fist into his own chest once again, striking the ribs above his heart. "I think I was kiddin' myself. What would I have done if I got there first? What would I say to her? What would I do? I got mad at you, but it was me that I hated. Did you kiss her ear like I should have? Did you talk to her while she passed on—like I should've been doin'? Did she say somethin' to you about me? Did she say I was cheatin' on her? Did she tell you a secret?"

Simon rose from his chair and approached Peter Keyes. He leaned over and whispered for a few seconds into the man's right ear. A grin appeared on the old man's face. He seemed about to burst with happiness. His entire body shook as he rose from his chair and threw his arms around the boy whom he had so cruelly tossed aside so long ago.

"Now I can stop sufferin'," he said with a deep sigh of relief. His eyes filled with tears. "Now I can finally stop sufferin'. Finally." He wiped his face with a sleeve, then inhaled deeply to compose himself. "I can't wait to tell Shayna." Then he fell silent for a few seconds. "Do you remember them feral cats that I told you about, the ones waitin' out there for the mice?"

He gestured toward the savannah, the huge expanse of land out beyond the cyclone fence. "Sometimes they're just these little bitty ten-pound cats, orange and striped and whatnot, but other times I look out there and I see somethin' else. I see lions—three of them. I saw one just now. I see that they're watchin' me close, studyin' my habits—measurin' up on me. They're thinkin' about the best way to bring me down. Hell, they're five hundred pounds each. What could I do? I know my time is comin'. I know they're here for me. At least now I know that things will be good for Sophia and for my kids. At least now I know that. I can't wait to tell Shayna. The lions can come. Let 'em come."

"Don't worry, Mr. Keyes," said Simon quietly as he and Zeke got up to leave. "When the time comes, I won't let them touch you."

"What did you say to him?" asked Zeke as the two men walked back to the car.

"I told him the truth," was Simon's answer. "I told him that he's given me the information I've always needed to keep her from hitting the ground. I told him that I'm going to catch her."

"Now, why didn't I know that," said Zeke sarcastically. "Keyes believed you, didn't he? Me, I don't believe it. I don't believe a word of it. It's like that card trick of yours. The cards never change at all. You only change the way I see them. It's some kind of hypnosis or suggestion. I only think that I saw four aces. I only think that I saw that ship, and I think I saw Chet Baker and those slaves, but . . ." he was suddenly silent. "Was that the *Zong*?" he asked as he strapped himself uneasily into the driver's seat. He seemed profoundly confused until the moment that his fingers touched the latch of his seatbelt. Then he was instantly overcome once again by the waves of nausea and a stabbing sense of urgency.

"Was that the *Zong* that I saw in that . . . that hallucination back on the highway?"

"Yes, it was," answered Simon.

"I swear I heard the husband and wife shout a single word as they jumped into the sea," said Zeke as he leaned forward and rested his forehead on the steering wheel. "I think I heard them shout 'Kassamila.' That was the boy's name, wasn't it? Kassamila. Oh, shit, now I'm going crazy, too. And the word that the two African men shouted to the little boy as he ran across the deck was 'haraku.' Why do I know that 'haraku' means hurry? How do I know that? I'm a Jew from Brooklyn. How can I possibly know that?"

Zeke was grinding his teeth as he spoke. His eyes were blinking almost rhythmically, and his right hand was twitching wildly. He released the buckle of his seatbelt, leaned toward Simon, and without asking for permission grabbed the leather-bound ledger from the open door of the glove compartment. He had always wanted to take a closer look at one of these books. Long ago he had seen one in Simon's briefcase and assumed that it was filled with poems that were under construction. Until Elena took him into the garage, he had never known that there were scores of books just like it. Simon made no effort to stop him. The investigator flipped through the pages and stared with astonishment at a dizzying array of numbers, dates, and times written on page after page after page.

There were thousands of entries neatly written in columns, hundreds more crammed into the margins, and even more scribbled near the metal binding coil. Still more entries were scrawled onto scraps of paper and taped to the pages. Were all of these grid coordinates nothing more than bits of random psychosis-induced nonsense?

"So this is what your mind looks like," he muttered under his breath.

Ezekiel Zacharias Stein slammed the ledger shut, closed his eyes, and mumbled to himself for a moment or two. His head tilted to the right, then to the left, as though he were deciding between two options. Then he opened the book to a set of entries somewhere near the center of the binder and jabbed his index finger at that page like a dart. He read the numbers beneath his finger, interpolating degrees, minutes, longitude, and latitude.

"Forty-eight degrees, eight minutes north latitude. One hundred and two degrees, twenty-one minutes . . ."

Before he could finish reading the coordinates, Simon whispered, "Wounded Knee. The slaughter of Hunkpapa and Miniconjou families by American cavalry."

Zeke's darting finger arbitrarily stabbed another set of numbers on the opposite page.

"Forty-four degrees, six minutes, and five seconds north latitude and nineteen minutes . . ."

"That is Srebrenica, the massacre of eight thousand Muslim men and boys."

"Forty-three point one degrees . . ."

"Matthew Shepard," said Simon, whose lips were quivering as

they formed those four syllables. "The person who discovered his nearly lifeless body mistook him for a scarecrow at first."

Zeke had a stunned look of belief and disbelief on his face. Now he spoke with a frenzy, spitting out numbers in a rapid staccato.

"Thirty point five-four-eight . . ."

"Bogue Chito Swamp in Mississippi," said Simon. "June 21st, 1964. The three civil rights workers."

"Thirty-seven degrees, thirteen minutes north latitude, and . . ."

"Iris Chang," said Simon almost silently. "Beautiful Iris."

"Two degrees, ten seconds east longitude . . ."

"Auvers-sur-Oise," answered Simon in the same quiet, confessional voice. "July 27th, 1890. The day that Vincent shot himself in a wheat field, then crawled to his bed to die."

"Thirty-five point one-three . . ."

"The Lorraine Motel, Memphis."

"Thirty-nine degrees, twenty-five minutes . . ."

"December 2nd in the year 1859," said Simon. "That was the hanging of John Brown."

"I suppose you're gonna tell me that you attended that hanging?" asked Zeke sarcastically.

"John wanted to die," said Simon solemnly. "He wanted to die for the slaves. He resisted me at first—until he glanced down from where we were in the sky. He spotted the scaffold and saw his head jerking violently to the left as his neck snapped. Then he realized that he had been given a chance that no one gets: a chance to look into the years ahead. He knew that I could answer some of his questions about the future of his country. He was overjoyed that a civil war began one year after the hangman placed the noose around his neck, but he was saddened when he saw how immense the presence of death would be. He cried when he saw that the war has never come to an end.

"He was sinewy and muscular—much lighter than I had ever

imagined he would be. Every painter made him look like a wild titan. He always seemed like a giant to me. In another age people would have built a religion around him. Right now he's lounging poolside, sharing an apartment with Malcolm X and Crispus Attucks. I have to say, John Brown looks really good in a Hawaiian shirt."

Zeke leaned forward again and pounded his forehead savagely against the steering wheel. There was confusion and frustration, even a faint trace of contempt, in his face.

"I want out of this!" he screamed. "This is all *mishegoss*, every *fercockte* word of it!" He slammed the steering wheel with both hands again. A drop of blood oozed from a small cut at his hairline. "The other night, the night when I first heard you on that prison radio show, those were recorded sound effects that I was hearing, weren't they—the dogs, the horses, and the shouting? Then there was the sound of that wind. Did you find a recording of a hurricane and dub it over your voice? There's no way that I could really be hearing Jesse Washington being rescued from a lynching that took place anyway, in spite of your efforts! History says the mob hung him and burned him to death."

"The history books don't even mention Jesse Washington," countered Simon savagely.

"I don't understand any of this," shouted Zeke. "I'm trying to understand. Jesse Washington died a horrible death, but he didn't. According to you, he didn't die that day in Waco, Texas. No, no, he's not moldering in the ground," he said with a mocking voice. "No, he's off somewhere hoisting a cold drink and wearing a Hawaiian shirt and luau shorts. Insanity! Who is this for?" shouted Zeke. "Who on earth does this help?"

"It's for me," answered Simon, his voice measured but filled with tension. His right hand had begun to quiver. "It helps me." He touched a quaking index finger to his forehead. "Every time I do it, I'm sane for another minute, another hour. Brick by brick, I build my own world—one that I can live with—even if it only exists for a microsecond in a single synapse. I learn something more about who I am. Every person I lift makes me a little more weightless. The people in Rouen built that fire in such a way that Joan of Arc didn't die quickly; she stayed alive and suffering for long, agonizing minutes. The good people down in Waco made it a point to pour that gasoline on Jesse Washington while he was still conscious and twitching.

"Every time I go flying to scenes like those, I winnow through the audience, going carefully from face to face. I look into the crowd at each person. I am terrified by the possibility, no, by the probability, that I will see my face there among them. My face there, gloating or glorying, smug and vacuous; my face blasé—or even worse, looking the other way. I am horrified that I might be a chameleon, my face and spirit—my life changing color to match my bishop's robes, my colonel's tunic, my sagging pants, or my shiny badge."

"Have you seen it there?" asked Zeke. "Have you ever seen your own face there?"

"Every day," said Simon quietly. "Every day I land on a scarred and pocked hill that I've landed on a million times. When I get there, I see, for the millionth time, a young boy who is lying on his back. He has a through-and-through GSW—a gunshot wound. His breathing is labored. Then it stops. His young eyes are staring but seeing nothing.

"When I look down at his belly, I can see straight through it. I can see the ground below his shattered spine." Simon took a deep breath. "There are bloody pieces of chocolate and caramel on the dirt beneath his shredded stomach sac. I look around that grisly scene, and I look from soldier to soldier, and there it is—my face. My face turned olive-drab. My brown Mexican face turned olive-drab. I had become a slave. Once I belonged to a squad, a gang, a group, a platoon, a generation—an era. Once I pulled a trigger and a little boy died. He was so harmless, so defenseless, and I followed orders.

There I was—a young killer, so devout in my green vestments."

Simon's eyes were closed, and his entire body was being wracked again and again by the recoil of the M-16 rifle against his right shoulder.

"Maybe if I can hear and see and learn about every cruelty of the past, then maybe . . . maybe I can be ready to hear cruelty and see cruelty in the here and now. We are all so blind in the present. Maybe I can be ready to point out callousness and call it by its proper name. Maybe I can see the very moment when I am relinquishing my own will—handing it over, lock, stock, and barrel, to my time, my place; to a mob, to a culture, to a queue, to a fashion—to an order being shouted over a walkie-talkie. Only if I know when I'm not free can I set myself free. If I am everybody . . . then I am nobody."

He slumped forward onto the Antikythera device. The effort required to answer Zeke's question had temporarily depleted his strength.

"Are these dreams?" asked Zeke. "Is it a dream?"

"These are all just fractured conjectures, Zeke," Simon answered weakly. "These are hallucinations, the babblings of a confused mind. I don't really know anything. I don't even know what I'm saying. I've been out of my mind for such a long time." The Mexican Flyboy shut his eyes, flexing the muscles in his jaw in an effort to regain control. There was silence for several minutes before anyone spoke again. "What did the little boy say as he jumped into the water?" Simon asked softly. "Do you remember what he said?"

"He shouted 'Umama,'" said Zeke, barely above his breath. "He shouted it twice. I heard it as clearly as I heard my alarm clock this morning." The question had stopped Zeke's aggressive cross-examination dead in its tracks. "He shouted for his mother. Somehow I know that the little boy can't swim, but I can see him kicking his legs and pulling himself downward with his thin arms, down into the darkest waters. He is searching the ocean floor for his parents. He is waiting impatiently for the air in his lungs to run out so that he can be with them.

"Shit! Those dark shapes down there on the bottom aren't coral—not finger coral or brain coral. Those aren't clusters of eels, those are arms and legs," cried Zeke. "Those aren't octopus eyes, those are faces! I see thousands of faces down there, thousands of barnacled teeth and worm-eaten eyes." His breathing had become arduous and irregular. He reeled, then lost consciousness.

"You know," said Simon softly as he pounded his own forehead with the heel of his right hand, "I am such an idiot! Such a stupid fool. It was right there in front of me, and I didn't see it. I never saw it. I have to go back. I have to move them! I have to move the two of them into the same cottage. It has taken me over forty years to realize that the old Portogee and the cook were lovers."

16

SOPHIA'S FALL

It was supposed to be a romantic and death-defying "jump into sunrise." It was all Peter's idea, just like leaving Georgia and moving back to the West Coast had been Peter's idea. In 1958 she had made promises to herself: to get as far away from the Pacific as she could get; to get as far away from men as she could get. She had sworn to herself that she would never again open her legs to anyone. Nothing good had ever come of it. She had vowed tearfully, solemnly, that she would never come back here. Now it was 1961 and she was back in California again.

"The West Coast is a skydiver's paradise," he had explained. "We gotta go! It's the place to be."

She had already jumped from an airplane twice—both times against her will. She had always had a fear of heights. Peter Keyes claimed that the moonlit jump into sunrise had been inspired by a high-altitude night jump back at Fort Benning when his entire battalion had hit the silk at the crack of dawn while yelling their famous war cry, "Death from above." No one knew that the jump was going to happen during a lunar eclipse.

Sophia glanced to her left and saw her dull but handsome fourth husband shouting manfully over the wind and the engine noise, his lips almost touching the ear of the ravishing young Veronica—his real reason for rushing out to the West Coast. Everyone on the plane knew that these two were in lust—even the pilot knew. The two lovebirds had been fooling around in semisecret for months. Articles of his clothing had been disappearing from his closet back at the base since early spring. Now the clothes were disappearing from the closet in their new apartment in Hayward. It was almost empty.

It had mattered to Sophia for a reflexive split second, but somewhere along the way a page had been turned. Prior editions of Sophia would have cared—would have been devastated and furious about his betrayal. A prior edition of her would have cut her own wrists superficially with a razor or swallowed half a bottle of sleeping pills just as she heard his car pulling up. She might even have attacked Veronica, but a new, updated, annotated version of Sophia simply didn't care enough to do any of those things. She smiled at poor, foolish Veronica, who was self-consciously, awkwardly, basking in the glow of Peter's ineptly concealed affections.

She wanted to warn her but thought better of it. Everyone has a right to learn from their own mistakes. Just then, all eight of the other jumpers rose to their feet and waddled like penguins to peek out of the tiny port-side windows. Their heavy gear and the maze of belts and straps made walking difficult. Sophia did not budge from her seat. She didn't have to look through a window to know that far to the east, the moon was vanishing.

Peter's fabulous plan had all nine skydivers dropping from the plane one behind the next, then immediately joining hands. At the silent count of ten, the two divers at either end of the line would hook up and lock their arms, forming a circle. The team would jump at the first hint of light and land while the sun was just creeping over the mountains. Peter winked at Veronica and laughed wickedly while he checked his camera to see if it had film. He looked through the viewfinder and focused the telephoto lens on the folding bench where his future former wife had been sitting. In an instant, the smile disappeared from his face and was replaced by a look of dull confusion. She wasn't there.

He looked around, quickly counting heads. She wasn't anywhere! Including himself, there were only eight jumpers in the plane. Peter was perplexed. He couldn't believe his eyes. He counted heads again, just to be sure. He looked at Veronica, who was covering her face with shaking hands, and the realization hit him: Sophia was an amateur—a goddamn novice. Hell, the last time out, she'd pissed her panties! This was only her third jump, and for some reason she had stepped out into the cold dawn air without waiting for the others—without even telling them what she was doing!

He looked at Veronica, who was sobbing now and staring down at her feet. She had been the only one to see Sophia finish putting on her makeup, calmly get up from her seat, and leap silently through the open door. But before she went, Sophia had looked directly into Veronica's eyes. On her face there was a look of infinite sorrow—or was it pity? Whichever it was, it had shaken Veronica to the core of her being.

"She's going to die! I know it!" Veronica had shouted, but no one had heard.

Two hundred and fifty yards directly below Veronica's jump boots, Sophia broke through the clouds at nine thousand feet and suddenly crashed through the vaulted leaded-glass ceiling of paradise—seemingly shattering an entire section of the shining, shimmering dome of a heaven that her father had described so many times. But to her surprise, nothing broke—no deadly shards of leaded glass flew—no precious icons tumbled from their columns to splinter on marble floors. Nothing happened—nothing at all.

She listened as carefully as the wind rushing through her helmet would allow, but she heard no seraphim, no silent singing, only the sad porcelain echo of a filling bedpan and the fluttering of starched yellowed sheets being tossed over a mattress and allowed to billow downward into perfectly folded hospital corners. Then, at eighty-five hundred feet, she was finally able to catch a snippet of conversation.

"Be careful over at bed nine, honey," one overworked nurse said warily to another. "That old preacher man's a real brute, an octopus if you know what I mean. He's got the grasping hands of Judas, and I've got bruises on my sweet ass to prove it."

"You know, whenever I go over there," said the second nurse, "I swear I can hear lions roaring. Most frightening thing I've ever heard. I'll tell you, I'm never goin' near that old man again. I'll trade you any three of your patients if you'll handle that one for me. Have you ever heard lions up close?"

"It's probably just his intestines growling," said the first nurse with a weary smile. "They say he used to be a preacher man. You've heard the rumors, haven't you? The operation that he got the other day would've killed a man half his age. Not him! He's goin' back home in three days. He's too mean to die. It won't be soon enough for me." The other nurse shook her head. "Everybody here is talkin' about it. They say he got his own daughter pregnant and his wife tried to commit suicide."

"If that's true," said the other nurse with a shiver, "I'm gonna start dumpin' his bedpan into his orange juice."

This had to be Daddy's precious heaven, thought Sophia as she fell farther downward. He always sermonized that it was some-place between the earth and the moon, a city of white walls bobbing lazily like a yacht, just above the clouds. Well, here she was, and it was nothing like he described in his sermons. No pearly this and no golden that. Hell, except for the piney-bleach smell of the hospital room, it was empty—no shining mansion on a hill, no eternal fish fries going on underneath the soft blue flicker of holy mosquito lights. Gabriel with his horn was nowhere to be seen.

She looked around and was astonished to see that her father's great hereafter was completely vacant. There were no buildings, no landlords, and not a single tenant. All the renters had given notice and moved out. Sophia herself had moved out when she was just thirteen.

She inhaled deeply through her nose, breaking out in a painful spasm of coughing when her lungs abruptly filled with foul air. What could that awful stench be? Then it came to her—it was that sickly, sickening odor. It was that old rotten reek of cheap lavender pomade mixing with his sweat. She stopped coughing and began to gag violently on the nauseating memory. How she detested that stink. It had the cocky, smug odor of a man who had never done an honest day's work, a man who was so chock-full of himself that there was no room in his life—or his heaven—for anybody else.

She fell another hundred feet, then covered her face with her arms and braced her body as she crashed straight through the green-shingled roof of that small church house. In the next split second she found herself gliding and banking above the pulpit and pews—doing figure eights while screaming at the parishioners who were sitting so primly in their seats. She began hollering at them not to waste another minute listening to that demon who was sermonizing up there at the podium.

"Don't you sing for him, Mrs. Merkel! Don't you dare sing for him, Mr. Fuchs!" she howled at the pious-looking people in their seats as she swooped over them and strafed them with words. "Don't you say prayers with that man! Every one of you knows deep inside that he's twisted. Those ain't even his real teeth! That's not even his hair! He's not a family man like he says. He's a guard at a prison, and I was one of his prisoners! There's nothing real about that man. He can't be happy unless someone else is suffering."

Sophia accelerated to a blinding speed, plunging past the pulpit and right through the wooden floor of the church. In an instant she found herself smashing through the tar-and-gravel roof and the flimsy rafters of that small house in Illinois. Then she jerked to a sudden stop and froze in place, hanging suspended in midair. There was stark terror in her face. She had just glimpsed something awful out of the corner of her eye. She closed her eyes tightly to keep from seeing it. Then she wrenched her head to the left with a savage jerk and forced herself to look. The woman hovering between the floor and the ceiling began to sob hysterically. There, on the bed, was what she had come to see—what she had never wanted to see ever again. There she was.

"There I am!"

There was that hideous old wound. There was that never-ending insult, that crippling injury that she thought had been buried beneath a hundred layers of scar tissue. Now it was ripped open again, bleeding and raw. With one hand over her mouth and tears streaming down into the lenses of her goggles, adult Sophia saw little Sophia's knobby young knees being pried apart and her shapeless child-body being crushed beneath the naked, sweaty weight of the lord of the house. The wrathful hand of God was covering her young mouth to stifle any screams that the neighbors might hear. The other hand was smearing her nascent breasts back and forth across her narrow, bony chest.

The petrified young girl on the bed turned her head and trained her tearful eyes on the bizarre apparition that had just appeared from out of nowhere. For an instant it looked like an angry seabird was soaring four feet above the floor and squawking in the wind. For a moment she forgot about the savage pain in her groin and her father's ecstatic groans.

When she was able to focus her disbelieving eyes, the little girl saw a woman wearing large goggles, a green helmet, and a forest-green jumpsuit. She was strapped into a heavy canvas harness that had some strange-looking buckles and latches on it. The woman's red hair had unfurled from beneath the headgear and was standing straight up as though a powerful wind were blowing up from the floor. The little girl's eyes grew even wider when she saw the flailing, whipping locks of crimson hair. It was just like her own!

The flying woman extended her right arm away from her body.

Clutching a circular metal handle in her left hand that was attached to the end of a cord, she used her right arm and both legs to maneuver into a position that would allow her to scream directly into the old man's ear.

"Leave her alone, you disgusting, dirty little man! Leave me alone, you filthy bastard!" Sophia cried out hatefully as she fell past her confused and frightened former self—as she dropped past her poor cowardly mother cowering on her knees in the barn and drowning in her own dark lamentations. The older woman listened to her husband's foul grunting while she sang a song, a lament as pitch-black as the bruises around her eyes and the cuts on her wrists.

"Don't you know? She'll never forget this! Never!" she sang. "She'll never have a moment of romance, not for the rest of her life. No romance—never! She'll be like me! She'll be just like me! Leave that baby girl alone!" The two wounded women, one on the ground and the other plummeting toward it, chanted together across a chasm of decades. Then the mother sang: "Leave her alone! Go dumb, baby. Go numb, baby. Pretend you're a mattress, honey, stuffed with nothin' but straw. Be a pillow or a sheet. Have no more sense than the Almighty give a bedspread! Your mama knows these things real good. Don't be yourself, and it can't hurt no more."

After falling three thousand feet, Sophia whipped and whirled out of control in the wailing air as she felt her twelve-year-old body suddenly bent in two by the profound pains of her first cesarean section. Still writhing in agony, she spun out of the hospital bed on a cross-current of air and wheeled herself out of that first maternity room and into an elevator that plunged straight down for a thousand feet. The free-fall didn't come to an end until she crashed through the shiny tin ceiling of a twenty-four-foot Airstream trailer parked somewhere in a shabby mobile home park on the outskirts of Decatur.

Sophia laughed and cried in the same breath when she caught sight of a six-year-old boy playing outside the trailer. There he was, playing like any other child! She remembered him now, his unloved childhood—her indecision and her unrelenting inner turmoil. As a mother she had loved the little boy. As a sister she had despised him. She looked into his young face and knew that he deserved to be loved. He deserved to be put into a sack and held under water until he drowned. Then she caught her first glimpse of herself at eighteen years of age—feeling married and all grown up.

There she was, the little homemaker frying neck bones and white flour for her first real husband. There was the groom, sitting on the stoop of the trailer reading the classified section. Sophia almost cried at the sight of him. My god, he was just a boy—a melancholy farm boy—a hapless, penniless fool who could never find work but had promised to adopt the child and give him a name.

"Don't do it!" she suddenly cried out to herself as she descended through the tiny kitchenette and past a foldaway bed where her eyes spotted the remnants of another image: the sight of herself and her husband, two naked, sweating children, one of them ineptly pretending at love, miming a family, playacting that empty cupboards are romantic, that "forever" never wears thin, while the other lies on her back feeling nothing—staring upward at nothing.

The girl in the trailer had been distracted for a second, having noticed something, having caught wind of something, having heard a wispy syllable or two of some words whispered in the air around her ears. For an instant she thought that she actually saw a woman suspended in the air next to the combination dining table and second bed. Her clothing and her red hair were flapping violently. Was it a chance reflection? Was it a ghost? Was it a mirage brought on by several kinds of hunger? Had she seen this woman before—somewhere—someplace?

"Don't do what?" the younger edition of herself had asked herself as she quietly turned each beef neck bone, one by one, in the melted fat and browning flour.

"Don't get married again, Sophia! But most of all, don't give up the little boy who is playing outside! Don't you toss him away like a piece of trash! Don't you turn your back on that little boy, or he'll become a ghost. He'll haunt you—he'll haunt everyone. Go put your arms around him right now, this second, and say that he isn't him. Say it to yourself over and over! Say that you'll never leave. Don't you see? He's not our father! He isn't him! Say it!"

Had the younger Sophia really heard those words? The younger woman wistfully twirled a finger through several loose strands of her hair—strands that were as red as flickering, licking flame. The older woman caught sight of her little son coming toward the Airstream. He looked so damn much like his father.

"He isn't him! He isn't him!"

The fully grown Sophia gasped in surprise and despair when the little boy's face appeared in a window. He had climbed a tree in order to spy on his mother. There was that face, the spitting image of his father—her father. Sophia screamed her grief, then fell through a timber floor, then through a white linoleum floor, and right past that mindless waitressing job in Atlantic City. Then she cracked through the greasy ceiling tiles of that moribund little diner in Uniontown.

She tumbled past the dim lights and blaring music of that hopeless topless bar in Boston, through the midst of a drunken wedding party in Las Vegas, and straight to the scene of that terrible car wreck on Highway 101 just north of Petaluma. She sliced through a cloud and found herself floating above herself as she stood alone by the gravesite at her second husband's funeral in Redwood City. The skydiver strained her eyes trying to get a better view of the inexpensive tiny headstone, but it was no use. She couldn't make out his name. They had been husband and wife for six hours, and she would never be able to remember his name.

"Where is your son? Where is your son?" she screamed at her grieving younger self. "I don't see the little boy. You've already done it, haven't you? Who was that man that was your husband for less than a day?" the falling woman implored the hungover bandaged and bewildered girl who was perched precariously close to the edge of a dark, dank hole that the two black gravediggers had not yet finished filling.

Sophia sobbed aloud, then pulled her arms into her sides, diving through the grassy lawn at the Chapel of the Chimes, falling past the faces and bedrooms of a hundred men in as many cities before she finally got to him. At last—alas—there it was in front of her, the face of the sweet little Hindu man who had built her a home out in the San Joaquin Valley of California. At the Rangoon Café, Sophia had finally found herself at the center of a real family. For the first time in her life, she had been in love.

He was the only man in the world who had ever been gentle to her and decent to her, and Sophia had been swept completely off her feet—but not by her doting third husband. She had fallen in love not with a man but with the new life burgeoning in her belly. But even that, like everything else in her life, would sour and go bad. In the end, her history, her curse, had hunted her down and found her. The thought of seeing that small, happy family—the thought of hearing the sweet laughter coming from their small rooms behind the Rangoon Café—made her sick to her stomach.

"I won't go there!" screamed the falling woman. "I can't go there. I just couldn't bear to see that. Not that!" she screamed. She pulled her arms in closer to her body, doubling her velocity so that she shot past that little restaurant on Mountain House Road at 150 miles an hour, but it didn't work quite as well as she had hoped.

Despite her desperate efforts, she caught a glimpse of her former self.

There she was with sweat pouring from her face, breasts, and legs while a doctor made an incision in her belly in order to remove a pair of premature twins that were as small and frail as kittens. In the hallway outside, her third husband was pacing nervously back and forth and praying silently. For the tiniest slice of a second, she glimpsed his dark face and saw something that almost stopped her heart. In his eyes she had seen hope and the unmistakable countenance of love.

"Please, not them. I couldn't bear to see them . . . any of them!"

Sophia began to sob uncontrollably, losing consciousness momentarily until she felt a new, angry wind rushing in from the direction of sunrise and rudely shoving the old fog-drenched wind out to sea. This dry, insolent onshore gale buffeted and battered her, then abruptly changed direction even while it was howling insults into her ears. She recoiled suddenly when she heard her father's cocksure wail woven into the twisting tempest.

Her arms burned as hot updrafts filled with millions of tiny fruit flies and moths began pelting her face and hands. Two or three dozen of them expired violently on her goggles, and a few perished in her mouth. Their lives were salty and bitter on her tongue—like her father's semen. She spat and spat again for a thousand feet, just as the face of the moon began to peek out from behind the shadow of the earth.

She suddenly remembered something very important that had almost slipped her mind: she had to keep her hand in a tight grip around the ripcord. She felt the surging heat of the morning thermals roiling upward like vertical waves from the warm brown soil beneath her and soon realized that the vague patterns below that she had first seen from six thousand feet higher were resolving into long rows of silvery irrigation pipes and row after row of green plants. That was not an airport down there, but a vineyard. Those weren't Piper Cubs, but tractors. She looked up and saw eight colorful parachutes spread out a half-mile above her. She laughed to herself. Peter hadn't anticipated this wild, errant wind. The jumpers had all been blown inland and would miss the landing zone by five miles or more.

Suddenly, like bats at sundown, every thought flew out of her mind. Her father was gone forever now, damned to a pauper's plot in Illinois—his sermons muffled by six feet of mud. Her sad mother and that anonymous husband in the graveyard in Redwood City were gone from memory. A few precious years of family life at the tiny Rangoon Café—her only moments of love in a wasted existence—were gone for all time, fossilized and disintegrating. Every thought was extinct now, except one.

Somehow Sophia sensed that someone could see her from down below. She strained her eyes trying to see him clearly, but she was still too high up to make out his features. Was he a man or a boy? Could it be him—the boy playing outside that trailer in Decatur? Could it be the man that Pete had seen by the rigging shack this morning? Had the person down below angrily ripped her name tag from her chute? Had he cut through a few of the risers or hatefully torn a hole in the silk? Did the person below have cold, heartless eyes? Had he found her yet again? She felt him tracking her trajectory across the sky, and she sensed his thoughts flying upward to meet her.

In that same unbearable, infinitesimal sliver of an instant, the boy a half-mile beneath her began sharing with her his own frantic dreams of flight. A moment later, she was shocked when she seemed to feel invisible arms clutching at her. Was he trying to kill her, or was he trying frantically to slow her fall? She smiled when she felt the unmistakable push of two small hands pressing up against her belly, trying with all their strength to stop her in midair.

She sensed the touch weakening in strength but still straining to help her. It wasn't him. This touch was gentle and caring. It couldn't possibly be him. For an instant she thought she glimpsed something fantastical—someone, a brown-skinned adult male, hovering at her side. It seemed as though he was just a few feet away. Then he vanished as quickly as he had appeared.

Realizing that she was about to slam into the earth face first, she grappled with a fierce, self-righteous wind, slapping its cheek until it lustfully twisted her and angrily pinned her shoulders—until it was her backside that was a hundred feet from the ground. Now it was her face and breasts and pretty toes that were pointed toward the clouds. She let go of the ripcord. She quickly tore off her helmet and goggles and let them go. She had to say something to this young boy, whoever he was. She had something to say to him, and she wanted her face and mouth to be exposed and in one piece in order to say it.

She saw the boy in her peripheral vision. She was very close to the ground. Knowing that her senses would soon be scrambled and leaking from the back of her skull, knowing that her torn lungs would push no air over vocal cords that had been snapped and shredded, she carefully placed each of her chosen words onto her tongue—at the very tip—and got them ready to burst forth, one after the other in the correct order.

One-third of a second before she died, she turned her head to catch a clear glimpse of the boy's face—to look straight into his terrified brown eyes. As she turned her head back to face the blue sky above, she spread her lips to let the words go free just as her ribs tore through her skin and through the cloth of her jumpsuit. The strange words reached his ears as the shadow abandoned the moon, just as dark blood exploded into the cavity that had once held her doubly cursed womb—into the glands that had once made the jinxed milk of her breasts—and finally gushed from the faintly pumping chambers of her unseen, unloved heart.

"She . . . isn't . . . me."

Then, in an unknowable place for an immeasurably small sliver of time, she sensed an infinitesimal breeze . . . no, it was a child's breath blowing across those things that would never again be her eyelashes.

17

THE *LUFTMENSCH*

Zeke bit his wrist to keep from gagging. He blinked his eyes and tried to think of anything but the human forms at the bottom of the sea—shapes that had made him so nauseous and forlorn. He inhaled deeply in order to catch his breath and gather his senses.

"What are these numbers down here?" he demanded as he pointed to a particular set of coordinates at the bottom of yet another crowded page. He desperately needed a distraction. The numbers had been circled vigorously, five, six, or seven times.

"No other numbers are circled that many times. It's no good. I can't work with you anymore," he blurted out angrily. Then his voice dropped to a whimper. "I want out of this madness! You're a *luftmensch,* you're *meshugge.* I've ignored all of this for years. I've put up with your eccentric, bizarre behavior for twenty-five years because you always seem to pull it together. You're a beat-up punch-drunk boxer who manages to put on the gloves on Friday night and slog it out for chump change.

"Knowing you is too much work for me." His voice was stressed, and his whole body quivered as he spoke. "It's just too much for me. If I keep hanging out with you, I know I'm going to be just as bonkers as you. Look at me. I'm in Sacramento. I'm in the parking lot of a convalescent home, and I swear I just saw a lion crouching out there in that field. A goddamn lion! It's a hundred and two degrees outside, and I'm covered with sea water and bird shit, and I'm hearing voices from the eighteenth century!"

In the next instant Zeke fell silent. It was then that he realized he had been screaming with all of his strength, and that at some point during his last outburst he had begun davening fiercely. He fell backward into the car seat and covered his eyes with his hands. After several minutes of quiet, he spoke again in a weak, raspy whisper.

"I never daven. Never. When I was a kid at Hebrew school, I swore I would never do it. How many of these ledgers do you have? I saw a lot of them in your garage."

"If you count the years before Hephaestus Segundo and I got the Antikythera device to work, I have ninety other volumes just like this one. Elena showed them to you, didn't she? I started the first ledger when I was nine years old. At first it was just a wish book, like a Sears catalogue sitting on a shelf in some field workers' outhouse in the Imperial Valley. Some of the first entries were rabbits and kittens—the dates when they died and the locations where the tractors ran over them. My very first entry was a list of fifteen names."

"Aren't you weighed down by this?" Zeke asked as he looked at the encircled numbers. "Aren't you devastated by all of this? You've forced yourself to study—to swallow and digest human tragedy and so much suffering. Even if what you do isn't real, isn't the responsibility of it crushing you?" He was no longer sure that he wanted to see how deep his friend's disturbance went. "I saw those eyes at the bottom of the ocean for only a second, and it felt like the weight of a hundred atmospheres was pressing down on me."

"It's exactly the opposite, Zeke. The other night when I hoisted Jesse Washington up and away from that lynch mob, I could feel my heartache diminishing with every foot of altitude that we gained. Don't you see? I gave something to Jesse that no one else has ever given him. I studied his life and memorized his death. I carefully located his place in time. I looked for him and found him—his exact location on the surface of the earth—when everyone else had pushed him aside or forgotten all about him. Someone should have been there for him, Zeke. Someone in Waco should have stepped forward. I tried to share his terror and his loneliness," he said with a voice that almost evaporated as he spoke.

Now Zeke knew that he was hearing the boy within Simon the man.

"Are you some kind of conjurer? Is it magic—the supernatural? Is it magical thinking?" asked Zeke.

"No," said Simon with a chuckle. "I'm just a Mexican with some Irish blood—and it certainly isn't what most would call magic. It's magic when you pray to the stratosphere for a new bike. It's magic when you thank the ionosphere for a timely home run or for a game-winning touchdown, when you stand on a smoking field of battle that is still soaking with sorrow and you give thanks. When you strap on a vest full of high explosives, then run into a market-place that is teeming with mothers and babies, all in the name of the Crab Nebula—that's magic."

"What good does this do for all of us?" asked Zeke.

"It isn't for all of us. It's for me. Like I told you, it's for me. It was supernatural once, long ago, before I began to find my props and my tools, before I gathered together my maps, my comics, my cape, and now the Antikythera machine. How can it be prestidigitation and legerdemain when I am the magician and I am the audience? How can it be magic when I am the rabbit and I am the hat—when I am sawing myself in half and putting myself back together? I really can't explain it to you or to me. It isn't magic, just my fierce desire to be free—to not be a man of my time. I refuse to be a slave anymore."

"What is this number here—the very first number on the very first page? Two degrees, ten minutes east longitude . . ."

"The Triangle Shirtwaist Factory in the Village in New York City," Simon said in a detached, almost mechanical whisper. "My mother read the story to me when I was a little boy. There was an awful fire, and the women couldn't get out of their workspaces because the doors had been padlocked. The floor bosses suspected that the women were taking needles and pieces of fabric home with them, so they locked them in so that their purses could be searched. That's when the fire happened. The photographs in the newspaper article showed forty broken bodies on the sidewalk. The women had jumped from the ninth and tenth floors. Beautiful dark-eyed girls from Italy."

"They make all of the Hawaiian shirts, don't they?" said Zeke snidely. "In this contorted, inverted universe of yours, the ladies of the Triangle Shirtwaist Factory have been unionized. They are living in Florida, making the Hawaiian shirts that the residents there all seem to be wearing. Did I hear you right the other night—did you take Jesse Washington to Boca Raton, to a section of Boca that you referred to as Mexican heaven? Isn't that what you said to the thousands of cynical, hardened convicts in San Quentin Prison? What will you tell them next, that Malcolm X is somewhere in Boca sporting a straw hat, a flowered shirt, and a necklace of orchids? He's hoisting a gin and tonic with Osawatomie John Brown?"

"John Brown doesn't drink," said Simon. "He thinks alcohol is unseemly. John and his brood of twenty children love hibiscus tea and mango juice. They had never tasted such things back in Kansas."

"You know I'm going to run those numbers that you have tattooed on your chest, don't you?" said Zeke almost inaudibly. "You know I'm going to find out what happened at that location. Then my work for you is done—over. I'll be through with all of this—forever.

"What is that number on the bottom of this page—another one that's circled six or seven times, but in red ink?" Zeke was sounding defeated. His voice was fading, almost fearful. He hadn't signed up for any of this. He was just an investigator who read Carl Jung assiduously and Bertrand Russell occasionally. He didn't want to be a rabbi. He didn't want to fight with winds. He didn't want a friend who was clearly off his rocker. Still, there was a hint of curiosity in his face. "What does that number mean? Fifty-two degrees, forty-five seconds . . . ?"

"Bergen-Belsen," said Simon in a gentle, almost vanishing tenor. "The concentration camp."

"The tent camp?" asked Zeke, who was suddenly trembling, his lips quivering with intensity. There were newly formed drops of sweat flowing down his cheeks and forehead.

"Is it the tent camp? It can't be."

"Nine degrees, twenty-eight point zero-eight seconds east," said Simon. "There's a small margin of error in those numbers."

"Have you been there yet?" asked Zeke. His face was rigid and his teeth were clenched. His eyes were open and suddenly very bloodshot.

"Have you been there yet?" he repeated. "Have you seen them?"

"Not yet," said Simon. "I've already searched through three of the tents. It takes so much energy to do because I can't bear to leave anyone behind. Eventually, everyone who died in that concentration camp will be taken to Florida. The new battery pack on the Antikythera device has its limits. The ancient components are self-powered, of course. Archimedes got very close to a perpetual motion device when he designed them. It's the modern components that soak up all of the energy.

"The people themselves are no problem. In their naked, emaciated condition, the people in the tents are easy to lift. It's like lifting kittens, Zeke. Just like lifting a litter of newborns—blind and shivering kittens. But by the time we get to Florida, they've gained back all the weight they had lost to disease and starvation.

"Thirty or forty of them gaining weight by the second can drain the circuitry if I'm not ready for it. On mass retrievals like Rwanda and Cambodia, I had to carry several heavy battery packs on my back. Hephaestus carried even more."

"Rwanda? Cambodia?" said Zeke. Now he was sure of it. This went far beyond friendship. Simon was truly a lost cause.

"Hephaestus Segundo is working on a smaller yet far more potent power source that uses tiny copper ingots, grappa, and curdled goat's milk. As for the two girls, I know the week, the month, and the year when it happened, but no one on earth knows the exact day, much less the hour." As Simon spoke, the anger seemed to drain from Zeke's face. "There was one witness who spoke with the younger girl through a barbed wire fence. It was the little girl's last known conversation with anyone. Current scholarship says it happened during the first week in May."

"Please," moaned Zeke with a muted intensity. His voice was breaking with resignation and sorrow—and a growing undercurrent of excitement. Then he stiffened and said, "Please don't go. Not there. Promise me you won't go back to Bergen-Belsen again. Let me do it. Let me."

"It's for me, Zeke. Don't you see it's for me? I'm the one who has been haunted all of my life." Now the Flyboy was screaming. "I do it just to wake up another morning, take a shower, put on a necktie, and go on living in this world. I'm not a joiner, Zeke. Don't you see?" he shouted into his friend's face. "I can't get in line. Not anymore. I see a mass of people cheering a hole in one or kneeling down to pray, and I am diminished by it. When I hear about people camping on the sidewalk to get into a department store, I feel nauseated.

"Shit, Zeke, don't you see? I do this thing just to keep on living—just to get by. How can I explain something when I can't even understand it myself? I've had it up to my ears with trauma-focused crap therapy and that cognitive-behavioral drivel they hand out at the army hospital. I couldn't swallow another fluoxetine pill or sertraline. Those things almost killed me. I don't want my serotonin selectively reuptaken and inhibited by anything. When I was a kid,

I had the weight of the world on me. Doctors and drugs couldn't cure what I had. It was up to me. I had to find a way to lessen that weight, ounce by ounce, day by day."

The Flyboy slumped in his seat and said nothing for a minute or two. When he spoke again, all of the anger and the intensity were gone. He turned his face to the door and spoke to the glass.

"I'm not someone who can caress a cell phone or worship a car. I want to know as much as I can and believe as little as possible. I can't bear to live only in my own time. I don't want amnesia. I don't want to be blind," he said in a low voice. "I want to know when I have become manacled by a belief. And now I've made things worse . . . or better. Goddamn it, I'm having a baby!" Simon abruptly shrieked at Zeke. "A little baby girl! What kind of father is someone like me going to be? I could ruin her life, too!"

He reached over and grabbed Zeke's arm, pulling him across the center console of the car until the two men's eyes were no more than six inches apart. "I have to catch Sophia. Then maybe I'll be a good daddy," said the Mexican Flyboy with bulging eyes and renewed intensity. "I have to get those two girls in Bergen-Belsen, those five hundred and four people at My Lai; then maybe I can be a decent father and a loving husband. Maybe I can be a free man. Maybe I'll stand a chance." He let go of Zeke's arm and used his free hand to cover his twisted face. For a minute, Simon seemed weary and ancient.

"The word 'we' is the most beautiful word there is," he said while turning his face away from Zeke. "Sometimes I imagine a family—Elena and the baby and me—we are a family. The word 'we' is the most beautiful word." He thought of the faces in the crowd in Waco and in Rouen. He saw the grunts trudging back from My Lai, looking as though nothing at all had happened. "The word 'we' is the ugliest word on earth."

"We humans have been turning gold into scrap iron for a long,

long time," said Zeke, who was suddenly feeling dizzy. His stomach ached, and he rubbed it. "That is the true falsification of metals. What was on that stick of gum?"

There was an old Irish tune starting to vibrate in Zeke's gorge. Simon began to sing the words of the song as he manipulated the controls on the Antikythera machine. The investigator had never heard the lyrics before, but he seemed to know them by heart. In the same instant, Zeke thought he saw a long line of waves breaking lazily along an endless strand of white beach. He thought he saw a man and a woman—two lithe and sinuous humans who were as black as living ebony, as supple as flexible obsidian. Zeke's jaw dropped. It was the young parents from the slave ship *Zong*. He could actually see their faces!

They were wearing colorful dappled shorts and orange thongs, Hawaiian shirts and leis of scarlet hibiscus blossoms. They were waving their arms wildly and running at full speed toward a young boy, who was screaming their names as he ran toward them, his arms open wide. All three were laughing hysterically and sobbing at the same time, their tears conjoining, mixing on their faces. They hugged each other for what seemed an eternity before they joined hands and walked together toward a small two-bedroom bungalow on a lovely lagoon.

"You're going to love it here, Kassamila. Look, there's a slide and a swing over there! You have your own bed. A soft, warm bed."

In another instant, none of them could remember why they had once been so incredibly sad—why their ankles had once been chafed to the bone and endlessly bleeding—why the chains on the swing had given them a moment of pause, a cold chill that was soon dispelled by a warm tropical breeze. Even their lovely skin had lost its memories of sores and running pustules.

"There's a sweet little Pequot family living next door, Kassamila," said the mother. *"I'm sure their boys would love to have a playmate."*

On their way home from the beach, the trio happened to pass a middle-aged Mexican magician who was walking—no, levitating—in the opposite direction. He had an odd blinking machine strapped to his belly, and he was smiling. All three nodded politely at him but said nothing. When they reached their home, they stared vaguely back at the magician, then shrugged in mild bemused confusion, as though they might once have known him—as though they might once have known his name.

"Do they live forever—these people in Boca Raton, do they live forever?"

"I don't know," said Simon. "I think they just live out their lives—the lives they would have had if people had left them alone. Funny, I've never asked myself that question. I learn about them. I study and honor them. Then I go get them. I collect them and bring them to Mexican heaven. They find each other, Zeke. They find one another and heal one another. They heal me. I've never thought beyond that. Does an eccentric have to think things through, Zeke? Is a shell-shocked weirdo like me really supposed to be consistent? Am I obliged to have a coherent plan? I'm Señor Tomás O'Bedlam, the Mexican-Irish madman. I don't have to have a comprehensive scheme."

"Now I've gone mad, too," said Zeke. "Completely mad." All of the color had drained from his face, and he was davening again and again. "I've lost my mind. I can feel it slipping away. Please," he begged again, "don't go back to Bergen-Belsen. Don't go back to the tent camp. Those tents have been in my dreams since I read her diary when I was a little boy. It broke my heart. I cried so much that my mother hid the book from me. It broke my heart. Those tents have always haunted me. Don't go there, Simon. Let me. Let me go."

18

MAGDALENA

Elena woke with a start. There had been an excruciating din in her dreams. Loud noises were still reverberating in her head as she lay staring at the ceiling. As her mind cleared, she could still hear the cries of desperate humans and the sounds of splashing. She took a deep breath and was relieved to find that it was air that was entering her lungs and not salt water. She quickly touched her forehead, then her neck and chest. She must have kicked off the sheets during the night. Her entire body was wet from her scalp to her toes. She lifted her forearm to her nose and sniffed, then sighed with relief. It was only cold sweat.

It slowly began to dawn on her that her breathing was heavy and there were sharp pains shooting through her stomach and into her groin. She tried to roll out of bed but couldn't do it. She tried again but was defeated by gravity and some indeterminate force that caused her to slump back into the mattress. Her left hand was clutched in Simon's right hand and he was squeezing it tightly. He hadn't done that in a long, long time.

She glanced at the luminous hands of the clock. It was five in the morning. The sky outside was still black. She felt confused and sensed that something about this morning was different—something besides the imminent birth of their daughter. Simon was usually gone by now.

"Are you asleep?" she asked in a whisper. She could see his body clearly, but she had no idea where his mind might be at that moment. "Are you here in this room with me?"

"No," he answered. "No, I am not asleep. Yes, I am right here." Then he added, "Is today the day? Are you having pains?"

"Yes," she answered. Simon's voice seemed remarkably lucid this morning, more tethered to the here and now than usual. "They're still pretty far apart, but today's the day. Sometime tonight, I think." Then, "It'll be tonight." She looked around the darkened room. Everything was there and ready: diapers, baby wipes, blankets the size of hand towels, a mechanical mobile, and a music maker for her small bassinet.

She noticed that Simon's hand was beginning to shake. She curled her sweaty fingers around it to calm the growing tremor. She couldn't tell if he was shaking out of fear, out of concern, or out of excitement. She hoped that it was all three. She felt dizzy for a moment. Then she understood that it was elation she was feeling. It was exhilaration and not panic. Her conscious mind had been in constant turmoil the last few weeks, but there was something growing and moving far beneath the havoc and humdrum of her daily life. After so many hours of pain and waiting, a glacial, irresistible calm was coming.

"Your clothing smells like the ocean," she whispered to her husband. "Have you been swimming in the bay? I think that odor on your suit caused me to have dreams about the sea last night—or was it that Antikythera device blinking on your chest? I have dozens of loud, vivid dreams every night. Some are enjoyable, but I don't think the ocean dreams were pleasant." She paused for a moment. "No, they were bad dreams—disturbing and far from pleasant. Now I'm certain of it. I had terrible dreams about some sort of antique ship. Everything was creaky and wet and smelly. Men were being cruel. That's all I can remember. It was very disturbing."

Then she paused for a moment to allow a thought to evolve in her mind and in her memory.

"You've been flying, haven't you?" she said. She nodded to herself in the dark as she realized something that should have been obvious all along. She finally recognized that the residual energy from Simon's flights radiated from the Antikythera device for days afterward, subsiding slowly, lingering there like the heat from an engine.

"Yes," he answered.

"The ocean," whispered Elena. "The little boy and his parents." Then, "I didn't go with you, did I? I don't feel sick at all."

"Zeke went," said Simon. "But that was six or seven days ago, and we were a long way from here—out on the highway. You shouldn't have been affected. There must be a lot of energy stored up in all of these gears and tubes. You know what? I've discovered that if I wear the machine at night, I sleep like a baby. It doesn't even have to be turned on. Apparently it has a different effect on you. There's a lot about this machine that I still don't understand. Are you all right?"

She nodded her head, then used a corner of the bedsheet to daub at the tears and perspiration glistening on her face.

"Remember your promise," she said quietly but forcefully. "After the baby has come out, I'm . . . we're going with you. The baby is coming, too."

The two said nothing for several long minutes before Elena spoke again.

"When I was a girl, Judy Garland made me cry," she whispered. "How could Dorothy do that—to herself, to all of us? Nat Turner made me cry. John Kennedy Toole. I think of him every time I smell exhaust fumes." She was whispering even more softly now, having an internal discussion. "Jonestown—two hundred children. All of those children . . ." She suddenly felt the kick of first one leg, then the other. The infant began turning her head downward—making early preparations for a grand entrance into the world.

"I'll call you when I head to the hospital," said Elena. "First I have to go visit my father. Today is the anniversary of his death." She almost sobbed as she said it. "Do you think it's a coincidence? Can it be just a coincidence? I wish he had lived long enough to see this baby—his only grandchild." She rubbed her enormous belly as she spoke. "I do miss my papa," she said. "I miss him so much. It's not fair. It's just not fair. He should be here for this, with his creaky old sextants and his oil bath compasses helping us map our way through all of this."

She cried softly as her mind flooded with a thousand iterations of her father's face. There he is tugging at a Chinese kite. There he is lovingly buttoning her favorite quilted coat. There are his footsteps at the front door—the sound of the key. Now his hand reaches in to turn out the light. He is bending to kiss her while she pretends to sleep. The sweet perfume of his map room fills her nostrils. She can see him in his favorite chair, not loving the maps so much as the human longing they represent—the desire to know. She can hear the careful crackle of ancient paper being fastidiously unfurled, and she can see the dance of his fingertips over every inch of its surface. The memories always sent pangs of longing and love through her body.

Simon released her hand, and she lay quietly for a few moments before rolling to her right and into a sitting position at the edge of the bed. Outside their bedroom window, the sky was turning from black to lavender. He watched her as she moved. Usually lithe and light-footed, she had to hold her breath and struggle to put on her left slipper. She inhaled and held her breath again, then tossed her right foot onto her left knee in order to reach it and slip on the soft pink shoe. She heaved herself to her feet and slowly crossed the room.

"Both schools have called," she shouted without turning back. "You haven't shown up for your classes this week, and your students are asking for their grades. I told them that the baby was due yesterday, and that seemed to satisfy them—for now."

He saw a meridian moving with her as she traveled—her swollen, discolored navel a meridian more prime than Greenwich. It marked a profound dividing line between this day and yesterday, between the darkness of night and the coming light of morning. He saw a quotidian, a common yet momentous thing, in her stupendous aching girth and in her enormous veined breasts, and he felt a new anxiety, a chained wave—a tsunami growing in the pit of his stomach. The fateful day was finally here, the day of reckoning—the adding up of wildly disparate things—the day when Simon Magus Vegas has a baby daughter.

As she started to enter the bathroom, she paused in the doorway. "I'm sorry about what happened at the prison," she said. "Maybe it happened in the hospital. I'm not sure. But I read about it in the newspaper yesterday—at least the first two paragraphs of the story. I know he was a monster, but I'm still sorry for his life, I guess—for his whole life and for the people in it."

The infant kicked again, then pressed her tiny hands against the living wall of her mother's belly. "She's coming soon!" shouted Elena. "She's coming soon. She says her father has to be there when she comes down. He's got to be there. With two hands at the ready, he's got to be there."

He heard the sound of the shower and the soft drone of the exhaust fan coming from the bathroom. For some reason, the sound of rain, the muffled squall behind the shower curtain, soothed and settled him. Lenny Hudson was dead. He would never again come screaming and shouting into the interview room. His tiny, sterile stainless steel cell would become someone else's home for life.

His final instructions, on file at the administration office, dictated that all of his worldly possessions were to be given to Simon Vegas. Lenny had put his signature on the instructions a full decade and a half before the day that Simon first came to see him on

Condemned Row. The warden had called the night before last to tell Simon that Lenny was dying in an ambulance that was headed for the emergency room at Marin General Hospital, the backup for the small medical facility in San Quentin.

"He's tried to kill himself," Warden Harris had pronounced solemnly.

Simon had dropped everything and driven out to the hospital. The warden was waiting there to greet him as he entered the intensive care unit. There were armed guards at the entrance, and Simon could see several others on the other side of the glass doors. When he pulled the white curtain aside, he could see that Lenny was chained to his deathbed. He stayed at the prisoner's side for four hours until the doctor officially pronounced him dead. The next morning, Simon had driven back to San Quentin to pick up all of Lenny's personal effects. Everything the deceased prisoner had owned had been placed in a single brown envelope and a small box.

"Not a carton like everybody else," the warden had explained, "just a measly manila envelope and this tiny box. And it's all yours, my man. Just sign here. All the years he was here, Lenny never received a letter or a postcard or a phone call. No one but lawyers ever came to visit him. He didn't want to die of old age. You know that, don't you? Now that the state has suspended all executions for budgetary reasons, he couldn't bear the thought of dying ancient and irrelevant. He needed his rage."

The Mexican Flyboy closed his eyes and listened to the soothing sound of the pelting shower. He realized that he had fallen asleep without undressing. He thought about Lenny Hudson, about how endlessly sad his face had been two days ago. He had looked desiccated, almost mummified, in those hospital bedsheets. The hard, dizzying maze of false identities, carefully constructed disguises, and hardened excuses had collapsed into a single deflated flaccid desire to let go—to let all of it go.

Simon sighed. He had something to do in the minutes before Elena stepped from the shower. He had one more flight to make before he could be ready to meet his daughter. He touched the controls of the machine and was instantaneously sucked upward into yet another wailing cyclonic vortex that was touching ground just above his bedspread, seemingly intent upon sweeping the body of the Mexican maniac into the stratosphere.

He let the wind come, taunting it with his fists. The wind had announced itself as Cockeyed Bob from New South Wales. Simon lay against the turnbuckle, arms open and taking every punch, letting the storm grow confident and cocky—the rope-a-dope. Bob drove his thumbs into the Mexican's kidneys twice, three times, sending a shiver of pain down Simon's back. He allowed the tempest to carry him along while it threw everything it had at him. Despite the pain, he wore the wind out over Santa Fe, then he turned on it in the air above El Paso. The Mexican Flyboy slapped the hurricane silly and left it abated and beaten.

—⌐

"Man, is that me down there?" asked the young man. "Yes," said Simon Magus Vegas, "that's you. You were shot in the neck. Your esophagus and windpipe were shredded, and the bullet clipped your spine. It's almost the same wound! You were shot in the neck twenty-two years after—well, you'll see."

"Shit, man, I look all tore up. Do they need that many doctors? There must be eight doctors down there."

"It often takes a lot of care and concern, and thousands of hours of study, experimentation, and practice to offset a single act of stupidity," said Simon.

"And who are those other people—the ones waiting off to the side?" asked the young man, who had not felt the verbal jab. "Why are they carrying duct tape and those white boxes?"

"Those people are here to harvest your organs," said Simon. "As soon as the head surgeon shakes his head and puts down his scalpel, his team will step away from the operating table, and the other people will step forward. Your heart, your kidneys, your eyes, and your liver will be cut out, put on ice, and sent to hospitals in three states.

"Do you see that monitor? Your brain is almost dead, but the rest of your body is still working. Come to think of it, it's not much of a change from your life before the gunshot. A little girl in Houston is slated to have your liver. Her name is Ruby. A kidney will be sent to a Professor Craig Werner up in Madison. A forty-year-old woman in Hawaii is scheduled to receive your eyes; her name is Sarah. If you die on that table, your mother will save her money like a miser so that she can visit every single recipient of your organs—just to touch a living piece of her only son. In Honolulu she will look into your eyes, and for the first time in years they won't look away angrily."

"So I'm dead—that's what you're saying. I died on that operating table down there. It was Arturo who shot me, you know. His street name is Loco Ratón. He was nothin' but a little Indio from a little shithole of a town just south of Juárez. Just a scrap. That's all he is—just a scrap. It was that little fuckup Arturo Gómez from the 7th Street Boys who put a cap in me when I wasn't lookin'."

"Stop being so damned trivial!" seethed the Flyboy. There was rage and supreme frustration in his face. Fulgencio Garza Junior recoiled at the sheer ferocity of the voice. "I'm a madman, don't you see?" explained Simon harshly. "There's nothing intrinsically valuable about life—yours, mine, or anyone else's. We say life is precious, but in truth, we all have to agree on its value, and honor that value or it has no value. People like you and Arturo Gómez make that agreement seem impossible. Don't you see?" He was screaming now. The young man was pulling away from him and cowering behind a small tower of surgical instruments.

"It's the only true covenant we have—the only one that means anything. It's the only covenant we've ever had. Don't be scared," Simon said softly. "I'm just truly disturbed, and I rave like this all the time. I can't stomach triviality and I can't stand joiners. You are both. Arturo Gómez didn't have any more choice than you did. Choice is an acquired taste, you see. You once had a perfectly good mind, Fulgencio. Why did you surrender it so cheaply?" Simon closed his eyes. "Why did you give up your whole life for a pocket full of candy bars—for a few pieces of chocolate and nougat? Why did you do that?"

"Chocolate candy?" asked Fulgencio. "What the fuck you talkin' about? There weren't no chocolate candy involved in none of this. I was wearin' my colors. I was wearin' my celadon, and he was wearin' that puce they wear over on his street. That's why he shot me. I woulda shot him back, but I didn't have my gun. Who the fuck are you anyway, man? And why are you interferin' with my death?"

Simon considered the words that had just been on his tongue and said, "I'm sorry. I wasn't really talking about you—but I guess I was. There was a little boy who walked through a minefield . . . oh, it doesn't matter right now. My name is Simon Magus Vegas. Have I introduced myself? Did you hear me mention your mother?"

Fulgencio nodded.

"Why didn't you ask me about her?"

"She's a mother!" he said angrily. "She had me, then she went to work and let me watch television and run the streets. She didn't make me go to school. I don't remember her ever bein' home with me. All she ever did was work and cook and . . . cry. When she was at home, she would cry and go on and on about my father. He was a good man and all that shit. She should've loved him and she should've married him and all that shit. Look, man, I never even seen the dude! Not once. Never seen him.

"Why should I give a shit about him? He didn't give a shit about me. He died somewhere far away from here a long time ago. He chose to go there. What's he got to do with me? And where's my mother now? She is probably deliverin' mail, gettin' home after dark, drinkin' cheap wine, and fallin' asleep in front of the TV!"

In the next instant, the blinding whiteness of the surgeons' gowns, the mercury lamps, and the Styrofoam boxes of the surgical theater had vanished. In its place was an epidemic of blackness— a darkness that was made even more obscure by a single green light.

"Hey, man, where the fuck are we? Qué chinga madre es esto? What is this thing?"

"Wait," said Simon forcefully. "This is a Chinook—a large helicopter. We're coming in for a landing. Be quiet and wait."

The two men crouched in the earsplitting gloom and waited until their eyes became accustomed to the lack of light. They braced themselves against the abrupt, sometimes savagely erratic movements of the vibrating machine that encased them.

"Is that my father there—sitting next to you?" the young man asked excitedly while pointing a finger across the interior of the chopper. "That's him! When I used to go through my mother's purse, I seen his picture inside this tiny metal case. Shit, he looks just like me! He's looking this way. Man, is he young! He's so young. Does he see us?"

"He is younger than you are. Yes, he does see us. Long ago he asked me if someone was sitting near the ramp, in the shadows. He thought someone was watching us. I never answered his question, but I looked into those shadows and I saw my future."

"You saw that you would be carryin' a weird gadget on your belly, wearin' funny outfits, and talkin' to dead people?" asked Junior, suddenly tensing up as the wheels of the chopper hit the ground. The heavy ramp began to yawn open, and the young troopers in the belly of the aircraft stood up. There was dread and stony resignation in their faces. This sortie didn't feel right. The world didn't make sense. This could be the end. There was a loud flurry of cracks and pops just meters from the Chinook. There were a hundred men outside firing their weapons. As the ramp slammed into the ground, the intensity and volume of the gunfire doubled, then tripled into a deafening roar.

"They're gonna stand up and walk out into that?" asked Junior. There was pain and disbelief in his eyes. "Are they fuckin' crazy?" His shattered voice box was emitting sounds of shock. This was no cowardly drive-by shooting. The gunfights in the streets back home in Port Arthur were kids' games compared to this. The two men watched as Private Fulgencio Garza kissed a small photograph, then rose from his seat. They watched as Simon pushed his friend back and switched places with him, heading down the ramp in front of a large, bulky machine.

Both watchers noticed that young Private Vegas had hastily stuffed a small piece of electronic equipment into his flak vest, and they saw stark terror in his face that grew with each step that he took toward the end of the ramp. As he passed by on his way down, Simon glanced to his right and nodded tensely to his older self. Sweat was pouring down his face as he stepped closer and closer to manmade insanity.

The two watchers witnessed the firefight, the wounded soldiers limping desperately back into the Chinook. They stared in horror as two young officers were mortally wounded. They watched the desperate struggle between Ajax Carruthers and Trooper Vegas over the life of Fulgencio Garza. An instant later, Junior glanced to his right and caught sight of the very bullet that would kill his father.

He saw it appear from a small stand of trees and fly in slow motion toward his young padre. He saw its rifling-induced spin and its arching trajectory—a tiny segment of a parabola. He screamed for the bullet to stop and watched helplessly as flesh, blood, and the same bullet, now deformed and even uglier, exited his father's throat and exploded through Simon's hand. He watched as the interior of the chopper filled with the fine pink mist and drizzle of his father's life. And he watched his father's head fall down to his chest, his once wet and perceptive eyes now dull and senseless.

Junior began to quake and shiver. The muscles in his neck and jaw had buckled and contracted with shock. His face was unrecognizable. He grabbed Simon's right hand and, through a sea of tears, looked closely at the ugly scars in the older man's palm and on the back of his hand: the proof—the living proof. This terrible, ugly thing had actually happened. It had happened to his father. This was why he had never come home. This was why he had never held his little boy, taught him how to fold a burrito or catch a baseball. To see his baby boy had been his papa's only desire in the last ticking seconds of his life.

So this was why his mother drank herself to sleep every night. Junior collapsed heavily into a corner under the weight of a single realization: things are real—they mean something—they have an effect. For every action, there is an equal and opposite reaction. His body began to shudder until it was wracked and wrenched with seismic waves of grief. His muscles cramped with sorrow. He wept each and every tear that he had refused to cry for most of his life.

The Mexican Flyboy rose from his hiding place and walked halfway down the metal incline. He could see himself coming up the ramp, and he could see Sergeant Carruthers lying on top of the doomsday device, throwing away his flak vest and pulling the tarp over himself. He watched as Private Vegas bent down to pick up a tiny piece of paper that had fallen onto the ramp. Simon approached himself.

"May I borrow this for a moment?" he asked himself.

"Yes," came the answer. "You can keep it."

He walked back to Fulgencio Junior and held a photo up in

front of the young man's eyes. Junior looked at the picture, then shut his eyes once more as the sound of gunfire died away. When he opened his eyes again, the Chinook was gone. The soldiers were gone. Even the body of his young father was nowhere to be seen. He looked around and found himself lying in a bed in a hospital room. There were bags of liquid hanging everywhere. There was a noisy monitor to his right, and several needles were taped to his right arm and to his neck.

He couldn't turn his head, but he moved his eyes to his left and saw his mother sitting in a chair next to the bed, so close that her head was resting on the sheets. Magdalena's eyes were closed. He looked into her pretty face, and for the first time in his life, saw the grief and the longing in residence there. He saw the young pregnant girl that she had once been. He saw the moment when she and Fulgencio's family had huddled together and opened that devastating letter from the Department of the Army.

Her eyes shot open when she sensed that someone was looking at her. She turned her head slowly until their eyes met. She saw his lips moving and leaned down to place an ear near his mouth. She was trembling.

Elena turned the shower off and cocked her head to listen. "That was the oddest thing," she said as she entered the bedroom with a towel on her head and another one wrapped around her body. "I could swear I heard a helicopter hovering just outside the bathroom window." No one answered. Simon was already gone.

He had gone to the city. He had crossed the Bay Bridge and gone to his office at San Francisco State College. Then he had gone to Café Zazie on Cole Street to have a late breakfast with Zeke. They talked for over two hours, and then Simon walked to his car and drove away. He crossed over the bridge again and followed the freeway to Berkeley. He took the Ashby Avenue exit and drove toward the hills until the large building appeared on his right. After parking the car on the third level of the elevated parking garage at Alta Bates Hospital, he walked down the stairs and across the road, all the while staring up at the fourth floor of the large building, the maternity floor. The smiling woman at the information desk told him to go to room 407.

When he went in, he could see Elena walking back and forth in the small area between the bed and the wall. She was straining to move, taking mincing steps and showing obvious pain. Things were happening faster than she had anticipated. Five or six of her closest girlfriends were sitting in the room chatting and eating while one woman walked with Elena, whispering and holding her left arm. Simon walked over to his wife, hugged her awkwardly, then sat down while two nurses who had just entered the room explained the options to Elena.

"Do you want a spinal block?" one of them asked.

"A spinal block? No, I don't think so," said Elena. I want to feel the baby when she comes out."

Her husband knew that the time of reckoning was drawing near.

"I'll take one," he said.

19

THE WINDS OF SAME

Zeke had gone on a trip earlier in the week. He had booked his flight three days after he and Simon interviewed Peter Keyes. He had taken his mother and all of her luggage to the airport for her flight back to New York, then boarded a plane to Phoenix, Arizona. He had rented a car and made the long drive into Greenlee County and up into the hills to the tiny mining town of Morenci. This morning Simon had sat quietly at Café Zazie and listened to his friend. He had always known that this moment was inevitable, even necessary, but he could hardly bear the words that Zeke was saying. He didn't touch his breakfast.

"I found an old man there," said Zeke. "He still lives in the same house at the crest of a hill. He's a hundred and three years old, and he still remembers you."

Simon was flabbergasted. "Señor Zarigüeya," he whispered in astonishment. "He's still alive? He was on his last legs when I knew him, and that was way back when I was nine years old. That old viejito kept practicing his own death, over and over again. 'Practice makes perfect,' he would say. Maybe that's why he's lived so long."

"His narcolepsy is in remission now," said Zeke. "He says it's cleared up because the real thing is coming. His narcolepsy has been shamed into the shadows by the close presence of genuine death. He calls his disease 'the pretender.' But here's the beauty part: he's got a girlfriend! He's gone and robbed the cradle. She's eighty-one years old and never wears a stitch of clothing. Walks around the house all day long as naked as you please. Not bad looking, either, for a gal with that much mileage on her. He told me that for most of his life, the mere sight of a woman's bared breasts would cause him to lose consciousness. It must have been so frustrating."

"I remember," said Simon. "He would look at the cover of a girlie magazine and pass out."

"Well, this little gal decided to fix that problem by putting her titties in front of his face twenty-four hours a day until the shock of seeing them wore off. It worked. Eventually the shock disappeared and only the pleasure stayed behind. Now the old guy has girlie magazines everywhere in his house. He was the happiest guy I've ever seen—until I asked him about your family."

Simon said nothing else for two hours, which was how long Zeke's monologue lasted. He listened to his friend and nodded his head quietly. Every few minutes he closed his eyes. As Peter Keyes had said, it had happened—all of it had happened. Those people had once existed. They had all been alive and filling his childhood home with love and the sweet sounds of life. When Zeke was done, Simon left forty dollars on the table, then walked silently to his car. He was on his way to the hospital, on his way to fatherhood.

Zeke pulled his friend's untouched plate of food to his side of the table but couldn't eat it. He sat quietly, using a fork to push a strip of bacon back and forth between a poached egg and a ginger pancake. Had he done the right thing? Had he meddled in his friend's life? Simon had demanded it—not with words but with actions, glaring clues left here and there. What he had found in Morenci had chilled him to the bone. How could young Simon have lived through that? How could anyone have lived through something like that? He looked up from the plate and caught a glimpse of his friend as he pulled out of the parking space and drove down Cole Street. How had he survived that day so many years ago? Had he survived? Was he a part of this world anymore?

He felt a touch on his left shoulder but ignored it. He only left the café when one of the waitresses, a cute little brunette, gave up tapping, grabbed his shoulder, and shook him to get his attention. She told him in her sweetest voice that the establishment was closed. Zeke rose from his chair and looked around. The other chairs had all been upended and were stacked up on the tables so that the floors could be mopped.

"Mr. Stein!" shouted the waitress after the investigator had walked a dozen steps toward Haight Street. "Is this your briefcase?" she asked. "You left it behind." It was Simon's. It was something that was never out of Simon's possession, much less out of his sight. Zeke picked up the leather briefcase and walked home. This wasn't a clue or a silent demand; this was an order, loud and clear.

In room 407, the doctor, a tall, handsome black man, had come and gone, then come back again. Simon had arrived at the hospital around two o'clock in the afternoon, and it was almost seven when the doctor announced, "We will give it fifteen more minutes, and then this baby has got to come out." A nurse to Simon's left pulled open a drawer and took out a device to which she attached a thin white tube that culminated in something resembling a miniature fez. Using this apparatus, the doctor would pull the baby down the canal and out into the world.

Simon watched as Elena took deep, heavy breaths, then pressed again with all of her strength, focusing her power on the distant, insensible, almost ineffable opening in her legs. The pain had been too much for too long. She had finally opted for the drugs. Now she pushed as an act of memory; she pushed and breathed and followed whispered instructions and encouragement from the doula and from her friends. She heard them all but acknowledged no one.

The doctor reappeared in the doorway. He was pulling on a pair of translucent white gloves. A nurse went up to him, and they spoke briefly. A second nurse approached and guided his arms through the armholes of a smock while the first nurse tied it behind his neck and back. When the doctor came into the room, Simon began to tremble. When the doctor knelt between Elena's legs, Simon began to whisper a song that grew in volume until everyone in the room could hear it clearly.

Elena turned toward her husband. In all the years of their marriage, she had never quite heard the song, only faint insinuations of it rustling the air around her ears. She had heard some of the lyrics on the PNFY radio broadcast. She had heard the melody a million times, but never so many clear words before tonight. All at once the song changed. The fluid lyrics were interspersed with tribal names and historic locations, abruptly tapped out on Simon's lips and tongue like the staccato of a flamenco dancer's hands and feet.

"What's wrong with him?" asked the doctor. "Is he all right?" Simon's singing was even clearer now, as distinct as a conversation a half-block away on a cold, windless autumn night. The doctor glanced at a nurse and said, "Ask him to keep it down."

"He's the father," said one of Elena's friends.

"He's just a little out of his mind, doctor," said Elena. "Right now, so am I. This is his time, too. Leave him be." The nurse returned to her post. The doctor shrugged and took the little fez that the second nurse had extended to him. He squeezed the tiny hat, then began inserting it into the birth canal.

> In Dublin's fair city where the girls are so pretty
> I first set my eyes on sweet Molly Malone . . .

"I'll put Hank Williams in an apartment with Paul Robeson, Sam Cooke, and Sappho," whispered Simon out loud between the lyrics of the song. "He'll be next door to Susannah McCorkle, Janis Joplin, and Aida. The music in that section of Boca Raton will be amazing! I'll just have to add a few more rooms to Jesse Washington's apartment and put Oscar Grant in there. He'll be able to talk across the fence with the Laotian family living on the other side. That portion of the complex is filled with Hussites, Sethians, and Gnostics, Japanese from Hiroshima, and two million Cambodians, all dressed for a day at the beach. Where should I put Sylvia Plath and her son?"

A nurse flipped a switch, and a small pump began to whirr. The soft sound froze Simon for a moment. Then the shaking and the singing began once again. Elena was pushing with all of her power. Her friends had gathered behind the doctor to watch as the baby came into the world. The doctor mumbled something, and a nurse switched on an apparatus, sending a focused beam of light into the cleft in Elena's thigh.

Zeke had gone to Morenci, to the exact coordinates that were written on Simon's belly. He had driven through the small mining town and parked at its only hotel. After a shower and a meal, he had gone to the tavern next door. Inside that tavern were old men who drank tequila, mezcal, and whiskey and passed their days spinning an epic poem about copper—old men who remembered.

"Hell, we know bits and pieces of it," one of the men had explained. "It was awful. It's old man Zarigüeya who knows it all. He was there for every minute of it. Whatever happened to that boy?"

"Your family once lived in a small house in the foothills on the far edge of town," Zeke had said during breakfast at Café Zazie. "There was no plumbing out there, so an indoor toilet was your mother's dream. What was her name again?"

"Siobhán Ó Floinn Vegas," answered Simon.

"Right, Siobhán Ó Floinn Vegas. It took years for your father to bring plumbing into the house. With the help of Siobhán's father, he built three pump houses just to get the water up into the hills as far as Señor Zarigüeya's house. Then he built a storage tank. It took a year longer to put in a septic tank. Señor Zarigüeya told me that your father truly loved your mother. He helped him run the pipes—almost half a mile. The three men dug the pit for the tank by hand. You had a drafty outdoor bathroom until you were almost nine years old."

"*She wanted a warm bathroom adentro, inside,*" *Señor Zarigüeya had explained to Zeke as he watched his beloved naked wife pouring grease into a coffee can, then returning a black iron pan to its place on the stove. A small mound of reddish chorizo was melting down in the center of the pan, and the sharp aroma filled the room. The old man waited for her to bend over a bit so he could see the soft flesh of her breasts that normally rested against her ribcage.*

"*Her breasts don't sag—not one bit. Qué milagro. It's a miracle. Don't you think she has nice breasts?*"

"*I think she does,*" *Zeke had answered. The woman at the stove smiled as she cracked an egg and held it above the pan until the perfect moment. A drop of grease spat upward from the pan and landed on her exposed belly. She danced away from the stove and wiped her stomach with a dishrag. The quick movement caused her breasts and nipples to distend, then to undulate in a way that made Señor Zarigüeya smile from ear to ear. She sighed and shook her head. She had been a schoolteacher in Globe for almost fifty years, and now she was spending her golden years as a topless dancer.*

"*The story is so sad,*" *said the woman as she dropped the second and third egg into the chorizo and began to scramble them together. "I can see their house from this window—what's left of it. Of course, I wasn't here when it happened. I was living in Globe back then. But everyone in Arizona heard about it. No one ever knew what happened to the boy.*"

"*So he built her a bathroom,*" *continued Señor Zarigüeya. "And what a bathroom it was! Oh, Simon's mother was a beauty. A famous beauty in these parts. She was mestiza, part Mexicana and part Irlandesa—part Irish with wild hair like living flame. Sometimes the sight of her hair would kill me, put me straight to sleep.*"

"He has narcolepsy," the naked woman explained without looking up from her cooking. "He has explosive catalepsy. Whenever he gets excited, he loses consciousness. He falls down wherever he is. He never has enough time to break his fall or to avoid hitting a pile of broken glass with his chin. It's like he's a marionette and someone up there cuts his strings. It has been such a curse. Every inch of his body has a scar or a stitch."

"If I'm remembering correctly, your mother's great-grandfather was named Bardán Ó Floinn," said Zeke. "Nowadays they would call him Brendan Flynn. He was a member of the famous Saint Patrick's Battalion, the San Patricio Batallón that fought against Zachary Taylor and his troops when the Americans invaded Mexico. He was captured at the convento de Churubusco and hanged on September 13th, 1847 . . . but the Mexican people still honor him and his fellow soldiers to this day."

"Bardán Ó Floinn's only son, Ciarón, left Mexico for good and built that house that still stands over there. I can't go near the place no more," added Señor Zarigüeya. "It hurts me too much. I take just three steps toward that house, and I feel my sickness coming on. The house is over that way." The old man had gestured in a vague direction toward a place of uncertain description. An unknown place best left unknown.

"His son Éamonn, your mother's father, was born in that house," said Zeke. "You slept in Éamonn's bed until he finally came back from his wanderings, then the two of you slept together. He told you amazing stories and taught you songs in Spanish and Gaelic. He taught you the song that Bardán Ó Floinn sang from the gallows. It was always on your mother's lips, and then it found new life on yours. Señor Zarigüeya told me that your pillows and bedsheets were green and had the shamrock and the Harp of Erin emblazoned on them."

"The boy's comida, his food was Mexican—his dreams were in Ghaeltacht."

As he listened to the investigative report, Simon could still feel the warmth of the old man's body. His raspy breath snagging on crooked, yellowing teeth had been the sweetest bouquet to young Simon's nose. He felt the stubble of his chin during un abrazo, and he saw the intensity of his eyes when the old man was deep into the twisted intricacies of a bedtime story. He could see weathered hands flitting, swooping, gesturing into the half-darkness above the pillows, gnarled fingers spinning the long yarn in the magical air over the old man's face. Then his mother's voice would flutter in from another world: *"Enough bedtime stories, Papa."*

"Really?" Papa Éamonn would call out. "Can there really be enough? I seem to remember . . ."

"Oh, just one more, then," Siobhán would say with a gentle sigh of surrender.

Simon inhaled deeply as Zeke spoke. Once upon a time, the world had been so safe.

"What's going on here?" the Flyboy asked the investigator. "Why are you telling me things that I already know?" It was not really a question. He inhaled deeply again.

"It's for me," answered Zeke. "This is for me."

Simon could still smell the cigarettes and the whiskey of that life lived so long ago. He could hear the soft, ragged snoring and see the unsteady rise and fall of faulty, reluctant lungs that had once inhaled the sulfur, the noxious powders, and the diesel fumes of the Battle of the Bulge. Simon wanted more than just memory. He always had. Memory was vaporous, weightless, as mercurial as quicksilver spilled from a cracked thermometer. The young boy's first years of acute and full self-awareness had coincided—almost to the day—with the final years of his grandfather's tempestuous life.

"I'm just a bag of bones now, me boyo—weak and harmless I am. But mind you, in my day I had a jab, a wicked left hook, and a smile full o' teeth. I thought that was all I needed to get on in life. But it's all drivel!

I broke your grandmother's heart with my drinking and my drivel. Too much uisce beatha," he said while drinking from an imaginary bottle, clenching his fingers and tipping his thumb toward his mouth. "I was as much a fool as the next man, and that is always a tragedy—a spine- less fool, bending to this wind, then that. That is the only eternal truth, Simon: all men are pendejos. We are fools. We follow each other. Have you seen those freedom marchers on the TV?"

Young Simon nodded that he had.

"They sing this song: 'We Shall Overcome.'" Éamonn hummed the tune for a bar or two. "I always wondered what it is that they're overcom- ing. Then one day I knew." The old man tapped the side of his head with a yellow, nicotine-stained finger. "It ain't a 'what,' it's a 'who.' Who do they have to overcome? They have to overcome us, that's who—you and me. I was cruel once—a stupid, cruel boy." His voice broke as he said it.

"I was wandering in Texas a long time ago and stopped in a little town. In the town center a black boy was hanging from a pole. A boy and his papa threw gas on him . . ." He could barely force the words from his mouth. His voice dropped down to a point below a whisper. "And some- one in the crowd shouted out for a match. I reached into my pocket for a match. I did that. I did that," he said with a sob into his pillow. "I did that."

"At first I couldn't strike that match, but someone else in the crowd called me a coward. Then someone else shouted that I was a Paddy cow- ard, so I struck the match and angrily tossed it. The young man—soakin' in gas—was hangin' from a pole, and I swear I saw his only good eye lookin' directly at me. He was lookin' at me! He seemed so surprised. So surprised." The old man buried his face in the pillow for a minute or two. "Jesse Washington! Oh, Jesse Washington!" the old man screamed into his pillow with every ounce of his strength. The entire bed shook with his spasms of grief.

"Promise me you'll step out of line, Simon, me boyo." He cupped the boy's face in his rough, craggy hands. "Promise me. Make sure you

step out of line, the farther the better. Look around you, and if a rank is formin', get out of it. Don't make my mistake, boyo. People will think you're mad if you do, but you won't be. The winds of same . . . the winds of sameness blew over me, and I bent with them. Don't be like me. Do it for your old Grandpapa Éamonn. Overcome yourself." The old man pressed the backs of his hands together and fluttered his fingers like a set of wings.

Elena began to push hard, with all of her waning strength and at shorter and shorter intervals. Beads of perspiration were covering her body and drenching the sheet beneath her back. The doctor between her legs was muttering, "Good. Good. Keep it up. Won't be long now." Elena lifted her right hand and whispered, "Simon. Simon." He stood up and walked to her side. He took her hand in his and kissed her knuckles.

"Not much longer," whispered the doula. Simon tensed up at those words. For a single moment his lips stopped moving, and the steady stream of semi-audible syllables superimposed over the Irish melody ceased, leaving the air about his ears ringing with the deepest calm.

"Not much longer."

20

BOCA RATON

Hank Williams entered the room with Simon at his side. Hank was wearing a black shirt that was covered with lavender orchids. He wore a pair of khaki shorts and orange sandals. His precious Silvertone was in the battered case that Simon had placed next to the great singer's feet. There was a large white hat in Hank's hand and a sheepish grin on his face as he looked at the people who had come to greet him and welcome him. He shook each hand that was extended to him and addressed each person with a short but heartfelt greeting.

"Mr. Robeson, so proud to meet you, sir. Mr. Guthrie, so pleased to see you. Mr. Caruso, so proud to meet you. Miss Smith, I've always loved your singin'. Jimmy Rodgers, you coulda been my kin. Mr. Cooke, so pleased to know you. Mr. Johnson and Mr. House, I'd a been nothin' without the two of you."

"Hank, I brought your car to Boca Raton," said Simon proudly.

"You did?" said Hank with a look of surprise and pleasure in his face. He turned around and looked at his most prized possession—a powder-blue 1952 Cadillac. "Oh, but my baby is so beautiful—all that chrome and hand-stitched white and powder-blue upholstery," he said with a wistful smile. "Thing is, I won't need her here. Give my car to your daughter, Simon. That pretty little baby's slidin' out of her mama right this very minute. Give it to her and tell her about all me."

Waiting to sing with Hank were hundreds of thousands of nameless and unknown singers, blues singers, gypsy bands, minstrels, starving buskers, and troubadours who had suffered so much for their songs. And behind them was an endless line of anonymous juke-joint crooners and

shouters, chain-gang chanteurs, and at their backs, ten thousand cas-
trati—all in Hawaiian shirts—all singing . . .

> *As she wheeled her wheelbarrow*
> *Through streets broad and narrow . . .*

"So, as I was saying," said Señor Zarigüeya, "her loving husband,
Augusto Vegas, finally built her a bathroom—a big, beautiful bathroom.
Its walls were twenty feet by twenty feet and almost doubled the size of
the house. She loved it so much. She burned the old outhouse down and
began to plan una despedida, a grand-opening party for her new toilet.
She hung magazine racks on the door and put maps on all four walls and
had one beautiful projection of the whole world tacked up to the ceiling.
There were bookshelves on every wall. Can you imagine that? She loved
poetry. It was a library! That's what it was! A library with hundreds of
books, and with a toilet built smack dab in the middle of it.

"I used that bathroom once and never wanted to leave. The whole
family used to gather in that bathroom after dinner and point at the
maps, read the poems, and look at hundreds of pictures by candlelight.
I remember there was a calendar to my left as I sat on the throne. It was
a giant calendar showing all the beaches of the world. Beaches in France
and Italy—everywhere. Every month was a new beach with endless
stretches of white sand. Her favorite was . . ."

"Boca Raton," interjected Zeke.

"Si, señor, but how did you know that? How could you possibly know
that? There is only one way you could know about Boca. You've seen
Simon, haven't you? He's alive, isn't he?"

The old man began to tremble and swoon. The woman at the stove
turned around and walked to the table. She stroked his hair to calm him
down. Her right breast lightly brushed his cheek.

"Yes, he's alive," said Zeke. "He lives in Oakland." It was then that
he noticed thousands of small, colorful magazines in the next room. Some
had been sheathed in plastic and mounted on the walls. There was one

tall stack of girly magazines and countless stacks of old comic books, all in perfect condition. Señor Zarigüeya was a collector.

"I have the first copy of the first edition of everything. Is he all right? Is Simon OK?" asked Señor Zarigüeya.

"He's found a machine. It allows him to fly. He's distilled a love potion. Everyone thinks he's lost his mind," answered Zeke. After briefly considering the investigator's words, the old man nodded his head and said, "Good. Very good." The nude woman carried two plates to the table and placed one in front of each man. Each plate held a steaming mound of chorizo con huevo that had been heaped on a corn tortilla. There was a dollop of salsa at the top. She gave each man a cup of coffee, then, using a tortilla as a spoon, began to eat from the small iron pan.

"On the door to the bathroom, Siobhán had painted two signs. One of them said 'siempre ocupado,' and the other said in big green letters, 'Mi Cielo Mexicano,' My Mexican Heaven. That woman would invite people—even strangers—into her house just so she could show them her beautiful baño. It had always been Siobhán and Augusto's dream to someday move to Boca Raton and live with the whole family in a little house on the beach. Siobhán was so tired of the high desert. They even invited me to come along—to come live with them. Can you imagine? We would all wear luau clothes and watch the sea as the sun went down. We would still be there drinking funny drinks and laughing when the sun came up again."

A darkness appeared on the face of the old man—an eclipse.

"Keirán hates to think about it," said the woman, "but he thinks about it every day—ten times a day. I've heard the story from him so many times that now it seems like my own memory."

"Keirán?" Zeke had asked.

"Keirán O'Hara Zarigüeya," the woman said with a smile. "Siobhán had also asked for a heater because her house, like this one, freezes in the wintertime," she continued. The smile on her face vanished. "Every year it ices up just like up in Flagstaff—only worse. Come December, we have to melt water on the stove just to wash our faces. She desperately wanted the house heated for her *despedida*, her bathroom party. She had invited all of their family members for dinner on New Year's Eve, and she knew they would drink themselves silly and have to sleep over. That's what the Mexicans and the Irish do, you know. She wanted a warm house for them. What woman doesn't?"

"There's the head," said the doctor as he lightly tugged at the vacuum extractor.

"Such a beautiful face," sighed someone in the hospital room.

It was the doula who had spoken those words, but everyone in the room heard a mysterious second voice singing the same words in close harmony.

It was Magdalena, Fulgencio Junior's mother, who had intoned the same syllables in perfect tempo and harmony with the distant words of the doula. She had chanted those words while waiting in another hospital, two decades ago and a thousand miles away—waiting for her son to come back from death.

"Such a beautiful face . . . just like his father's," Magdalena had whispered. She shivered when her gaze fell upon the sutures below his jaw. She would never know that his father had died of a similar but even more ghastly wound to the neck. Then she noticed that her son's eyelashes began to flick and flutter almost imperceptibly after her breath had crossed over them. He was trying to say something! She moved an ear to within an inch of his lips.

"Te quiero, mamá." Young Fulgencio mouthed the words tenderly. More air than sound came from his dry, cracking lips and from his stitched throat and windpipe. "No te preocupes. Papá está en la Florida. I saw him. I saw mi papa! We are there with him. He is so happy to be with us. The two of you were married . . . by a rabbi! He is finally happy, Mama."

His mother had mouthed the words "Florida" and then "married." Then she had fainted and fallen in slow motion to the floor.

Simon had walked past the guard at the foot of the bed and toward the pillow that cradled Lenny Hudson's head. The guard moved to stop the Mexican Magus, but the warden grabbed his arm and shook his head no. The guard nodded and stepped back. Simon bent over Lenny. He could see the purple bruising around his neck and the pieces of thread still embedded in his paper-white skin. There were no bars, no overhead fixtures or hooks anywhere in his cell. There were no bedsprings, no hard edges to be found.

He had been doing his customary set of pushups just after ten o'clock. A guard walking by on a fifteen-minute rotation had shined his flashlight into Lenny's cell and had seen him in the "up" position, preparing to lower himself slowly until his chest just touched the floor. The guard had seen this sight a thousand times before. Lenny's pushups were always arduous and slow—meant to punish the pecs and triceps. After the guard had passed, the prisoner wrapped his thin homemade rope around the tiny flush handle on the stainless steel toilet. He lowered himself until the rope tightened on his trachea, then folded his hands together across his chest, the left hand crossing the right. He straightened his legs and back until they were flat and rigid.

"If Lenny dies, the cause of death would have to be willpower," said Warden Harris. "Any other human being would have lost consciousness and fallen over in a heap, but not Lenny—not him. When the guards finally went into his cell a quarter-hour later, he was as straight and as stiff as a board. The doctor thinks he's brain-dead. There's a faint pulse, but it's only getting fainter."

The Flyboy bent down over the prisoner's body and blew softly across his eyelids. On a day long, long ago, these same two people had been standing in the same vineyard watching the same woman's body being placed into an ambulance. From his hiding place behind a John Deere tractor, Lenny had seen Simon the boy climb into the ambulance and bend over his mother, Sophia—bending in the same way he was bending now—blowing across her eyelashes just as he was blowing now—just as the white sheet was being pulled over her face—his face. When Simon pulled back a few inches, he could see that one or two hairs of Lenny's lashes flickered afterward, when there was no wind to move them. Simon bent forward again.

"Liam . . . Liam Hanlon, you once said you would tell me who I am," said the Flyboy into Lenny's left ear. The prisoner began to shiver when he heard the rare sound of his true name. Simon could see Lenny gathering together every last iota of his strength and funneling that tiny force toward his voice box, to his purple lips and wooden tongue. Lenny turned his head just a fraction of an inch and, in a monumental act of will, forced three frail words past a coffin lid that was slamming shut: "You . . . ain't . . . me."

> Crying cockles and mussels,
> Cathars and Tutsis,
> Ibo and Cheyenne,
> Alive, alive-O.

Simon had carefully opened the letter. It was one of only three items that he found in Lenny's—Liam's—property envelope. Below it there was a blank postcard that had been mailed to India. He unfolded the pages of the letter and read the words that he found there, then placed it back into its tattered cover. The paper was worn thin, tearing at the folds, and the handwriting had grown faint. It had been written to her, to Sophia, by her husband, Damodar. Not many days ago, Simon had gone into the archives in San Joaquin County and pulled out the autopsy photos of the two boys who were murdered at the fruit stand in Tracy.

Despite their different sizes and different last names, Raju and Singh, the boys had looked identical in their faces and expressions. They looked like twin brothers, not like the unrelated adopted boys that the parents had claimed they were. Now Simon knew that they had been brothers from the same womb. The frightened woman must have changed her children's names sometime after their birth so that their half-brother Liam—Lenny—could never find them.

The family had lived in a remote little hotel on an obscure back road. She had been the waitress in the café, and he had done all of the cooking. She had washed the bedsheets, and he and the boys were responsible for maintaining the hotel rooms. Damodar had planted a small garden out back, and the family had sold their fresh vegetables from a small stand near the road.

She had dyed her hair blonde and always wore sunglasses. The strategy had worked for over a decade. But somehow Lenny had come across the small café in the barren foothills and had set about destroying a family. The instant she learned about the deaths of her sons on her car radio, Sophia Hanlon had turned the car around and headed east.

"Run!" she had screamed at her husband from a phone booth in Nevada. "He'll kill you, too. Run!" Damodar had told the police about Sophia's oldest son, but he had never been told his name—first or last. Sophia had never told him where the older boy had been born or raised. It seemed that Damodar knew nothing at all about her past life. The police could find no evidence to link anyone to the killing. For a week or two, they had suspected the father. A warrant was issued for the mother, but it soon died a bureaucratic death. Within a month's time, everyone in the valley had forgotten about the two Indian boys who had breathed their last in a dusty aisle between the half-priced zucchini and the ripening eggplants.

For two weeks, Sophia had driven aimlessly until she found herself at the army base in Fort Benning, Georgia, where she got a job as a waitress at the bowling alley. Two days later, she served a double order of pigs in a blanket with a double side order of corned beef hash to a man named Peter Keyes. Her sad, frightened husband had sailed back to India to be at his mother's side after the unexpected death of his father. His entire family back home had been eagerly anticipating his arrival with his two beautiful American sons.

After a few months in India, he received a single postcard from the army base in Georgia. Nothing was written on it, but he recognized her handwriting and sailed home immediately. Perhaps it was a message. Perhaps she wanted him to come back. Maybe she was going back to their home. When he got back to California, the motel rooms, the tables, the seats at the food counter, the entire universe was empty. She had never returned. She never would. He sat down on a stool at the empty breakfast counter and began to write the letter that Sophia would read over and over again for years to come.

He rewrote and revised it on his way back home, then mailed it from India. He had addressed the envelope to general delivery at the army base and hoped that she would get it. He wrote the letter that she would place on top of her parachute after Peter Keyes had returned it to the rigging shack. He wrote the love letter that Lenny would keep under his mattress while he waited to die.

In order to plunge the dagger even deeper into his mother's heart, Lenny had killed that fellow inmate at Corcoran Prison in broad daylight and had confessed to the murders in Tracy. He had stabbed that inmate to death for the sole purpose of receiving the death penalty. "Do I know you?" the doomed prisoner had asked casually while standing in a food line. "Ain't you from Illinois?" Lenny's own death was to be the coup de grace. Sophia would become Rachel who had lost all of her children. She would become La Llorona. She would be sentenced to life without the possibility of peace.

Though Lenny had watched her fall from the sky that morning so long ago, his mind had never accepted her abrupt change to his plans. What had his mother been doing up there in the sky? Making a choice? She had always run from him before. Lenny had gone back to the scene of the crime, back to the small café. It had been abandoned and run down, but he had found one thing: the postcard that

Damodar had left on the lunch counter. Lenny had gone to Georgia, then he had followed his mother back to California.

She had always kept the chase alive. But this time she wasn't playing by the rules! Five hundred feet from the ground, she was calling it quits. She had done it again! She had abandoned him again. Still, his unquenchable desire for revenge had discounted her death completely. In his dreams, she lived on to suffer through his years of appeals. She would have decades of sleepless nights waiting for his date with the gas chamber, then his date with lethal injection. She would have to live through three or four stays of execution. Then she would have to endure that awful day and those anguished minutes before midnight.

Now that the death penalty had been suspended indefinitely, there was only one way to punish his mother. A death by natural causes would be worthless to him. What would a stroke or a heart attack do to her? Suicide was a message. She would have to come to San Quentin and claim the body. She would have to open the lid of the coffin and look down at him. She would see his crushed trachea and purple neck. She would see what she had done to him. It was the second-best option. Once he had been a boy playing on the front steps of a trailer—a boy cursed with his father's face.

Simon reached into the large envelope and pulled out a tiny scrap of ripped cloth: a name tag that had been ripped from a parachute. Sophia Hanlon. The letter had been addressed to Sophia Chabra and had been sent from overseas to the army base in Georgia. The postmaster had tacked the envelope to the bulletin board next to the building's entrance. The board was adjacent to the entrance to a bowling alley that boasted of having the fastest pin-setting machines and the biggest pancakes in Georgia. It was a love letter written to recount and celebrate a few precious years of happiness.

It was a love letter written to a guilt-ridden, sorrowful wife who was running from her past, and from two innocent children who had died terrible deaths because of what she had done so long ago. For years, only a cheerless dark man in India could conjure up all of their images and the true names of the boys. Now Simon knew her real name, and he knew precisely where her body had plowed into the earth. Now he knew the true names of the boys: not Raju or Singh, but Chabra—Manohar and Anil Chabra. All of this had gone into logbook number ninety-one.

When he dropped the name tag into the manila envelope, he chanced to notice something at the bottom, something that had been wedged into a fold at the very base. Simon turned the envelope over, and it fell out. It was a small lock of fiery red hair that had been secured by a piece of purple thread. It had been tied into a tiny bow by a mother's hand. How long had Lenny—Liam—been dyeing his hair? How had he managed to color it on death row?

The Flyboy sighed. He opened the small box that had been the only other item in Lenny's property. Inside it he found a copy of the only book of poetry that Simon Vegas had ever published. He leafed through it and found Lenny's handwritten notes on every page. There was no hate or anger in those notations, only things that any college student might write. Somehow Liam Hanlon had kept track of Simon Vegas for all these years. Someone at the vineyard—one of the Mexican workers—must have given Simon's name to Lenny. It had probably been Germán, the angry man with the missing ear.

Zeke had searched the databases, combing the archives of every newspaper in Illinois. He had found the stories about the murder of Patrick Hanlon, a defrocked minister who had been suspected of child molestation and of incest. The old man had gone mad as his once thriving congregation dwindled away. He was bedridden when he died. His wife had witnessed the brutal stabbing in the bedroom but would never speak to anyone about what she saw. It was assumed that she had been struck mute by grief.

She had been washing clothes in the kitchen sink when it happened. Sensing his presence, she had raised her head, then her eyes. She had looked at her grandson's face and, knowing his intentions, she had nodded toward a certain room. She had never been suspected of doing it herself. There was not a single speck of blood on her apron, and the wide crimson trail led out of the bedroom window and onto the porch. She must have been the one who got word to Sophia that her mad son had gone hunting, that he had killed his own grandfather—his father.

"He told me he's coming for you, Sophia. Hide, my baby. Hide."

Lenny had once shouted to Simon that he had killed more than three.

"Strangest thing happened," the warden had said. "The guard who pulled aside the curtain when all those heart monitor and brain monitor alarms went off swears he saw Marilyn Monroe holding Lenny in her arms. He swears by it. I wish I'd seen that. We gave him a week off."

"There's the chin!" the doctor exclaimed. "Now, Elena, I'm going to need you to push just once more. Put all of your strength into it. Focus all of your energy on this spot."

> She was a fishmonger, but sure 'twas no wonder
> For so were her father and mother before
> And they each wheeled their barrow
> Through streets broad and narrow
> Crying Pequots and Bantus, alive, alive-O . . .

Simon heard Elena take a deep breath, then hold it as she funneled all of her energy toward the emerging face.

> Philistines and Hittites,
> Alive, alive-O.
> Crying Seminoles and Apaches,
> Alive, alive-O.

Amorites and Hivites,
The children of Dresden,
Sodom and Gomorrah,
Alive, alive-O.

The Mexican Flyboy watched through the grape leaves as the solitary skydiver plummeted downward, her mind awash in memories. He could see her turning in midair, preparing to strike the hard ground—preparing to land a blow against the bedeviled dust that had spewed her forth four decades before. She was falling past someone way up there. He could see someone hovering by her side as she fell. He could see himself doing as he had done countless times before. But this time he knew her name, and he knew where she was in time and in place. At the convalescent home, he had whispered into Peter Keyes's aged ear that the boy in the vineyard had told Sophia that someday he would come back and catch her. Now he would keep that promise.

He knew the story of her life. She wasn't just a nobody rolling into a grave. No one is that. He had longed to know her name just as he had longed to know the names of the other five thousand people who had been crucified that same day—the names of all of the people in Riga and Bergen-Belsen—the women and children at Washita River who had cowered in their tents at the approach of General Custer and the glorious 7th Cavalry—nameless Indian babies about to be impaled on white picket fences. Sophia Hanlon, falling, falling.

"His papa had brought in a propane stove from the mine and set it up in the middle of the house to keep everybody warm. He knew how to use the thing," said Señor Zarigüeya. "He'd used it in the mine a thousand times before. I guess some piece needed cleaning or some other piece had a bad part—a bad valve or something. Anyway, sometime in the night the flame went out—but the gas kept coming. It was nobody's fault. Nobody's fault!" he cried. "Nobody to blame. Well . . . you know

what happened then." He clenched his fists and fought to remain conscious.

His wife handed him a kitchen towel, and the old man blew his nose. "Simon used to work for me, you know. I would pay him two bits an hour to help me out. When all those Irish Mexicans arrived and started kickin' up and drinkin' those funny tropical drinks, I couldn't take it. I was having so much fun that I passed out and hit my head on a table edge. I still have the scar."

He used a bumpy, veined hand to part his hair and show an ancient cicatrix that had steadfastly refused to allow new follicles to grow on its surface.

"Little Simon had to take me home, bandage up my forehead, and give me my medication. That stuff used to give me terrible constipation. We both fell asleep on my bed. In the morning . . . I'll never forget it," he said with a sniffle. "I'll never forget it." Tears began to flow from his eyes, and his cheeks began to puff with the exertion of the memory that had haunted his mind for years. It had taken up residence in his consciousness and demanded to be heard from every day. But he had seldom been called upon to enunciate it, to describe all of its brutal cutting edges, every contour of its sorrowful form.

"I always used to say to him, 'Just blow on my eyelashes.' Sopla tu aliento en mis pestañas. Si tiemblan aunque sea levemente. If they twitch, even the tiniest bit, then I'm still alive. Sabrás que no he muerto. Then cover me against the sun and especially against the winds. Después cúbreme del sol y del vendaval. He must've done that for me a hundred times.

"Anyways . . . the boy went home alone and found them all, all fifteen of them." The old man's face turned red as his mind prepared to say the words that he knew he must say. His voice broke as he tried to speak. "He . . . must've been alone . . . with his dead family . . . for an hour before I got there. Alone! So alone! Who could be more alone? When I got there, I forced myself to stay alive." Señor Zarigüeya clenched his fists.

"I used every ounce of my willpower to keep alive. I could smell all that propane everywhere. I covered my face with a rag, and I looked for the boy. What my eyes saw! What I saw! Oh, god, why can't good people have what they want?" He drew a sleeve across his flooding eyes. "Why can't they? Then I saw him. He was moving from one body to the next, blowing on their eyelashes again and again and again. I could see his spirit trying to break, trying so hard to break apart. I saw the flesh beneath his skin shivering. But something kept it together—something." The old man began to sob. "I taught him to do that, you know—blow on eyelashes. Then he would know if he needed to carry me home to bed or to call an undertaker."

The woman left her position by the stove and walked toward the old man. She put her arms around him and hugged him tightly.

"There he was, that little boy moving from his mama to his papa to his sisters, his aunties and uncles, blowing on eyelashes. They were all there, every one of them in flip-flops and Hawaiian shirts, still smiling from their fabulous party. All cold and asleep forever. Not a tear. Not a tear. The tears were inside . . . in his heart. They were in his heart, you see. He was so alone. So alone. He left that same day, and I have never seen him since. He didn't wait for the ambulance or the sheriff. He walked down the road that you came up and never once looked back. Qué triste. Bhí sé go holc. It was so sad."

Zeke had walked the hundred steps to the Vegas home. He had walked through weeds and windblown refuse and, after shoving the front door open, had finally stood in that room—the dark space at the center of Simon's melancholy. He had found ground zero, the single room at the epicenter of his friend's sorrow. But where was the source of his strength?

Zeke turned in a full circle. It was as if the noisy, giggling guests had all left the party for a moment to go outside and see a partial eclipse of the moon. All of the glasses and plates were still on the table. The meat had long since fossilized, and the tequila had dried into a dark amber residue in the bottom of every glass. No coyotes had moved in—no owls or pigeons had taken up residence.

He had walked down a short hallway into her Mexican heaven, and after spending a moment marveling sadly at the amazing work that Simon's mother had done in her precious bathroom, he had taken down the yellowed calendar, carefully rolled it up, and put it into his briefcase. He spun in a circle when he suddenly heard the excited voices of children who were poring over maps, a mother reading a travelogue, and a father reading aloud from the Travels of Marco Polo.

He heard the voices of two young girls—and a boy. He distinctly heard a young boy reciting Yeats. He heard the flush of a toilet and a round of laughter. Here was Simon's wellspring of strength, his touchstone. Here was the fledgling place where the boy's flights had begun. He walked to a bed and took a green and yellow pillowcase, then walked slowly back to Señor Zarigüeya's house.

"He asked me for a few comic books that he could read on his journey to who knows where. As you can see, I've been collecting them all my life. I'm gonna leave them all to Simon. I told him to take what he wanted, but he only wanted the magicians. He took five; that's all he wanted—five comics. I gave him a cloth sack with fifty-five comics and all the money I could spare. He had a few shirts and socks and the little magician's cape that his mama had sewn for him. How I miss that boy. I miss him so. I'll never see him again."

"Yes, you will," said Zeke softly as he rose from the table. The naked woman was crying. "Yes, you will."

"Where's the father? Papa, come over here," shouted the doctor excitedly. "Does the father want to catch her?" The words seemed to stun Simon. Then the doctor shouted again. "Do you want to catch her?"

"Yes!" shouted Simon. He released Elena's hand and leapt toward her feet. "Yes, yes, yes. All my life I've wanted to catch her. All my life." He stood still for an instant to let a nurse stretch gloves over his fingers, then knelt down next to the doctor. He swooned at the wondrous sight. There she was, a beautiful baby emerging from one world and entering the next. The baby's grayish-blue eyes moved from side to side. There were so many people waiting for her.

"Are you ready to catch her?"

Simon nodded three times—four times, yes. He had been longing to do this for over forty years. "Put your hands down here," instructed the doctor, who demonstrated with his own hands. Like a giant brown hummingbird, the Flyboy hovered above the trellises, the vines, the furrows, and above the wrinkled soft corrugations of the bedsheets. He shoved aside a sudden flow of rude, bellicose winds, punched another in the face, then reached out his hands and finally—finally—clutched her just as she flashed by, just as she slid out of her mother. Finally.

"So little weight—we have so little weight," he sighed as he held her—held them both. In desperation he had wrapped his arms around her just as she fell to a point within a hundred feet of the vineyard—within an inch of the sopping mattress in the delivery room. As his baby began to cry her first joyful cry, he heard Sophia, too. He heard the sad woman's final words sent flying from her lips—three lone survivors on a fragile lifeboat of warm breath, but this time he heard the words clearly and understood them: three words meant for his ears —three words of comfort that could only make sense forty-five years into the future: "She isn't me."

Simon held the wet, shining baby while the doctor lifted the cord and asked, "Do you want to cut it?" A pair of scissors appeared from somewhere. There was a snip and a cloth and a whiff of medication. A lifelong knot was tied. Then Simon stood with his untethered baby in his hands, their faces just inches apart.

After that deathly silent house in Morenci; after that sorrowful vineyard; after that loud, horrid night on the shuddering Chinook and that small singing boy crawling after candy through the concertina wire; after so many years of pruning, weeding, and harvesting the pain from his soul, pulling it from the vine person by person, the universe had all at once been put level . . . for just a time . . . for a brief moment, the fulcrum had moved all the way to the center, and the whole world was in balance.

For the first time in a lifetime, *un coup de foudre*; amor a primera vista—de relámpago, head over heels. All of those savage winds, all of those cruel blows, could not equal a breath from this tiny, squirming weight. No prop wash could drown out this little cry. For the first time in his life, Simon had been battered not by grief, but by joy—for the first time, by wonder.

"Did you see him in heaven?" asked Fulgencio Junior's sobbing, laughing mother.

"No, Mama, Papa's not in heaven. He's gone to a better place—en Boca Raton, in a beautiful place of tropical cottages."

Simon kissed his little girl's face, her chin, her eyes. It was a spontaneous, heartfelt act. He kissed her tiny cheeks until the age-spotted fingers of a nurse began tugging at his hands. "Let the mother see her," said a gentle voice.

"Nothing divine, my little girl, but the choice to never cause suffering," sang the Mexican Flyboy as he handed his beautiful daughter to her smiling mother. Elena's hands brushed against her husband's, and the new parents looked at each other, seeing their partner, their lover, for the first time in years. He sang softly the song of his ancestor on the gallows.

> *She died of a fever and no one could save her*
> *And that was the end of sweet Molly Malone*
> *But her ghost wheels her barrow*
> *Through streets broad and narrow*
> *Crying Incas and Arawaks,*
> *Alive, alive-O*

Crying Armenians and Druids,
Crying Copernicans,
And Albigensians,
Mayans, Mandinkas,
Alive, alive-O.

"Nothing deathless but stupidity. No sin but sameness. Nothing evil but surrender—when the will is relinquished. No perdition but the possession of things. Nothing divine but the person stepping out of line. Nothing holy but the inevitability of science and the persistence of art. Nothing sacred but this moment of love. Nothing divine but stepping out of line.

She is beautiful," he whispered.

"Kineahora," whispered voices in the room and far, far, far beyond.

EPILOGUE

Zeke had gone crazy staring at the beckoning briefcase. He had come home from his breakfast with Simon and had cavalierly tossed the leather bag into a closet near his front door. Then he had fidgeted and wasted time for an hour before moving it to a place beneath his desk, and from there to a location beneath the kitchen table. The calendar from Siobhán's Mexican heaven was now hanging on the wall above the dish rack. He planned to have it framed and give it to Simon. The pillowcase had been folded up and put in a pocket on the side of the briefcase.

Driven to distraction by the picture on the calendar and by the buzzing and clicking under the table, he had finally ripped the briefcase open, and with trembling fingers he had carefully removed the Antikythera device—along with a small clay vial with an ancient black cork stuck in its throat. Was this really the *aurum potabile* that so many men had spent their lives searching for? He grabbed the Mexican bandido's bandoliers, thought for a moment, then returned them to the briefcase.

He walked to a hall closet and pushed all of the clothing aside. He pulled out the antique wooden case that had belonged to his grandfather. He opened it and removed a shawl that was white with blue markings. There were knotted tassels hanging from both ends. He carefully placed the tallith around his neck and across his shoulders. He arranged the two ends so that they fell down the front of his body. He carefully tied the tassels to the rings that Simon had installed on the device. He reached into a small bag that hung from the closet door and pulled out a dorje pendant. He tied it around his neck using a sisal string. Next he walked to his bookshelf, where he found a special book. He opened it and pulled out a tiny scrap of paper that was nestled between pages 3 and 4. He looked at it with reverence. It was a mandala drawn by Carl Jung himself. Zeke placed it gingerly into a breast pocket.

He had done the research days ago. He had pored over Simon's notebook, and after several hours of laborious hunting, he had finally found her entries. Now the madness was fully upon him. He had found her. She was there in the ninetieth book at fifty-two degrees, forty-five minutes, and twenty-eight seconds north latitude. She was there at nine degrees, fifty-four minutes, and twenty-eight seconds east longitude. He had carefully studied the supplemental entry in Simon's ninety-first logbook and had been able to tease out a set of dates.

Four had been crossed off. That meant that Simon had already made four trips. Trembling with excitement, Zeke entered the last date and time into the machine, then began to gag and swoon when the lights on the device started to glow and the kitchen walls around him began to distort and bend light like a hall of mirrors at a carnival. He put a drop of *aurum potabile* into a cup of cold coffee and swallowed it all in a single gulp.

The final numbers in Simon's last ledger had been the right ones. He shot up over Marin County and streaked over the Atlantic before descending through the clouds above war-torn Europe. There, in the center of a fenced compound not thirty feet below him, was the tattered, frost-covered canvas covering of their tent. Zeke gasped when he saw it. The two little girls, bony and starving, were lying in hard wooden boxes that some bill of lading had described as a suitable bed. Each filthy blue-skinned shadow wore a thin rag that the official inventory had listed as a blanket.

The daughters of Otto and Edith Frank were shivering and wheezing with the cold and eating rotten scraps that a logistical clerk and his officemates had described in their carefully planned menus as food. The girls' faintly beating hearts were failing in compliance with what one man, then one committee, then an assembly, a congregation, a convocation, a cadre, a tribunal, a quorum, and a commission had decided was a solution to a problem. In accordance with the tenor of the times, with the purpose of the camp, the two sisters were dying, their stomachs shriveled to the size of a walnut. Their skin clung to their bones like the paper on a wet kite.

After being assaulted by five stalking winds, Zeke had dashed downward to the ground. He had flown all the way from the West Coast of America to this horrid place just seconds before the end. Simon and Hephaestus had done their work well. The machine was functioning perfectly. He hovered beneath the canvas and lifted Margot and Annelies out of that carefully handcrafted horror. He lifted them away from the iron fists and metal hands that were already grasping at their ankles and their wrists, preparing to toss them onto the heap. The two little girls were blind and trembling and weightless. Simon Magus Vegas, the Mexican Flyboy, was right, and Friedrich Nietzsche was wrong. We *can* bear remembrance. We *can* bear it. It was easy—as easy as lifting kittens from a eucalyptus stump.

"Where are we going, sir? To the death house?" asked little Anne, whose formerly purple, cracked lips had turned pink. "If you wait another minute or two, you won't have to kill us. I can barely hold my head up."

"Not the death house. You're going to a new home," he said gently to two young girls whose never-to-bud breasts were suddenly budding—two young girls whose typhus-eaten skin was beginning to glow with inner radiance—two young girls whose dry, yellowed eyes were beginning to shimmer. Zeke could smell the perfume of youth on their breaths.

"Vader en moeder?"

"Everyone is there," answered Zeke, who was wearing a black hat and a long brown coat. His sideburns were dangling loosely in front of his ears.

"Moortje?" asked one of the girls.

"Da kat?" said Zeke. "She's there, too. I fed her this morning. All of the helpers are there, too. You'll live next door to Joan and her little Vietnamese butterfly boy," he said to the young girls, who were now hugging and crying with happiness. "Do you remember Sadie from the tent camp?" asked Zeke. The girls nodded excitedly. "She's living there with her cousin Queenie."

"Sadie! We're going to see Sadie!" they shouted with glee. Sadie was a fellow prisoner who had given half of her rations to the little girls. The hefty, buxom young woman had shriveled away to nothing in only a few months. She had died in Margot's arms. The two girls had used her enormous brassieres as pillows. Her enormous panties had been their bedsheets.

"Sophia, her husband, and their three sons live across the street. You can play with them and with Kassamila and with two really nice men who have only one ear. There are a hundred million little Chinese girls to play with. Lot's wife, Edith, lives just across the fence from you. She has remarried, you know. Her new husband is Baruch de Spinoza, and she is so much happier with his kind of god. And on the other side of your apartment is a large unit with fifteen Irish Mexicans who never stop having parties. They have a stupendous bathroom."

"Vijftien Mexicanen!" cried Annelies, clapping her hands with glee as Ezekiel Zacharias Stein cut his airspeed and radioed ahead for clearance to fly into Mexican airspace. He could see that the girls had attained their normal weight and vitality. They were so beautiful. He was laughing. He was laughing.

Like lifting kittens.